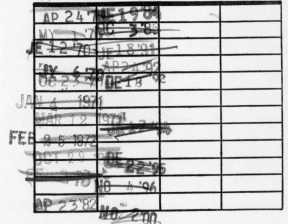

THE
# BEST
AMERICAN SHORT STORIES
## 1969

THE

# BEST

AMERICAN SHORT STORIES

# 1969

*&*

*the Yearbook of*
*the American Short Story*

EDITED BY

MARTHA FOLEY

AND

DAVID BURNETT

Houghton Mifflin Company
Boston
1969

"The Eldest Child" by Maeve Brennan. First published in *The New Yorker.*
Copyright © 1968 by The New Yorker Magazine, Inc.

"Play Like I'm Sheriff" by Jack Cady. First published in *Twigs.* Copyright
© 1968 by Bruce B. Brown, Editor, *Twigs,* Hilltop Editions, Pikeville College
Press.

"Murphy's Xmas" by Mark Costello. First published in *Transatlantic Review.*
Copyright © 1968 by Mark Costello.

"Walking Wounded" by John Bart Gerald. First published in *Harper's Magazine.* Copyright © 1968 by John Bart Gerald.

"The Foreigner in the Blood" by Mary Gray Hughes. First published in
*Esquire.* Copyright © 1968 by Esquire, Inc.

"The Boy in the Green Hat" by Norma Klein. Reprinted from *Prairie
Schooner.* Copyright © 1968 by the University of Nebraska Press.

"Happiness" by Mary Lavin. First published in *The New Yorker.* Copyright
© 1968 by The New Yorker Magazine, Inc.

"The Boat" by Alistair MacLeod. Reprinted from *The Massachusetts Review,*
Vol. IX, No. 2, Spring 1968. Copyright © 1968, by the Massachusetts Review,
Inc.

"The Day the Flowers Came" by David Madden. Originally appeared in *Playboy* magazine. Copyright © by HMH Publishing Co., Inc.

"Pictures of Fidelman" by Bernard Malamud. First published in *The Atlantic
Monthly.* Copyright © 1968 by The Atlantic Monthly Company, Boston, Mass.
Reprinted with permission.

To
MARY LAVIN

# Foreword

THIS PAST YEAR the most notable trend in the American short story, and certainly the noisiest, has been the hullabaloo among publishers, editors and critics over the state of its health. All because a few slick magazines concentrating on Madison Avenue advertising revenues, which had been going more and more to television, nearly eliminated fiction from their contents. Madison Avenue prefers soap opera to literature with the excuse that readers do. But there are eighty-six magazines in this country, and I have carefully counted them, culling many others without high literary standards, which publish good short stories. Unfortunately the general public and certainly advertising executives overlook them because they do not appear on newsstands and cannot afford, even if they wished, expensive promotion campaigns.

The event which caused a lot of the discussion was the death of the *Saturday Evening Post,* once primarily a fiction magazine. MacLennan Farrell, its fiction editor who has done a magnificent job, wrote me this letter from which he has given me permission to quote. He writes: "I don't know whether what we were doing was right or wrong. I do know that our readers didn't like being dragged into the twentieth century but that doesn't make us wrong for trying. We didn't come up with new versions of Penrod and Sam or Tugboat Annie or Scattergood Baines or Alexander Botts, though God knows they asked us to — or even to reprint the old ones. Bellow they didn't like, or Miller or O'Connor or Singer or

Roth or Humphrey or Algren or O'Faolain, or the scores of other
writers who use the short story for a current purpose. Whether we
were too early or too late I don't know. We didn't try to sell this
year's schlock writers. Maybe we should have. Mostly we published stories we ourselves admired and enjoyed — which still seems
to me a reasonable thing to do. The reasons for the *Post's* demise
are complex and in many ways unattractive, but I do think its
editors if not its managers, stood in honor at the end."

Indeed they did. His letter reminded me of what another editor
told me years ago. She was the editor of *The Golden Book,* once a
thriving magazine, devoted to reprinting short stories. It had to
cease publication in the thirties because, the editor explained, it
had run out of material which appealed to its readers. As long as
it reprinted stories from a period extending approximately from
1890 to 1912 its readers were happy. Every time the magazine tried
to publish stories of a later date there were complaints. Those
*Golden Book* readers did not want the very stories for which *Post*
readers clamored.

I do not have all the answers but I think an important one is
the conditioning of children in school to feel reading is a chore
when it should be a joy. The number of people who never open a
book after leaving school and college is appalling. This was true
long before moving pictures and television. The denigration of
fiction as frivolous and inferior to nonfiction by many uninformed
public men is also injurious to the serious novel and short story.
The damage, though, mostly begins in schools. Books, victims of
critical murder, are corpses on which students are taught to per-
form autopsies. It is my conviction after teaching for twenty years
in a university English department that children should be let
loose among all kinds of books to read as they please and for the
fun of it. They'll soon learn to separate the good from the bad.
I have seen it happen.

As for television, I am afraid I have come to agree with J. D.
Salinger. When he told me he would never permit any of his
stories to be televised I protested, "But if all good writers take
your attitude, television will be as bad as Hollywood." He
answered, "The writing was on the wall before the wall was even
there."

Again advertising rears its ugly head. What if commercials make a bedlam of the air which belongs to all the people? What if children are inured to crime and violence by what they are shown? Even taught how to commit them? What if the stories are the old soap opera tripe? How are the ratings? How are the money changers in the Temple?

Lamenting the passing of the *Post*, Stewart Alsop, one of its long time contributors, compared the situation of fiction writers with that of poets on the grounds that poetry died when it ceased to be profitable. Oh, those Temple money changers! Of course he quoted Dr. Johnson's "No man except a blockhead ever wrote except for money," ignoring, like most people, that Dr. Johnson was poking fun at himself. Although in debt for years he kept on writing for the love of it and never did become solvent until he was fifty-three years old and then only because he was granted a government pension. There are more poets writing and being published right now in this country than ever before in its history. They are not getting much money but then neither are the editors or publishers of our literary magazines. Most of them give their time and work absolutely free. Anyone reading those magazines learns there is another America far apart from Madison Avenue and one of which we can be proud.

As for trends in the short story itself, there is little reference to Vietnam. As is usual with all wars, the important writing is done afterward. With this war there is undoubtedly greater opposition among writers, who feel deeply and painfully about it. Here television has done some good by bringing home the suffering of peasant women and children, the agony of the helpless old as they see their villages destroyed, the horror and uselessness of war itself.

For the last couple of years this anthology has noted the growth of the supernatural in stories, ghosts, talking animals, werewolves, and the like. This year there has been a remarkable number of stories centering around dreams. Not, thank heaven, the old device of a character having an extraordinary adventure and waking up to find it was only a dream but dreams as a more tangible part of the story.

There is, too, the well-known fact which has continued to be true that our Jewish writers at last have come into their own. It was only a few years ago that I was consoling some of my Jewish students at Columbia, whose good work was being rejected, by telling them that their turn was coming. Once it was New England writers who predominated, then came the Middle Western, then the Southern and now it is the Jewish.

There have been more stories with humor in them, both black humor and white. When I edited a magazine I discovered that every time I described a story as hilarious there was an outburst from readers who couldn't see anything humorous about it. I learned the reader has to be taken unaware, surprise being a basic part of humor.

Segregation of the sexes is still practiced by the girlie magazines. "Abandon all womanliness ye who enter here!" No feminine authors are allowed. The women's magazines which continue to publish much low-grade fiction are more broad-minded. Men are more than welcome to write for them. They even go to the other extreme by permitting little that is adverse about male characters. But women can be bitches in their stories. An editor explained that although her readers were nearly all women she had to be careful not to print anything derogatory about male characters. There can be no wonderful villains as in all fiction of yore. "Our publisher and top executives are men," she declared. "They wouldn't like it." I, personally, refuse to believe that modern men, even publishers, have become so namby-pamby.

This foreword began with the noting of the death of the *Post*. There was a happier event this year. The *Hudson Review*, a superb example of how fine our better magazines can be, celebrated its twentieth anniversary. I don't remember a single inferior story appearing in its pages.

I am grateful to the editors who have kept this anthology supplied with copies of their magazines and to their authors for generously granting us reprint rights. The editor of any new magazine is urged to send copies to us.

The editors and staff of Houghton Mifflin Company are entitled to gratitude for their help. Finally, tribute is paid to the memory of Edward J. O'Brien, who founded this anthology.

MARTHA FOLEY

# Contents

# Contents

THE

# BEST

AMERICAN SHORT STORIES

## 1969

# MAEVE BRENNAN

## *The Eldest Child*

(FROM THE NEW YORKER)

MRS. BAGOT had lived in the house for fifteen years, ever since her marriage. It was on a narrow street, a dead end, in the suburbs of Dublin. Her three children had been born there, in the upstairs front bedroom, and she was glad of that, because her first child, her son, was dead, and it comforted her to think that she was still familiar with what had been his one glimpse of earth — he had died at three days. At the time he died she said to herself that she would never get used to it, and what she meant by that was that as long as she lived she would never accept what had happened in the mechanical subdued way that the rest of them accepted it. They carried on, they talked and moved about her room as though when they tidied the baby away they had really tidied him away, and it seemed to her that more than anything else they expressed the hope that nothing more would be said about him. They behaved as though what had happened was finished, as though some ordinary event had taken place and come to an end in a natural way. There had not been an ordinary event, and it had not come to an end.

Lying in her bed, Mrs. Bagot thought her husband and the rest of them seemed very strange, or else, she thought fearfully, perhaps it was she herself who was strange, delirious, or even a bit unbalanced. If she was unbalanced she wasn't going to let them know about it — not even Martin, who kept looking at her with frightened eyes and telling her she must try to rest. It might be better not to talk, yet she was very anxious to explain how she felt. Words did no good. Either they did not want to hear her, or they were not able to hear her. What she was trying to tell them seemed very simple to her. What had happened could not come to an end, that was all. It could not come to an end. Without a memory, how was the baby going to find his way? Mrs. Bagot would have liked to ask that question, but she wanted to express it properly, and she thought if she could just be left alone for a while she would be able to find the right words, so that she could make herself clearly understood — but they wouldn't leave her alone. They kept trying to rouse her, and yet when she spoke for any length of time they always silenced her by telling her it was God's will. She had accepted God's will all her life without argument, and she was not arguing now, but she knew that what had happened was not finished, and she was sure it was not God's will that she be left in this bewilderment. All she wanted was to say how she felt, but they mentioned God's will as though they were slamming a door between her and some territory that was forbidden to her. But only to her; everybody else knew all about it. She alone must lie quiet and silent under this semblance of ignorance that they wrapped about her like a shroud. They wanted her to be silent and not speak of this knowledge she had now, the knowledge that made her afraid. It was the same knowledge they all had, of course, but they did not want it spoken of. Everything about her seemed false, and Mrs. Bagot was tired of everything. She was tired of being told that she must do this for her own good and that she must do that for her own good, and it annoyed her when they said she was being brave — she was being what she had to be, she had no alternative. She felt very uncomfortable and out of place, and as though she had failed, but she did not know whether to push her failure away or comfort it, and in any case it seemed to have drifted out of reach.

She was not making sense. She could not get her thoughts sorted out. Something was drifting away — that was as far as she could go in her mind. No wonder she couldn't talk properly. What she wanted to say was really quite simple. Two things. First, there was the failure that had emptied and darkened her mind until nothing remained now but a black wash. Second, there was something that drifted and dwindled, always dwindling, until it was now no more than a small shape, very small, not to be identified except as something lost. Mrs. Bagot thought she was the only one who could still identify that shape, and she was afraid to take her eyes off it, because it became constantly smaller, showing as it diminished the new horizons it was reaching, although it drifted so gently it seemed not to move at all. Mrs. Bagot would never have dreamed her mind could stretch so far, or that her thoughts could follow so faithfully, or that she could watch so steadily, without tears or sleep.

The fierce demands that had been made on her body and on her attention were finished. She could have met all those demands, and more. She could have moved mountains. She had found that the more the child demanded of her, the more she had to give. Her strength came up in waves that had their source in a sea of calm and unconquerable devotion. The child's holy trust made her open her eyes, and she took stock of herself and found that everything was all right, and that she could meet what challenges arose and meet them well, and that she had nothing to apologize for — on the contrary, she had every reason to rejoice. Her days took on an orderliness that introduced her to a sense of ease and confidence she had never been told about. The house became a kingdom, significant, private, and safe. She smiled often, a smile of innocent importance.

Perhaps she had let herself get too proud. She had seen at once that the child was unique. She had been thankful, but perhaps not thankful enough. The first minute she had held him in her arms, immediately after he was born, she had seen his friendliness. He was fine. There was nothing in the world the matter with him. She had remarked to herself that his tiny face had a very humorous expression, as though he already knew exactly what was going on. And he was determined to live. He was full of fight. She had felt him fight toward life with all his strength, and then again, with all her strength. In a little while, he would have recognized her.

What she watched now made no demands on anyone. There was no impatience there, and no impatience in her, either. She lay on her side, and her hand beat gently on the pillow in obedience to words, an old tune, that had been sounding in her head for some time, and that she now began to listen to. It was an old song, very slow, a tenor voice from long ago and far away. She listened idly.

*Oft in the stilly night,*
*Ere slumber's chain has bound me,*

*Fond memory brings the light*
*Of other days around me . . .*

Over and over and over again, the same words, the same kind, simple words. Mrs. Bagot thought she must have heard that song a hundred times or more.

*Oft in the stilly night,*
    *Ere slumber's chain has bound me,*
*Fond memory brings the light*
*Of other days around me;*
    *The smiles, the tears,*
    *Of boyhood's years,*
*The words of love then spoken;*
    *The eyes that shone*
    *Now dimmed and gone,*
*The cheerful hearts now broken.*

It was a very kind song. She had never noticed the words before, even though she knew them well. Loving words, loving eyes, loving hearts. The faraway voice she listened to was joined by others, as the first bird of dawn is joined by other birds, all telling the same story, telling it over and over again, because it is the only story they know.

There was the song, and then, there was the small shape that drifted uncomplainingly from distant horizon to still more distant horizon. Mrs. Bagot closed her eyes. She felt herself being beckoned to a place where she could hide, for the time being.

For the past day or so, she had turned from everyone, even from Martin. He no longer attempted to touch her. He had not even touched her hand since the evening he knelt down beside the bed and tried to put his arms around her. She struggled so fiercely against him that he had to let her go, and he stood up and stepped away from her. It really seemed she might injure herself, fighting against him, and that she would rather injure herself than lie quietly against him, even for a minute. He could not understand her. It was his loss as much as hers, but she behaved as though it had to do only with her. She pushed him away, and then when she was free of him she turned her face away from him and began crying in a way that pleaded for attention and consolation from someone, but not from him — that was plain. But before that, when she was pushing him away, he had seen her face, and the expression on it was of hatred. She might have been a wild animal, for all the control he had over her then, but if so she was a wild animal in a trap, because she was too weak to go very far. He pitied her, and the thought sped through his mind that if she could get up and run, or fly, he would let her go as far as she wished, and hope she would come back to him in her own time, when her anger and grief were spent. But he forgot that thought immediately in his panic at her distress, and he called down to the woman who had come in to help around the house, and asked her to come up at once. She had heard the noise and was on her way up anyway, and she was in the room almost as soon as he called — Mrs. Knox, a small, red-faced, gray-haired woman who enjoyed the illusion that life had nothing to teach her.

"Oh, I've been afraid of this all day," she said confidently, and she began to lift Mrs. Bagot up so that she could straighten the pillows and prop her up for her tea. But Mrs. Bagot struck out at the woman and began crying, "Oh, leave me alone, leave me alone. Why can't the two of you leave me alone." Then she wailed, "Oh, leave me alone," in a high strange voice, an artificial voice, and at that moment Mr. Bagot became convinced that she was acting, and that the best thing to do was walk off and leave her there, whether that was what she really wanted or not. Oh, but he loved her. He stared at her, and said to himself that it would have given him the greatest joy to see her lying there with the baby in her arms, but although that was true, the reverse was not true — to see her lying there as she was did not cause him terrible grief or anything like it. He felt ashamed and lonely and impatient, and he longed to say to her, "Delia, stop all this nonsense and let me talk to you." He wanted to appear masterful and kind and understanding, but she drowned him out with her wails, and he made up his mind she was acting, because if she was not acting, and if the grief she felt was real, then it was excessive grief, and perhaps incurable. She was getting stronger every day, the doctor had said so, and she had better learn to control herself or she would be a nervous wreck. And it wasn't a bit like her, to have no thought for him, or for what he might be suffering. It wasn't like her at all. She was always kind. He began to fear she would never be the same. He would have liked to kneel down beside the bed and talk to her in a very quiet voice, and make her understand that he knew what she was going through, and that he was going through much the same thing himself, and to ask her not to shut him away from her. But he felt afraid of her, and in any case Mrs. Knox was in the room. He was helpless. He was trying to think of something to say, not to walk out in silence, when Mrs. Knox came around the end of the bed and touched his arm familiarly, as though they were conspirators.

"The poor child is upset," she said. "We'll leave her by herself awhile, and then I'll bring her up something to eat. Now, you go along down. I have your own tea all ready."

Delia turned her head on the pillow and looked at him. "Martin," she said, "I am not angry with you."

He would have gone to her then, but Mrs. Knox spoke at once. "We know you're not angry, Mrs. Bagot," she said. "Now, you rest yourself, and I'll be back in a minute with your tray." She gave Martin a little push to start him out of the room, and since Delia was already turning her face away, he walked out and down the stairs.

There seemed to be no end to the damage — even the house looked bleak and the furniture looked poor and cheap. It was only a year since they moved into the house, and it had all seemed lovely then. Only a year. He was beginning to fear that Delia had turned against him. He had visions of awful scenes and strains in the future, a miserable life. He wished they could go back to the beginning and start all over again, but the place where they had stood together, where they had been happy, was all trampled over and so spoiled that it seemed impossible ever to make it smooth again. And how could they even begin to make it smooth with this one memory, which they should have shared, standing like an enemy between them and making enemies out of them. He would not let himself think of the baby. He might never be able to forget the shape of the poor little defeated bundle he had carried out of the bedroom in his arms, and that he had cried over down here in the hall, but he was not going to let his mind dwell on it, not for one minute. He wanted Delia as she used to be. He wanted the girl who would never have struck out at him, or spoken roughly to him. He was beginning to see there were things about her that he had never guessed at and that he did not want to know about. He thought, Better let her rest, and let this fit work itself out. Maybe tomorrow she'll be herself again. He had a fancy that when he next approached Delia it would be on tiptoe, going very quietly, hardly breathing, moving into her presence without a sound that might startle her, or surprise her, or even wake her up, so that he might find her again as she had been the first time he saw her, quiet, untroubled, hardly speaking, alone, altogether alone and all his.

Mrs. Bagot was telling the truth when she told Martin she was not angry with him. It irritated her that he thought all he had to do was put his arms around her and all her sorrow would go away, but she wasn't really angry with him. What it was — he held her so tightly that she was afraid she might lose sight of the baby, and the fear made her frantic. The baby must not drift out of sight, that was her only thought, and that is why she struck out at Martin and begged to be left alone. As he walked out of the room, she turned her face away so that he would not see the tears beginning to pour down her face again. Then she slept. When Martin came up to the room next time, she was asleep, and not, as he suspected, pretending to be asleep, but he was grateful for the pretense, if that is what it was, and he crept away, back downstairs to his book.

Mrs. Bagot slept for a long time. When she woke up, the room was dark and the house was silent. Outside was silent too; she could hear nothing. This was the front bedroom, where she and Martin slept together, and she lay in their big bed. The room was made irregular by its windows — a bow window, and then, in the flat section of wall that faced the door, French windows. The French windows were partly open, and the long white net curtains that covered them moved gently in a breeze Mrs. Bagot could not feel. She had washed all the curtains last week, and starched them, getting the room ready for the baby. In the dim light of the streetlamp, she could see the dark roof line of the row of houses across the street, and beyond the houses a very soft blackness, the sky. She was much calmer than she had been, and she no longer feared that she would lose sight of the small shape that had drifted, she noticed, much farther away while she slept. He was traveling a long way, but she would watch him. She was his mother, and it was all she could do for him now. She could do it. She was weak, and the world was very shaky, but the light of other days shone steadily and showed the truth. She was no longer bewildered, only dull, and the next time Martin came to stand hopefully beside her bed she smiled at him and spoke to him in her ordinary voice.

# JACK CADY

## *Play Like I'm Sheriff*

(FROM TWIGS)

SUNSET LAY behind the tall buildings like red and yellow smoke. The cloud cover was high. Shadows of the buildings fell across the circle that was the business center of downtown Indianapolis. The towering monument to war dead was bizarre against the darkening horizon. On it figures writhed in frozen agony, except when they caught the corner of his eye. Then they seemed to move, reflecting his own pain.

About the circle a thousand people hurried. The winter cold was non-directional as the circle enclosed the wind and channeled it here and there. The temperature was nearly freezing. Lights in store windows began to glow with attraction and importance. Everywhere there was movement.

He stood before a store window, a young man of slight build with uncut black hair, looking at coats. There was tension about his eyes. Occasionally his mouth moved. Muttering. Then his face would tense under a surge of mental pressure.

The mannequins in the window smiled; tiny female smiles dubbed on faces above plaster breasts and too-narrow legs. Some of the coats were gaily colored. Others were black with fur collars. Some were fur. The wind hailed against his thin work jacket but he was not cold. He was accustomed to weather much harder than the kind blowing.

There was no question in his mind that he was a little insane. He sobbed. Not because he was insane, but because his wife had not ever had a nice coat. Only a few times had she had really nice dresses. He felt a deep and very personal shame. She had come so far with him. He sobbed, trying to divert his thoughts and remembering that he had read that madness was never admitted. He wondered if anyone else had ever admitted it to themselves. He thought of the man who would be his wife's new husband and wondered if he would buy her fine clothes.

Farther down the street he believed there might be another store. He walked slowly, looking. Unhappiness depressed his body so that he walked with a slight stoop. Before he found another store a girl idled along beside him, walking slowly, just fast enough.

"Hello," she said, and smiled a little cleaver of a smile. He was taken by the look of her, but in his mind there was no inventory. He was conscious only of a female image. It was very general. Light and dark hair mixed. A slim girl with a pretty face. He was fooled at first, vaguely wondering if she were lost and wanted direction. The word direction sang in his head and caused him to smile.

"Hello," he told her. He walked at the same pace. She fell in beside him. It seemed almost as if they were going somewhere. As if there was a place to go and something that must be done when they arrived.

She was silent for a little while. "Do you know," she said finally, "I've come from home with practically no money. I could stand a drink. Or a sandwich." Her voice had started softly. It ended strained.

He looked at her. "Come on. It's cold here."

In the half light of the bar she seemed younger and more unhappy. He took time to look, surveying her across the table while he felt in his pocket for the fifteen dollars that must buy restaurant food and bus fare to work for the next four days. He found himself wanting the girl. He found himself wanting to go home, reacting familiarly with despair as he realized for some thousandth time that it was impossible.

As always with women he was shy. Now he did not know how to tell her. He did not want to miscall her and edged around it. "I'm pretty broke, myself," he told her. "Will be all this week."

She did not leave. She did not seem disturbed about the money. "I'll pay for the drinks. The money part wasn't true. I have some."

"I don't understand."

She suddenly seemed smaller. Almost like a child. "Talk," she said. Her voice was also smaller. She looked at him as if she were lost. "Talking to. There's lonesome in the wind. I walked to the bus station, and there was lonesome in the crowd. Like something evil hovering . . . I haven't talked to anyone for more than a week."

Her voice, as much as what she said, told him. He looked directly at her. "You're crazy, too. You've found a good ear. A good voice."

"Yes, crazy. I just want to know that someone cares. Cares just something. Want you to know. Want me to know." She hesitated. "You are so unhappy. Look so unhappy. I wouldn't have been able to speak otherwise."

"Maybe no one does care. You said it. There's lonesome all over."

She watched him. Her coat hanging beside the booth was new. "Norma," he said. "Norma Marie."

"It isn't, but I know what you mean."

A crowd of couples came through the doorway. They were laughing. He watched them then looked at her. "What do they know?" he asked.

"How to pretend," she said. "I don't really like to drink. Let's go."

They walked a long way off the circle to a parking lot. The wind pressed at the back of his legs. The girl wore no hat. Her hair was blowing.

The car was good but not new. She drove it for a long time out of the center of town. He wondered if he was supposed to make love to her, then wondered if he could. Instead of touching her he lit a cigarette and passed it. His hand was trembling.

"No," she said, taking the cigarette. "I don't think so. At least not now." She smiled at him and he felt ashamed, felt himself withdrawing into recollections of another time which held more shame. "I'll do better," he told his wife under his breath. The girl touched his hand.

"Talk," she told him. "Talk away at the lonesome first. Maybe that's all it will be."

"Do you tell me or do I tell you?"

"I don't know." She drove slowly for several minutes. He watched the streets and then the sky where the clouds seemed to be lowering. There was no light except along the streets.

She turned a corner. He realized suddenly that she was also nervous, more than she had been. "My house is down this block," she told him. "I have a whole house."

"You don't even know my name."

"I think it's Johnnie. If it isn't, lie to me."

"You guessed right," he lied. "But I haven't been called that in years." He thought it sounded authentic.

"You lie good," she told him.

"Only to myself."

The house was a tall white frame. The driveway and porch were dark. She parked the car at the back of the drive.

"My grandmother's house," she told him. "Then mother's. Then mine. Any sound will be grandma trying to get out of the attic." She laughed faintly.

"You mean haunted?" He watched her, wondering at her nervousness and at himself. The pressure of his hurt, the tension in his mind, was not relaxed but was relaxing. He quickly pulled the hurt to him because it was his and familiar. "Haunted?" He wondered if she were not worse than himself.

"Sure. Ghosts get as lonesome as people." She tried to smile and it did not work. "At least, I think they must." She stared through the windshield at the sky. "I think it will snow."

She turned to him, the tension seeming to break a little with controlled excitement. "I pretend a lot. Since I was little . . . Well, for a while I didn't pretend. Yes, I did. But now I pretend a lot. Like when you were little you know, and you said 'Let's play like I'm the sheriff and you don't know I'm here and you come around that corner.' . . ."

"I remember."

"All right. Now, I'll play like Norma and you play like Johnnie and we'll go into our house and I'll fix dinner. And while I fix dinner you can sit in the kitchen and talk. And be friendly. And good, and tell me how well I'm doing, because . . ." She turned to him. Her eyes held tears that she would not allow to come. "Because he never did, you know."

"But, you pretended." He could not help interest.

"Of course. Didn't you?"

The question alarmed him. He sat watching the sky through the windshield and was quiet for a long time. Finally he turned toward her. "Yes, but I called it lying to myself."

"It is. Do you like the real way better?"

"No." The longing for something that could not be came back hard. He felt it, then fought it, surprising himself. "All right. Pretend." He opened the door on his side and she watched him. He got out, walked in front of the car and around to open the door for her. When she got out it was with a smile that he believed, and not a muscular gesture. "You never did that before," she whispered.

"I will now," he told her. "I will show you more care now, but I'm sorry for before."

"Don't be sorry." She took his hand and they walked around the old house. "People should use their front doors," she told him, "it makes them more important."

The house looked like a museum. The furniture was of mixed periods. He recognized some as old and valuable. There was antique glassware sitting about. The rooms were ordered and neat.

"We are the fourth generation in this house," she said. "It's always good to think that."

"I don't know much about my family," he said truthfully.

"I know," she told him, "but that's not important. As long as we're proud of us."

He took her coat, holding it and looking about.

"Thank you," she said. "The closet under the front stairway will do." She moved from him, through a series of rooms to the back of the house. He hung the coat and his jacket in the closet, which was empty except for an old trench coat. He looked at the coat, thinking it long enough to fit him but made for a heavier man. Then he walked through the rooms where she had gone. He found her working at the counter in the kitchen. The kitchen was modern, contradicting the rest of the house. He stood, not quite knowing what was expected of him. "Can I help you?"

"No," she smiled. "Just sit with me." Her movements at the counter seemed natural and nearly familiar. She looked at him seriously, then hesitated. "I'm glad to have you home." Her voice was faint, but it seemed clearly determined.

He was surprised, then remembered. "I'm glad to be home."

There was a different kind of worry on her face. "I was afraid. Well, you like Charlotte too well. I wish she were married."

He looked at her. "Not that well. A friend."

"Too well, and she's awfully crude."

"Yes," he said. "I wish she would move. Tough. Very hard."

"She's been gone since you left, and I thought."

"Of course. But, here I am."

"Sometimes. Oh, I'm sorry. Sometimes you're hard and I don't understand."

He was startled and then defensive about being charged with something he could never be. "I'll not be that, not anymore. I'm different now, you know. I've stopped losing my temper." He wondered if he were saying right. The girl had her back turned, working rapidly. Then she turned to face him. Her face held shame.

"I'm sorry about something, too. I was going to kill myself if I didn't find you tonight. You'd been gone so long."

He was startled. "How long has it been?"

"Nearly five months. Your mother called last night and said you were on the coast. She wanted the rings back. She wasn't kind." She turned back to work. "How did you get home so soon?"

"I flew." He did not understand his action, but he rose and walked to her. He touched her shoulder.

"Sometimes," she said, "you used to touch me here." She placed his hand in her hair. "It's all right if you muss it." He touched gently under and about her hair.

"Thank you," she said, then turned to him with a pretended smile because the hurt was deep in her eyes. "Now go," she told him, "or go hungry."

"I'd rather go hungry."

Her hands shook over the bowl. "Thank you again," she said. He returned to his chair. "Kill yourself?" He wondered, thinking that she was even more troubled than himself. Then he denied it out of an obscure loyalty to his own trouble. He wondered if there were not more complications than he could handle, and he wondered that he cared.

"My grandmother was so happy," she said. "This fine house, fine husband and nice children. But my mother was not. So I locked her in the attic."

"Your mother?"

"No. You know when we buried her. But grandma died when I was little. I helped carry her things to the attic. They told me . . . I don't know. Whatever you tell children. But she has lived in the attic ever since. But I locked the door. Against losing her, you know."

"But, kill yourself?"

"By going to sleep. In a special way. Someday, and that day was tonight, I think, it would have come on so very lonesome. With you gone. With you gone. And only people to talk to who wanted to buzz at you. Friends, you know." Her back was still turned. He watched her tense, then clench her hands and he heard the bitterness in her voice. Then her hands relaxed a bit. Her voice was low and strained. Worse, he thought, than it had been.

"When no one cares. What to do?"

"What were you going to do?" He was surprised at the softness of his voice.

"Get the key and unlock the door. Then I was going up the steps. Very narrow. Very straight. And I'd go quietly and catch her asleep. And I'd say 'Grandma, grandma,' and she would come, like when I was little . . . I had a dog once, remember I told you, but he died. That dog loved me. I played with him when I was a little girl. And grandma loved me — and, she'd touch me and hold me and make me like a little girl again, because, because . . ." Her speech stumbled and the tensions moved to tears and heavy weeping. "Because I'm so damn lousy — at being a woman."

He moved to her quickly around the counter and held her while she wept. She was tense in his arms. Her body seemed slim nearly to thinness. He was confused. Wondering who. Wondering what was her name.

"Norma," he said, and held her closer.

She raised her head to look at him while still weeping. "Do you want me? Will you want me? I'll do so very badly." She lowered her head. "But I'll try. Because I'm crazy now. I'll be lots better crazy." -

"Wait," he told her. "Come now, calm down." He felt nearly afraid. "Come, sit down." He moved to try to lead her to a chair.

"No," she told him. "It's all right. It will be all right." She moved back toward him. He smoothed her hair as he held her. They stood for several minutes until her weeping subsided. Then she turned and left, to come back with a handkerchief. She was trying to smile.

"I took my vacation to find you. The whole two weeks."

The continued pretense made him angry. He reacted in a way familiar to him and became very quiet. It occurred to him that she needed him more than he needed her. It was a strange and warm feeling to be needed. Then it occurred to him that he might be lying to himself again.

"I changed jobs." He paused. "The other wasn't that good anyway." A rush of misgiving overcame him. He had surprised himself by having been taken by the pretense. "I wanted to do better."

"Better?"

"Not right away." He heard shame in his voice. "In a little while you get raised."

"Don't worry about money. Oh, please, not now. Don't worry." She turned to the window then turned back with a tiny laugh.

"See," she told him, "I was right. It's snowing."

He stood and went to the window. The snow was light and carried by the wind. "A light fall," he said.

"It will get heavier." She was placing silver and dishes on the table. "I just have wine." Her voice was apologetic.

"Just a little," he told her. She looked up quickly.

"The table looks so pretty," he said.

"Thank you."

"And the house looks nice."

"I kept it for when you came. Now we'll eat before it's cold."

The meal went well. They ate quickly. She seemed more at ease to him. Once or twice the unfamiliarity of his surroundings surprised him. Or he looked at the girl and recoiled at the pretense. When that happened memories of his wife and memories of his loss and aimlessness came back. His mind would try to recede each time into the trouble. Instead, he would speak.

"When I was little," he told her, "we'd watch a snow like this. Kid hungry, you know. If it were early in the year, like tonight, Dad would watch for a while. If it got heavy he'd get the sleds out of the barn. We'd polish the runners."

"Great Grandfather died on a night like this," she told him.

"When I was very little. I mostly remembered the snow. I've always loved it. Like a fresh beginning in the morning."

"You've always lived here?"

"Always here." She looked at him reproachfully, maintaining the pretense. "I didn't know you ever lived on a farm. You should have known about Great Grandfather."

"Yes."

She smiled, then stood to clear the table. "But I'll tell you something the cousins never told you. He didn't come to Indiana because of the oil wells. He left Philadelphia in front of a shotgun."

"Girl?"

"The family skeleton. No, that's not kind to say. Because the girl died soon after. I don't know how."

He helped to clear the table while she placed dishes in the sink. "He was an old rip, I guess. But I've always loved the snow."

While she ran water in the sink he moved to help her. She turned, surprised, but said nothing. They worked together quietly. He stacked the dry dishes on the counter. When the work was done she began putting them away.

"Do you know," she said, "I'm so tired. I seem to get tired quicker, lately."

He watched her. Unsure. "I figured it out because I'm the same way. Every minute you're awake you're tensed up, burning energy. I sleep a lot."

"Good," she said. "Come with me." She took his hand and they walked slowly through the house to ascend the front stairway. At the top of the stairs she hesitated. He stood beside her, moving away a short distance. He did not hold her hand.

"No," she said. "That way is the door to the attic." There was some quality of determination in her voice. She took his hand and led him down a hall to the front bedroom. The room was very dark until she pulled the shades at the front window. Tall trees stood bare before the house, partially obstructing a streetlight. The snow fall was getting heavier. It was still being pushed by the wind.

"Please stand here," she said and squeezed his hand. He stood, watching through the window and listening to her movement about the room.

When she spoke her voice was faint. "You used to like to watch me but I was shy. I still am but not so much."

He stood watching the snow. The onetime familiar feeling of excitement filled him as the snow swirled about the streetlight. When she stepped beside him she was naked to the waist.

"I love you," she said, "I was so stupid to doubt." Her breasts were lighted by the faintness of the snow-shrouded streetlight. They were shadowed underneath. The light fell across her face and hair so that he saw that she was beautiful with the prettiness. Her face seemed even more sensitive than before. Then across her face there seemed a small realization of fear.

"We stood this way once," she murmured.

He nodded, saying nothing, but knowing that with the fear and the pretense he could not make love to her.

"Would you like to sleep now?" he asked.

"Yes." She smiled. The fear vanished as she saw his understanding. "But, first. Hold me, please." He put his arm about her waist then moved to touch her.

"Thank you," he said, and he did not know why.

"Come." She led him to the bed which was on a darkened side of the room. She lay down and he removed his shoes then lay beside her. He did not touch her. They were quiet. He listened to her breathing. It seemed to him that the darkened room was filled with questions and the questions were mostly about himself.

"Norma?"

"Yes."

"Are you still pretending?"

"I'm not sure. In parts, I think."

He paused. "I always blamed myself, you know. Never figured anyone was wrong but me."

He touched her hand. It was relaxed and did not respond. Her breathing was quiet. For a moment he felt badly. "Maybe I was right," he said. "Nobody does care. Maybe nobody cares for anybody."

"Don't," she said. "You're feeling wrong. Not for you they don't care that way. Maybe they don't care. Not for me. But each cares that no one cares for the other."

"That isn't enough, is it?"

"No. That isn't enough. But it's enough to keep yourself from dying. And, thank you."

"My mind gets so full of the other . . ." He realized what she had said. He tried to draw back a small feeling of pride.

"And mine," she told him. "But pretend seems to be what I've been doing most of my life. Can you pretend a thing until it's real?"

"I think it's what we haven't learned." He touched her hand again. This time she held his. "In the morning when we get up I'll say hello to you. I'll say, 'I love you, Norma' and you'll say . . ."

"I'll say, 'I love you, Johnnie.' "

"And I'll go to work."

"If the streets aren't impossible I'll drive you. Then I'll go back to work. And when work is over . . ." She stopped. He wanted badly to tell her that at least he was really wondering about tomorrow.

"You don't know," he told her instead.

"That's the truth. Yes. That's the truth. I don't. Maybe it's how hard you pretend, Johnnie." She turned to him and whispered her shyness. "Before we sleep, will you pretend something if it doesn't hurt? Will you kiss me and say good night and call me Catherine? Not Cathy, but Catherine. Then I'll pretend for you and call you . . ."

He held her and kissed her. He was surprised at her response in the short kiss. Her body against his seemed in some way familiar. He did not know if it was the familiarity of the form of Norma who was not there or the familiarity of the stranger who was. There was a rush of pressure in his mind. He had lived with it for so long. Now he fought it back.

"Thank you, Catherine," he told her. "And, something that just occurred. Maybe you have to love yourself a little first, Catherine."

She touched his hair. His hand felt necessary to him against her back. He wondered what his hand meant to her.

"Pretend, Catherine," he whispered gently. "Good night, Catherine," he said.

# MARK COSTELLO

## Murphy's Xmas

(FROM THE TRANSATLANTIC REVIEW)

### I

MURPHY'S DRUNK on the bright verge of still another Christmas and a car door slams. Then he's out in the headlights and in bed waking up the next afternoon with Annie kissing his crucified right fist. It's blue and swollen, and when he tries to move it, it tingles, it chimes and Annie says, How did you hurt your hand? Did you hit somebody?

Murphy waits while that question fades on her mouth, then the room glitters and he sniffs the old fractured acid of remorse asking: Was I sick?

Yes.

Where?

On the floor. And you fell out of bed twice. It was so terrible I don't think I could stand it if it happened again promise me you won't get drunk anymore, Glover had to teach both of your classes this morning you frighten me when you're this way and you've lost so much weight you should have seen yourself last night laying naked on the floor like something from a concentration camp in your own vomit you were so white you were blue

is the color of Annie's eyes as Murphy sinks into the stars and splinters of the sheets with her, making love to her and begging her forgiveness which she gives and gives until Murphy can feel her shy skeleton waltzing away with his in a fit of ribbons, the bursting bouquets of a Christmas they are going to spend apart and

bright the next morning they rise in sweet sorrow to part for

Christmas; she to her parents' home in Missouri, he to haunted
Illinois.

Murphy holds her head in his hands and whispers: I can't leave
you. I won't be able to sleep. I know I won't. I'll get sick. I need
you Annie.

She squeezes his shoulders, kisses his cheeks and tells him he can
do it. It's only for two weeks. Good-bye. And be careful. Driving.

The door slams, the windows rattle, and Annie walking through
the snow is no bigger than her cello which she holds to her shoulder,
a suitcase bangs against her left knee and the door opens and there's
Glover jangling the keys of his Volkswagen, offering again to drive
Murphy's family into Illinois for him.

Stricken by swerving visions of his son strewn across the wet December roadside, his toys and intestines glistening under the wheels
of semi-trucks, Murphy says no, he will drive and as he takes the
proffered keys, Glover says: Is Annie gone already? I was supposed
to give her a cello lesson before she left

then he leaves, the door slams and Murphy hates him, his By-
ronesque limp through the snow, his cello and his Volkswagen and
sobriety. Rubbing his right fist, Murphy goes to the kitchen and
drains a can of beer. Then he packs his bag and lights out for his
abandoned home.

## II

Now the trunks are tied down and the Volkswagen is overladen
and they roll out of Kansas into Missouri with the big wind knocking
them all over the road while vigilant Murphy fights the wheel and
grins at the feather touches of his five-year-old son who kisses his
neck and romps in the back seat, ready for Christmas.

In Mexico, Missouri, his ex-wife looks at his swollen right fist and
says: Tsk-tsk. You haven't grown up yet have you. Who did you
hit this time?

Into the face of her challenge, Murphy blows blue cigarette smoke.

When they cross the mighty Mississippi at Hannibal, she looks up
at the old, well-kept houses, pats her swollen stomach and says:
Maybe I could come here to live, to have my baby.

Murphy's son rushes into the crack of her voice. And he doesn't
stop asking him to come back and be his daddy again until Murphy
takes Dexamyl to keep awake and it is dark and his son is asleep and

the Volkswagen hops and shutters over the flat mauve stretches of
Illinois.

At Springfield, where they stop to take on gas, the fluorescent light
of the filling station is like the clap of a blue hand across the face.
Murphy's son wakes and his wife says: This is where President
Lincoln lived and is buried.
Where?
In a tomb. Out there.
She points a finger past his nose and Murphy makes a promise he
knows he can't keep: I know what. Do you want to hear a poem,
Michael?
With his son at the back of his neck all snug in a car that he should
never have presumed to borrow, he drives through Springfield trying to remember "When Lilacs Last in the Dooryard Bloom'd."
But he can't get past the first stanza. 3 times he repeats "O powerful western fallen star," and then goes on in prose about the coffin
moving across the country with the pomp of the inloop'd flags,
through cities draped in black until his son is asleep again and
    that coffin becomes his wife's womb and from deep in its copious
satin Murphy hears the shy warble of the fetus: *you are my father,
you are my father,* the throat bleeds, the song bubbles, Murphy is
afraid enough to fight. He looks at his wife and remembers the wily
sunlight of conception, the last time he made love to her amid the
lace iron and miniature American flags of the Veterans' Cemetery
(it's the quietest place I know to talk, she said) while the crows
slipped across the sun like blue razor blades and the chatter of
their divorce sprung up around them
    stone and pine, lilac and star, the cedars dusk and dim: *well it's
final then, we're definitely going to get a divorce?* Murphy said *yes,*
for good? *yes* and his wife caught him by the hip as he turned
away *well it's almost dark now so why don't we just lay down and
fuck once more for old time's sake here on the grass come on there
are pine needles and they're soft*
    *Did you take your pill?*
    *Yes*
    *Ok, but no strings attached* and
    three and a half months later Murphy is informed that he is going
to be a father again and again, hurray, whoopee now

Murphy drives across slippery Illinois hearing a carol of death until the singer so shy becomes a child he will never hold or know, and the sweet chant of its breath gets caught in the whine of the tires as he imagines holding the child and naming it and kissing it, until it falls asleep on his shoulder — *how could you have tricked me this way? how could you have done it?*

That question keeps exploding behind Murphy's eyes, and when they hit his wife's hometown, he stops the car in front of a tavern and says: I can't do it.

What?

Face your parents.

He gets out: I'll wait here. Come back when you're unloaded.

His wife says *wait a minute,* and Murphy slams the door. He walks under the glittering *Budweiser* sign and she screams: I can't drive. I don't even know how to get this thing in reverse . . .

Push down.

Child!

Murphy hovers over the car: *I'm not a child!* and the motor roars, and the gears grind, and the Volkswagen hops and is dead. A red light flashes on in the middle of the speedometer and Murphy turns to the wakening face of five-year-old Michael: Are we at grandma's yet daddy?

He slams his swollen right fist into his left palm: Yes we are!

Then he gets in and takes the wheel. And he drives them all the way home.


But he doesn't stop there. Murphy roars northwest out of Illinois into Iowa in search of friends and gin he can't find. Then he bangs back across the Mississippi, cuts down the heart of Illinois, and holes up in the YMCA in his wife's hometown, within visiting distance of his son.

Whom he loves and doesn't see. He keeps telling himself: *I think I'll surprise Michael and take him to the park this afternoon,* then he races down to the gym to run in circles and spit against the walls. He sits in the steam room, watches the clock and slaps his stomach, which is flat, but on the blink. To ease his pain, he drinks milk and eats cottage cheese and yogurt and calls Annie long distance in Missouri: God I love you and miss your body Annie I haven't slept for two days and she says: Guess what?

What?

Glover was through town and gave me a cello lesson, he's a great guy his

gifts are stunning and relentless, he limps off to take your classes when you're too drunk to stand up in the morning — his hair is scrubbed, his skin cherubic, his wrists are opal and delicate; right now Murphy would like to seize them and break them off. Instead he says: Is he still in town?

Who?

Glover.

Heavens no, he just stopped through for about two hours are you all right?

Yes.  Listen Annie I love you

Murphy slams the phone down and bounds back upstairs to his room in the YMCA to sit alone while his cottage cheese and yogurt cartons fill up with snow on the window ledge and he imagines Annie back in their rooms in Kansas.  When she walks across the floor her heels ring against the walls and every morning Murphy hears her before he sees her standing at the stove, her hair dark, her earrings silver, her robe wine, her thighs so cool and the pearl flick of her tongue is like a beak when she kisses him

Murphy tastes unbelievable mint and blood and

imagines Glover limping across the floor of the living room with two glasses of gin in his hands.  The betrayal is dazzling and quick. Bending under Glover's tongue, Annie whispers *no, no,* and as she goes down in their bed, her fingers make star-shaped wrinkles in the sheets

Murphy slams his fist down on his YMCA windowsill.  Then popping them like white bullwhips over his head, he stuffs his towels and clothes into his bag, and lights out of there on lustrous Highway 47.  The night is prodigal, the inane angels of the radio squawk out their 1000 songs of Christmas and return.  Bearing down on the wheel, Murphy murders the memory of Annie and Glover with the memory of his father, whom he has betrayed to old age, the stars and stripes of the U.S. MAIL.

Composing them on the back of his American Legion 40 *and* 8 stationery, Murphy's father sends quick notes *BY AIR* to his grandson saying: I was feeling pretty low x until I got the pictures you drew for me Michael boy x then I bucked up x God bless you x I miss you x give my love to your daddy x who

unblessed and rocking in the slick crescents of Dexamyl and fatigue, is on his way home for still another Christmas. Now as he drives, he notes the dim absence of birds in the telephone lines, and thinking of the happy crows that Michael draws with smiles in their beaks, Murphy sees his father stumbling under the sign of the cross, crossing himself again and again on the forehead and lips, crossing himself on his tie clasp, wandering in a listless daze across the front lawn with a rake in his hands, not knowing whether to clean the gutter along the street or pray for his own son who has sunk so low out in Kansas.

It is just dawning when Murphy breaks into the mauve and white outskirts of his dear dirty Decatur where billboards and *Newport* girls in turquoise are crowned by the bursting golden crosses of Murphy's high school then

he's home. Pulled up and stopped in his own driveway. And sitting there with his hands crossed in his lap he feels agog like a buddhistic time bomb about to go off, about to splinter and explode inside the dry sleep of his parents, the tears will smoulder, the braying angels of insomnia will shatter around the childless Christmas tree, there will be a fire, it will sputter and run up the walls and be Murphy's fault. Sitting there he feels hearts beginning to pump in the palms of his hands and he doesn't want to let anybody die

as he knocks on the dry oaken door of his parents' home and is welcomed with open arms and the sun rising behind his back

Inside the sockets of his mother's eyes, there are mauve circles and they have had the living room walls painted turquoise. Murphy blinks, shakes his father's hand, and his mother leads him into the kitchen.

There he drinks milk, eats cottage cheese and kisses his mother's hands. She cries and wants him to eat a big breakfast. With tears in her eyes, she offers him bacon, eggs, cornbread, coffee, butter chunk sweet rolls and Brazil nuts. When Murphy shakes his head she says: I think you're making the biggest mistake of your life, I think you'll live to regret it. Patricia is a lovely girl, you have a

wonderful son and another child on the way. Isn't there any hope
of you getting back together? I pray night and day and can't get
little Michael off my mind. What's ever going to happen to him and
the new child? Oh I wish I were twenty years younger

After breakfast they go shopping, and for his Christmas present
Murphy picks out three packs of stainless steel razor blades and a
pair of black oxford basketball shoes. Then he slips off for a work-
out at his high school gym. The basketball team is practicing and
Murphy runs in wide circles around them, not bothering a soul.

Left to himself that afternoon, he drinks rum and eggnog and
plays with the remote controls of the color television set. Then he
roams the house and neighborhood and everything has changed.
The sheets of his bed are blue. On the walls, where once there were
newspaper photographs of himself in high school basketball uniform, there are now purple paintings of Jesus Christ kneeling on
rocks in the Garden of Gethsemane. Every place he looks, in cor-
niced frames of diminishing size, there are color photographs of
Murphy in tight-collared military attire. As he looks, the photographs get smaller and smaller and there is always a snub-nosed
statue of St. Francis of Assisi standing there, to measure himself by.

Up and down the block, birds bang in and out of bird feeders.
The withering neighbors have put up fences within fences within
fences. Half-drunk, Murphy keeps hitting the wrong switches and
floodlights glare from the roof of the garage and light up the whole
backyard. All night long his father keeps paying the encroaching
Negro carolers not to sing. Finally Murphy gets up from the sofa,
and smiling, announces that he's going out. Taking his rum and
eggnog with him, he sits in the Volkswagen and drinks until 3 o'clock
in the morning. Then he gets out, vomits on the curb, and goes
back inside

Where his mother is awake in a nightgown of shriveled violet,
with yellow spears of wheat sewn into the shoulders like cross-staves
of static lightning about to go off and how
will Murphy hold her when she stops him on the carpet outside his bedroom door to tell him that she loves him, that he will
always be her son no matter what happens she is so sorry that he
had to leave his wife and children for

a mere girl, it is unbelievable that

in his hands her small skull buzzes and even before she mentions the fact of Annie, Murphy is holding Annie's skull in his hands and the sinking wings of his mother's sweet shoulders are Annie's shoulders in his mother's nightgown sinking: What are you talking about?

That girl you're living with.  She called tonight

on Christmas Eve

Murphy hears the old familiar bells of his father's fury gonging

Your father answered, he was furious

Mother I'm not living with anyone

Michael I know you are

then the small lightning of her nightgown begins to strike across her shoulders and she is sobbing against his throat and Murphy is in bed holding his lie like a sheet up to his chin: Mother I told you I'm not living with anyone

Stroking his leg through the blankets, she disregards the crocked insomnia of his eyes, and makes him promise to try to sleep: Do you promise now?

Yes mother, I promise

and she leaves him sleepless between the blue sheets with Christ kneeling on the wall, the scent of his mother's hand cream on the back of his neck and he hears her alone in her room coughing like a wife he has lost at last and picking at her rosary beads all night long

There is no sleep

or peace on earth. But with the muzzy dawn Murphy rises and goes to church with his parents. In the choir loft, the organs shutter; in his pew, Murphy shivers and sniffs the contrition of Christmastide. All around him the faithful kneel in candle smoke and pray; all day long Murphy kneels and shuffles around trying to get Annie *long distance,* trying to tell her *never to call him at home again.* Then at 7 p.m. the phone rings and Murphy's simmering 70-year-old father answers it hissing: Long distance, for you

By the time Murphy hangs up, his father is dizzy. He staggers through the rooms slamming doors while Murphy's mother follows him whispering: Mike your blood pressure, your blood pressure

Then in the living room they face each other: The bitch! Calling here on Christmas Day! The little bitch!

Murphy turns to his mother and says, *I'm leaving* and his father spins him by the shoulder: You're not leaving, *I* am!

They both leave. Murphy by the back, his father by the front. Storm doors slam, crucifixes rattle on the walls. Murphy's father rounds the corner and screams: Come back here!

His voice is higher than Murphy has ever heard it, and the wind pulls at their clothes while they walk toward each other, his father in a slanting stagger, his overcoat too big for him, his eyes filled with tears.

I'm an old man. I'm dying. You won't see me again. Go back to your family, don't abandon your son.

Murphy reaches for his shoulder and says *Dad I can't* and his father slaps his hand away

*Michael Murphy*. You have a son named *Michael Murphy* and you tell me you can't go back to him?

Murphy lifts his hand and starts to speak, but his father screams: *Phony!* You're a phon*eee,* do you hear me?

They are at the door and Murphy's mother, in grief and her night-gown, pulls them in. His father stumbles to the wall and hits it: You phony. You ought to be in Vietnam!

Murphy's laughter is curdled and relieved. He slaps his hands together and screams: That's it, that's it!

Then he spins and bolts toward the back door, with his mother screaming: Michael! Where are you going?

To Vietnam, god damn it! To Vietnam

Which isn't far. 150 miles north. From a motel room deep in her own hometown, Murphy calls his wife and when he asks her to come over she says: Why *should* I come over?

You know why. I'm going out of my mind.

Be my guest.

*Click*

She opens the door during half-time of a TV football game and neither of them say a word as their clothes fly in slurred arcs onto the bed. Then standing naked in front of her, Murphy hunches up with holy quietude and smiles and breathes as he holds a glass of gin and tonic to her lips and she drinks and smiles as the lime-skin nudges her teeth and she nods when she's had enough. While her mouth is still cool, Murphy kisses her tongue and gums and wants to push the bed against the wall and then to drive all the other guests to insomniac rack and ruin by humping and banging the bed with wet good health against the wall all afternoon but

his wife is sunk in an older despair. She runs her fingers up the vapid stack of Murphy's spine and says: You *are* handsome. I love to touch you.

Bare-chested Murphy turns on it, and the quick trick of her flattery gets them into bed, where to the pelvic thud of the inner-spring, she sucks on the spare skin of his collar bone and says: Tell me that you love me. You don't have to mean it. Just say it . . .

Murphy would like to, but he can't. Both memory and flesh legislate against him. He looks down, and like painted furniture, his wife's ribs now seem chipped by a 1000 kicks; when he takes them in his mouth, her nipples taste as tight and deprived as walnuts; within the pregnant strop of her stomach against his, Murphy can feel the delicate strophes of Annie's waist, and moving like a pale liar before his wife's bared teeth, he remembers the beginning of the end of their marriage; the masks, mirrors and carrots that began to sprout around their bed like a bitter, 2 am, Victory garden, one that Murphy had planted all by himself and was going to pick and shake in his wife's face on the sparkling, sacrosanct morning that he left for good and ever. Caught in the dowdy mosaics of their bedroom mirror, they would get down on their hands and knees and as the orange joke of a carrot disappeared between her legs, his wife would turn and ask, *who are you?* and Murphy would smile down from behind his mask and say: *who are you?* Then his smile would rot in his opened mouth, and Murphy *became* his impersonations; he played and moaned within an adultery so hypothetical it stunk and smoked the bedroom ceiling up like the induced death of love between them *HARDER, OH HARDER* now Murphy and his father are standing outside the motel room window looking in at Murphy's marriage like peeping toms and his father is ordering Murphy back into the bed but Murphy resists and all of his reasons are rosy and shrill like a schoolboy he screams: *I wouldn't swap Annie for anybody, do you hear me, not anybody* and his father, in tears and death screams: *Not for your son? Not for Michael Murphy? I'M*
*COMING*

and Murphy opens his eyes to endure his wife's orgasm like a slap across the face *OH THANK YOU GOD, OH THANK YOU*

Thanking her with whispers and pecks about the neck and ears,
Murphy sweeps his wife out into the brittle December afternoon and
bright the next morning he picks up his son to take him home, 150
miles south, to his grandmother. Michael's raucous teeth glitter in
the rearview mirror of the VW, and as they rattle into Decatur,
Murphy loves him so much, he can't stop or share him with anybody just yet: I know what Michael. Do you want to go to the zoo
before we go to grandma's? Yes

he does. Right now. And Murphy, full of grins and flapdoodle,
takes him there. He buys Michael a bag of popcorn, and as he goes
back to the car to flick off the headlights, he turns to see the popcorn falling in white, jerky sprays among the ducks and geese.

The whole pause at the zoo is that way: spendthrift, inaugural
and loving. Murphy squats and shows Michael how to feed the
steaming billy goat with his bare hands. He flinches and giggles at
the pink pluck of his lips, then they race over to look through the
windows at the pacing leopards. Bare-handed and standing there,
Murphy wonders how he would defend his son against a leopard.
He can feel his fists and forearms being ripped away, but also he can
feel his son escaping into the dusk and dim of the elm trees that
surround the zoo.

Then he gets zany and amid giggles and protests, Murphy drives
the borrowed VW up over the curb and through the park to grandmother's house they go with the radio blaring: help I need somebody's help then

suddenly it's darker and cooler and their smiles are whiter when
the subject changes like a slap across the face to

Michael's dreams. 5 years old in a fatherless house, he sleeps
alone and dreams of

snow. Murphy pulls him into the front seat, sets him on his lap
and turns off the radio. Holding him too tight, he says: what kind
of snow Michael?

*You know.* The kind that falls.

What do you dream?

That it's covering me up.

Then Michael begins to cry and says: I want somebody to sleep
with me tonight and tomorrow night. I want *you* to sleep with me
daddy.

Murphy does. Three nights they stay in his parents' house and
Murphy sleeps between the blue sheets while Michael sucks his
thumb and urinates the first night against Murphy's leg, giving him
the chance to be patient father loving his son

he carries him to the bathroom with sure avowals and tender
kisses: That's all right Michael boy, dad will take care of you

Always?

Always

and Murphy's mother is there in her nightgown in the stark light
of the bedroom changing the sheets, putting down towels, kissing her
grandson, wishing she were twenty years younger

In the lilac morning, quick with clouds and sunlight, Murphy
and his mother and son go uptown. Standing in front of laughing
mirrors in the Buster Brown Shoe Store, Murphy and Michael
grow fat and skinny and tall and short together, then go to see Pin-
nochio not in the belly of a whale

but in the outer space of sure death and forgiveness, they eat
silver sno-cones and Murphy is finally able to eat steak while his
father roams through the rooms presenting his grandson with a
plastic pistol on the barrel of which an assassin's scope has been
mounted.

Compounding that armament with love, he displays, on the last
afternoon, Murphy's basketball clippings. Spreading them out
for his grandson on the bed, he whispers, smiles and gloats until 5
year old Michael can't help himself. He walks over to Murphy and
says: Grandpa says you were a great basketball player and played
on TV

is that right daddy?

That's right Michael, then they

are leaving. Clasping his toys to him, Michael cries pained and
formal tears. Murphy stands on the curb, the wind is in his eyes,
and the apologies are yet to be made. Overhead the streetlight clangs
and they are standing on the same corner where Murphy used to sit
under the streetlight at night on the orange fire hydrant twirling
his rosary beads like a black propeller over his head waiting for his
parents to come home and light up the dark rooms with their voices
and cigarettes then

he would see their headlights coming up the street and he would
rise and put away his rosary beads to greet them now

he takes off his gloves and puts out his right hand to his father
and says: Dad, I'm sorry.

When his apology cracks the air, his mother begins to cry. Grateful for that cue, his father takes his hand and says Good bye, good
luck, God bless you

## III

Out there in Kansas the next afternoon, under a sere and bene-
dictory sun, Murphy's Christmas comes to an end. He tools west
away from home and the holidays, southwest toward the snaggled
conclusion of still another New Year. His family rides in a swarm
of shredded Kleenex, Cracker Jack and terror referred

is terror refined: like the crucial envoy of his grandfather, Michael,
sweet assassin, holds his plastic pistol to the base of Murphy's skull
and says: Daddy? Why don't you come back and be my daddy?

Terse and perspirate, Murphy's wife takes a swipe at the pistol,
but Michael moves out of her reach, and keeping it trained on the
back of his father's skull, he repeats his question: Why don't you
come back daddy?

Before he can think or excuse himself, Murphy says, *Because.*
Because why?

Because mommy and I fight

You're not fighting now.

In tears and on her knees, Murphy's wife lunges into the back
seat and disarms her son. But he begins to cry and find his ulti-
matum: Daddy

I'm too shy to have a new daddy, I want you to be my daddy, and
if you won't come back and be my daddy

I'm going to kill you.

The moment of his threat is considered. And then it is fore-
gone. Out of his fist and index finger, Michael makes a pistol and
a patricide: Bang, bang, bang

you're dead daddy

you're dead

Coffin that passes through lanes and streets, Volkswagen that
blows and rattles under the new snow's perpetual clang, here,
Murphy hands over his sprig of lilac and return, his modicum of
rage and disbelief.

Certain that his son's aim was shy and hypothetical, he stops the
Volkswagen in front of his apartment, flicks off the headlights, slams
the door and hears the
   dual squawk of tuned and funereal cellos
   their notes curdle the snow, splinter the windows with a welcome
so baroque and sepulchral, Murphy can't stand it. Roaring toward
the door, he imagines Annie and Glover sitting on stiff-backed chairs,
their cellos between their legs, their innocence arranged by Bach,
certified by
   the diagonal churn of their bows on string, the spiney octagons
of their music stands, the opal bone and nylon of Annie's knees.
Murphy rattles the door with his fist, and for a moment their music
needles his rage, then squeaks to a stop. In turquoise slacks and
sweater, with a smile brimful of tears and teeth so bright, Annie
throws open the door and how
   will Murphy return her kiss, while blurred in the corner of his
eye, Glover scurries, gathering up his cello and his music: *Happy
New Year did the car run all right* he takes the proffered keys and
   guilty of nothing but his embarrassment
   he says *don't mention it* as he leaves, slams out the door and
   left in the rattled vacuum of that departure, Murphy has no one
to beat up or murder, no one on whom to avenge his Christmas; he
is left with only the echo of the music, a suspicion founded on nothing but a cherub's limp and hustle through the chiming snow.

   In bed, Annie is a sweet new anatomy of hope and extinction.
She kisses him, the *Newport* flood of her hair gets in his eyes, and
Murphy cracks an elegiac and necessary joke: *Annie you'll never
leave me for Glover will you?* She tells him not to be silly then
   Murphy kisses her, and in a rush of flesh and new avowals, he puts
everything in to his lovemaking but his
   heart
   which hangs unbelievable and dead in his ribs, all shot to smithereens by Michael.

   Outside the new snow falls and inside it is over. Annie is asleep
in his arms and Murphy lies sleepless on a numb and chiming cross
of his own making. On the walls there are no praying Christs, the
turquoise Gethsemanes of Decatur are gone forever. The clock

drones, the womb whirrs, the shy trill of his wife's gestation comes to Murphy through the pines like Michael calling to him: *Sleep with me tonight and tomorrow night daddy* the cradle's eloquence depends on pain, it is sewn in lilacs and shocks of wheat. Shy charlatan, Murphy sneaks up to it and in a room full of white, white sunlight, he looks in at his newborn child, and cannot look away or kid himself, his fatherhood is the fatherhood

of cottage cheese, the retreating footprints of snow and yogurt up his father's spine, the borrowed Volkswagen that will never run out of gas or plastic pistols. Then the dry bells of the furnace begin to hiss against Murphy's ankles, and he hears the whistling pines, the clangorous tombstones of the Veterans' Cemetery. Flapping their arms like downed angels in the middle of winter, Murphy and Annie make love and forgive each other until their ears and eyesockets fill up with snow

then Michael stands over them, takes aim at Murphy and makes his final declaration: Bang

bang, bang

you're dead daddy

you're dead

## IV

And for the first time in his life, Murphy lies there and knows it.

# JOHN BART GERALD

## Walking Wounded

(FROM HARPER'S MAGAZINE)

WE HAVE a very gutsy chaplain on our base. It was Sunday morning in one of our little Air Force churches with thin walls and runty steeples so they won't scrape the bellies of planes coming in too low, and the chaplain, a major, was up there entertaining us. Chaplains are always more entertaining than civilian preachers. For one thing they have a sense of humor about themselves. Now our chaplain was making jokes about hawks and doves, I can't remember them exactly because I'm not very political. But he was making everyone in that church nervous, from airman basic to the commander who sat in the front row with his wife. My own wife was giggling because she hates the war like sin and only understood the jokes on her own side. But when everyone was feeling uncomfortable, the major leaned over with the Bible open in his two large hands and said, "Are not five sparrows sold for two farthings, and not one of them is forgotten before God? But even the very hairs of your head are all numbered. Fear not therefore, ye are of more value than many sparrows."

You better believe it. I slipped my fingers through the buttons of my shirt and held the cool metal of my dog tags against my heart.

My own name is Dunbar and the three stripes on my sleeve feed my wife and the baby. I don't like war. But I don't hate it either. The way I see it everything's a fight. The little creatures war on each other; when I was little I used to shoot robins and stuff them back between the rocks of the old silo foundation — until my father caught me because they smelled so bad. So I know myself. I know what I mean. That doesn't mean I'm glad, which is why I'm a medical specialist instead of a load master.

Of course the war hurts me. There's a lot of difference between killing robins and people. Like one night when I was working the air-evac ward a guy told me this story.

"Palletti and me were standing in the middle of the street after our squad went through this village when a slope woman comes up to me and knocks her hands together. 'Boom-boom,' she says. She points to her hut and says, 'Boom-boom.' So I laugh and jiggle my balls and follow her back to her hut; only as she goes in I watch her step over a wire across her door. I just turn around and walk back to Palletti. But she comes out after me and tugs at my arm saying, 'Boom-boom, boom-boom.' Her dress was open. I pushed her off and shot her up the front. Then I took off a grenade and rolled it smooth through the door of her hut and it blew out two kids. I didn't mind the woman so much."

Now I've never forgotten that story but to be honest, when I think of it now it sort of bores me. It's another one of those things you see on TV if you finish supper too early, and I have too many stories. But at the time I walked off the ward and drank my coffee down in the basement with my hand shaking. And I suppose if I had been any younger I would have cried out at God. I hated the war and didn't want anything to do with it.

But just as I was getting off my twelve-hour shift, the lieutenant asked me if I could report for parade duty. And that was no question. So I drove home and changed, and there I was dead on my feet out in the middle of the airfield. Music whispered out to us from near the grandstands, echoing off transport planes, while we checked our buttons, our shaves, the set of our caps, grumbling before we made the turn, some guys still palming their cigarettes and my own belt cutting into my gut. The stands were filled with patches of greens and pinks, women and kids in Sunday best, and we marched down toward them with the music growing louder, the ranks sharpening around me, setting our shoulders, digging our heels into the pavement, feeling out our places in the block so we wouldn't stand out wrong, and my own foot hitting right with the beat of the bass drum. The brass thumped in our guts, there was a lot of high snappy razzing as the reviewing stand loomed up. The "Eyes Right" went off like a shot — our heads all snapped together. And there was some general I've never seen a picture of, and the women. But we were off down the landing strip with every guy's heel splitting the second, our arms together and eyes straight ahead, until the music began to fade with the strong breeze and a kind of life went out of us in a long breath.

You see the military isn't so different from any kind of work, except sucking around doesn't help you get ahead so much. In fact the way I see it, everybody's life is like the military service and getting more so. You make scratch or you get rubbed out. We're all part of one great machine. So I feel a little ahead of a lot of people who don't see that yet.

Which is why on Sunday morning I leave my pajamas on the bathroom floor and sit on the toilet lid polishing my low shoes with spit and bits of toilet paper. I put on a clean blue shirt which cuts into my neck. My blues only fit when I joined six years ago, before I started drinking. I close my pants. I button the four insignia buttons up my front staring in the mirror at the yellow-and-red good-conduct ribbon which could be pinned to my skin — as Marsha once said in bed. And polishing my visor, we start off to church.

But someday I will breathe in deep and burst the buttons off my chest and split the zipper and rip the stripes and all that goddam blue stuff off my body and stand out there on the flight line naked before all the world. Even if I'm old and fat.

There was a guy once on the wards whose legs were full of metal and pus, with a fever of a hundred and four. He kept showing me a dirty scrap of paper with the words on it he wanted for his stone:

> *As here I lie*
> *So must you be.*
> *Look straight ahead*
> *And follow me.*

But he was gone the next day and I never found out whether he lived or died.

There's no loose brass around that late, no chickenshit, just the medical busses and ambulances lined up at the edge of the dark. I don't really mind sitting out there in the dead of night. I clear myself a space in the litter stays on the bus floor, or, if I can, take the warm place on top of the heating unit thrumming away, while we wait. I talk some, doze, look out at silhouettes of the huge cargo planes and the runway flat out into the night. Way out there on the other side of the globe the war burns like a slow fire. And I'm safe here with my wife and kid.

When the plane lands we roll out to pick up the cargo. There aren't any windows so when the back of the plane drops away from under the tail, light spills into the fresh air like a wound opening. We back right in and walk out into the plane's belly. Stretchers are stacked from top to bottom and past them the walking wounded stare out at us, looking for home.

We let the flight medics take down the litters one at a time and put them on the tailgate. Then we pick them up and stack them two or three high along each side of the bus. I could direct it in my sleep. One two three lift with the litter, keeping it level, always careful where I put my feet because the only wrong I can do is drop one. And lose my stripes. Still I could do it in my sleep.

Though before I lift I look into the man's face. When the plane lands and decompresses sometimes the wounds open up. As for the guys themselves, I wouldn't fight them in a bar. After battle they shouldn't look like kids anymore, like half-time at a football game, sweating. Wounded without beards. I don't get used to that.

I also look in their faces for pain because sometimes they have pieces of metal in their bodies and it hurts them to move. I'm careful with the guys who still feel anything. Sometimes a man's face does something very private and I don't look at him anymore.

That night they brought out a Marine lieutenant — I could hear him crying back in the stomach of the plane. He was on the tailgate breathing hard, arms and shoulders naked under a light blanket while we stood over him in our parkas. And he said, "Wait a minute, let's wait a minute," because he didn't want us to move him. But a lot more guys had to come out.

"Sorry to be such a pussy," he said as I lifted. I could feel the noises in my bones. I jammed the litter handle into the wall clasp and locked it. The lieutenant screamed. I didn't mean to jolt him but I was sweating. I knew the guy too well. He said, "You boys make it hard for a man to be a hero."

Because of his sounds the bus moved out extra slow over the pavement. Some officer was up front welcoming the troops home in the

name of the Air Force, the base commander, the squadron, telling
them where they were and what time it was. The guys lay there
listening to the bullshit up front and the Marine's noises in the
back, making peace in their own little worlds, running fingers
over the bandage, trying to look out the window at the dark, or
staring up at white pant legs in the aisle and swaying bottles of dex-
trose. Some just lay there staring straight up at the green canvas of
the litter overhead as though they were scared the guy's blood
would seep through and drip on them.

I always look at their faces. I can't stop looking at their faces.
At one time I thought I was looking for guys I knew. Or I was
curious what a face looked like, forty-eight hours after the kid's
blown up. Until on a drunk I was trying to remember what one
of them looked like, just one, and all I could remember in that
whole line of litters I've been unloading was my own face, one after
another on those green stretchers I take out of the guts of those
planes.

When the kid pulled my pant leg I crouched down beside him.
"Take the straps off me, Sarge," he said, "I want to look outside."
But I was lighting a cigarette and didn't want to take the straps off
him. I'd have to strap him down again for unloading. And I didn't
know what his wound was. I've learned not to look. I saw there
was only enough bulk for one leg under his blanket so I gave him
a cigarette. We smoked.

At first wounded guys are like anyone, before they learn to live
with their wounds, use mechanical limbs or change their own bags.
Because they really aren't any different. Until we look at them too
much, or look away. Or they know we're afraid to look under the
covers. But the kid didn't realize that yet. I told him he didn't
want to look outside anyway because it was dark and looked like
any other air base with the grass turning yellow because we were
going into winter. There was miles and miles of concrete empty
as the shopping center on Sunday afternoon. Though I knew that
wasn't much to tell a man he's come home to. So I said we had a
good PX and you could get stereo sets there now and tape recorders at a big discount. And every day we had a happy hour over
at the NCO club, which my wife said was how I got my gut. And
there was a color TV set on the ward.

When they first come off the plane some of them ask to be set

down so they can feel American soil again. They don't think about
the concrete. But this kid was black as ashes and that made it harder
to explain what was out there. I didn't know why I was telling
him anyway so I stopped. You really come home to your own people. All I know is I go home to Marsha just waking up or if she's
up I watch her feeding the baby. And that's a good thing, I don't
care what anybody thinks.

Maybe because I was silent the kid said, "They sending you over,
Sarge?"

When I thought of that I felt the fire was spreading through
the middle of my own life too, and Marsha was waiting with me at
the edges. "How would I know?"

"You going if they send you?" said the kid.

I was quiet. It's not the kind of question you ask in the service.
At one time or another every guy thinks of not going, but he won't
admit it. Unless he's a fool. So I just looked at the kid thinking
you can't tell with colored guys, and sorry I gave him a cigarette.
After all, I've always loved my country. I guess I still love her, right
or wrong, because a lot of her's wrong. I've seen that many guys
shot up for nothing. For officers who said it's necessary, it's necessary. And sometimes it was necessary to cut off a leg. I tried to
smile at the kid.

He didn't smile back. He rolled his head on the white pillow
and said, "Don't go, man." Why was he telling me? He said it
again and I thought he was being political, trying to sell me something. "Don't go," he kept saying. Until I realized that was what
he had to tell me, like the other guys had their war stories, it was
the only thing he knew anymore.

But I didn't want the kid to think that with only one leg. And
I didn't want him to say it out loud because he could get into trouble. And I guess I didn't want to hear him, so I stood up.

The Marine was crying. The bus joggled down the uneven road
and everyone had to listen. Two medics were trying to hold his
litter steady but it didn't help. And we don't carry drugs on the
bus. And anyway you can never be sure with guys like that, they
might just be screaming for an extra shot. Only I couldn't ignore
it. I was sweating again.

The kid pulled my pant leg so I squatted down and said, "You
take it easy, soldier."

"You hear him crying?" said the kid as though I had no ears.
I said I heard him and it was tough.
"But it's not so tough."
"I'll tell him that," I said, sick of this kid.
"No, listen in," he said, holding his black hand in the air as
though he could catch the sound. I watched his hand move. I could
have bashed his head in for conducting his own band. Until I listened to the lieutenant. They were regular even cries like someone remembering screams from long ago. Or someone trying them
on, waiting for something worse. The guy didn't really believe
in his own screams. Because the pain was there but the real pain
was that it didn't hurt yet. It didn't hurt enough. And that was
scaring. I saw why it cut into me so bad. We hit a crack and the
marine screamed again loud. And I can still hear it. But if I let it
get to my heart I'll explode.

When things are bad I get efficient. Maybe that's my training.
I pushed the cart down the long waxed corridor to Ward 4, then
down past the isolation rooms to open bay and squared the litter
longside the bed. Sometimes the guys can move over themselves,
but for him I had to bring two medics in for help. We hung the
bottle up by his bed. I untied the bag of urine. One pulled the
blanket where the guy was all right on top but from his stomach
down was wrapped in old bandages.

We had to lift all of him at once. Ignoring the smell I slipped
both arms under his legs, the warm bandages soaked through on
my skin. When we started to lift my hands sunk up into the gauze
letting out the smell as something trickled into the bends of my
arms. But I kept telling the guy it was all right until he was on the
bed.

When I took the cart out to the stack of litters and peeled off
the yellow sheet, pus had soaked through to the canvas. The smell
was still with me. I try to explain that smell to my wife but I never
can. It's too strong to really breathe so you don't get used to it. It
smells like hot urine, or milk gone sour. Like dead birds or something stinking up the foundation. A lot of guys smell because
they're dressed just off the battlefield, and it takes an anesthetic to
change some bandages. So for a while the sickness in there just
gets older and older.

I washed up in the utility room and rinsed with a handful of alcohol swabs, before I went out for the next.

When the buses were unloaded and the ward full, I took a cup of coffee and watched the Red Cross lady ask each guy where he was from and did he want to call home free. Each did, so she brought the phone stand around and stood listening, smiling while the guy said yeah Mom I'm okay.

The doctor and nurse came through and I got my assignments. The first was a petty officer who had less than a fifty-fifty chance, the doctor thought. If someone looks like he's really going to die we move him to another ward. I looked in at his door and the man was sitting there cranked halfway up in bed with no shirt on but his bandages and a sheet over his legs. There were lines of sweat running between the bandages. His temperature was too high. I went to the utility room to wash up and brought back the dressing cart.

"Hello, bright eyes," the man said.

I started to tell him just what I was going to do with the dressing cart but he said just go ahead and do it. So I broke out the sterile towels and laid them around the shrapnel wounds on his chest. I'm a good medic and when I start working I almost enjoy it. The old bandages were stuck to the wounds. I broke out an irrigation set, poured in hydrogen peroxide, stuck an emesis basin up under the first wound, and squeezed the fluid over his bandage. I took my time so the bandages could soak and lift off easy. And I tried to get the guy talking so he wouldn't be thinking about what hurt. It wasn't easy for him to speak but he tried, flying his chopper so low his skids parted the grass because when you were flying that low Charlie couldn't see you to shoot, until he came all of a sudden on a clearing with a lot of people and cows.

I broke open one of the disposable suture sets and put on gloves, which are about the thickness of medium grade prophylactics. With forceps I lifted off the old dressing with just a little pull so the man broke sentence, and then picked it right up again. Someone fired a shot at him so he angled off and came in over the horns of the cattle with his guns open. And if he felt bad about it I wasn't really listening. I did another wound, then another, until the bandages were all off the guy's chest and he was sitting there with a line of holes up his side and across under his tit filled with yellow packing. And I thought of changing that too but it was in pretty tight and the petty officer said he'd just as soon kill me if I touched those. So I asked him how come he caught shrapnel when he was supposed to be up in a helicopter.

Then I cleaned what I could with normal saline, dressed the wounds with clean stuff and started on the guy's legs, while he sat there, his face gleaming with sweat, his body burning up under my hands, moving his hard jaw like some guy on the next barstool at the NCO club, circling around the cows and the little people.

Back on the ward the colored kid had found some crutches and was trying to make the TV set work, but it was only five in the morning and nothing much was on. So he stood in the middle of the ward and hopped around flapping his crutches like a stork for anyone who cared to watch him. "Goddam," he said to me, "you ever see a one-legged nigger dance?"

One guy had a leg cast up over his hip and a little hatch in the cast like a manhole cover, right in the middle of his thigh. There was a neat circle filled with red meat and a slit in that. The swab went into the leg all of five inches, disappeared down into that hole and came out again yellow. And all the while the guy just sat there looking very cool with a little black mustache over his smirk.

Then another guy's stump had to be treated, but that was clean work and I considered myself lucky because there was a man down the way who had put a gun under his chin and the whole lower half of his face was missing. I finished breakfast early. I didn't go straight back to the ward, they put you right to work. Some nights when the load is light we take turns sleeping in the linen room and the morning doesn't hit so bad.

I walked into the ambulatory ward where the men were just getting up. The TV was off; I slumped in a chair facing the dead tube. The sky was burning pale clear blue out past the window. Marsha and I were nestled in some warm green hollow with sunlight filtering in through the grass. Something very good was about to happen to us.

I was listening to a detailed explanation of shooting elephants with a bazooka. I opened my eyes. I looked at the kid, husky, crewcut, with the new-type combat boots. He was in good shape so I said to him, "What's wrong with you?"

He turned to look at me and held down his hand. The shaking
started at the elbow. "Nerves," he said.

He was a psychiatric patient. I looked hard at his natural blue
eyes not so different from the sky staring back at mine.

"I could have killed the guy who woke me. I don't know how
I'm going to wake up," he said. I figured if he was that violent
they would have him in restraints.

"You're doing all right," I said.

"No," he said. "I hate too much."

Well, I pushed down in my chair and shut my eyes again. "Hate,"
I said, "is no simple thing."

"You weren't there," said the kid.

I was sorry I said anything.

"We used to bring back ears."

"Yes I've heard that," I said. As a matter of fact I've heard just
about everything.

"You didn't walk into the clearing," the kid said, "and see our
guys hung up by their feet. They were all dead, except one, because they hung there all night. There was blood all down their
stomachs. And I looked at the one guy for about a minute before I understood what they did to him. Charlie cut the things off
and stuffed them in his mouth, and ragged his mouth to keep them
there. The sergeant told me to cut him down. The name stenciled on his fatigues was Henderson, I never saw him before. A
couple of my buddies held him and I cut him down. He lay on the
ground opening and closing his eyes, I wouldn't touch him. The
corpsman took the things out of his mouth and the guy said, 'Kill
me, just shoot me,' with the blood dried on his teeth. I got sick.
Our sergeant said go over the other side of the clearing. I turned
my back, and Sarge shot him."

I wasn't going to have any peace. "Well I got to get back to
work," I said and stood up. I only had an hour more anyway.

The psychiatric patient said, "Yeah, I'm sorry," and put out his
hand, trembling. I shook hands with him and walked back to my
ward. I guess I felt a little sorry for the guy. His story was such an
old story they probably told it in basic to scare the new recruits. Or
he read it somewhere. But I knew the kid must have done something nasty to be pushing it around as his own, that kid with his

body still whole and strong. His body was still whole and strong. That means a lot where I work.

When I got back to the project the baby was still asleep and Marsha in bed. I undressed. My whites had yellow stains on the front so I stuffed them in the laundry bag. Then I washed and climbed into bed. I lay on my back. Marsha was awake and she turned over and put her leg over mine, and put her head against my neck while I stared up at the ceiling. I wasn't ready for sleep. "Do you want a drink?" she said. I shook my head. She put her hand up behind my neck and we lay there. I looked at her black hair and soft skin, but I didn't feel anything. I put my hands on her shoulders and then along her sides and lifted her. She brought my head into her breasts. But I didn't feel a thing. I put my hands around her breasts. I pressed her around my face. And I held on for dear life. But I wasn't there. I was breathing in the smell of old wounds. Until I put my palms against my face and realized where the smell came from. As though the wounds had become part of my own skin. I took my hands away and sat up on the edge of the bed, staring down at my own naked body.

Because that's all I have left. I am alive. I'm breathing.

# MARY GRAY HUGHES

## The Foreigner in the Blood

(FROM ESQUIRE)

THE DAUGHTER of Leon Esteban, yes *the* Leon Esteban, committed him to a private sanatorium for elderly incompetents in July. She, Clara Rasmussen, for that was the name of the man she had married and was the name she used even professionally, signed the committing forms as a member of his family and his potential guardian, and two other doctors signed the psychiatric reports required by the law, a model law, too, which Esteban himself had drawn up for the state years ago. It was all done "according to Esteban," as his colleagues used to joke. And indeed the precipitating incident, the immediate cause of his committal, made a case as classic as any of those in his textbooks.

"Who is that strange man in my house?" he had said over the phone to his secretary and assistant. "I tell you there is a stranger in the house," and the *s*'s of his speech hissed heavily, as they did more and more the last few years. The secretary at once asked what he meant and what was he talking about, and as she began asking questions it seemed there was only some misunderstanding or other, and he said it was all quite all right and that he was on his way up to bed. She told him he had been working too hard, which was true. Two nights later he called her again, waking her from a deep sleep. "I tell you there is a strange man in my house. Who is he? What is he doing here?" By the time she was awake enough to begin talking to him and questioning him, the matter seemed again of no importance. Some shadows he had seen. In the morning she did not mention it, and neither did he. It was not until the third time he called her, in the afternoon this time, crying out, "Who is this man? I am afraid, understand? Afraid. There is a strange man here in the hall beside me," that she remembered the phone was in front of the large hall mirror, and that it was himself he saw.

She had gone at once to his home, and she had stayed with him, without protest from him either, until Clara could cancel her appointments and get a plane out from New York.

Esteban's doctor agreed Esteban must have more care now than in the past. A little more care in circumstances somewhat different, somewhat more careful of him, and he could continue his life much as before. It was decided he would be best off in some good private home. He could continue his work there and everything would be made easier for him. Many arrangements had to be made, and both women were enormously busy. Any number of homes and special hospitals for the old or sick had to be investigated and one selected. Esteban's books, papers, and notebooks had to be sorted, since he could not take them all with him. And there were the legal papers. They worked night after night to get it all done. Esteban worked with them, and seemed tactfully grateful for their help.

He said so, sometimes. Then again, he would be quite different.

"You enjoy it too much," he said to them. "You, you women. Interviewing hospitals. Signing papers. You love it."

"Now, now, you know you don't mean that," his secretary said, not so much as lifting her head from the drawer where she was going through notes of his early cases and throwing out duplicates. But Clara Rasmussen looked hard at him, her father, this clever man. How much in fact was he failing? How much of that was the querulousness of age, and how much was sheer malice, the irresistible dig? He'd always loved to tease her by making fun of her seriousness, her conscientiousness, her hard work. It was only by this she had got ahead. She hadn't his brilliance. She knew she was a drudge, but she was competent. She had published. Little Earnesta, he called her. He had done it pleasantly enough, but she had winced. How much of what he said now was intended? Did he really think she enjoyed committing him? As she stared at him, his long dark face split open like an apple with a white grin.

"Well, little Clahra," he said, for so the name came out on his foreign tongue. "Well? You were always the one who liked measurements, no? Have you decided? Am I 100 percent certifiable? Or 99 percent? Or maybe . . . 63 percent?"

"Papa, stop it. Tell me which of these books you want to take. Pick out which ones you want. If you change your mind, I can always bring you different ones later."

"Later? What do you mean later? How long are you staying?" So hopefully, so anxiously and hopefully, completely different from his manner the second before.

On the spur of the moment, because of his face, she said, "All summer. Peter can come out and spend his vacation here, and I'll stay here all summer."

And Esteban spun away from her and half-ran out of the room.

"He's so up and down, so all mixed up," Clara said to the secretary.

"Now, now, never mind. He's old, you know, Clara," she answered.

When the time came Clara drove Esteban to the Home in his car, which was piled with books and files and, in suitcases and on hangers, quantities of Esteban's lovely clothes. He was to have a corner room. Clara had seen to that. And she had replaced the dark green, flowered curtains with plain good white ones. She had not been able to get them to repaint the light green walls.

From a few steps into the center of the room Esteban stood surveying it. In his linen suit, among the institutional furniture, surrounded by short-sleeved attendants bringing in his belongings, he was completely out of place.

"Well, do you like it? Is it all right, do you think? Papa?" Master, she might have called him. Teacher. A giant in the field. He had known Freud. He would certainly see the farce in it, that he should be here, in the little corner room with good curtains at the two windows (special rate for two windows) and not enough bookshelf room to hold even the books that he, Esteban himself, had written.

"I couldn't get them to paint the walls yet," Clara said. "But I could have a painter come in and do it. I'm sure of that."

"You can't change everything. See, am I not being good?"

"Papa, stop that. Stop. If you don't like it, I'll take you right out. You know that. We can make other arrangements . . . oh

yes we can, don't look like that. You could stay at home, if you want.
I could shift my practice here."

"And Peter? Nonsense, Clahra. No such thing. Some things
now I must give up. It must be. Let strangers deprive me of things,
that is better than your doing it. Now, send Alice soon to help me
with the typing. And you must again be my assistant until I am settled. It will be fine, yes? Only, you are sure they understand about
all this, and you and Alice are to come and go as we please? Good.
One thing, tell that little man, the fat one, what's his name?"

"Hoffman."

"Tell him to stay away from me. I don't like that little fat man."

"But he's the director," she said. "He's not really fat. He's quite
good. Really. He told me they were honored to have you here.
He knows your work."

"Ha ha ha. Honored, fine. Honored. I know that type. He's
my jailer, Clahra. Only I don't have to like him. Remember? All
the best analysts say that. I don't have to like anyone for such a
thing."

It turned out to be unfortunate about the director's name. Esteban said he could never remember it, or never remember it correctly. He delighted in making variations on it: Hausmann, Haus-
frau, Hauptman, Helpman. Even Faust. But occasionally he was
genuinely not able to remember the name, and his sharp bright
face would bunch up with the effort, as if something were jammed,
and in an instant he would grow old, ancient, before one's eyes.
Yet other than this, he accepted it remarkably well, Clara thought.
He worked long hours in his corner room, dictating from his old
notes and correcting the drafts of typescripts. He called for one
volume after another to check references or reread papers. The finished papers piled up on his desk with Clara working hard as his
assistant, as she had years ago, but with a great difference now. She
had her own career and her own life, which had to be kept up as
well.

She established her family in Esteban's home and took over the
few patients he still had. She commuted by jet to New York each
week to take care of her own practice. She had never had such a
busy, expensive life of such sophistication. She loved the jets and
all the rituals of flying: the care, the cocktails, the good food. She

had never felt so solemnly adult, so important. And everywhere people in her profession knew of her father's trouble and how she was managing it. Everyone asked about him, and as in her early days as a practicing analyst she had amused psychiatrists with stories of the great Esteban's problems with American pronunciation, or American slang, now she told over and over the classic story of how he had not recognized himself in the mirror, and so had been committed. It was a remarkable story. Whenever she told it there would be a pause of silence afterward. Then she would be asked how he was doing, and she would tell of his fights with Hope-man. It went over very well. Too well. She found it hard to stop. One rainy wretched day she realized she had twice, in different groups at a New York cocktail party, brought the conversation around so that she could tell her story on Esteban. And that's what it had become — a story on Esteban.

"Enjoying it too much?" Esteban had said. Was she? Probably. Yes, probably, damn him. He knew. Hadn't he written, in a famous paper, *If only the young would take as their revenge the damage time will inflict upon their parents, they would not need to indulge in those actions or thoughts which sully their minds with guilt.* The word "sully" had been particularly admired in analytic circles. When Clara first read the paper (she was the most talented of his protégés at this time, and his "closest critic," it amused him to say) she said only, assuming as she often did the right to a much greater understanding of the United States than he, a foreigner, could have, "Papa, you never will understand Americans must do something themselves. They don't get satisfaction from anything that just happens. They are first and always doers."

He had laughed. So many American words, like "doer," amused him. But he had not changed anything in the paper. Sometimes he made changes when she had suggestions, most often he did not. And everything he did was successful anyway. Everyone admired him.

Except at the Home. At the Home, Esteban was beginning to have difficulties. When she visited him and found him working, as she always did, and worked with him, he seemed as active and agile, as excited about his work and as alert, or almost as alert, as ever. It seemed then only because of some matter of strange convenience that he should be living in a tiny corner room in a Home for the senile and deranged. Yet the staff told her other things: that he could never remember how to get to the dining hall and an attendant had to be sent for him. That he didn't want to change out of his clothes at night and get into his pajamas. That he threw things on the floor. Petty little things. Institutional offenses. Half deliberate, she suspected, done with the malice of the angry but sane. He had always liked jokes. If these were stranger ones, pettier ones, who could blame him? All the silly rules of the place, all the dull people staffing it. He was bound to hit back. *She* had no trouble with him.

Yet one of their complaints about him, she could see, did give them real trouble. That was his dislike for the director. It was amusing to call Hoffman names behind his back, but lately Esteban had begun doing it openly, and often before other patients. It disturbed them, the director said. "Half-man," Esteban yelled at him, right in the common living room. And when Hoffman went on by, Esteban had spat after him onto the floor. It was foolish, childish, Clara told Esteban. He didn't need to do that sort of thing. He could avoid Hoffman if he wished.

"Don't worry," Esteban said. "You always worry too much. Bring me some oranges, Clahra. We never get any decent fruit in this place. Bring me some Spanish oranges I can suck on," and he held his hand up before his face with the fingers curved around an imaginary orange, "something I can get some juice out of."

Blood oranges, he meant. She bought a net sack of them at the market south of town.

"What a gloomy name for an orange," her husband said. "Who wants to eat blood? It's that old macabre Latin sense."

"He's not Latin. He's Spanish," Clara said, but she wasn't paying much attention. She was packing food in a small kit. Her husband watched with a bland weighing eye and from time to time would reach in and rearrange a box or the thermos so that it would fit compactly. He was much better at this sort of thing than she was. He often came along, chatting with her and helping when she tidied the house or put away the clothes because he was the better at it and because it was a pleasant time to talk. He was a geologist who ran a small firm that did consulting for oil companies. He knew nothing of analysis. Her work was always an amazement to him, as was his to her, and they constantly brought each other gifts of novel information and delighting, fresh ideas, for their minds, like most of the hours of their days, ran along quite separately but side by side, with hundreds of ties across. Her father, however, was not one of them and, with Esteban, Rasmussen shared nothing.

"I'm taking him out for a drive," she said. "I hate seeing him cooped up in that place all the time. It must get on him. It gets on me. All those dreadful people, sick and old or addled. And the dimwitted staff. I can't work with him there anymore." She could not focus on him, she meant. She felt she could not seem to see him, could not get through to him to do any real work, anything that was not the simplest routine.

"Well, be careful."

"Don't be silly, he's my father," she said.

Esteban was not expecting her. He was standing by one of the two windows. He was without jacket and tie, and he was leaning forward with his hand touching the screen. It was a heavy one of the sort that could not be opened from the inside. She was sure it had not been there when she had taken the room.

"Papa," she said. He seemed disconcerted by her being there. "I came early," she said. "It's Sunday . . . and I'm quite early."

"Yes. All right. I was thinking. I have been thinking of the meanings of the disrobing of Christ."

"Good heavens."

"Have you thought about it? Think about it."

"Okay, if I have to. But later. I've got a surprise."

He brightened. "Oh, listen, Clahra, I have a surprise. I, too. Such a funny thing this morning. Let me tell you. It's really very funny. Hoffman came to see me. He came in," and he began to mimic Hoffman, for despite his accent and his sharp Spanish face, he had a gift for mimicry and could catch the voice and look of his victim. " 'Ah, ah, ah now, good morning now, ah now, Dr. Esteban.' He's never learned I am not an M.D. We weren't in those days," he said. Then he switched roles again, drooping his shoulders and pushing out a nonexistent tummy. " 'My dear Dr. Esteban, I wonder if, ah now, you couldn't help me out.' You see the direction, Clahra? I am to help the big director. Oh I am to be flattered." She began to smile. What a fool Hoffman was to think he could try anything like that with Papa. "So I, I keep a straight still face, very still . . . like in a session, understand? 'I'm in need of some references for a paper,' he says. 'I've been doing a little, ah now, ah now, work, ha ha.' He can't even come out and say the word decently. He doesn't know the meaning of the word and knows it, so he gives a little apologetic laugh, 'ha ha,' when he says 'work.' 'I've been doing a little work, ha ha,' he says, 'with chlorpromazine among our more, um, ah now, elderly patients here.' All the time I am blank, a blank face, but just beginning to let it go a little stupid, a little slack and stupid. Not too much. 'My assistant seems to remember some work along these lines done in a Veteran's hospital. We thought perhaps you, ah now, perhaps you might remember . . .' He had even set me such a simple task, you see, so I could give the answer and get the prize. That paper by Belanjian and Emerson. Oh just the right degree of difficulty. But recent, to test how much I remembered recently."

"Oh, Papa, really you can't be sure of that!" But she could not help laughing, too. He was impossible, her father.

"On he goes," Esteban said, "giving me all the clues, more and more, suggesting a name, even their names, and I get a bit stupider, a bit slacker. He calls the names out, and I stare. And oh he is happy. He begins to smile. I am foolish, he thinks. I am foolish and he is quite sure. He smiles, you see, he thinks he knows just how the mind is gone. He is happy, he is certain. He is ready to go. I let him take a step, another, then I straighten my face, stern, stern, the look of a father to an errant son, indignation, the hard stare, and I say, in good medical Latin, the words for gullible fool, sucker you know. And I spell it for him. Don't worry, he'll look it up. I know the type. Ah it was perfect, perfect. He doesn't know, you see, how much I meant it, how much of what he was saying I comprehended totally. He doesn't know if I am foolish or joking or lucky. All his certainty gone. Ha ha ha ha. Hoffnut."

"Oh Papa!" But she was laughing with him and was elated, too. "You're impossible," she said. But what did Hoffman expect, that Esteban was some ordinary slobbering old man?

"We'll celebrate," she said. "I've been tied to a desk all week and I want to get out. Let's have a picnic snack, out at Mt. Schyler

Park like we used to do. Get some air. Do us both good. We can take something to work on and work with clear heads. Just like we used to do years ago. We can take some of the notebooks Alice has typed up. Let's take some of the early New York ones. You get them, and whatever else you want, and I'll go tell someone on the staff."

"Ask permission you mean?" Esteban said.

"Yes." She laughed, but with him. "All right, yes. From old Half-brow." And she left the room smiling still.

But permission was not so easy to get. She did have to see Hoffman. She could not just tell a secretary. And Hoffman was against it. In his office, behind his desk, he seemed a nice, sensible, rather heavyset man trying to do his job, and some of her elation left her. He did not want Esteban to go out.

"I don't see why," she said. "How do you find him, then? Isn't he doing well? Doctor?" she added, switching sides.

"I find his condition discouraging and deteriorating, frankly, Doctor."

"You have to make allowance that he has always been, well, eccentric. He's always liked his little jokes."

He waved all that aside. There went Leon Esteban, his wave said. "No no, I'm not talking about that," he answered her. "He's showing difficult signs. We feel, we have found, that he needs very careful handling. More than I think you realize."

"What exactly do you mean?"

"A phase comes over him now and then when he is extremely excitable and frenzied. He gets difficult. I mean physically, Doctor. We have all come to recognize it. We call it his hyena phase."

She hated him. For its accuracy. It was true. She had seen it herself. She had seen it the night they were boxing his notebooks and he had said she enjoyed it too much. Yes, she had. She had seen it, but she had not named it and so had forgotten it. Now she would always know it. No, it was too horrible. She refused.

"I don't agree," she said. "I don't agree at all. You've forgotten how depressing this place can be to someone used to a quite different life. You don't realize how confining, I mean intellectually of course, it can be for a man like my father. He needs to get out more. To be free of nurses and staff and administrators. I think he should be taken out much more. I feel I have been very remiss in not having done so before. I am sure it will help him."

"Where do you want to take him?"

"I thought I'd start with a little picnic in Mt. Schyler Park. We used to go there frequently."

"You want to take him yourself? Alone?"

"Of course. Oh, Dr. Hoffman, he's a tiny, old man. Come now."

"I am against it. Absolutely against it. But I don't feel I can refuse you if you are set on it. I do insist, however, you take my car. Yes, I insist. It's equipped for such purposes. It has two doors only, and both have special locks which are difficult to open and which are set down low. I'll show you how they work. I insist that you take it."

"What took you so long?" Esteban asked when she got back. He was fully dressed, standing, and plainly fretful from waiting.

"Silliness," she said.

"They didn't want to let me go, did they?"

"It just took time to get some arrangements made. You know how these places are, Papa. They excrete red tape."

He became more relaxed as they left the white stucco building. She had been right to take him out. She was sure. She kept talking as they walked to the car and got in, and apparently he attached no importance to the change of car. He rode beside her with obvious and excited pleasure. And he looked so nice. She felt ashamed that she had not taken him out long before.

They reached the park after about a half-hour drive and she paid the fifty-cent entrance fee and started up the low slopes of the mountain. Clara intended to stop at one of the lower picnic areas, but Esteban asked her to go higher. He wanted to see the scrub cedar where it was thick and smelled good, he said, up near the top.

"All right," she said, and turned the car and began the winding drive upward.

"Go way up," he said. "That's right, to the little parking place just below the peak. It's not a steep drive, Fidélia."

She jumped, startled, but his face was blank, unnoticing. He gave no sign of the slip. There was nothing sharp, nothing crafty in his face.

At the topmost picnic area, where it was rocky and there was dense scrub cedar, she drove the car gently off the highway, bumping slowly over the rough half-rock half-grass terrain, and stopped as close as she could get beside one of the picnic tables.

"Hmmm, I love the air up here," she said. "I haven't come enough. We must do this more often." She got out and began unloading the little basket of food and utensils and the notebooks and papers he had brought.

Esteban got out, too, and walked slowly around the open picnic area, and then wandered over to stand by one of the little green cedars, seemingly with his hands buried in it. She had taken all their things out of the car and was trying to arrange them on the table in some order, aware she was never as neat as he.

"Well," she said. "I don't know if we'll get any work done here, but it is nice. You know I came up here once on a geology field trip. That was a long time ago. We were hunting fossils. They brought us in a bus and parked it down at the first picnic area, and we had to hike up the rest of the way. You know I'm terrible at that sort of thing, and after a few hundred feet I was panting like a haying machine. At first I was one of the ones in the lead, but gradually everyone went past me. Two of the boys tried to haul me along, but finally that wouldn't do, either. We'd come to find little fossil snails and sea animals. All things that could be found here because of the fault that runs this side of town. Well, I'd had it. I couldn't go a foot further, dragged or not, and I just sat down on a rock and gasped. To hell with it, I thought. I could hear them all marching along, higher and higher, and I sat on my rock gasping and staring at my feet, and right there, between my feet, were fossils." She laughed at the memory. "I found as many fossils as anyone. They went scrabbling all over the mountain, in and out among bushes, and I just sat picking up fossils from between my feet. You know, I should have brought a couple of blankets, or an air mattress. This bench is going to be hard after a while."

He was still standing almost into the branches of the cedar. Smelling it? Holding it? Good Lord, could he be urinating in it?

"Shall we have something to eat first, or do you want to go over some of these notes?"

"No, no. Fidélia," he said.

"Papa. You know I'm Clara."

He smiled at her. A sweet smile at first, but with something sly developing in it. It stayed on his face too long. And he was standing so far away from her. Halfway across the picnic area from her, and halfway behind that bush. Was he playing a game? Or what?

She sat on the bench. She opened a notebook, then another one. But she could not bring it off. She could not read them. He was watching her.

"I'm Clara," she said.

"Don't worry," he said. "Don't worry. You were always such a worrier. You were always afraid I'd make a mistake in a paper. Change this, you said, change that. Look out, Papa, look out." Mimicking her voice and a little earnest nodding gesture of her head. Oh, he was good at it. "This might be wrong, Papa. Or that. You were good at finding my mistakes."

"It was how we worked," she said. "You wanted me to do it. You didn't even want me to go away to New York. Remember?"

"Remember?" he mimicked. "No. You liked finding the mistakes. You were one for measurement, and you liked finding the mistakes." He was relishing the hurt.

"That's not so, Papa." She stood up. Instantly he was around the bush and further away from her with the little scrub cedar between them. He peered over the top of it at her, watching her, his eyes liquid and shining, pouring out malice from the sharp, the hyena face.

"Look, Papa," she began. Then, "Let's eat."

"Look, Papa," he said. "Let's eat."

"Stop it."

"Stop it."

She could not stand the way he looked, and took two quick steps toward him, but he flitted away, completely out of sight this time. She had lost him. She rushed, ran, to the bush, and on then to the next one. But her high heels (why had she worn them? But every time she had gone to see him, every time, she had dressed up, had dressed in heels and stockings and a pretty dress), the useless heels slid and lost traction and threw her off balance and she skittered to a stop. She could not run. She could not possibly catch him. Where was he?

"Clahra," he called.

She turned her head. He was across the picnic area. On the other side near the car. How had he got there so fast? Thank God she had automatically put the key in her pocket. From just this side of the car he was watching her.

"Professor Esteban," she said sharply.

"No no." He laughed. "No no no. I wrote that one, remember? *Systems of Approach and Treatment.* Esteban and Holloway. Page 328 of the revised edition. Ha ha ha."

"All right. Papa, then. Help me, Papa." But he shook his head, threw off the plea, and watched her, waited, expectant and still.

She began walking in his general direction, but not directly toward him. Moving instead so she might be able to cut him off if he started back for the scrub cedars. She had to get him. He could so easily get hurt here. He could fall or get lost. He was a small old man, no matter his fancy clothes or his quickness. She came closer to him, but he laughed and moved back to keep a bush between them, and there he stood, poised and waiting and expectant again, watching her over the top of the bush. If she could get close enough she could reach over and grab him. The scratchy little stiff branches would give way. She could reach through them for him. Again she walked closer to him, but slowly. She was beginning to perspire. Deliberately she slowed her pace, broke it up, made it irregular, but moved closer.

"Bye bye," he said, and ducked his head, bent over, and was gone from sight. She rushed after him, quickly quickly, teetering on the high heels, trying to cut between the bushes and perhaps surprise him. Quick quick, cut him off, get him. And she slid again, stumbled, and caught herself only by grabbing a limb of one of the cedar bushes and hanging onto the green bristly thing.

"Hell," she said.

There was a noise beside her. She raised her head and just above her — he must have been standing on a rock — was Esteban. Right there, on the other side of the bush she was holding. He was delighted. Delighted. He stuck his face forward between

the bushes, with his eyebrows arched and his eyes wide, in a pan-
tomime, a child's exaggeration of surprise. "Peek-a-boo," he
shouted in her face, and jerked back, doubled over, and was out of
sight.

In despair and rage she crashed through the side of the bush
after him and so suddenly that she saw him, stretched out her hand
for him as he ran doubled over, crafty, animallike, and she almost
had hold of him, almost had him, and then her heel caught and
held this time, in the scrub bush, and she was thrown forward
and down with the full force of her plunge after him, and she
crashed hard onto one knee, crying out.

Silence.

Then, "Oh oh oh," she said.

"Are you . . . all right?" she heard. An old man's voice. An
old man's weak voice. "Clahra?"

She did not answer. No reply to this plea and pretense of sanity. Shaken, hurt, bleeding, covered with dirt, her stocking torn,
trembling all over outside, she was like marble inside, cool and
hard and one piece. Watching her blood ooze through the
wide scrape on her knee, through her ripped stocking, coming up
like red grass out of the brown torn stocking, soothing and holding her knee, rubbing the hurt, rocking back and forth and
watching the blood, she knew her father was an old man deranged in his senility. Was mad. "Oh oh oh," she said, rocking her
knee, holding it. "Oh oh," but saying it automatically for inside
she was still and certain and calm. From her pocket she took a
Kleenex and sopped the blood, sopped and sopped it. "Oh
oh oh." More blood. Oozing blood. And it was Esteban who had
written, *Remember how ancient and how deep is the fear of madness, of this terrible derangement of our very selves. Illness, even
death seem natural to us. Part of the life of the body. But insanity, in all forms, comes as a foreigner rising in our own blood,
and is the more horrifying because of the very intimacy of its
strangeness.*

Slowly she stopped the ooze of blood. Slowly her outer trembling ceased. The blood, the dirt on her, her weakness, her
apparent hurt, these were her weapons now.

Slowly, slowly, with great fatigue and great difficulty, barely able to do it, she pulled herself up and moved over to sit on a rock. There she sat, hunched forward, a lump of despair and hurt and shattered strength. She did not answer his two or three callings of her name. She did not look up when he came nearer. She sat.

Slowly she reached into her pocket and brought out cigarettes. Slowly, shakily, she fished out one cigarette. Then dropped it, reached for it, couldn't lift it, and began again fumbling for another. Finally she got it out, tried to put it in her mouth, seemed unable to do so, and rested, both arms limp on her legs, head down, too weak to smoke. Again she put the cigarette in her mouth, raised her head, and began searching clumsily for a match. first in one pocket, then in another, then back to the first.

"You have a match?" she said.

"Oh yes," he said. "I am allowed the tiny sort." And he approached. Was it going to be this simple? No. From a few steps away he tossed the packet to her. But he did not step back. He stayed. She seemed hardly to notice where the matches had fallen. Then with great slowness and fatigue, she reached down, found them, dropped them, got them again. She lit one, and it went out. She lit another, it held, and with it finally she got the cigarette lit. She inhaled slowly, deeply, then let her head slump down as before. Exhausted. Helpless. The sun blazing on her.

"Want one?" she asked him, her voice dull, indifferent.

"Oh no," he said. But still he did not move away. He shifted back and forth, standing first on one small rock and then on another. More and more restless. It was no fun now. She sat. He moved back and forth, this rock, then that one, then this one, but all within a tiny space, like a butterfly. More and more quick and restless. "Oh no no," he said. "I am not allowed to smoke. You should know that. I'm surprised at you. You wouldn't really offer me a cigarette, would you? You should know better."

She poked at the dirt with one hand, paying no attention to him. She was slumped so far forward it seemed she could not even see him.

"You wouldn't really offer me one, would you? Are you hurt? Not if you can smoke. You should give it up. It's bad for you. Why don't you give it up? It poisons the entire body. You may already have cancer. Do you know that? Do you cough much?

Women are susceptible to it, too. Especially women of your
build. On the heavy side. You should lose some weight. I never
put on weight. Smoking is bad for your eyesight, too. You have
very bad eyesight, Clahra. You can't see nearly as well as I. I can
see far better. I have perfect eyesight. You can't see that line of
trees across the valley," he swung his arm out to point at them,
"but I, I can make out what kind of trees they are and I can see,
in among them, yes, I can see some, oh, some, let me see—" and
in that instant she was up and had thrown herself forward and on
him, arms and body spread around him like a net, springing and
jumping on him all before he could no more than turn his head
around toward her in surprise, and then they both went down,
clumping together onto their knees with her arms wrapped
around him. She had him. She had him and held him fiercely.
Such a frail little old man, a thin bony little man. Yet she stood
up and jerked him with her, holding and handling him more
roughly, she knew, than she had to, but she was not able to stop.
She turned him around and tugged down his jacket, the lovely
pale linen jacket, until it was halfway down his arms, pinning
them.

"Ah, Clahra," he said. "Too much. It's melodrama. Your tim-
ing was good, but don't do this, it's silly."

"Stop it. Stop that," she said. "Don't pretend you're joking. I'm
not Hoffman, and you stop pretending you are playing a game. It
won't do. You have to have help, Papa."

"Ha ha ha ha ha."

But she would not let herself mind. She took him to the car and
put him into the back of it, and reached across the seat to fasten
one lock and then through the window to lock the other door.
Probably Esteban could open them. Probably he had invented
the locks. But it would take him time to do it and she would be
able to get back to the car before he got out. She gathered up
the picnic lunch, the books and papers and shoved them into the
trunk. Mustn't leave anything in the car for him to throw at her.
Then she unlocked the door, got in, and settled herself behind
the wheel, leaving Esteban in the back like a prisoner. It was
terrible, but it was safe, and it was right. What if he had come to
harm through her? What if he had been hurt because she had
been stubborn and insisted he was perfectly competent. Thought

he was joking! She would never have forgiven herself if some harm had come to him through her.

"I'm sorry, Papa. I have to make sure you aren't hurt. You understand that. I know you do. Papa?"

He sulked and would not answer. She turned the rearview mirror so he could not find a place to sit where she could not see him by glancing at it.

"Who was Fidélia?" she asked.

He would not answer.

"Come on, Papa. Talk to me." But he would not. He sat in the middle of the back seat staring with venom at the back of her neck. So they rode, in silence, back to the Home.

Once there, as they drove into the parking area before the stucco building, he became more cheerful. When she helped him out of the car he asked, "Is it about five?"

"Just four-thirty," she said. She let an attendant take him to his room, and she went to sign him in.

"Have a little trouble?" Hoffman asked, distinctly pleased.

She was dirty. Her hair was down. Her knee and stocking were crusted with blood. "Yes," she said. "But it was nothing that I couldn't handle."

"All the same, you better not take him out again."

"No."

She insisted on taking care of Esteban and helping him change his clothes, and she sent the male nurse out of the room. But Esteban refused to put on his pajamas and robe. "They always want me to do that, to prevent it, but I won't do it, I won't," he said. He was near bursting into tears, and here, where he was safe, among his books and papers and the books that he had written, seeing him nearly crying she lost all her inner firmness, and she let him do whatever he wished. She helped him select and put on one of his fine suits.

"Now," he said. "Do I look all right? Is it all nice?"

"You look fine, fine. But why the blue shirt with it?"

His face turned crafty and he smiled slyly at her and stroked the shirt with his fingertips.

"Wear what you want, please," she said. "Shall I tidy some of the books? Wait, where are you moving that chair? It's heavy."

"Here. Over here, with the light, in range of . . . of . . . it,"

and he nodded at it. The mirror, he meant. "Here in its focus,"
he said. "Hurry, hurry, little one, it's almost time."

"Time for what?"

He looked all around the room, first at the door and at each
of the two windows, and then he said, lowering his voice and
with his eyes and face hyena sharp, "Closer. Now, listen," he whispered, "Fidélia." (Oh it was not her name. And it was not one of
the names he had called her when she was small and her hair still
fair and eyes, he said, that were green, and he would pick her
up and rub his nose on her and call her his little golden penny, his
little green pine tree. It was not even the name of her mother. It
was not the name of anyone she knew.) "Listen, they mustn't
hear. They try to stop me, but they can't. They'd find mistakes
. . . ha ha ha . . . but on Sunday, and sometimes special during
the week, I speak to the whole world. Me, I'm on," and he nodded at the mirror, "on TV."

Her mouth, her eyes broke wide in dismay. Oh Papa, oh dear
God, oh it was so usual, it was so mundane, so unoriginal, so common, oh dear God, it was so trite.

He was watching her, greedy for her amazement, her awe.

"Well, I . . . I . . . uh, Papa, I . . ."

"Shh, shh, quick," and he seated himself in the chair, very erect
and proud and stiff, the mirror reflecting him in profile. He
pulled, tugged on her arm, pulled her down saying, "You must
get out of range, get out of range, yes, yes," the *s*'s hissing. "Soon
it starts, soon I will be on and you can see it, yes, yes," and from the
corner of his eye he watched his profile in the mirror. "Any
minute now, see," he said to her. So proud. "Well? Well, little
one?"

"How nice. It's nice. It's great for you," she said, for he had
written, "Don't argue with the old." "Do you like doing it?" she
asked, for *Indulge the senile,* he had said in that book that was
the textbook of their science. "What . . . tell me what . . . oh
God, what channel are you on, Papa?" Hadn't he written, *Allow
them the pleasures of their sad fantasies, for how shall it harm
you?*

Oh Papa no, you were wrong, it's not like that, it's not, it's not.

"Lower," he said. "Down lower," pulling her arm.

"Papa," she said. "Shh, shh," he hissed, still pulling on her arm.

"Papa," she whispered, "Papa," and her head came to rest against his sharp and bony knee, his hard old bony knee. "Shh," he said, "shh, shh," but gently now, soothing her, petting her with his hand, stroking her hair with his hand over and over again, tenderly, automatically, abstractedly, his mind elsewhere.

# NORMA KLEIN

## *The Boy in the Green Hat*

(FROM PRAIRIE SCHOONER)

"THE STRANGEST thing happened in the park today," his wife said.
Lange, standing in the entrance hall, had thought she was about
to take his coat and hang it up, but she just stood staring at him
with her large, lustrous eyes which, with their milky gray color,
had a peculiar, almost manic intensity. He went to hang it up himself. He had had a difficult day at work but, even if he had not,
he was always taken aback, unpleasantly, by his wife's habit of
bursting out with her "events of the day" before he had had a
chance to relax, make himself a drink, and ease out of the strain
of his own worries. Of course, he reminded himself, hunting for
a sturdy, wooden hanger — he was always telling her to throw
out these twisted, metal ones — she was alone all day or most of
the day with only the maid or their five-year-old son, Avram, to
talk to. This explained why her need to communicate to him was
so much greater than his need to communicate to her. He found
a hanger, draped the coat over it, and started into the kitchen.
"What was it that happened?" he said.
"This boy," she said, "this boy in a green hat."
"What boy?" He opened the refrigerator door and withdrew
the Rose's Lime Juice with which he intended to make himself a
gimlet. It would have been nice, too, he could not help thinking,
if she had thought of preparing his drink for him, having it ready
when he came home.
"There was this boy," she said. She stood near the refriger-

ator, watching him, her arms crossed tensely over her breasts. "He kept following Avie and me."

"Following you?" Lange, selecting a large glass, measured out a precise amount of vodka. He always kept the vodka chilling so that no ice cubes would be necessary.

"Yes," she said, her voice breathless, shrill, insistent. "He followed us."

"From where to where?"

"Well, first in the playground. He kept circling around Avie — "

"Talking to him?"

"No."

"Then, what?" The drink prepared, Lange walked out after her, into the living room. He sat down on the large scarlet couch and arranged himself comfortably. It was an enormous room, almost circular, with a terrace running halfway the length of the apartment. Lange's advertising company allowed him to deduct the rent from his income tax. From the couch, without even stepping onto the terrace, a wide expanse of New York was visible. Now, at dusk, with the lights on in the living room and this soothing darkness, the faint, glimmering lights of the city, the first sips of the drink which was perfectly cold and as he liked it, soothed Lange's nerves. He turned to his wife more genially, crossed his legs and said, with almost guilty attentiveness, "How old was this boy?"

"I'd say he was nine or ten," she said. She remained standing, as though hovering over him, like a bird about to take flight.

He motioned to the couch beside him, but she shook her head, evidently too absorbed in her story to sit. "Well, there's nothing so unusual about a boy of nine or ten being in the playground," he said.

"Yes, but he followed us," she said. "Later we went down to One Hundredth Street. I told you — I was going to meet Janie McGregor there. And I was sitting, talking to her and looked up — there he was again."

"Maybe his mother just happened to go down there too."

"But he had no mother," she said.

"Really?" Lange sipped his drink reflectively, trying to listen and to piece it all together. "Still, he could have been playing by himself at that age."

"Maybe. But why would he follow us?" Her eyes, fixed on him, were demanding, impatient.

"I don't *know* why," said Lange, impatient himself. "Need there have been a reason? Anyway, if he wasn't harming you, why does it matter?"

"But he might have! He might have!" Her voice became so agonized that he set down his drink. "He was staring so."

Lange stood up and put his arm around her. He felt that her whole body was trembling uncontrollably; she was terrified. "Have a sip of my drink," he said quietly.

She took the drink and mechanically, as though it were medicine, swallowed what remained in the glass.

"You're tired," he said, half suggesting this possibility as a partial explanation; she was three months pregnant and, although it scarcely showed, he felt it might have told already on her nerves.

"No," she said stubbornly. "No, it isn't that."

She was always cleverer than he expected, seeing through these attempted excuses on his part; he felt defeated. The pleasantness of the half hour in which he was to have had his drink, a half hour he had looked forward to almost throughout the day, was marred. He thought of making himself another drink, then decided against it. A few minutes later the maid announced that dinner was ready.

After dinner he went into his son's room to say good night to him. Katherine was inside, discussing something with the maid. His son's room was almost as large as their own master bedroom. Gaily colored paintings hung on the wall. In the corner was his bed, painted bright red and decorated by hand with Amish designs.

"So, how's the boy?" he said, coming to sit down beside him.

"Okay," Avie said cheerfully.

He was always surprised at his son's good nature, his outgoingness. Perhaps he expected that somehow the boy was doomed to become some combination of himself and his mother, whereas, on the contrary, he seemed far better adjusted than either of them, at ease with strangers, rarely intimidated.

"I hear you went to the park today," he said. "Wasn't it cold?"

"No-o," the boy replied, considering. "It rained later," he said after a minute.

"Who'd you play with?" Lange asked. "Was Billy there?"

"Ya, we played a little."

"What'd you play?"

"Oh, different things."

"Were there a lot of kids there?"

"Sure." Avie lay back, looking at his father with large, dark eyes.

Lange felt confused by the directness of this glance. He hesitated, then said very quickly, as though it were of no importance, "Was there some boy in a green hat?"

"What boy?" Avie said.

"Was anyone — trying to bother you? You know — "

"Nobody had a green hat," he said.

"You just played with Billy?"

"Ya."

Lange sat there, abstracted, not speaking. He stared at the wall where a tapestry of a shocking pink bull hung slightly off center. Its eye, a vivid purple shade, seemed unusually bright and angry, even though the dark room muted the color.

"Aren't you going to tell me a story?" Avie said.

Lange started. Then he said, stroking his son's pajama-clad foot, "I really can't tonight, Av. I've got to do a lot of things. To-morrow — tomorrow I'll tell you one — twice as long if you like."

"OK." The boy accepted this readily and burrowed down under his covers as he always did before going to sleep. Lange tucked him in, kissed him lightly on the cheek, and left the room.

Standing in the hall outside the boy's room, Lange frowned. A dead end. What would Avie know or remember anyway? There were so many children — he didn't keep track of all of them. Oh let it go, he thought, impatient with himself. But he couldn't, not so easily. He felt he had to know if there had been a boy in a green hat.

Katherine was standing in the living room, looking out over the terrace. He approached and said in a quiet voice, "You feel better now?"

For a minute she didn't reply. Her body, next to his, seemed very still and languid, almost limp. "Yes, I feel fine," she said in a vague voice.

"You can get to bed early," he suggested. "Read in bed."

"Yes." Again her voice had that dreamy, not quite paying attention quality.

"I might go in my study," Lange said. "I have some papers to go over. I'll be in later. Should I carry the TV into the bedroom?"

To this also she agreed. He left her in the bedroom, getting undressed to take her nightly bath.

He did go to his study, but only for a few minutes. If he could have worked, he would have — he had not been lying about having things to do — but he was restless and distracted and merely sat at his desk, drumming on the broad teak surface with his fingers. Then he had an idea. Leaving the room quietly, he took his coat from the hall closet and, equally quietly, closed the door behind him. There was a chance Katherine would miss him, but it was unlikely. If he hurried, he would be up before she had finished her bath. He knew that often she liked to soak there for at least half an hour. He could, he thought, waiting for the elevator, have used the study phone, but there was the chance she might lift it up to make a call herself and, although the study was sound-proofed with a double layer of Portuguese cork, he would not have felt completely safe.

Outside it was gray and rainy, unusually cold for April. He hurried across the street, ducking his head to shield himself from the rain. Most of the stores along the block were still open, the delicatessen, the beauty parlor which was reputedly a hangout for all the call girls of the neighborhood; he had always looked with suspicion and curiosity at its glossy exterior of spun-glass wigs and artificial nails. He went into the drugstore. The middle-aged Jew behind the counter smiled at him genially. Usually he would have stopped to exchange a word. Now he just smiled, trying not to seem curt and ducked into the phone booth at the back of the store.

It was a small booth with no stool. For a moment Lange stood there, staring at the advertisement glued to the inside of the booth. "Have you made your ten calls?" it read. "Groceries? In-vitations? Business Matters?" Under which category, he wondered, did his present call belong? He withdrew from his pocket the slip of paper on which he had written the number, inserted two nickels, and dialed. He was in luck; Janie answered.

"Hello, Janie? Sol Lange."

"Sol! Hi! How *are* you?"

"Fine, very well." He hesitated.

"Bill isn't here," she said quickly. "He's at a meeting. Did you want to leave a message for him?"

Lange cleared his throat. "No, actually, I wanted to ask you, Janie. There's a favor I wanted to ask — well, not a favor, I just wanted to find out — You were in the park with Katherine today, weren't you?"

"Yes, yes, I was," she said, sounding mildly surprised.

"How did she seem to you? I mean, did she seem — nervous or upset in any way?"

"Upset?" She paused just a second, then said, "Maybe a little keyed up. Nothing much."

"Did she by any chance mention anything to you about a boy in a green hat?"

"No-o, not that I remember."

"I see." He was silent a moment, staring out of the booth at a customer who was coming in to get a newspaper. "Well, could you tell me this, then? Did you yourself happen to notice a boy in a green hat — you know, just playing in the park anywhere."

"A boy in a green hat," she said, obviously trying to remember.

"Think a minute. There's no hurry."

There was silence at both ends of the line for several moments. Then Janie said, "Yes, yes, I did, come to think of it."

Lange swallowed hard; his heart was beating quickly. "You did?" he said, trying to keep the eagerness from his voice.

"Yes, I remember now."

"How old would you say he was?"

"Oh, maybe seven."

Seven — nine; that was close enough. A tremendous relief settled over him. He said, "Thanks so much, Janie . . . Listen, just one more thing, though — how long after Katherine arrived did this boy appear? Do you happen to recall that?"

"Oh, he was there before she came," Janie said right away without any hesitation.

"Before she came?"

"Yes, he was there all afternoon."

"You're *sure* of that?"

"Yes, positive. Well, I know his mother, Mrs. Model — I was even talking with her earlier in the afternoon."

"He has a mother?" Lange said, dismayed.

Janie laughed. "Well, of course he has a mother! Sol, don't be silly! He has a sister, too — they were playing together."

"A sister, too." He frowned, despair and unquiet seizing him again. "Then it may not be the same boy," he said, troubled.

"What boy? What do you mean?" she said. "What is this all about?"

Lange hesitated. In general he did not discuss his wife with anyone, but now he was compelled, not so much by closeness to Janie McGregor, as from a desire to talk to someone about it, to hear what they might have to say, to create order out of this chaos. "It's — " he began slowly. "Well, you remember when Katherine went into the hospital the last time?"

"Bellevue?"

"No, the time after that when she was just in Mount Sinai for a few months. Right after Avie was born."

"Yes, I remember."

"Well then, then the thing that started it off, or seemed to, was her imagining that certain people were following her — sometimes real people, people we knew, but sometimes just imaginary people. But she would describe them in great detail — what they wore, what they looked like. Maybe she was describing people she had really seen on the street, maybe taking bits of this person and that and combining them. Anyway, she would become obsessed with these people, what they were doing, what they wanted of her — "

"Paranoia," Janie said quickly, proud, Lange thought, to be able, so quickly, to put a label on it; this annoyed him.

"In a sense," he said impatiently. "There's more to it than that."

"Of course."

Again her tone irritated him; he wondered if this whole thing wasn't a mistake. She was obviously delighted to be hearing all of this, to be treated as confidante — she had always resented his abruptness with her, he knew. But he felt compelled to go on, having gone this far. "Well, at that time, when she was released, the doctor said this was one thing I ought to be watchful for — this tendency to imagine people, that it might be the beginning of something."

"I see," Janie said. She added, "Katherine is always so observant of people, anyway."

What did that have to do with it! Oh, he regretted this! What folly to talk to this woman! "Anyway, that's all," he said quickly, wanting to get off the phone. "So I just wanted to check with you about this boy."

"Yes, yes, well, I'm glad you did, Sol." Even her use of his first name bothered him as some attempt at an unwarranted intimacy. "And listen, if anything should happen, I'll let you know."

"I doubt that it will," he said, trying to be genial and at the same time trying to discourage her from getting further involved. "Thank you, anyway."

Going upstairs, he felt angry with himself. What had been the purpose of that? What had it accomplished? Was there any point, really, in playing private detective, tracking down all these minor clues which, nine times out of ten, might mean nothing?

The long, carpeted corridor of the floor on which he lived was silent. There had always seemed to Lange something faintly ominous about that long corridor. It was so totally impersonal, each door marked only by a number or possibly a mat placed outside. It was as though the coldness and uniformity must conceal in each case, as in his own, some peculiarities going on within, fights, tensions of one kind or another. Perhaps such people, he thought, musing on this, perhaps people who had something to hide selected these buildings unconsciously, wanting to conceal themselves in their bland uniformity like animals hiding under a rock.

He returned to his study, moving quietly through the darkened apartment. He decided to stay there just a little while, long enough so that he could then enter the bedroom and feel calm and collected. He took up the papers he had been trying to study before he had gone down and was just beginning to get absorbed in them when the door opened. "Janie McGregor called," Katherine said, standing in the study door.

Lange started; he had imagined, hoped, she might be asleep. But she stood at the door, alert as a sentry, her body outlined in the transparent nightgown, her hair bound up sleek and tight in a turban.

"Janie McGregor?" he said, uneasy. "What did she want?"

"She was just calling to invite us over for dinner in two weeks." She paused, still not moving an inch from the doorway. "She said she had just spoken to you."

He was silent one second, then said, "Yes, I called her. Well, I wanted to speak to Bill, really, but he wasn't in."

"I came in here after she called, but you weren't here." She gazed at him with an intense, inexorable glance. "Why did you call from downstairs?"

"I was down — to get an evening paper," Lange said quickly, remembering in a flash that he had forgotten to get the paper. "And I thought I'd just call from there."

"She said you called about me."

Damn the woman! Damn her to eternal hell! And damn himself for his idiot foolishness in trusting her to keep her mouth shut for one second. He sat at his desk, fury making him clench his fists, at the same time knowing he was trapped now.

She stepped further into the room, closer to the desk. "Didn't you believe me?" she said. "About the boy? Didn't you believe me?"

He frowned painfully. "I wasn't — sure." He paused. "I *wanted* to believe you," he said, staring at her intently and inwardly willing her to believe him.

She smiled at him strangely, her face in the tight turban, oriental, mysterious, the eyes seeming elongated like the eyes of an Arab woman. "You never have faith in me," she said. "Never."

"I do have faith in you," Lange said. He stood up and went over to comfort her. He felt that his touch, more than what he could say in words, would calm her.

But she drew back as soon as he had laid his hand on her arm. "You never do," she said. "You never have. Right from the first time. You always think of me as someone crazy, not to be trusted. I always sense it."

"It's not true," he said. "You simply think that."

"No." She shook her head. "I can tell. I always sense that in you. You act as though I were some wild animal that could never be trained."

"But I want you to get well," he said, trying to make his voice quiet and patient. "Surely you can't doubt that . . . And not just for your sake," he felt compelled to add. "For mine. For our children."

"But I never will," she said in a desperate voice, "because you'll never trust me. And one can't get well without trust."

He said nothing, touched by some truth in this. "I have trust," he said, reaching out for her again.

"You pretend to have trust," she said. "It isn't the same thing."

Lange was silent, tired, finally, of denials, of disguises. "Perhaps you're right," he said. "I only pretend to. That's so." He stood, exhausted, staring at her.

He had expected that this confession would arouse her still further, but suddenly, as though the words were a needle which he had sunk into her arm, bringing sudden peace, she became quiet. She let him approach her and, as they went inside, her whole body went limp and unresisting while he, in a kind of stilled fury, tried to vent on her body the anger he felt, not so much at himself, or even at her, but at her illness which, like a knife, lay between them, making trust and belief impossible.

The next Saturday he took Avie to the park alone; Katherine was at home preparing for a dinner party they were to give that evening. The weather had suddenly cleared, turned mild, although it was still hazy and not quite spring. He walked alone, feeling in a good mood, relaxed, having slept well, his nerves at rest. The playground was crowded with pretty young mothers, chatting beside carriages and, perhaps due to the spring weather, they looked to him unusually fresh and attractive in their brightly colored coats and scarves. He stood to one side of the playground while Avie went off on his tricycle, pedaling furiously. Lange stared around, bemused, at the children playing, digging in the large sandbox with their shovels. Then suddenly his eyes stopped roaming and stared. Right near the sandbox, standing to one side, leaning against a tree, was a boy in a green wool hat. He might have been

playing and stopped or was just about to play, but now he stood
with a peculiar, dreamy expression, watching the other children.
Lange's throat felt dry. He stood motionless, staring at the boy. At
that moment Avie came peddling over and announced that he
wanted something to eat. "Yes, we'll go back," Lange said hastily.
"It's time for lunch."

"But we just came," the boy wailed. "We just got here."

"We have to go back. Your mother's expecting us," Lange said
and hurried his son out of the playground and up the hill to their
house.

At home Katherine was in the kitchen, standing at the counter,
slicing tomatoes. Lange came into the kitchen, his coat still on.

"Was it nice out?" she asked.

"Yes, quite nice," Lange said. He paused a moment. "But, Kath,
you were right. I saw that boy. The one you mentioned. . . . The
boy in the green hat," he added as she continued to look at him
with a blank, uncomprehending expression.

But when she spoke her voice was bland and unrevealing; she
continued to slice the tomatoes. "What boy do you mean?" she
said.

# MARY LAVIN

## *Happiness*

(FROM THE NEW YORKER)

MOTHER HAD a lot to say. This does not mean she was always talking but that we children felt the wells she drew upon were deep, deep, deep. Her theme was happiness: what it was, what it was not; where we might find it, where not; and how, if found, it must be guarded. Never must we confound it with pleasure. Nor think sorrow its exact opposite.

"Take Father Hugh." Mother's eyes flashed as she looked at him. "According to him, sorrow is an ingredient of happiness — a *necessary* ingredient, if you please!" And when he tried to protest she put up her hand. "There may be a freakish truth in the theory — for some people. But not for me. And not, I hope, for my children." She looked severely at us three girls. We laughed. None of us had had much experience with sorrow. Bea and I were children and Linda only a year old when our father died suddenly after a short illness that had not at first seemed very serious. "I've known people to make sorrow a *substitute* for happiness," Mother said.

Father Hugh protested again. "You're not putting me in that class, I hope?"

Father Hugh, ever since our father died, had been the closest of anyone to us as a family, without being close to any one of us in particular — even to Mother. He lived in a monastery near our farm in County Meath, and he had been one of the celebrants at the Requiem High Mass our father's political importance had demanded. He met us that day for the first time, but he took to drop-

ping in to see us, with the idea of filling the crater of loneliness left
at our center. He did not know that there was a cavity in his own
life, much less that we would fill it. He and Mother were both
young in those days, and perhaps it gave scandal to some that he
was so often in our house, staying till late into the night and, indeed, thinking nothing of stopping all night if there was any special reason, such as one of us being sick. He had even on occasion
slept there if the night was too wet for tramping home across the
fields.

When we girls were young, we were so used to having Father
Hugh around that we never stood on ceremony with him but in
his presence dried our hair and pared our nails and never minded
what garments were strewn about. As for Mother — she thought
nothing of running out of the bathroom in her slip, brushing her
teeth or combing her hair, if she wanted to tell him something she
might otherwise forget. And she brooked no criticism of her behavior. "Chastity was never meant to take all the warmth and
homeliness out of their lives," she said.

On this point, too, Bea was adamant. Bea, the middle sister, was
our oracle. "I'm so glad he *has* Mother," she said, "as well as her
having him, because it must be awful the way most women treat
them — priests, I mean — as if they were pariahs. Mother treats
him like a human being — that's all!"

And when it came to Mother's ears that there had been gossip
about her making free with Father Hugh, she opened her eyes
wide in astonishment. "But he's only a priest!" she said.

Bea giggled. "It's a good job he didn't hear *that*," she said to me
afterward. "It would undo the good she's done him. You'd think
he was a eunuch."

"Bea!" I said. "Do you think he's in love with her?"

"If so, he doesn't know it," Bea said firmly. "It's her soul he's
after! Maybe he wants to make sure of her in the next world!"

But thoughts of the world to come never troubled Mother. "If
anything ever happens to me, children," she said, "suddenly, I
mean, or when you are not near me, or that I cannot speak to you,
I want you to promise you won't feel bad. There's no need! Just
remember that I had a happy life — and that if I had to choose my
kind of Heaven I'd take it on this earth with you again, no matter
how much you might annoy me!"

You see, annoyance and fatigue, according to Mother, and even illness and pain, could coexist with happiness. She had a habit of asking people if they were happy at times and in places that — to say the least of it — seemed to us inappropriate. "But are you happy?" she'd probe as one lay sick and bathed in sweat, or in the throes of a jumping toothache. And once in our presence she made the inquiry of an old friend as he lay upon his deathbed.

"Why not?" she said when we took her to task for it later. "Isn't it more important than ever to be happy when you're dying? Take my own father! You know what he said in his last moments? On his deathbed, he defied me to name a man who had enjoyed a better life. In spite of dreadful pain, his face *radiated* happiness!" said Mother, nodding her head comfortably. "Happiness drives out pain, as fire burns out fire."

Having no knowledge of our own to pit against hers, we thirstily drank in her rhetoric. Only Bea was skeptical. "Perhaps you *got* it from him, like spots, or fever," she said. "Or something that could at least be slipped from hand to hand."

"Do you think I'd have taken it if that were the case!" Mother cried. "Then, when he needed it most?"

"Not there and then!" Bea said stubbornly. "I meant as a sort of legacy."

"Don't you think in *that* case," Mother said, exasperated, "he would have felt obliged to leave it to your grandmother?"

Certainly we knew that in spite of his lavish heart our grandfather had failed to provide our grandmother with enduring happiness. He had passed that job on to Mother. And Mother had not made too good a fist of it, even when Father was living and she had him — and, later, us children — to help.

As for Father Hugh, he had given our grandmother up early in the game. "God Almighty couldn't make that woman happy," he said one day, seeing Mother's face, drawn and pale with fatigue, preparing for the nightly run over to her own mother's flat that would exhaust her utterly.

There were evenings after she came home from the library where she worked when we saw her stand with the car keys in her hand, trying to think which would be worse — to slog over there on foot or take out the car again. And yet the distance was short. It was Mother's days that were too long.

"Weren't you over to see her this morning?" Father Hugh demanded.

"No matter!" said Mother. She was no doubt thinking of the forlorn face our grandmother always put on when she was leaving. ("Don't say good night, Vera," Grandmother would plead. "It makes me feel too lonely. And you never can tell — you might slip over again before you go to bed!")

"Do you know the time?" Bea would say impatiently, if she happened to be with Mother. Not indeed that the lateness of the hour counted for anything, because in all likelihood Mother *would* go back, if only to pass by under the window and see that the lights were out, or stand and listen and make sure that as far as she could tell all was well.

"I wouldn't mind if she was happy," Mother said.

"And how do you know she's not?" we'd ask.

"When people are happy, I can feel it. Can't you?"

We were not sure. Most people thought our grandmother was a gay creature, a small birdy being who even at a great age laughed like a girl, and — more remarkable — sang like one, as she went about her day. But beak and claw were of steel. She'd think nothing of sending Mother back to a shop three times if her errands were not exactly right. "Not sugar like that — that's *too* fine; it's not caster sugar I want. But *not* as coarse as *that,* either. I want an in-between kind."

Provoked one day, my youngest sister, Linda, turned and gave battle. "You're mean!" she cried. "You love ordering people about!"

Grandmother preened, as if Linda had acclaimed an attribute. "I was always hard to please," she said. "As a girl, I used to be called Miss Imperious."

And Miss Imperious she remained as long as she lived, even when she was a great age. Her orders were then given a wry twist by the fact that as she advanced in age she took to calling her daughter Mother, as we did.

There was one great phrase with which our grandmother opened every sentence: "if only." "If only," she'd say, when we came to visit her, "—if only you'd come earlier, before I was worn out expecting you!" Or if we were early, then if only it was later, after she'd had a rest and could enjoy us, be *able* for us. And if we brought her flowers, she'd sigh to think that if only we'd brought them the previous day she'd have had a visitor to appreciate them, or say it was a pity the stems weren't longer. If only we'd picked a few green leaves, or included some buds, because, she said disparagingly, the poor flowers we'd brought were already wilting. We might just as well not have brought them! As the years went on, Grandmother had a new bead to add to her rosary: if only her friends were not all dead! By their absence, they reduced to nil all *real* enjoyment in anything. Our own father — her son-in-law — was the one person who had ever gone close to pleasing her. But even here there had been a snag. "If only he was my real son!" she used to say, with a sigh.

Mother's mother lived on through our childhood and into our early maturity (though she outlived the money our grandfather left her), and in our minds she was a complicated mixture of valiance and defeat. Courageous and generous within the limits of her own life, her simplest demand was yet enormous in the larger frame of Mother's life, and so we never could see her with the same clarity of vision with which we saw our grandfather, or our own father. Them we saw only through Mother's eyes.

"Take your grandfather!" she'd cry, and instantly we'd see him, his eyes burning upon us — yes, upon *us*, although in his day only one of us had been born: me. At another time, Mother would cry, "Take your own father!" and instantly we'd see *him* — tall, handsome, young, and much more suited to marry one of us than poor bedraggled Mother.

Most fascinating of all were the times Mother would say, "Take me!" By magic then, staring down the years, we'd see blazingly clear a small girl with black hair and buttoned boots, who, though plain and pouting, burned bright, like a star. "I was happy, you see," Mother said. And we'd strain hard to try and understand the mystery of the light that still radiated from her. "I used to lean along a tree that grew out over the river," she said, "and look down through the gray leaves at the water flowing past below, and I used to think it was not the stream that flowed but me, spread-eagled over it, who flew through the air! Like a bird! That I'd found the secret!" She made it seem there might *be* such a secret, just waiting to be found. Or she dreamed that she'd be a great singer.

"We didn't know you sang, Mother!"

"Like a crow," she said.

Sometimes she used to think she'd swim the Channel.

"Did you swim *that* well, Mother?"

"Oh, not really — just the breaststroke," she said. "And then only by the aid of two pig bladders blown up by my father and tied around my middle. But I used to throb — yes, throb — with happiness."

Behind Mother's back, Bea raised her eyebrows.

What was it, we used to ask ourselves — that quality that she, we felt sure, misnamed? Was it courage? Was it strength, health, or high spirits? Something you could not give or take — a conundrum? A game of catch-as-catch-can?

"I know," cried Bea. "A sham!"

Whatever it was, we knew that Mother would let no wind of violence from within or without tear it from her. Although, one evening when Father Hugh was with us, our astonished ears heard her proclaim that there might be a time when one had to slacken hold on it — let go — to catch at it again with a surer hand. In the way, we supposed, that the high-wire walker up among the painted stars of his canvas sky must wait to fling himself through the air until the bar he catches at has started to sway perversely from him. Oh no, no! That downward drag at our innards we could not bear, the belly swelling to the shape of a pear. Let happiness go by the board. "After all, lots of people seem to make out without it," Bea cried. It was too tricky a business. And might it not be that one had to be born with a flair for it?

"A flair would not be enough," Mother answered. "Take Father Hugh. He, if anyone, has a flair for it — a natural capacity! You've only to look at him when he's off guard, with you children, or helping me in the garden. But he rejects happiness! He casts it from him."

"That is simply not true, Vera," cried Father Hugh, overhearing her. "It's just that I don't place an inordinate value on it like you. I don't think it's enough to carry one all the way. To the end, I mean — and after."

"Oh, don't talk about the end when we're only in the middle," cried Mother. And, indeed, at that moment her own face shone with such happiness it was hard to believe that her earth was not her Heaven. Certainly it was her constant contention that of hap-

piness she had had a lion's share. This, however, we, in private,
doubted. Perhaps there were times when she had had a surplus of
it — when she was young, say, with her redoubtable father, whose
love blazed circles around her, making winter into summer and ice
into fire. Perhaps she had a brimming measure in her early married years. By straining hard, we could find traces left in our minds
from those days of milk and honey. Our father, while he lived,
had cast a magic over everything, for us as well as for her. He held
his love up over us like an umbrella and kept off the troubles that
afterward came down on us, pouring cats and dogs!

But if she did have more than the common lot of happiness in
those early days, what use was that when we could remember so
clearly how our father's death had ravaged her? And how could we
forget the distress it brought on us when, afraid to let her out of
our sight, Bea and I stumbled after her everywhere, through the
woods and along the bank of the river, where, in the weeks that
followed, she tried vainly to find peace.

The summer after Father died, we were invited to France to stay
with friends, and when she went walking on the cliffs at Fécamp
our fears for her grew frenzied, so that we hung on to her arm and
dragged at her skirt, hoping that like leaded weights we'd pin her
down if she went too near to the edge. But at night we had to
abandon our watch, being forced to follow the conventions of a
family still whole — a home still intact — and go to bed at the
same time as the other children. It was at that hour, when the
coast guard was gone from his rowboat offshore and the sand was as
cold and gray as the sea, that Mother liked to swim. And when she
had washed, kissed, and left us, our hearts almost died inside us
and we'd creep out of bed again to stand in our bare feet at the
mansard and watch as she ran down the shingle, striking out when
she reached the water where, far out, wave and sky and mist
were one, and the grayness closed over her. If we took our eyes off
her for an instant, it was impossible to find her again.

"Oh, make her turn back, God, please!" I prayed out loud one
night.

Startled, Bea turned away from the window. "She'll *have* to turn
back sometime, won't she? Unless . . . ?"

Locking our damp hands together, we stared out again. "She
wouldn't!" I whispered. "It would be a sin!"

Secure in the deterring power of sin, we let out our breath. Then Bea's breath caught again. "What if she went out so far she used up all her strength? She couldn't swim back! It wouldn't be a sin then!"

"It's the intention that counts," I whispered.

A second later, we could see an arm lift heavily up and wearily cleave down, and at last Mother was in the shallows, wading back to shore.

"Don't let her see us!" cried Bea. As if our chattering teeth would not give us away when she looked in at us before she went to her own room on the other side of the corridor, from where, later in the night, the sound of crying would reach us.

What was it worth — a happiness bought that dearly.

Mother had never questioned it. And once she told us, "On a wintry day, I brought my own mother a snowdrop. It was the first one of the year — a bleak bud that had come up stunted before its time — and I meant it for a sign. But do you know what your grandmother said? 'What good are snowdrops to me now?' Such a thing to say! What good is a snowdrop at all if it doesn't hold its value always, and never lose it! Isn't that the whole point of a snowdrop? And that is the whole point of happiness, too! What good would it be if it could be erased without trace? Take me and those daffodils!" Stooping, she buried her face in a bunch that lay on the table waiting to be put in vases. "If I didn't hold their beauty absolute and inviolable, do you think I could bear the sight of them after what happened when your father was in hospital?"

It was a fair question. When Father went to hospital, Mother went with him and stayed in a small hotel across the street so she could be with him all day from early to late. "Because it was so awful for him — being in Dublin!" she said. "You have no idea how he hated it."

That he was dying neither of them realized. How could they know, as it rushed through the sky, that their star was a falling star! But one evening when she'd left him asleep Mother came home for a few hours to see how we were faring, and it broke her heart to see the daffodils out all over the place — in the woods, under the trees, and along the sides of the avenue. There had never been so many, and she thought how awful it was that Father was missing them. "You sent up little bunches to him, you poor dears!" she said. "Sweet little bunches, too — squeezed tight as posies by your little fists! But stuffed into vases they couldn't really make up to him for not being able to see them growing!"

So on the way back to the hospital she stopped her car and pulled a great bunch — the full of her arms. "They took up the whole back seat," she said, "and I was so excited at the thought of walking into his room and dumping them on his bed — you know, just plomping them down so he could smell them, and feel them, and look and look! I didn't mean them to be put in vases, or anything ridiculous like that — it would have taken a rainwater barrel to hold them. Why, I could hardly see over them as I came up the steps; I kept tripping. But when I came into the hall, that nun — I told you about her — that nun came up to me, sprang out of nowhere it seemed, although I know now that she was waiting for me, knowing that somebody had to bring me to my senses. But the way she did it! Reached out and grabbed the flowers, letting lots of them fall — I remember them getting stood on. 'Where are you going with those foolish flowers, you foolish woman?' she said. 'Don't you know your husband is dying? Your prayers are all you can give him now!'

"She was right. I *was* foolish. But I wasn't cured. Afterward, it was nothing but foolishness the way I dragged you children after me all over Europe. As if any one place was going to be different from another, any better, any less desolate. But there was great satisfaction in bringing you places your father and I had planned to bring you — although in fairness to him I must say that he would not perhaps have brought you so young. And he would not have had an ulterior motive. But above all he would not have attempted those trips in such a dilapidated car."

Oh, that car! It was a battered and dilapidated red sports car, so depleted of accessories that when, eventually, we got a new car, Mother still stuck out her hand on bends, and in wet weather jumped out to wipe the windscreen with her sleeve. And if fussed she'd let down the window and shout at people, forgetting she now had a horn. How we had ever fitted into it with all our luggage was a miracle.

"You were never lumpish — any of you!" Mother said proudly.
"But you were very healthy and very strong." She turned to me.
"Think of how you got that car up the hill in Switzerland!"

"The Alps are not hills, Mother!" I pointed out coldly, as I had
done at the time, when, as actually happened, the car failed to make
it on one of the inclines. Mother let it run back until it wedged
against the rock face, and I had to get out and push till she got going again in first gear. But when it got started it couldn't be stopped
to pick me up until it got to the top, where they had to wait for
me, and for a very long time.

"Ah, well," she said, sighing wistfully at the thought of those
trips. "You got something out of them, I hope. All that traveling
must have helped you with your geography and your history."

We looked at each other and smiled, and then Mother herself
laughed. "Remember the time," she said, "when we were in Italy,
and it was Easter, and all the shops were chock-full of food? The
butcher shops had poultry and game hanging up outside the doors,
fully feathered, and with their poor heads dripping blood, and in
the windows they had poor little lambs and suckling pigs and young
goats, all skinned and hanging by their forefeet." Mother shuddered. "They think so much about food. I found it revolting. I
had to hurry past. But Linda, who must have been only four then,
dragged at me and stared and stared. You know how children are
at that age; they have a morbid fascination for what is cruel and
bloody. Her face was flushed and her eyes were wide. I hurried
her back to the hotel. But next morning she crept into my room.
She crept up to me and pressed against me. 'Can't we go back, just
once, and look again at that shop?' she whispered. 'The shop where
they have the little children hanging up for Easter!' It was the
young goats, of course, but I'd said 'kids,' I suppose. How we
laughed." But her face was grave. "You were *so* good on those
trips, all of you," she said. "You were really very good children in
general. Otherwise I would never have put so much effort into rear-
ing you, because I wasn't a bit maternal. You brought out the best
in me! I put an unnatural effort into you, of course, because I was
taking my standards from your father, forgetting that his might
not have remained so inflexible if he had lived to middle age and
was beset by life, like other parents."

"Well, the job is nearly over now, Vera," said Father Hugh. "And you didn't do so badly."

"That's right, Hugh," said Mother, and she straightened up, and put her hand to her back the way she sometimes did in the garden when she got up from her knees after weeding. "I didn't go over to the enemy, anyway! We survived!" Then a flash of defiance came into her eyes. "And we were happy. That's the main thing!"

Father Hugh frowned. "There you go again!" he said.

Mother turned on him. "I don't think you realize the onslaughts that were made upon our happiness! The minute Robert died, they came down on me — cohorts of relatives, friends, even strangers, all draped in black, opening their arms like bats to let me pass into their company. 'Life is a vale of tears,' they said. 'You are privileged to find it out so young!' Ugh! After I staggered onto my feet and began to take hold of life once more, they fell back defeated. And the first day I gave a laugh — pouf, they were blown out like candles. They weren't living in a real world at all; they belonged to a ghostly world where life was easy: all one had to do was sit and weep. It takes effort to push back the stone from the mouth of the tomb."

Effort. Effort. Ah, but that strange-sounding word could invoke little sympathy from one who had not learned yet what it meant. Life must have been hardest for Mother in those years when we older ones were at college — no longer children, and still dependent on her. Indeed, we made more demands on her than ever then, having moved into new areas of activity and emotion. And of friends! Our friends came and went as freely as we did ourselves, so that the house was often like a café — and one where pets were not prohibited but took their places on our chairs and beds, as regardless as the people. And anyway it was hard to have sympathy for someone who got things into such a state as Mother. All over the house there was clutter. Her study was like the returned-letter department of a post office, with stacks of paper everywhere, bills paid and unpaid, letters answered and unanswered, tax returns, pamphlets, leaflets. If by mistake we left the door open on a windy day, we came back to find papers flapping through the air like frightened birds. Efficient only in that she managed eventually to conclude every task she began, Mother's methods always seemed to outsiders incapable of accomplishing anything whatever. In an attempt to keep order elsewhere, she made her own room the clearing house into which the rest of us put everything: things to be given away, things to be mended, things to be stored, things to be treasured, things to be returned — even things to be thrown out! By the end of the year, the room resembled an obsolescence dump. And no one could help her; the chaos of her life was as personal as an act of creation — one might as well try to finish another person's poem.

As the years passed, Mother rushed around more hectically. And although Bea and I had married and were not at home anymore, except at holiday time and for occasional weekends, Linda was noisier than the two of us put together had been, and for every follower we had brought home she brought twenty. The house was never still. Now that we were reduced to being visitors, we watched Mother's tension mount to vertigo, knowing that, like a spinning top, she could not rest till she fell. But now at the smallest pretext Father Hugh would call in the doctor and Mother would be put on the mail boat and dispatched for London. For it was essential that she get far enough away to make phoning home every night prohibitively costly.

Unfortunately, the thought of departure often drove a spur into her and she redoubled her effort to achieve order in her affairs. She would be up until the early hours ransacking her desk. To her, always, the shortest parting entailed a preparation as for death. And as if it were her end that was at hand, we would all be summoned, although she had no time to speak a word to us, because five minutes before departure she would still be attempting to reply to letters that were the acquisition of weeks and would have taken whole days to dispatch.

"Don't you know the taxi is at the door, Vera?" Father Hugh would say, running his hand through his gray hair and looking very dishevelled himself. She had him at times as distracted as herself. "You can't do any more. You'll have to leave the rest till you come back."

"I can't, I can't!" Mother would cry. "I'll have to cancel my plans."

One day, Father Hugh opened the lid of her case, which was strapped up in the hall, and with a swipe of his arm he cleared all the papers on the top of the desk pell-mell into the suitcase. "You can sort them on the boat," he said, "or the train to London!"

Thereafter, Mother's luggage always included an empty case to hold the unfinished papers on her desk. And years afterward a steward on the Irish Mail told us she was a familiar figure, working away at letters and bills nearly all the way from Holyhead to Euston. "She gave it up about Rugby or Crewe," he said. "She'd get talking to someone in the compartment." He smiled. "There was one time coming down the train I was just in time to see her close up the window with a guilty look. I didn't say anything, but I think she'd emptied those papers of hers out the window!"

Quite likely. When we were children, even a few hours away from us gave her composure. And in two weeks or less, when she'd come home, the well of her spirit would be freshened. We'd hardly know her — her step so light, her eye so bright, and her love and patience once more freely flowing. But in no time at all the house would fill up once more with the noise and confusion of too many people and too many animals, and again we'd be fighting our corner with cats and dogs, slugs, bats, mice, and even bees. "Don't kill it!" Mother would cry if we raised a hand to an angry wasp. "Just catch it, dear, and put it outside. Open the window and let it fly away!" But even this treatment could at times be deemed too harsh. "Wait a minute. Close the window!" she'd cry. "It's too cold outside. It will die. That's why it came in, I suppose! Oh dear, what will we do?" Life would be going full blast again.

There was only one place Mother found rest. When she was at breaking point and fit to fall, she'd go out into the garden — not to sit or stroll around but to dig, to drag up weeds, to move great clumps of corms or rhizomes, or indeed quite frequently to haul huge rocks from one place to another. She was always laying down a path, building a dry wall, or making compost heaps as high as hills. However jaded she might be going out, when dark forced her in at last her step had the spring of a daisy. So if she did not succeed in defining happiness to our understanding, we could see that whatever it was, she possessed it to the full when she was in her garden.

One of us said as much one Sunday when Bea and I had dropped around for the afternoon. Father Hugh was with us again. "It's an unthinking happiness, though," he caviled. We were standing at the drawing room window, looking out to where in the fading light we could see Mother on her knees, weeding in the long border that stretched from the house right down to the woods. "I wonder how she'd take it if she were stricken down and had to give up that heavy work!" he said. Was he perhaps a little jealous of how she could stoop and bend? He himself had begun to use a stick. I was often a little jealous of her myself, because although I was married and had children of my own, I had married young and felt the weight of living as heavy as a weight of years. "She doesn't take enough care of herself," Father Hugh said sadly. "Look at her out there with nothing under her knees to protect her from the damp ground." It was almost too dim for us to see her, but even in the drawing room it was chilly. "She should not be let stay out there after the sun goes down."

"Just you try to get her in then!" said Linda, who had come into the room in time to hear him. "Don't you know by now anyway that what would kill another person only seems to make Mother thrive?"

Father Hugh shook his head again. "You seem to forget it's not younger she's getting!" He fidgeted and fussed, and several times went to the window to stare out apprehensively. He was really getting quite elderly.

"Come and sit down, Father Hugh," Bea said, and to take his mind off Mother she turned on the light and blotted out the garden. Instead of seeing through the window, we saw into it as into a mirror, and there between the flower-laden tables and the lamps it was ourselves we saw moving vaguely. Like Father Hugh, we, too, were waiting for her to come in before we called an end to the day.

"Oh, this is ridiculous!" Father Hugh cried at last. "She'll have to listen to reason." And, going back to the window, he threw it open. "Vera!" he called. "Vera!" — sternly, so sternly that, more intimate than an endearment, his tone shocked us. "She didn't hear me," he said, turning back blinking at us in the lighted room. "I'm going out to get her." And in a minute he was gone from the room. As he ran down the garden path, we stared at each other, astonished; his step, too, was the step of a lover. "I'm coming, Vera!" he cried.

Although she was never stubborn except in things that mattered, Mother had not moved. In the wholehearted way she did everything, she was bent down close to the ground. It wasn't the light only that was dimming, her eyesight also was failing, I thought, as instinctively I followed Father Hugh.

But halfway down the path I stopped. I had seen something he had not: Mother's hand that appeared to support itself in a forked branch of an old tree peony she had planted as a bride was not in fact gripping it but impaled upon it. And the hand that appeared to be grubbing in the clay in fact was sunk into the soft mold. "Mother!" I screamed, and I ran forward, but when I reached her I covered my face with my hands. "Oh Father Hugh!" I cried. "Is she dead?"

It was Bea who answered, hysterical. "She is! She is!" she cried, and she began to pound Father Hugh on the back with her fists, as if his pessimistic words had made this happen.

But Mother was not dead. And at first the doctor even offered hope of her pulling through. She lived for four hours. But from the moment Father Hugh lifted her up to carry her into the house we ourselves had no hope, seeing how effortlessly he, who was not strong, could carry her. When he put her down on her bed, her head hardly creased the pillow.

Like the days of her life, those four hours that Mother lived were packed tight with concern and anxiety. Partly conscious, partly delirious, she seemed to think the counterpane was her desk, and she scrabbled her fingers upon it as if trying to sort out a muddle of bills and correspondence. No longer indifferent now, we listened, anguished, to the distracted cries that had for all our lifetimes been so familiar to us. "Oh, where is it? Where is it? I had it a minute ago! Where on earth did I put it?"

"Vera, Vera, stop worrying," Father Hugh pleaded, but she waved him away and went on sifting through the sheets as if they were sheets of paper. "Oh Vera!" he begged. "Listen to me. Do you not know — "

Bea pushed between them. "You're not to tell her!" she commanded. "Why frighten her?"

"But it ought not to frighten her," said Father Hugh. "This is what I was always afraid would happen — that she'd be frightened when it came to the end."

At that moment, as if to vindicate him, Mother's hands fell idle on the coverlet, palm upward and empty. And, turning her head, she stared at each of us in turn, beseechingly. "I cannot face it," she whispered. "I can't! I can't! I can't!"

"Oh, my God!" Bea said, and she started to cry.

"Vera. For God's sake listen to me," Father Hugh cried, and pressing his face to hers, as close as a kiss, he kept whispering to her, trying to cast into the dark tunnel before her the light of his own faith, hope, and charity.

But it seemed to us that Mother must already be looking into God's exigent eyes. "I can't!" she cried. "I can't!"

Then her mind came back from the stark world of the spirit to the world where her body was still detained, but even that world was now a whirling kaleidoscope of things which only she could see. Suddenly her eyes focused, and, catching at Father Hugh, she pulled herself up a little and pointed to something we could not see. "What will be done with them?" Her voice was anxious. "They ought to be put in water anyway," she said, and, leaning over the edge of the bed, she pointed to the floor. "Don't step on that one!" she said sharply. Then, more sharply still, she addressed us all. "Have them sent to the public ward," she said peremptorily. "Don't let that nun take them; she'll only put them on the altar. And God doesn't want them! He made them for *us* — not for Himself!"

It was the familiar rhetoric that all her life had characterized her utterances. For a moment we were mystified. Then Bea gasped. "The daffodils!" she cried. "The day Father died!" And over her face came the light that had so often blazed over Mother's. Leaning across the bed, she pushed Father Hugh aside. And, putting out her hands, she held Mother's face between her palms as tenderly as if it were the face of a child. "It's all right, Mother. You don't *have* to face it! It's over!" Then she who had so fiercely forbade Father Hugh to do so blurted out the truth. "You've finished with this world, Mother," she said, and, confident that her tidings were joyous, her voice was strong.

Mother made the last effort of her life and grasped at Bea's meaning. She let out a sigh, and, closing her eyes, she sank back, and this time her head sank so deep into the pillow that it would have been dented had it been a pillow of stone.

# ALISTAIR MacLEOD

## *The Boat*

(FROM THE MASSACHUSETTS REVIEW)

THERE ARE TIMES even now, when I awake at four o'clock in the morning with the terrible fear that I have overslept; when I imagine that my father is waiting for me in the room below the darkened stairs or that the shorebound men are tossing pebbles against my window while blowing their hands and stomping their feet impatiently on the frozen steadfast earth. There are times when I am half out of bed and fumbling for socks and mumbling for words before I realize that I am foolishly alone, that no one waits at the base of the stairs and no boat rides restlessly in the waters by the pier.

At such times only the gray corpses on the overflowing ashtray beside my bed bear witness to the extinction of the latest spark and silently await the crushing out of the most recent of their fellows. And then because I am afraid to be alone with death, I dress rapidly, make a great to-do about clearing my throat, turn on both faucets in the sink and proceed to make loud splashing ineffectual noises. Later I go out and walk the mile to the all-night restaurant.

In the winter it is a very cold walk and there are often tears in my eyes when I arrive. The waitress usually gives a sympathetic little shiver and says, "Boy, it must be really cold out there; you got tears in your eyes."

"Yes," I said, "it sure is; it really is."

And then the three or four of us who are always in such places at such times make uninteresting little protective chitchat until the dawn reluctantly arrives. Then I swallow the coffee which is always bitter and leave with a great busy rush because by that time I have to worry about being late and whether I have a clean shirt and whether my car will start and about all the other countless things one must worry about when he teaches at a great Midwestern university. And I know then that that day will go by as have all the days of the past ten years, for the call and the voices and the shapes and the boat were not really there in the early morning's darkness and I have all kinds of comforting reality to prove it. They are only shadows and echoes, the animals a child's hands make on the wall by lamplight, and the voices from the rain barrel; the cuttings from an old movie made in the black and white of long ago.

I first became conscious of the boat in the same way and at almost the same time that I became aware of the people it supported. My earliest recollection of my father is a view from the floor of gigantic rubber boots and then of being suddenly elevated and having my face pressed against the stubble of his cheek, and of how it tasted of salt and of how he smelled of salt from his red-soled rubber boots to the shaggy whiteness of his hair.

When I was very small, he took me for my first ride in the boat. I rode the half mile from our house to the wharf on his shoulders and I remember the sound of his rubber boots galumphing along the gravel beach, the tune of the indecent little song he used to sing and the odor of the salt.

The floor of the boat was permeated with the same odor and in its constancy I was not aware of change. In the harbor we made our little circle and returned. He tied the boat by its painter, fastened the stern to its permanent anchor and lifted me high over his head to the solidity of the wharf. Then he climbed up the little iron ladder that led to the wharf's cap, placed me once more upon his shoulder and galumphed off again.

When we returned to the house everyone made a great fuss over my precocious excursion and asked, "How did you like the boat?" "Were you afraid in the boat?" "Did you cry in the boat?" They repeated "the boat" at the end of all their questions and I knew it must be very important to everyone.

My earliest recollection of my mother is of being alone with her in the mornings while my father was away in the boat. She seemed to be always repairing clothes that were "torn in the boat," preparing food "to be eaten in the boat" or looking for "the boat" through our kitchen window which faced upon the sea. When my father returned about noon, she would ask, "Well how did things go in the boat today?" It was the first question I remember asking, "Well how did things go in the boat today?" "Well how did things go in the boat today?"

The boat in our lives was registered at Port Hawkesbury. She was what Nova Scotians called a Cape Island boat and was designed for the small inshore fishermen who sought the lobsters of the spring and the mackerel of summer and later the cod and haddock and hake. She was thirty-two feet long and nine wide, and was powered by an engine from a Chevrolet truck. She had a marine clutch and a high speed reverse gear and was painted light green with the name *Jenny Lynn* stenciled in black letters on her bow and painted on an oblong plate across her stern. Jenny Lynn had been my mother's maiden name and the boat was called after her as another link in the chain of tradition. Most of the boats that berthed at the wharf bore the names of some female member of their owner's household.

I say this now as if I knew it all then. All at once, all about boat dimensions and engines, and as if on the day of my first childish voyage I noticed the difference between a stenciled name and a painted name. But of course it was not that way at all, for I learned it all very slowly and there was not time enough.

I learned first about our house which was one of about fifty which marched around the horseshoes of our harbor and the wharf which was its heart. Some of them were so close to the water that during a storm the sea spray splashed against their windows while others were built farther along the beach as was the case with ours. The houses and their people, like those of the neighboring towns and villages, were the result of Ireland's discontent and Scotland's Highland Clearances and America's War of Independence. Impulsive emotional Catholic Celts who could not bear to live with England and shrewd determined Protestant Puritans who, in the years after 1776, could not bear to live without.

The most important room in our house was one of those oblong old-fashioned kitchens heated by a wood and coal burning stove. Behind the stove was a box of kindlings and beside it a coal scuttle. A heavy wooden table with leaves that expanded or reduced

its dimensions stood in the middle of the floor. There were five
wooden homemade chairs which had been chipped and hacked by
a variety of knives. Against the east wall, opposite the stove, there
was a couch which sagged in the middle and had a cushion for
a pillow, and above it a shelf which contained matches, tobacco,
pencils, odd fish hooks, bits of twine, and a tin can filled with bills
and receipts. The south wall was dominated by a window which
faced the sea and on the north there was a five-foot board which
bore a variety of clothes hooks and the burdens of each. Beneath
the board there was a jumble of odd footwear, mostly of rubber.
There was also, on this wall, a barometer, a map of the marine area
and a shelf which held a tiny radio. The kitchen was shared by all
of us and was a buffer zone between the immaculate order of ten
other rooms and the disruptive chaos of the single room that was
my father's.

My mother ran her house as her brothers ran their boats. Everything was clean and spotless and in order. She was tall and dark
and powerfully energetic. In later years she reminded me of the
women of Thomas Hardy, particularly Eustacia Vye, in a physical way. She fed and clothed a family of seven children, making
all of the meals and most of the clothes. She grew miraculous
gardens and magnificent flowers and raised broods of hens and
ducks. She would walk miles on berry-picking expeditions and
hoist her skirts to dig for clams when the tide was low. She was
fourteen years younger than my father whom she had married when
she was twenty-six, and had been a local beauty for a period of ten
years. My mother was of the sea as were all of her people, and her
horizons were the very literal one she scanned with her dark and
fearless eyes.

Between the kitchen clothes rack and barometer a door opened
into my father's bedroom. It was a room of disorder and disarray.
It was as if the wind which so often clamored about the house succeeded in entering this single room and after whipping it into tur-
moil stole quietly away to renew its knowing laughter from without.

My father's bed was against the south wall. It always looked rumpled and unmade because he lay on top of it more than he slept
within any folds it might have had. Beside it, there was a little
brown table. An archaic goose-necked reading light, a battered

table radio, a mound of wooden matches, one or two packages of tobacco, a deck of cigarette papers and an overflowing ashtray cluttered its surface. The brown larvae of tobacco shreds and the gray flecks of ash covered both the table and the floor beneath it. The once-varnished surface of the table was disfigured by numerous black scars and gashes inflicted by the neglected burning cigarettes of many years. They had tumbled from the ashtray unnoticed and branded their statements permanently and quietly into the wood until the odor of their burning caused the snuffing out of their lives. At the bed's foot there was a single window which looked upon the sea.

Against the adjacent wall there was a battered bureau and beside it there was a closet which held his single ill-fitting serge suit, the two or three white shirts that strangled him and the square black shoes that pinched. When he took off his more friendly clothes, the heavy woolen sweaters, mitts and socks which my mother knitted for him and the woolen and doeskin shirts, he dumped them unceremoniously on a single chair. If a visitor entered the room while he was lying on the bed, he would be told to throw the clothes on the floor and take their place upon the chair.

Magazines and books covered the bureau and competed with the clothes for domination of the chair. They further overburdened the heroic little table and lay on top of the radio. They filled a baffling and unknowable cave beneath the bed, and in the corner by the bureau they spilled from the walls and grew up from the floor.

The magazines were the most conventional: *Time, Newsweek, Life, MacLeans, The Family Herald, The Reader's Digest.* They were the result of various cut-rate subscriptions or of the gift subscriptions associated with Christmas, "the two whole years for only $3.50."

The books were more varied. There were a few hard-cover magnificents and bygone Book of the Month wonders and some were Christmas or birthday gifts. The majority of them, however, were used paperbacks which came from those second-hand bookstores which advertise in the backs of magazines: "Miscellaneous Used Paperbacks 10¢ Each." At first he sent for them himself, although my mother resented the expense, but in later years they came more and more often from my sisters who had moved to the

cities. Especially at first they were very weird and varied. Mickey
Spillane and Ernest Haycox vied with Dostoyevsky and Faulk-
ner, and the Penguin Poets' edition of Gerard Manley Hopkins arrived in the same box as a little book on sex technique called *Getting the Most Out of Love*. The former had been assiduously
annotated by a very fine hand using a very blue-inked fountain pen
while the latter had been studied by someone with very large
thumbs, the prints of which were still visible in the margins. At
the slightest provocation it would open almost automatically to
particularly graphic and well-smudged pages.

When he was not in the boat, my father spent most of his time
lying on the bed in his socks, the top two buttons of his trousers
undone, his discarded shirt on the ever ready chair and the sleeves
of the woolen Stanfield underwear, which he wore both summer
and winter, drawn halfway up to his elbows. The pillows propped
up the whiteness of his head and the goose-necked lamp illumi-
nated the pages in his hands. The cigarettes smoked and smoul-
dered on the ashtray and on the table and the radio played constantly, sometimes low and sometimes loud. At midnight and at
one, two, three and four, one could sometimes hear the radio, his
occasional cough, the rustling thud of a completed book being
tossed to the corner heap, or the movement necessitated by his sitting on the edge of the bed to roll the thousandth cigarette. He
seemed never to sleep, only to doze and the light shone constantly
from his window to the sea.

My mother despised the room and all it stood for and she had
stopped sleeping in it after I was born. She despised disorder in
rooms and in houses and in hours and in lives, and she had not
read a book since high school. There she had read *Ivanhoe* and
considered it a colossal waste of time. Still the room remained, like
a solid rock of opposition in the sparkling waters of a clear deep
harbor, opening off the kitchen where we really lived our lives,
with its door always open and its contents visible to all.

The daughters of the room and of the house were very beautiful.
They were tall and willowy like my mother and had her fine fa-
cial features set off by the reddish copper-colored hair that had
apparently once been my father's before it turned to white. All of
them were very clever in school and helped my mother a great deal
about the house. When they were young they sang and were very

happy and very nice to me because I was the youngest and the family's only boy.

My father never approved of their playing about the wharf like the other children, and they went there only when my mother sent them on an errand. At such times they almost always overstayed, playing screaming games of tag or hide-and-seek in and about the fishing shanties, the piled traps and tubs of trawl, shouting down to the perch that swam languidly about the wharf's algae-covered piles, or jumping in and out of the boats that tugged gently at their lines. My mother was never uneasy about them at such times, and when her husband criticized her she would say, "Nothing will happen to them there," or "They could be doing worse things in worse places."

By about the ninth or tenth grade my sisters one by one discovered my father's bedroom and then the change would begin. Each would go into the room one morning when he was out. She would go with the ideal hope of imposing order or with the more practical objective of emptying the ashtray, and later she would be found spellbound by the volume in her hand. My mother's reaction was always abrupt, bordering on the angry. "Take your nose out of that trash and come and do your work," she would say, and once I saw her slap my youngest sister so hard that the print of her hand was scarletly emblazoned upon her daughter's cheek while the broken-spined paperback fluttered uselessly to the floor.

Thereafter my mother would launch a campaign against what she had discovered but could not understand. At times although she was not overly religious she would bring in God to bolster her arguments saying, "In the next world God will see to those who waste their lives reading useless books when they should be about their work." Or without theological aid, "I would like to know how books help anyone to live a life." If my father were in, she would repeat the remarks louder than necessary, and her voice would carry into his room where he lay upon his bed. His usual reaction was to turn up the volume of the radio, although that action in itself betrayed the success of the initial thrust.

Shortly after my sisters began to read the books, they grew restless and lost interest in darning socks and baking bread, and all of them eventually went to work as summer waitresses in the Sea Food Restaurant. The restaurant was run by a big American concern from Boston and catered to the tourists that flooded the area during July and August. My mother despised the whole operation. She said the restaurant was not run by "our people," and "our people" did not eat there, and that it was run by outsiders for outsiders.

"Who are these people anyway?" she would ask, tossing back her dark hair, "and what do they, though they go about with their cameras for a hundred years, know about the way it is here, and what do they care about me and mine, and why should I care about them?"

She was angry that my sisters should even conceive of working in such a place and more angry when my father made no move to prevent it, and she was worried about herself and about her family and about her life. Sometimes she would say softly to her sisters, "I don't know what's the matter with my girls. It seems none of them are interested in any of the right things." And sometimes there would be bitter savage arguments. One afternoon I was coming in with three mackerel I'd been given at the wharf when I heard her say, "Well I hope you'll be satisfied when they come home knocked up and you'll have had your way."

It was the most savage thing I'd ever heard my mother say. Not just the words but the way she said them, and I stood there in the porch afraid to breathe for what seemed like the years from ten to fifteen, feeling the damp moist mackerel with their silver glassy eyes growing clammy against my leg.

Through the angle in the screen door I saw my father who had been walking into his room wheel around on one of his rubber-booted heels and look at her with his blue eyes flashing like clearest ice beneath the snow that was his hair. His usually ruddy face was drawn and gray, reflecting the exhaustion of a man of sixty-five who had been working in those rubber boots for eleven hours on an August day, and for a fleeting moment I wondered what I would do if he killed my mother while I stood there in the porch with those three foolish mackerel in my hand. Then he turned and went into his room and the radio blared forth the next day's weather forecast and I retreated under the noise and returned again, stamping my feet and slamming the door too loudly to signal my approach. My mother was busy at the stove when I came in, and did not raise her head when I threw the mackerel in a pan.

As I looked into my father's room, I said, "Well how did things go in the boat today?" and he replied, "Oh not too badly, all things considered." He was lying on his back and lighting the first cigarette and the radio was talking about the Virginia coast.

All of my sisters made good money on tips. They bought my father an electric razor which he tried to use for a while and they took out even more magazine subscriptions. They bought my mother a great many clothes of the type she was very fond of, the wide-brimmed hats and the brocaded dresses, but she locked them all in trunks and refused to wear any of them.

On one August day my sisters prevailed upon my father to take some of their restaurant customers for an afternoon ride in the boat. The tourists with their expensive clothes and cameras and sun glasses awkwardly backed down the iron ladder at the wharf's side to where my father waited below, holding the rocking *Jenny Lynn* in snug against the wharf with one hand on the iron ladder and steadying his descending passengers with the other. They tried to look both prim and windblown like the girls in the Pepsi-Cola ads and did the best they could, sitting on the thwarts where the newspapers were spread to cover the splattered blood and fish entrails, crowding to one side so that they were in danger of capsizing the boat, taking the inevitable pictures or merely trailing their fingers through the water of their dreams.

All of them liked my father very much and, after he'd brought them back from their circles in the harbor, they invited him to their rented cabins which were located high on a hill overlooking the village to which they were so alien. He proceeded to get very drunk up there with the beautiful view and the strange company and the abundant liquor, and late in the afternoon he began to sing.

I was just approaching the wharf to deliver my mother's summons when he began, and the familiar yet unfamiliar voice that rolled down from the cabins made me feel as I had never felt before in my young life or perhaps as I had always felt without really knowing it, and I was ashamed yet proud, young yet old and saved yet forever lost, and there was nothing I could do to control my legs which trembled nor my eyes which wept for what they could not tell.

The tourists were equipped with tape recorders and my father sang for more than three hours. His voice boomed down the hill and bounced off the surface of the harbor, which was an unearthly blue on that hot August day, and was then reflected to the wharf and the fishing shanties where it was absorbed amidst the men who were baiting their lines for the next day's haul.

He sang all the old sea chanties which had come across from the Old World and by which men like him had pulled ropes for generations, and he sang the East Coast sea songs which celebrated the sealing vessels of Northumberland Strait and the long liners of the Grand Banks, and of Anticosti, Sable Island, Grand Manan, Boston Harbor, Nantucket and Block Island. Gradually he shifted to the seemingly unending Gaelic drinking songs with their twenty or more verses and inevitable refrains, and the men in the shanties smiled at the coarseness of some of the verses and at the thought that the singer's immediate audience did not know what they were applauding nor recording to take back to staid old Boston. Later as the sun was setting he switched to the laments and the wild and haunting Gaelic war songs of those spattered Highland ancestors he had never seen, and when his voice ceased, the savage melancholy of three hundred years seemed to hang over the peaceful harbor and the quiet boats and the men leaning in the doorways of their shanties with their cigarettes glowing in the dusk and the women looking to the sea from their open windows with their children in their arms.

When he came home he threw the money he had earned on the kitchen table as he did with all his earnings but my mother refused to touch it and the next day he went with the rest of the men to bait his trawl in the shanties. The tourists came to the door that evening and my mother met them there and told them that her husband was not in although he was lying on the bed only a few feet away with the radio playing and the cigarette upon his lips. She stood in the doorway until they reluctantly went away.

In the winter they sent him a picture which had been taken on the day of the singing. On the back it said, "To Our Ernest Hemingway" and the "Our" was underlined. There was also an accompanying letter telling how much they had enjoyed themselves, how popular the tape was proving and explaining who Ernest

Hemingway was. In a way it almost did look like one of those unshaven, taken-in-Cuba pictures of Hemingway. He looked both massive and incongruous in the setting. His bulky fisherman's clothes were too big for the green and white lawn chair in which he sat, and his rubber boots seemed to take up all of the well-clipped grass square. The beach umbrella jarred with his sun-burned face and because he had already been singing for some time, his lips which chapped in the winds of spring and burned in the water glare of summer had already cracked in several places producing tiny flecks of blood at their corners and on the whiteness of his teeth. The bracelets of brass chain which he wore to protect his wrists from chafing seemed abnormally large and his broad leather belt had been slackened and his heavy shirt and underwear were open at the throat revealing an uncultivated wilderness of white chest hair bordering on the semi-controlled stubble of his neck and chin. His blue eyes had looked directly into the camera and his hair was whiter than the two tiny clouds which hung over his left shoulder. The sea was behind him and its immense blue flatness stretched out to touch the arching blueness of the sky. It seemed very far away from him or else he was so much in the fore-ground that he seemed too big for it.

Each year another of my sisters would read the books and work in the restaurant. Sometimes they would stay out quite late on the hot summer nights and when they came up the stairs my mother would ask them many long and involved questions which they re-sented and tried to avoid. Before ascending the stairs they would go into my father's room and those of us who waited above could hear them throwing his clothes off the chair before sitting on it or the squeak of the bed as they sat on its edge. Sometimes they would talk to him a long time, the murmur of their voices blend-ing with the music of the radio into a mysterious vaporlike sound which floated softly up the stairs.

I say this again as if it all happened at once and as if all of my sisters were of identical ages and like so many lemmings going into another sea and, again, it was of course not that way at all. Yet go they did, to Boston, to Montreal, to New York with the young men they met during the summers and later married in those faraway cities. The young men were very articulate and handsome and wore fine clothes and drove expensive cars and my sisters, as I said, were very tall and beautiful with their copper-colored hair and were tired of darning socks and baking bread.

One by one they went. My mother had each of her daughters for fifteen years, then lost them for two and finally forever. None married a fisherman. My mother never accepted any of the young men, for in her eyes they seemed always a combination of the lazy, the effeminate, the dishonest and the unknown. They never seemed to do any physical work and she could not comprehend their luxurious vacations and she did not know from whence they came nor who they were. And in the end she did not really care, for they were not of her people and they were not of her sea.

I say this now with a sense of wonder at my own stupidity in thinking I was somehow free and would go on doing well in school and playing and helping in the boat and passing into my early teens while streaks of gray began to appear in my mother's dark hair and my father's rubber boots dragged sometimes on the pebbles of the beach as he trudged home from the wharf. And there were but three of us in the house that had at one time been so loud.

Then during the winter that I was fifteen he seemed to grow old and ill at once. Most of January he lay upon the bed, smoking and reading and listening to the radio while the wind howled about the house and the needlelike snow blistered off the ice-covered harbor and the doors flew out of people's hands if they did not cling to them like death.

In February when the men began overhauling their lobster traps he still did not move, and my mother and I began to knit lobster trap headings in the evenings. The twine was as always very sharp and harsh, and blisters formed upon our thumbs and little paths of blood snaked quietly down between our fingers while the seals that had drifted down from distant Labrador wept and moaned like human children on the ice floes of the Gulf.

In the daytime my mother's brother who had been my father's partner as long as I could remember also came to work upon the gear. He was a year older than my mother and was tall and dark and the father of twelve children.

By March we were very far behind and although I began to work very hard in the evenings I knew it was not hard enough and that there were but eight weeks left before the opening of the season on May first. And I knew that my mother worried and my uncle was uneasy and that all of our very lives depended on the boat being ready with her gear and two men, by the date of May the first. And I knew then that *David Copperfield* and *The Tempest* and all of those friends I had dearly come to love must really go forever. So I bade them all good-bye.

The night after my first full day at home and after my mother had gone upstairs he called me into his room where I sat upon the chair beside his bed. "You will go back tomorrow," he said simply.

I refused then, saying I had made my decision and was satisfied.

"That is no way to make a decision," he said, "and if you are satisfied I am not. It is best that you go back." I was almost angry then and told him as all children do that I wished he would leave me alone and stop telling me what to do.

He looked at me a long time then, lying there on the same bed on which he had fathered me those sixteen years before, fathered me his only son, out of who knew what emotions when he was already fifty-six and his hair had turned to snow. Then he swung his legs over the edge of the squeaking bed and sat facing me and looked into my own dark eyes with his of crystal blue and placed his hand upon my knee. "I am not telling you to do anything," he said softly, "only asking you."

The next morning I returned to school. As I left, my mother followed me to the porch and said, "I never thought a son of mine would choose useless books over the parents that gave him life."

In the weeks that followed he got up rather miraculously and the gear was ready and the *Jenny Lynn* was freshly painted by the last two weeks of April when the ice began to break up and the lonely screaming gulls returned to haunt the silver herring as they flashed within the sea.

On the first day of May the boats raced out as they had always done, laden down almost to the gunwales with their heavy cargoes of traps. They were almost like living things as they plunged through the waters of the spring and maneuvered between the still floating icebergs of crystal white and emerald green on their way to the traditional grounds that they sought out every May. And those of us who sat that day in the high school on the hill, discussing the water imagery of Tennyson, watched them as they passed back and forth beneath us until by afternoon the piles of traps which had been stacked upon the wharf were no longer visible but were spread about the bottoms of the sea. And the *Jenny Lynn* went too, all day, with my uncle tall and dark, like a latter-day Tashtego standing at the tiller with his legs wide apart and guiding her deftly between the floating pans of ice and my father in the stern standing in the same way with his hands upon the ropes that lashed the cargo to the deck. And at night my mother asked, "Well, how did things go in the boat today?"

And the spring wore on and the summer came and school ended in the third week of June and the lobster season on July first and I wished that the two things I loved so dearly did not exclude each other in a manner that was so blunt and too clear.

At the conclusion of the lobster season my uncle said he had been offered a berth on a deep-sea dragger and had decided to accept. We all knew that he was leaving the *Jenny Lynn* forever and that before the next lobster season he would buy a boat of his own. He was expecting another child and would be supporting fifteen people by the next spring and could not chance my father against the family that he loved.

I joined my father then for the trawling season, and he made no protest and my mother was quite happy. Through the summer we baited the tubs of trawl in the afternoon and set them at sunset and revisited them in the darkness of the early morning. The men would come tramping by our house at 4:00 A.M. and we would join them and walk with them to the wharf and be on our way before the sun rose out of the ocean where it seemed to spend the night. If I was not up they would toss pebbles to my window and I would be very embarrassed and tumble downstairs to where my father lay fully clothed atop his bed, reading his book and listening to his radio and smoking his cigarette. When I appeared he would swing off his bed and put on his boots and be instantly ready and then we would take the lunches my mother had prepared the night before and walk off toward the sea. He would make no attempt to wake me himself.

It was in many ways a good summer. There were few storms and we were out almost every day and we lost a minimum of gear and seemed to land a maximum of fish and I tanned dark and brown after the manner of my uncles.

My father did not tan — he never tanned — because of his reddish complexion, and the salt water irritated his skin as it had for sixty years. He burned and reburned over and over again and his lips still cracked so that they bled when he smiled, and his arms, especially the left, still broke out into the oozing saltwater boils as they had ever since as a child I had first watched him soaking and bathing them in a variety of ineffectual solutions. The chafe-preventing bracelets of brass linked chain that all the men wore about their wrists in early spring, were his the full season and he shaved but painfully and only once a week.

And I saw then, that summer, many things that I had seen all my life as if for the first time and I thought that perhaps my father had never been intended for a fisherman either physically or mentally. At least not in the manner of my uncles; he had never really loved it. And I remembered that, one evening in his room when we were talking about *David Copperfield,* he had said that he had always wanted to go to the university and I had dismissed it then in the way one dismisses his father's saying he would like to be a tightrope walker, and we had gone on to talk about the Peggotys and how they loved the sea.

And I thought then to myself that there were many things wrong with all of us and all our lives and I wondered why my father, who was himself an only son, had not married before he was forty and then I wondered why he had. I even thought that perhaps he had had to marry my mother and checked the dates on the flyleaf of the Bible where I learned that my oldest sister had been born a prosaic eleven months after the marriage, and I felt myself then very dirty and debased for my lack of faith and for what I had thought and done.

And then there came into my heart a very great love for my father and I thought it was very much braver to spend a life doing what you really do not want rather than selfishly following forever your own dreams and inclinations. And I knew then that I could never leave him alone to suffer the iron-tipped harpoons which my mother would forever hurl into his soul because he was a failure as a husband and a father who had retained none of his own. And I felt that I had been very small in a little secret place within me and that even the completion of high school was for me a silly shallow selfish dream.

So I told him one night very resolutely and very powerfully that I would remain with him as long as he lived and we would fish the sea together. And he made no protest but only smiled through the cigarette smoke that wreathed his bed and replied, "I hope you will remember what you've said."

The room was now so filled with books as to be almost Dickensian, but he would not allow my mother to move or change them and continued to read them, sometimes two or three a night. They came with great regularity now, and there were more hard covers, sent by my sisters who had gone so long ago and now seemed so distant and so prosperous, and sent also pictures of small red-haired grandchildren with baseball bats and dolls which he placed upon his bureau and which my mother gazed at wistfully when she thought no one would see. Red-haired grandchildren with baseball bats and dolls who would never know the sea in hatred or in love.

And so we fished through the heat of August and into the cooler days of September when the water was so clear we could almost see the bottom and the white mists rose like delicate ghosts in the early morning dawn. And one day my mother said to me, "You have given added years to his life."

And we fished on into October when it began to roughen and we could no longer risk night sets but took our gear out each morning and returned at the first sign of the squalls; and on into November when we lost three tubs of trawl and the clear blue water turned to a sullen gray and the trochoidal waves rolled rough and high and washed across our bows and decks as we ran within their troughs. We wore heavy sweaters now and the awkward rubber slickers and the heavy woolen mitts which soaked and froze into masses of ice that hung from our wrists like the limbs of gigantic monsters until we thawed them against the exhaust pipe's heat. And almost every day we would leave for home before noon, driven by the blasts of the northwest wind, coating our eyebrows with ice and freezing our eyelids closed as we leaned into a visibility that was hardly there, charting our course from the compass and the sea, running with the waves and between them but never confronting their towering might.

And I stood at the tiller now, on these homeward lunges, stood in the place and in the manner of my uncle, turning to look at my father and to shout over the roar of the engine and the slop of the sea to where he stood in the stern, drenched and dripping with the snow and the salt and the spray and his bushy eyebrows caked in ice. But on November twenty-first, when it seemed we might be making the final run of the season, I turned and he was not there and I knew even in that instant that he would never be again.

On November twenty-first the waves of the gray Atlantic are very very high and the waters are very cold and there are no signposts on the surface of the sea. You cannot tell where you have been five minutes before and in the squalls of snow you cannot see. And it takes longer than you would believe to check a boat that has been running before a gale and turn her ever so carefully in a wide and stupid circle, with timbers creaking and straining, back into the face of storm. And you know that it is useless and that your voice does not carry the length of the boat and that even if you knew the original spot, the relentless waves would carry such a burden perhaps a mile or so by the time you could return. And you know also, the final irony, that your father like your uncles and all the men that form your past, cannot swim a stroke.

The lobster beds off the Cape Breton coast are still very rich and now, from May to July, their offerings are packed in crates of ice, and thundered by the gigantic transport trucks, day and night, through New Glasgow, Amherst, St. John and Bangor and Portland and into Boston where they are tossed still living into boiling pots of water, their final home.

And though the prices are higher and the competition tighter, the grounds to which the *Jenny Lynn* once went remain untouched and unfished as they have for the last ten years. For if there are no signposts on the sea in storm there are certain ones in calm and the lobster bottoms were distributed in calm before any of us can remember and the grounds my father fished were those his father fished before him and there were others before and before and before. Twice the big boats have come from forty and fifty miles, lured by the promise of the grounds, and strewn the bottom with their traps and twice they have returned to find their buoys cut adrift and their gear lost and destroyed. Twice the Fisheries Officer and the Mounted Police have come and asked many long and involved questions and twice they have received no answers from the men leaning in the doors of their shanties and the women standing at their windows with their children in their arms. Twice they have gone away saying: "There are no legal boundaries in the Marine area"; "No one can own the sea"; "Those grounds don't wait for anyone."

But the men and the women, with my mother dark among them, do not care for what they say, for to them the grounds are sacred and they think they wait for me.

It is not an easy thing to know that your mother lives alone on an inadequate insurance policy and that she is too proud to accept any other aid. And that she looks through her lonely window onto the ice of winter and the hot flat calm of summer and the rolling waves of fall. And that she lies awake in the early morning's darkness when the rubber boots of the men scrunch upon the gravel as they pass beside her house on their way down to the wharf. And she knows that the footsteps never stop, because no man goes from her house, and she alone of all the Lynns has neither son nor son-in-law that walks toward the boat that will take him to the sea. And it is not an easy thing to know that your mother looks upon the sea with love and on you with bitterness because the one has been so constant and the other so untrue.

But neither is it easy to know that your father was found on November twenty-eighth, ten miles to the north and wedged between two boulders at the base of the rock-strewn cliffs where he had been hurled and slammed so many many times. His hands were shredded ribbons as were his feet which had lost their boots to the suction of the sea, and his shoulders came apart in our hands when we tried to move him from the rocks. And the fish had eaten his testicles and the gulls had pecked out his eyes and the white-green stubble of his whiskers had continued to grow in death, like the grass on graves, upon the purple, bloated mass that was his face. There was not much left of my father, physically, as he lay there with the brass chains on his wrists and the seaweed in his hair.

# DAVID MADDEN

## *The Day the Flowers Came*

(FROM PLAYBOY)

J. D. OPENED HIS EYES. A woman was talking to him. A man began
talking to him. Through the pain in his head, in his eyes, he saw
his own living room ceiling. Who were these people? Why was he
on the couch? On the coffee table sat an empty Jack Daniel's fifth
and two glasses. Why two? The voices went on talking to him.
"Yes?" he asked.

Chimes. As he raised himself up to answer the front door, a magazine slipped off his chest and flopped onto the pale rose carpet.
*True.* Light through the wide window clashed on his eyes. The
chimes. He stumbled to the wall, pulled the drape cord, darkened
the room. Light flickered from the television set in the corner. The
man and the woman who had been talking to him were talking to
each other in a family situation comedy series. The husband was
greeting a neighbor at the door. But J. D. still heard chimes.

Going to the door, he wondered why he wasn't at the office. Labor Day. Where were Carolyn? Ronnie? Ellen?

The sudden smell of flowers, thrust at him in red profusion as
he opened the door, made J. D. step back. "Carolyn, flowers!" No,
she was gone. With the kids.

"This the Hindle residence?"

"My wife's in Florida."

The young man hooked the basket handle over J. D.'s arm and
started back down the walk.

A printed message: *"My deepest sympathy."*

"Hey, come back here, fella."

"Something wrong?"

"Yeah, wrong house."

"You just said you were Mr. Hindle."

"Nobody dead here, pal. Wrong Hindle, maybe. You better check."

J. D. handed the young man the basket. He took it and walked back to his truck.

Sunlight on endless roofs below glared up at J. D. as he paused a moment on his porch, which was at the crest of a roll in the Rolling Hills Homes community. Blinking, he went in and turned off the TV, picked up the bottle and the glasses and started to the kitchen to find coffee. As he passed the front door, the chimes sounded.

The young man again with the flowers.

"I checked and double-checked, Mr. Hindle. They're for you."

"Listen, nobody died here. The card's unsigned and the whole thing's a mistake. OK?" J. D. shut the door and went on to the kitchen. Through the window over the sink, he saw the delivery boy get into his truck without the flowers.

They stood on the porch, red, fresh, redolent. About to leave them there, J. D. saw a familiar car come down the street, so he took the roses and set them just inside the door.

Every morning since they had moved into this house three years ago, J. D. had found coffee in the pot as dependably as he had seen daylight in the yard. This morning, daylight hung full and bright in the young birch tree, but the pot was empty. When he found the coffee, he realized he didn't know how to operate the new model percolator. When he finally found the instant coffee, he was exhausted. The drinking he had done last night had a double impact because it had been solitary, depressing.

Now, how did the damned *stove* work? The latest model, it left him far behind. The kitchen was a single, integrated marvel — or mystery — princess pink. The second outfit since they had built the house. For Carolyn, it had every convenience. On the rare occasions when J. D. entered the kitchen, he simply dangled in the middle of the room, feeling immersed in a glimmer of pink that was, this morning, a hostile blur.

He let the hot water in the bathroom washbowl run, filled the plastic, insulated coffee mug, spooned instant coffee from the jar into the cup and stirred, viciously. The first sip scalded his tongue; the second, as he sat on the edge of the tub, made him gag. Perhaps four teaspoonfuls was too much.

In the hall, he slipped on Ronnie's plastic puzzle set strewn over the already slickly polished floor, and the pain of hot coffee that spilled down the front of his shirt made him shudder.

His feeling of abandonment seemed more intense than his feeling of contentment yesterday as he watched Carolyn and the kids board the plane. Sitting on the couch, he tried to see their faces.

Chimes startled him.

A different deliveryman stood on the porch, holding a green urn of lilies, using both hands, though his burden looked light.

"What do you want?"

"You J. D. Hindle?"

"Yes."

"Flowers."

"In God's name, what *for?*"

"I think there's a card."

J. D. set the coffee cup on the hall table and took a card out of its tiny white envelope: *"We extend our deepest sympathy to you in your recent bereavement. James L. Converse, Manager, Rolling Hills Homes."*

"Wait a moment, will you?"

Leaving the man holding the lilies, J. D. went to the telephone in a confusion of anger and bewilderment and dialed Converse's number. His office didn't answer. Labor Day. His home didn't answer. Gone fishing, probably.

"Everything OK?"

"I can take a joke," said J. D., taking the flowers. He tipped the deliveryman. He set the lilies beside the roses.

But as he showered, the more he thought about it, the less he felt *inclined* to take a joke like this.

Out of razor blades. In this world's-fair deluxe bathroom exhibit, he knew there was a blade dispenser concealed in the fixtures somewhere. When he found it, he would probably be delightfully amazed. Since Carolyn always saw to it that his razor was ready, he had had no occasion to use the dispenser. But he remembered it as one of the bathroom's awesome features. He pushed a button. Pink lotion burped out onto his bare toes. He ripped a Kleenex out of a dispenser under the towel cabinet. It seemed that the house, masterfully conceived to dispense with human beings, had not really existed for him until this morning, now that its more acclimatized human beings had temporarily vacated it.

Where were his underclothes, his shirts, his trousers — which Carolyn had waiting for him on the mobile valet gizmo every morning? In the first three houses they had had — each representing a major step in the insurance company's hierarchy — he had known where most things were and how to operate the facilities. He remembered vividly where his shirts used to hang in the house in Greenacres Manor. As second vice-president, perhaps he spent more time away now, more time in the air. Coming home was more and more like an astronaut's reentry problem.

His wristwatch informed him that two hours had been consumed in the simple act of getting up and dressing himself — in lounging clothes, at that. As he entered the living room again, he heard a racket in the foyer. When he stepped off the pale rose carpet onto the pinkish marble, water lapped against the toe of his shoe. The roses lay fanned out on the marble. A folded newspaper, shoved through the brass delivery slot, lay on the floor. When J. D. picked it up, water dripped on his trousers.

He removed the want-ad section and the comics and spread them over the four-branched run of water, stanching its flow.

He wished the chill of autumn had not set in so firmly. How nice it would be to sit on the veranda and read the morning paper leisurely in the light that filtered through the large umbrella. He opened the drapes a little and sat in his black leather easy chair. The cold leather chilled him thoroughly. He would have to turn the heat on.

On page two, as he clucked his tongue to alleviate the bitterness of the second cup of instant coffee on the back of his tongue, he read a news report twice about the death of Carolyn Hindle, 36, and her children, Ronald H. Hindle, 7, and Ellen Hindle, 9, in a hurricane near Daytona Beach, Florida. Survived by J. D. Hindle, 37, vice-president of——

"I'm sorry, all lines to Florida are in use."

"But, operator, this is an emergency."

"Whole sections of the Florida coast, sir, are in a state of emergency. Hurricane Gloria —— "

"I *know* that! My wife —— "

"And with Labor Day . . . Do you wish me to call you when I've contacted the Breakers Hotel, or do you wish to place the call later?"

"Call me."

J. D. flicked on the television and gulped the cold instant coffee. It was a mistake. They had mistakenly listed survivors instead of victims. Or perhaps they were only — the phone rang — missing.

"Mr. Hindle, on your call to the Breakers Hotel in Florida, the manager says that no one by the name of Carolyn Hindle is registered there."

"Well, she *was* a little uncertain in her plans."

"She didn't say exactly where she would be staying?"

"No, she left rather impulsively, but —— Listen, could you ask if she *has* been there?"

"I did, sir. She hasn't."

That opened up the entire state of Florida. On television, games and old movies, but no word of the hurricane. He would have to take the day off and try, somehow, perhaps through the Red Cross, to track her and the children down. Chimes.

On the porch stood the first delivery boy, long-stemmed roses again in a basket.

"This time I'm certain, Mr. Hindle."

J. D. accepted them. On the card was written in lovely script: *"They are just away. Our heartfelt sympathy. The Everlys."*

J. D. picked up the roses that had spilled, put them in their basket and hooked both baskets of roses over his arms and carried the urn of lilies with them into the living room. Still, there was something wrong. Flowers so soon, so quickly? He looked up the newspaper's phone number and dialed it.

"I'm just the cleaning lady, mister. They put out the paper, then locked up tight."

Just as J. D. placed the receiver in its cradle, the ringing phone startled him.

"Mr. J. D. Hindle?"

"Yes."

"Western Union. Telegram."

"Read it, will you?"

"Dearest Jay: The kids and I are having wonderful, wonderful time. We all miss you. But we may return sooner than planned. Love and kisses, Carolyn, Ronnie and Ellen."

"I knew it, I knew it! God, God . . . When was that telegram sent?"

"This morning."

"What time, exactly?"

"Hour ago. Eight o'clock. You want me to mail it?"

"What?"

"Some people like to keep a record."

"Yes. Please do. And thank you very much."

The flowers smelled like spring now and he bent over them and inhaled, his eyes softly closed. Then, glancing down at the newspaper on the floor, he became angry. He dialed the home of the editor of the suburban paper.

"Are you certain?"

"Listen, Mr. Garrett, it's *your* accuracy that's being questioned. That telegram was dated today and sent an hour ago. Now, I want to know where your information came from. What town? Why? This house is full of flowers."

"Well, if we're in error, Mr. Hindle, we'll certainly print a correction in tomorrow's paper. Meanwhile, I'll investigate the matter immediately and call you back when I've tracked something down."

"I'll be waiting."

Chimes. J. D. picked up the flowers again and carried them to the door. The odor was good, but they breathed all the oxygen, and the overtone of funerals still emanated from them. He would unload them all on whichever deliveryman it was *this* time.

Bill Henderson stood on the porch holding a tray covered with a white cloth. "Nancy sent you something hot, Jay."

"That was sweet of her, Bill. Excuse me." J. D. set the flowers outside on the porch. "Come in." J. D. was smiling. He was aware that Bill noticed he was smiling.

"We were about to risk our lives on the freeway today, to visit Nancy's people, when we saw the newspaper. Jay, I —— "

"Thanks, Bill, but save it. It's a mistake. A stupid mistake. I just heard from Carolyn."

"What? You mean she's OK? She called?"

DAVID MADDEN 123

"Yes. Well, she sent a telegram from Florida an hour ago. Didn't even mention the hurricane."

"That's odd. Must be on everybody's *mind* down there."

"Yeah, a little inconsiderate, in a way. She might know I'd be worried about that."

"Maybe the telegram was delayed. The hurricane and all."

"What're you trying to say?"

"Nothing."

"Why can't it be the *newspaper* that's wrong?"

"Well, it just doesn't seem likely."

"I gave that editor hell. He's going to call back. Look, let's shut up about it, OK? I've got a hangover from drinking alone last night."

"Why didn't you call me? We could have had a few hands of poker."

"Yeah. Why didn't I? It was a strange night. And now all this flood of flowers this morning. My stomach's in knots. Have a cup of coffee with me before you hit the highway."

"OK, then I guess we may's well go ahead with our trip."

Lifting the white cloth from the tray, J. D. felt an eerie sensation in his stomach that the sight of the smoking food dispelled. "I'm going to eat this anyway, OK? Not enough coffee for both of us. You have this and I'll make some more instant for myself."

Running the water in the bathroom basin again, waiting for it to get steaming hot, J. D. heard the telephone ring. "Hey, Bill, you mind getting that for me?"

J. D. spooned coffee into the plastic mug and watched it stain the water. Steam rising made his eyes misty. Bill was a blur in the bathroom door. J. D. blinked the tears from his eyes. Bill's face was grimly set.

"What's the matter with *you?*"

"That was the editor. He thought I was you, so he started right in with his report. The story . . . checks out . . . through Associated Press. He made other inquiries and found out that the . . . the bodies are being shipped back tonight by plane."

J. D. slung the cup and coffee into the tub and with the same hand, clenched, slugged Bill in the mouth.

"What's the matter with you, Jay? Didn't you want me to tell —— "

"You son of a bitch! You made the whole thing up. I see the whole thing now. It was you, back of it all. Your masterpiece. Not just one more stupid practical joke. You put *everything* into *this* one."

"You think I'd do a terrible thing like that just for laughs?"

"Not until now, I didn't. Why else would you come around? You had to see how it was getting to me. OK, I fell for it. All the way. So far, I'm still sick, and I'll *be* sick all day."

"Jay, you better get out of this house. You're not used to being alone here. Nancy and I will stay home. You come on over with me and ——— "

"You're the one that better get out of here, before I kill you!"

Staring up at J. D., Bill got to his feet. Without looking back, he walked out, leaving the front door open.

Still so angry he could hardly see or walk straight, J. D. went into the living room and flopped onto the couch, satisfied that all the pieces of the puzzle were now in place. The mixture of emotions that had convulsed him was now a vivid anger that struck at a single object. Seeing the tray of food, no longer steaming, on the footrest of his leather chair, he leaped to his feet and took the tray into the bathroom and with precise flips of his wrist, tossed the eggs, toast, coffee, jelly, butter and bacon into the toilet and flushed it. Over the sound of water, he heard the chimes.

With the tray still in his hands, he went into the foyer, where the door still stood open. Among the flowers he had set out on the porch stood a woman, smartly dressed. She held a soup tureen in both gloved hands. The sight of the tray surprised her and she smiled awkwardly, thinking, perhaps, that she had come at the end of a line and that J. D. was ready for her. She started to set the tureen on the tray, saying, "I'm Mrs. Merrill, president of your PTA, and I just want you to know ——— " But J. D. stepped back and lowered the tray in one hand to his side.

"A stupid, criminal joke has been played here, Mrs. Merrill. I won't need the soup, thank you. Come again when my wife is home. They're having a wonderful time in Florida."

"With that horrible hurricane and all?"

"Yes, hurricane and *all.*"

J. D. shut the door and turned back and locked it.

He closed the drapes and lay down on the couch again. His head throbbed as though too large for his body. Just as his head touched the cushion, the telephone rang. He let it. Then, realizing that it might be Carolyn, calling in person, he jumped up. It stopped before he could reach it. As he returned to the couch, it started again. Maybe she was finally worried about the hurricane, about *his* worrying about it.

"Mr. Hindle, this is Mr. Crigger at Greenlawn. It is my understanding that you have not yet made arrangements for your dear wife and chil —— "

Seeing three red-clay holes in the ground, J. D. slammed the receiver in its cradle.

Chimes. J. D. just stood there, letting the sound rock him like waves at sea. Among the flowers that crowded the porch stood the first delivery boy.

"If you touch those chimes one more time . . ."

"Listen, mister, have a heart, I'm only doing what I was told."

"*I'm* telling you ——" Unable to finish J. D. jerked the basket of flowers from the young man's hands and threw it back at him. He turned and ran down the walk, and J. D. kicked at the other baskets, urns and pots, until all the flowers were strewn over the lawn around the small porch.

He slammed the door and locked it again. Standing on a chair, he rammed his fist against the electric-chimes mechanism that was fastened to the wall above the front door. The blow started the chimes going. He struck again and again, until the pain in his hand made him stop.

Reeling about the house searching for an object with which to smash the chimes, J. D. saw in his mind an image from a Charlie Chaplin movie he had seen on the late show one night in the early years of television: Charlie entangled in modern machinery on an assembly line. The film moved twice as fast in his head. He found no deadly weapon in the house nor in the garage that adjoined the house. Seeing the switch box he cut off the current.

Lying on the couch again, he tried to relax. He thought of people passing, of more people coming to offer their condolences, of the flowers strewn like gestures of insanity in the yard. Carolyn would be shocked at the stories she would hear of the flowers in the yard; for until they all knew the truth, it would appear to the neighbors that J. D. had no respect, no love, felt no remorse for his dead family.

He went out and gathered the flowers into one overflowing armful and took them into the house and put them in his leather easy chair. Then he brought in the baskets, urns and pots.

He had heard that lying on the floor relaxed tense muscles and nerves. He tried it. He lay on the carpet, arms and legs sticking straight out. After a few shuddering sighs, he began to drift, to doze. He recalled the funerals of some of his friends. Somewhat as these people today had approached him, he had approached the wives and families of his departed friends. For the important families, he had attended to insurance details himself. How artificial, meaningless, ridiculous, even cruelly stupid it all seemed now.

Coldness woke him. The room was black dark. The cold odor of roses and lilies was so strong he had to suck in air to breathe. He rolled over on his belly and rose on his hands and knees, then, holding onto the couch, pulled himself up.

Weak and shivering, he moved across the floor as though on a deck that heaved and sank. When he pulled the cord, the drapes, like stage curtains, opened on icy stars, a luminous sky.

None of the light switches worked. Then he remembered throwing the main switch in the garage. Using matches, he inched along until he found the switch.

Perhaps if he ate something, to get strength.

In the refrigerator, stack of TV dinners. The pink stove gleamed in the fluorescent light of the kitchen. The buttons and dials, like the control panel of an airplane, were a hopeless confusion.

He was astonished that the first week in September could be so cold. Perhaps it had something to do with the hurricanes. Arctic air masses or something. What did he know of the behavior of weather? Nothing. Where was the switch to turn on the electric heat? He looked until he was exhausted. Perhaps he had better get out of the house for a while.

Sitting behind the wheel, his hand on the ignition, he wondered where he could go. A feeling of absolute indecision overwhelmed him. The realm of space and time in which all possibilities lay was a white blank.

As he sat there, hand on key, staring through the windshield as if hypnotized by the monotony of a freeway at night, he experienced a sudden intuition of the essence of his last moments with Carolyn. Ronnie and Ellen in the back seat, Carolyn sat beside J. D., saying again what she had said in similar words for weeks and in silence for months, perhaps years, before that: "I must get away for a while. Something is happening to me. I'm dying, very, very slowly; do you understand that, Jay? Our life. It's the way we live, somehow the way we live." No, he had not understood. Not then. He had only thought, How wonderful to be rid of all of you for a while, to know that in our house you aren't grinding the wheels of routine down the same old grooves, to feel that the pattern is disrupted, the current that keeps the wheels turning is off.

The telephone ringing shattered his daze. He went into the house.

Seeing the receiver on the floor, he realized that he had only imagined the ringing of the phone. But the chimes were going. He opened the door. There was only moonlight on the porch. Then he remembered striking at the chimes with his fist. Something had somehow sparked them off again.

As he stood on the threshold of his house, the chimes ringing, he looked out over the rooftops of the houses below, where the rolling hills gave the development its name. From horizon to horizon, he saw only roofs, gleaming in moonlight, their television aerials bristling against the glittering stars. All lights were out, as though there had been a massive power failure, and he realized how long he must have slept. He looked for the man in the moon, but the moon appeared faceless. Then, with the chimes filling the brilliantly lighted house at his back, he gazed up at the stars; and as he began to see Carolyn's face and Ronnie's face and Ellen's face more and more clearly, snow began to fall, as though the stars had disintegrated into flakes, and he knew that he would never see his wife and children again.

# BERNARD MALAMUD

## *Pictures of Fidelman*

(FROM THE ATLANTIC)

FIDELMAN pissing in muddy water discovers water over his head. Modigliani wanders by searching by searchlight for his lost statues in Livorno canal. They told me to dump them in the canal, so I dumped them. *Ne ha visto? Niente.* How come that yellow light works underwater? Hashish. If we wake we drown, says Fidelman. *Chants de Maldoror.* His eyeless face drained of blood but not yellow light, Modi goes up canal as Fidelman drifts down.

Woodcut. Knight, Death and the Devil. Dürer.

*Au fond il s'est suicidé.* Anon.

Broken rusting balls of Venus. Ah, to sculpt a perfect hole, the volume and gravity constant. Invent space. Surround matter with hole rather than vice versa. That would have won me enduring fame and fortune and spared me all this wandering.

Cathedral of Erotic Misery. Schwitters.

Everybody says you're dead, otherwise why do you never write? Madonna Adoring the Child. Mater Dolorosa. Madonna della Peste. Long White Knights. Lives of the Saints. S. Sebastian, arrow collector, swimming in bloody sewer. Pictured transfixed with arrows. S. Denis, decapitated. Pictured holding his head. S. Agatha, breasts shorn clean, running enflamed. Painted carrying both bloody breasts in white salver. S. Stephen, crowned with rocks. Shown stoned. S. Lucy tearing out eyes for suitor smitten by same. Portrayed bearing two-eyed omelet on dish. S. Catherine, broken apart on spiked wheel. Pictured married to wheel. S. Laurence, roasted on slow grill. *I am roasted on one side. Now turn*

*me over and eat.* Shown cooked but uneaten. S. Bartholomew,
flayed alive. Standing with skin draped over skinned arm. S.
Fima, eaten by rats. Pictured with happy young rat. S. Simon
Zelotes, sawed in half. Shown with bleeding crosscut saw. S. Genet
in prison, pictured with boys. S. Fidel Uomo, stuffing his ass with
flowers.

Still Life with Herrings. S. Soutine.

He divideth the gefilte fish and matzos.

Drawing. Flights of birds over dark woods, sparrows, finches,
thrushes, white doves, martins, swallows, eagles. Birds with human
faces crapping human on whom they crap.

Wood sculpture. Man holding sacrificial goat. Cubist goat with
triangular titties. Goat eating hanged goat.

The enigma of Isador Ducasse. Man Ray.

In this time Fidelman, after making studies of the work of Do-
natello, in particular of the Annunciation carved in stone for the
church of S. Croce, the S. George in armor, with all the beauty of
youth and the courage of the knight, and the bald man known
as Il Zuccone, from figures in the facade of Giotto's Campanile,
about whom it was said the sculptor, addressing his creation, would
cry out, Speak, Speak: In this time the American began to work in
original images dug into the soil. To those who expressed astonishment regarding his extraordinary venture, Fidelman is said to
have replied, Being a poor man I can neither purchase nor borrow hard or soft stone; therefore, since this is so, I create my figures as hollows in the earth. In sum, my material is the soil, my
tools a pickax and shovel, my sculpture the act of digging rather
than carving or assembling. However, the pleasure in creation
is not less than that felt by Michael Angelo.

After attempting first several huge ziggurats that because of the
rains tumbled down like Towers of Babel, he began to work laby-
rinths and mazes dug in the earth and constructed in the form of
jewels. Later he refined and simplified this method, building a
succession of spontaneously placed holes, each a perfect square,
which when seen together constituted a sculpture. These Fidelman exhibited throughout Italy in whatsoever place he came.

Having arrived in a city carrying his tools on his shoulder and a
few possessions in a knotted bundle on his arm, the sculptor
searched in the environs until he had come upon a small plot of

land he could dig on without the formality of paying rent. Because this good fortune was not always possible, he was more than
once rudely separated from his sculptures as they were in the act
of being constructed, and by the tip of someone's boot, ejected
from the property whereon he worked, the hollows then being
filled in by the angry landowners. For this reason the sculptor
often chose public places and dug in parks, or squares, if this were
possible, which to do so he sometimes pretended when questioned
by officials of the police that he was an underground repairman
sent by the municipality. If he was disbelieved by these and
dragged off to jail, he lay several days recuperating from the efforts of his labors, not unpleasantly. There are worse places than
jails, Fidelman is said to have said, and once I am set free I shall
begin my sculptures in another place. To sum up, he dug where
he could, yet not far from the marketplace where many of the inhabitants of the city passed by daily, and where, if he was not un-
lucky, the soil was friable and not too hard with rock to be dug.
This task he performed, as was his custom, quickly and expertly.
Just as Giotto is said to have been able to draw a perfect freehand
circle, so could Fidelman dig a perfect square hole without measurement. He arranged the sculptures singly or in pairs according
to the necessity of the Art. These were about a braccio in volume,
sometimes two, or two and a half if Fidelman was not too fatigued.
The smaller sculpture took from two to three hours to construct,
the larger perhaps five or six; and if the final grouping was to con-
tain three pieces, this meant a long day, indeed, and possibly two
of continual digging. There were times when because of weari-
ness Fidelman would have compromised for a single braccio piece;
but in the end Art prevailed and he dug as he must to fulfill those
forms that must be fulfilled.

    After constructing his sculptures, the artist, unwinding a can-
vas sign on stilts, advertised the exhibition. The admission re-
quested was ten lire, which was paid to him in the roped-off en-
tranceway, the artist standing with a container in his hand. Not
many were enticed to visit the exhibition, especially when it
snowed or rained, although Fidelman was heard to say that the
weather did not the least harm to his sculptures, indeed, sometimes
improved them by changing texture and volume as well as affect-
ing other qualities. And it was as though nature, which until now

was acted upon by the artist, now acted upon the Art itself, an unexpected but satisfying happening, since thus were changed the forms of a form. Even on the most crowded days, when more than several persons came to view his holes in the earth, the sculptor earned a meager sum, not more than two or three hundred lire at most. He well understood that his bread derived from the curious among the inhabitants, rather than from the true lovers of Art, but for this phenomenon took no responsibility since it was his need to create and not be concerned with the commerce of Art. Those few who came to the exhibit, they viewed the sculptures at times in amazement and disbelief, whether at the perfect constructions or at their own stupidity, if indeed they believed they were stupid, is not known. Some of the viewers, after gazing steadfastly at the sculptures, were like sheep in their expression, as if wondering whether they had been deceived; some were stony-faced, as if they knew they had been. But few complained aloud, being ashamed to admit their folly, if indeed it were folly. To the one or two who rudely questioned him, saying, Why do you pass off on us as sculpture an empty hole or two? the artist, with the greatest tact and courtesy, replied, It were well if you relaxed before my sculptures, if you mean to enjoy them, and yield yourself to the pleasure they evoke in the surprise of their forms. At these words he who had complained fell silent, not certain he had truly understood the significance of the work of Art he had seen. On occasion a visitor would stop by to compliment Fidelman, which he received with gratitude. Eh, maestro, your sculptures touch my heart. I thank you from the bottom of my own, the artist is said to have replied, blowing his nose to hide the gratification that he felt.

There is a story told that in Naples in a small park near the broad avenue called Via Carraciola, one day a young man waited until the remaining other visitor had left the exhibit so that he might speak to the sculptor. Maestro, said he most earnestly, it distresses me to do so, but I must pray you to return to me the ten lire I paid for admission to your exhibit. I have seen no more than two square holes in the ground and am much dissatisfied. The fault lies in you that you have seen only holes, Fidelman is said to have replied. I cannot, however, return the admission fee to you, for doing so might cause me to lose confidence in my

work. Why do you refuse me my just request? said the poorly
attired young man, whose dark eyes, although intense and comely,
were mournful. I ask for my young babes. My wife gave me money
so that I might buy bread for our supper, of which we have little.
We are poor folk, and I have no steady work. Yet when I observed
the sign calling attention to your sculptures, which though I
looked for them I could see none visible, I was moved by curiosity,
an enduring weakness of mine and the cause of much of my
misery. It came into my heart that I must see these sculptures, so I
gave up the ten lire, I will confess, in fear and trepidation, hoping to be edified and benefited although fearful I would not be. I
hoped that your sculptures, since they are described on the banner as new in the history of Art, might teach me what I myself
must make in order that I may fulfill my desire to be great in Art;
but all I can see are two large holes, the one deeper by about a
braccio than the other. Holes are of no use to me, my life being
full of them, so I beg you to return the lire that I may hasten to
the baker's shop to buy the bread I was sent for.

After hearing him out, Fidelman is said to have answered, I do
not as a rule explain my sculptures to the public, but since you are
an attractive young man who has turned his thoughts to becoming
an artist, I will say to you what your eyes have not seen, in order
that you may indeed be edified and benefited.

I hope that may be so, said the young man, although I doubt it.

Listen before you doubt. Primus, although the sculpture is more
or less invisible it is sculpture nevertheless. Because you can't see
it doesn't mean it isn't there. As for use or uselessness, rather
think that that is Art which is made by the artist to be Art. Secun-
dus, you must keep in mind that any sculpture is a form existing
at a point radiating in all directions; therefore since it is dug
into the Italian earth the sculpture vibrates overtones of Italy's
Art, history, politics, religion; even nature as one experiences it in
this country. There is also a metaphysic in relation of down to
up, and vice versa, but I won't pursue that matter now. Suffice to
say, my sculpture is not unrelated, though not necessarily purpose-
fully, to its environment, whether seen or unseen. Tertius, in
relation to the above, it is impossible to describe the range of
choices, conscious or unconscious, that exist in the creation of a
single sculptured hole. However, let it be understood that choice,

as I use the word in this context, means artistic freedom, for I do
not in advance choose the exact form and position of the hole;
it chooses me. The essential thing is to maintain contact with it
as it is being achieved. If the artist loses contact with his hole,
than which there is none like it in the universe, then the hole
will not respond and the sculpture will fail. Thus I mean to show
you that constructs of a sculpture which appear to be merely holes
are, in truth, in the hands of the artist, elements of a conceptual
work of Art.

You speak well, maestro, but I am dull-witted and find it difficult to comprehend such things. It would not surprise me that I
forgot what you have so courteously explained before I arrive at
the next piazza. May I not therefore have the ten lire back? I
will be ever grateful to you.

Tough titty if you can't comprehend Art, Fidelman is said to
have replied. Fuck off now.

The youth left, sighing, without his ten lire, nor with bread
for his babes.

Not long after he had departed, as it grew dusk, the sculptor
took down the banner of his exhibit and gathered his tools so
that he might fill in the sculpture and leave for another city. As
he was making these preparations a stranger appeared, wrapped
in the folds of a heavy cloak, although winter still hid in its
cave and the fields were ripe with grain. The stranger's nether
limbs, clothed in coarse black stockings, were short and bowed,
and his half-concealed visage, iron eyes in a leather face, caused
the flesh on Fidelman's neck to prickle and thicken. But the
stranger, averting his glance and speaking pleasantly, yet as though
to his own hands, and in the accent of one from a foreign land,
graciously prayed the sculptor for permission to view his sculpture,
the effect of which he had heard was extraordinary. He explained he had been delayed on board ship in the bay and apolo-
gized for appearing so late in the day. Fidelman, having recov-
ered somewhat from his surprise at the stranger's odd garments and
countenance, is said to have replied it made no difference that he
had come late so long as he paid the admission fee.

This the stranger did forthwith with a gold coin for which he
neither asked nor received change. He glanced fleetingly at the
sculpture and turned away as though dazzled, the which the sculp-

tor is said to have wondered at. But instead of departing the exhibit now that he had viewed it, however hastily, the stranger
tarried, his back to that place where the sculpture stood fixed in the
earth, the red sun sinking at his shoulders. As though reflecting
still upon what he had seen, he consumed an apple, the core of
which he tossed over his left shoulder into one of the holes of the
sculpture, an act that is said to have angered Fidelman although
he refrained from complaint; it may be because he feared this
stranger was an agent of the police, so it were better he said nothing.

If you'll excuse me, said the stranger at last, please explain to
me what mean these two holes that they have in them nothing
but the dark inside?

The meaning lies in that they are as they seem to be, and the
dark that you note within, although I did not plan it so or put it
there, may be thought of as an attribute of the aesthetic, Fidelman
is said to have replied.

So what then did you put there?

To wit, the sculpture.

At that the stranger laughed, his laughter not unlike the bray
of a young goat. All I saw was nothing. To me, if you'll pardon
me, is a hole nothing. This I will prove to you. If you will look in
the small hole there is now there an apple core. If not for this
would be empty the hole. If empty would be there nothing.

Emptiness is not nothing if it has form.

Form, if you will excuse me my expression, is not what is the
whole of Art.

The hole with an *h*?

No, with a *w*.

One might argue that, but neither is content if that's what you
intend to imply. Form may be and often is the content of Art.

You don't say?

I do indeed.

The stranger spat on both of his hands and rubbed them together, a disagreeable odor rising from them.

In this case I will give you form.

Since the stranger stood now scarce visible in the dark, the sculptor began to be in great fear, his legs, in truth, trembling.

Who are you? Fidelman is said finally to have demanded.

I am also that youth that he is now dead in the Bay of Naples, that you would not give him back his poor ten lire so he could buy bread for his babies.

Also? Are you not also the devil? the sculptor is said to have cried out.

I am also him.

*Quid ego feci?*

This I will tell you. You have not yet learned what is the difference between something and nothing.

Bending for the shovel, the stranger smote the horrified Fidelman with its blade a resounding blow on the head, the sculptor toppling as though dead into the larger of the two holes he himself had dug. He-whom-Fidelman-did-not-know then proceeded to shovel in earth until the sculpture and its creator were extinguished.

So it's a grave, the stranger is said to have muttered. So now we got form but we also got content.

Collage. The Flayed Ox. Rembrandt. Hanging Fowl. Soutine. Young Man With Death's Head. Van Leyden. Funeral at Ornans. Courbet. Bishop Eaten by Worms. Murillo. Last Supper, Last Judgment, Last Inning.

I paint with my prick. Renoir. I paint with my ulcer. Soutine. I paint with my paint. Fidelman.

One can study nature, dissect and analyze and balance it, without making paintings. Bonnard. Gouache. Unemployed Musician. Fidelman.

Painting is nothing more than the art of expressing the invisible through the visible. Fromentin. Indefinite Divisibility. Tanguy. Definite Invisibility. Fidelman.

I'm making the last paintings which anyone can make. Reinhardt. I've made them. I like my paintings because anyone can do them. Warhol. Me too.

Erased de Kooning Drawing. Rauschenberg. Erased Rauschenberg. de Kooning. Lithograph. Eraser. Fidelman.

Modigliani climbs and falls. He tries to scale a brick wall with bleeding fingers, his eyes lit crystals of heroin, whiskey, pain. He climbs and falls in silence.

My God, what's all that climbing and falling for?

For art, you cretin.

Thunder and lightning.

Portrait of an Old Jew Seated. Portrait of an Old Jew in an Armchair. Rembrandt. It beats walking.

Then I dreamt that I woke suddenly, with an unspeakable shock, to the consciousness that someone was lying in bed beside me. I put my hand out and touched the soft naked shoulder of a woman; and a cold gentle little woman's voice said: I have not been in bed for a hundred years. Raverat. The rat killer. Rembrandt. *Elle m'a mordu aux couilles.* Modigliani.

Mosaic. Piazza Amerina, Sicily. IVth Cent. A.D. All that remains after so long a time.

Susskind preacheth up on the mountain, a piece of green palm branch behind his head. (He has no halo, here the mosaic is broken.) Three small cactus plants groweth at his bare feet./ Tell the truth. Dont cheat. If its easy it dont mean its good. Be kind, specially to those that they got less than you. I want for everybody justice. Must also be charity. If you feel bad give charity. Must also be mercy. Be nice, don't fight. Children, how can we live without mercy? If you have no mercy for me I shall not live. Love, mercy, charity. Its not so easy, believe me.

\*

At the bottom of the brown hill they stand there by the huge lichenous rock that riseth above them on the top of which is a broad tree with a twisted trunk./ Ah, Master, my eyes watereth. Thou speakest true. I love thy words. I love thee more than thy words. If I could paint thee with my paints, then would my heart soar to the gates of heaven. I will be forever thy disciple, no ifs or buts./ This is already iffed. If you will follow me, follow. If you will follow must be for Who I Am. Also please, no paints or paintings. Remember the Law, what it says. No graven images, which is profanation and idolatry. Nobody can paint Who I Am. Not on papyrus, or make me into an idol of wood, or stone, not even in the sand. Dont try, its a sin. Here is a parable: And the Lord called unto Moses and spoke to him, Moses, come thou on this mountain and I will show Myself so thou mayst see Me, and none but thee; and Moses answered: Lord, if I see Thee, then wilt Thou become as a graven image on mine eye and I be blind. Then spake the Lord, saying, Thou art my beloved Son, in whom I am

well pleased, and for this there is no Promised Land./ What's the
parable of that? Its more a paradox, Id say./ If you dont know its
not for you./ Tell me, Master, art thou the Living God? Art thou
at least the Son of God?/ So we will see, its not impossible./ Art
thou the Redeemer?/ This could be also, I'm not sure myself.
Depends what happens./ Is thy fate ordained?/ I act like I Am.
Who knows my fate? All I know is somebody will betray me.
Don't ask how I know, I know. You dont but I do. This is the difference./ It is not I, Master, I will never betray thee. Cast me out
now if thou believest I speak not the TRUTH./ What happens will
happen. So give up your paints and your brushes and follow me
where I go, and we will see what we will see. This we will see./
Master, tis as good as done.

*

Fidelman droppeth into the Dead Sea all his paints and brushes,
except one. (A piece of the blue sea is faded.)

*

(In this picture) As Susskind preacheth to the multitude, on the
shore of the green sea of Galilee where sail the little ships of the
fisher men, as even the red fishes and the white fishes come to
listen at the marge of the water, the black goats stand still on
the hills, the painter, who hideth behind a palm tree, sketcheth
with a coal on papyrus the face and figure of the Master./ If I could
do a portrait of him as he is in this life I'll be remembered forever
in human history. Nobody can call that betrayal, I dont think, for
its for the good of us all./ My child, why do you do that which I
forbade you? Dont think I cant see you, I can. I wish I couldnt
see what I see, but I can.

*

The painter kneeleth on his knees. (A few tesserae are missing
from his face, including one of the eye, and a few black stones
from his beard.)/ Master, forgive me. All I meant to do was pre-
serve thy likeness for a future time. I guess it gotteth to be too
much for me, the thought that I might. Forgive, forgive in thy
mercy. Ill burn everything, I promise, papyrus, charcoal, a roll of
canvas I have hid in my hut, also this last paintbrush although a fa-

vorite of mine./ Listen to me, there are two horses, one brown, the other black. The brown obeys his master, the black does not. Which is the better horse?/ Both are the same./ How is this so?/ One obeys and the other does not, but they are both thoroughbreds./ You have an oily tongue. If I cant change you I must suffer my fate. This is a fact./ Master, have no further worries on that score, I am a changed man down to my toenails I give thee my word.

*

Fidelman speaketh to himself in a solitary place in Capernaum./ This talent it is death to hide lodged in me useless. How am I ever going to make a living or win my spurs? How can I compete in this world if both my hands are tied and my eyes blindfolded? Whats so moral about that? How is a man meant to fulfill himself if he isnt allowed to paint? Its graven image versus grave damages to myself and talent. Which harms the most there is no doubt. One can take just so much./ He gnasheth his teeth. He waileth to the sky. He teareth his cheeks and pulleth out the hairs of his head and of his beard. He butteth his skull against the crumbling brick wall. On this spot the wall is stained red with blood./ Satan saith Ha Ha.

*

As Susskind sat at meat he spoke thus. Verily I say, one of you who eats now at this table will betray me, dont ask who./ His followers blusheth. Their faces are in shades of pink. No one blusheth not. Fidelman blusheth red./ But if he knows, it cant be all that wrong to do it. What I mean is Im not doing it in any sneaky way, that is, for after all he knows./ He that has betrayed me once will betray me twice. He will betray me thrice./ Fidelman counteth on his fingers.

*

He is now in the abode of the high priest Caiaphas./ (Here the mosaic is almost all destroyed. Only the painters short-fingered pale hand survives.) Fidelmans heavy hand is filled with thirty-nine pieces of silver.

*

The painter runneth out to buy paints, brushes, canvas.

\*

On the Mount of Olives appeareth the painter amid a multitude with swords, staves, and lengths of lead pipe. Also come the chief priest, the chief of police, scribes, elders, the guards with dogs, the onlookers to look on. Fidelman goeth to the master and kisseth him full on the lips./ Twice, saith Susskind./ He wept.

\*

He hath on his head a crown of rusty chain links. A guard smiteth his head and spitteth on his eye. In mockery they worship Sussking./ Its a hard life, he saith./ He draggeth the beam of the cross up a hill. Fidelman watcheth from behind a mask.

\*

12 12 12 12 12 12 12 12 12 12 12 12 12 12 12 12 12 12 12 12 12 12 12
369 369 369 369 369 369 369 369 369 369 369 369 369 369 369 369 369
veyizmirveyizmirveyizmirveyizmirveyizmirveyizmirveyizmirveyizmir
12369 12369 12369 12369 12369 12369 12369 12369 12369 12369 12369

\*

Fidelman painteth three canvases. The Crucifixion he painteth red on red. The Descent from the Cross he painteth white on white. For the Resurrection, on Easter morning, he leaveth the canvas blank.

\*

P
tOtem
L
E
Suss
King

*Je vous emmerde.* Modigliani.

Oil on wood. Bottle fucking guitar? Bull impaled on flagpole? One-eyed carp stuffed in staring green bottle? Clown spooning dog dung out of sawdust? Staircase ascending a nude? Black-stockinged

whore reading pornographic book by lamplight? Still life: three
apple cores plus one long gray hair? Boy pissing on old man's
shoe? The blue disease? Balding woman dyeing her hair? Buggers of Calais? Blood oozing from ceiling on foggy night?

Rembrandt was the first great master whose sitters sometimes
dreaded seeing their portraits. Malraux. I is another. Rimbaud.
1. Watercolor. Tree growing in all directions. Nothing nameable
taxonomically speaking, like weeping willow with stiff spotted
leaves, some rotted brown-green. Otherwise stylized apple-green-to-
gold leaves. Not maple or sycamore same though resembling both,
enlarged, painted to cover whole tree from roots to topmost spotted
leaf. The leaves are the tree. Branches like black veins, thins to
thicks, visible behind or through leaves. No birds in tree, not rook
or raven. Impression is of mystery. Nothing more is seen at first but
if viewer keeps looking tree is cleverly a human face. Leaves and
branches delineate strained features, also lonely hollow anguished
eyes. What is this horror I am or represent? Painter can think of
none, for portrait is of a child and he remembers happy childhood,
or so it seems. Exactly what face has done, or where has been, or
knows, or wants to know, or is or isn't experiencing, isn't visible,
nor can be explained as tone, memory, feeling, or something that
happened in later life that painter can't exactly recall. Maybe it
never happened. It's as though his face is hiding in a tree or pretending to be one while waiting for something to happen in life
and that something when it happened was nothing. Nothing much.
2. Triptych. Woodcut. It's about forbidden love. In the first
black-and-white panel this guy is taking his sister in her black-and-
white bathrobe. She squirms but loves it. Can be done in white-
and-black for contrast. Man Seducing Sister or Vice Versa. The
second panel is about the shame of the first, where he takes to mas-
turbating in the cellar. It's dark so you can't see much of his face
but there's just enough light to see what he's up to. Man Spilling
Seed on Damp Cellar Floor. Then here in this third panel, two
men doing it, each with his three-fingered hand on the other maul-
stick. This can be inked darkly because they wouldn't want to be
seen. 3. Then having prepared it for painting he began to think
what he would paint upon it that would frighten everyone that saw
it, having the effect of the head of Medusa. So he brought for that
purpose to his room, which no one entered but himself, lizards,

grasshoppers, serpents, butterflies, locusts, bats, and other strange animals of the kind, and from them all he produced a great animal so horrible and fearful that it seemed to poison the air with its fiery breath. This he represented coming out of some dark rocks with venom issuing from its open jaws, fire from its eyes, and smoke from its nostrils, a monstrous and horrible thing indeed. Lives of the Painters. 4. Figure; wood, string, and found objects. Picasso.

Incisore. The cylinder, the sphere, the cone. Cézanne. The impact of an acute angle of a triangle on a circle promises an effect no less powerful than the finger of God touching the finger of Adam in Michaelangelo. Kandinsky.

Fidelman, etcher, left a single engraving of the series called A Painter's Progress. Originally there were six copper plates, drypoint, all with their prints destroyed, how or why is not known. Only a single imperfect artist's proof entitled "The Cave" survives. This etching represents a painter at work, resemblance to whom easily may be guessed. Each night, according to a tattered diary he had kept for a while, he entered the cave in question through a cellar he had the key to, when all the lights in the old clapboard house, several boards missing, were out, curtains thickly drawn over each narrow window. The painter in the etching worked all night, night after night, inch by slow inch covering the rough limestone surface of the voluminous cave at the end of a labyrinth under the cellar, with intricate designs of geometric figures; and he left before dawn, his coming and going unknown to his sister, who lived in the house alone. The walls and part of the roof of the huge cave that he had been decorating for years and years and estimated at least two more to go before his labors ended, were painted in an extraordinary tapestry of simple figures in black, salmon, gold-yellow, sea-green and apricot, although the colors cannot of course be discerned in the three-toned engraving — a rich design of circles and triangles, discrete or interlocking, of salmon triangles encompassed within apricot circles, and sea-green circles within pale gold-yellow triangles, blown like masses of autumn leaves over the firmament of the cave.

The painter of the cave, wearing a leafy loincloth as he labored, varied the patterns of the geometric design. He was at that time of his life engaged in developing a more intricate conception of circles within circles of various hues and shades including copper red and light olive; and to extend his art further, of triangles within triangles within concentric circles. He drove himself at his work, intending when his labor was done to climb the dark stairs ascending to his sister's first floor and tell her what he had accomplished in the cave below. Bessie, long a widow, all her children married and scattered across the continent, her oldest daughter in Montreal, lived, except for occasional visitors, mostly the doctor, alone in the old frame house she had come to as a young bride, in Newark, New Jersey. She was at this time ill and possibly dying. Nobody he could think of had told her artist-brother, but he figured he somehow knew. Call it intuition. It was his hope she would remain alive until he had completed his art work of the cave and could at last see how it had turned out.

Bessie, he would say, I did this for you and you know why.

Fidelman worked by the light of a single dusty one-hundred-watt bulb, the old-fashioned kind with a glass spicule at the bottom, dangling from a wire from the ceiling of the cave, that he had installed when he first came there to paint. For a long time he had distrusted the bulb because he had never had to replace it, and sometimes it glowed like a waning moon after he had switched it off, making him feel slightly uneasy and a little lumpy in the chest. He suspected a presence, immanent or otherwise, around; though who or why, and under what circumstances, he could not say. Nothing or nobody substantial. Anyway, he didn't care for the bulb. He knew why when it began, one night, to speak to him. How does a bulb speak? With the sound of light. Fidelman for a while did not respond, first because he couldn't, his throat constricted; and second, because he suspected this might be he talking to himself; yet when it spoke again, this time he answered.

Fidelman, said the voice of, or from within, the bulb, why are you here such a long time in this cave? Painting — this we know — but why do you paint so long a whole cave? What kind of business is this?

Leaving my mark is what. For the ages to see. This place will someday be crowded with visitors at a dollar a throw. Mark my words.

But why in this way if there are better?

What would you suggest, for instance?

Whatever I suggest is too late now, but why don't you go at least upstairs and say hello to your poor sister who hasn't seen you in years? Go before it is too late, because she is now dying.

Not quite just yet I can't go, said the painter. I can't until my work is finished because I want to show her what I've accomplished once it's done.

Go up to her now, this is the last chance. Your work in this cave will take years yet. Tell her at least hello. What have you got to lose? To her it will be a wonderful thing.

No, I can't. It's all too complicated. I can't go till I've finished the job. The truth is I hate the past. It caught me unawares. I'd rather not see her just yet. Maybe next week or so.

It's a short trip up the stairs to say hello to her. What can you lose if it's only fourteen steps and then you're there?

It's too complicated, like I said. I hate the past.

So why do you blame her for this?

I don't blame anybody at all. I just don't want to see her. At least not just yet.

If she dies she's dead. You can talk all you want then but she won't answer you.

It's no fault of mine if people die. There's nothing I can do about it.

Nobody is talking about fault or not fault. All we are talking about is to go upstairs.

I can't I told you, it's too complicated, I hate the past, it caught me unawares. If there's anything to blame I don't blame her. I just don't want to see her is all, at least not just yet until my work here is done.

Don't be so proud my friend. Pride ain't spinach. You can't eat it so it won't make you grow. Remember what happened to the Greeks.

Praxiteles? He who first showed Aphrodite naked? Phidias, whose centaur's head is thought to be a self-portrait? Who have you got in mind?

No, the one that he tore out his own eyes. Watch out for hubris. It's poison ivy. Trouble you got enough, you want also blisters? Also an electric bulb doesn't give so often advice so listen with care. When did you hear last that an electric bulb gave advice? Did I advise Napoleon? Did I advise Van Gogh? This is like a miracle, so why don't you take advantage and go upstairs?

Well, you've got a point there. There's some truth to it, I suppose. I might at that, come to think of it. As you say, it's not everybody who gets advice in this way. There's something biblical about it if I may say. Furthermore, I'm not getting any younger, and besides I haven't seen Bessie in years. Plus I do owe her something, after all. Be my Virgil, which way to up the stairs?

I will show you which way but I can't go with you. Up to a point but not further if you know what I mean. A bulb is a bulb. Light I got but not feet. After all, this is the Universe, everywhere is laws.

Fidelman slowly goes up the stone, then wooden, stairs, lit generously from bottom clear to top by the bulb, and opens the creaking door into a narrow corridor. He walks along it till he comes to a small room where Bessie is lying in a sagging double bed.

Hello, Bessie, I been downstairs most of the time but I came up to say hello.

Why are you so naked, Arthur? It's winter outside.

It's how I am nowadays.

Arthur, said Bessie, why did you stop writing for so long? Why didn't you answer my letters?

I guess I had nothing much to write. Nothing much has happened to me. There wasn't much to say.

Remember how Mama used to give us an apple to eat with a slice of bread?

I don't like to remember those things anymore.

Anyway, thanks for coming up to see me, Arthur. It's a nice thing to do when a person is so alone. At least I know what you look like and where you are nowadays.

Bessie died and rose to heaven, holding in her heart her brother's hello.

Flights of circles, cones, triangles.

End of drypoint etching.

The ugly and plebeian face with which Rembrandt was ill favored was accompanied by untidy and dirty clothes, since it was his custom, when working, to wipe his brushes on himself, and to do other things of a similar nature. Jakob Rosenberg.

If you're dead how do you go on living?

*Natura morta:* still life. Oil on paper.

# MATTHEW W. McGREGOR

## Porkchops with Whiskey and Ice Cream

(FROM THE VIRGINIA QUARTERLY REVIEW)

WE GOT OFF the streetcar at a corner in a part of the city I did not know and crossed at the traffic light as the streetcar slowly rumbled away. It had been warm in the car and now it was cold and I huddled down into my brother's sheepskin coat, thrusting my arms deep into broken pockets to close my fingers against the gritty remains of cookies and dirt.

"Hurry up, you," said my father, and I stumbled against the curbing to follow him across the other street and down to where the hospital loomed in the winter twilight. But we turned up a sidestreet a block before we came to the hospital and I looked up at my father. He only muttered impatiently, more to himself than to me. Then, where the alley crossed the street, he turned and looked both ways before entering the darkness. The snow had not been cleared in the alley as it had been in the streets and there were icy ruts made by autos to be carefully negotiated. My father picked his way, not even looking back at me, so far as I could see in the darkness, until we came to the street along which the hospital sided. He waited an impatient moment for me to come up with him.

"Noo," he said, "we've got to be quiet, ye understand?"

I was frightened but I nodded. It was very cold and the hospital lights only emphasized the strangeness of this part of town. I wished I had not begged to come with my father; had not enlisted my mother's aid in gaining his grudging consent. He looked down at me now as though he understood this but that it was too late.

"Bloody foolishness," he said, but then he took my arm and led me across the street and into the alley's darkness.

"Noo," he said, "ye must walk quiet. Ye must understand we're not to put Ned in trouble wie his job. He's no supposed to have visitors. I don't know why the bloody woman insisted ye come along," he muttered, looking down the alley again.

He turned and crept silently down the alley, holding my cold hand and shaking my arm when, once, I slipped on some ice. We were in the rear of the hospital now with the alley separating it from the garages and yards of houses fronting on the next street. A dog barked. The lights of the many-roomed hospital only made the alley darkness more so. Halfway down the block-long, three-storied building, we came silently until my father suddenly halted and stood rigid as the lights of a car suddenly appeared at the further end of the alley. Frightened, I stumbled against my father and heard him curse. But it was only a driver using the alley to turn around an old car, apparently, for the dim, yellow lights didn't carry down to where we stood. We waited a moment, after the car left, my father watchful before proceeding to where a weak light bulb shone nakedly over a concrete stairwell leading to a metal door.

Grasping the iron piping leading down the stairs, my father stepped quietly to the door and I followed. Raising himself on his toes, he peered up and down the alley before trying the metal door which yielded with only a small noise. Pushing me impatiently, he followed me through the door which he closed softly, raising the latch and letting it slip with, again, only a small sound.

We were in a dimly lit corridor which smelled of ashes and of what I did not know was ether but which I did not like. We went down the corridor quietly, down more concrete steps and along another corridor to some steps leading to a landing where another metal door barred the way.

My father gave a gently listening tap, tap, tap on the door and then clicked the latch softly to open it.

Now, all was brightness and warmth; the hissing of steam in asbestos-covered piping that ran crazily over the ceiling and into the walls; the clicking and clacking of metal expanding under heat pressure; the smell of steam-heat, coal, and ashes and of basement and the sight of a huge furnace room with, there below us, halfway up another long, concrete staircase, Neddie Bates with a hand raised in greeting, his bald head shining pinkly. He waved us down, a smile gentle on his thin, worn face.

We followed him down, this slight, but erect man who was proud to share what he had with us and with his other friends. Hot pipes hissed and spluttered. Neddie's suspenders made a dark X across the worn, blue workshirt. His trousers were as wide as any Dutchman's. Still, he walked in erect dignity past the roar and mutter of the furnace and past it to a warm, clean space fitted with apple and orange crates and Neddie's simple cot. Hung nearby were the tools of his trade: long, stiff pokers, huge scoop shovels, ash rakes, wrenches of all kinds and sizes and wheeled metal boxes, some mounded over with ashes.

In the cleared space sat Johnny Caroline, who bulged his eyes at us while taking a long, slow pull at what I knew was a jug of forbidden whiskey. Jimmy McNair sat glaze-eyed before the grim furnace with the look of a man just in from the cold.

"Ah," said my father, pleased now, "a bit of a bottle."

"Half a bloody gallon," chuckled Neddie. He turned and checked a gauge and then another, touched a valve, and took a quick, hand-shaded peer into the furnace. Watching, still shivering a little, I thought of how we could all be blown to smithereens. What a huge boiler, and what if it went? I thought of that huge volcanic force erupting and spewing all of us, like lava running and pouring hot over Detroit's long, cold streets; hardening to be run over by automobiles.

I looked at my father but he only nodded, sagely and satisfactorily, as a man who knows his trade will approve the efforts of another who knows his.

"That's the proper thing for a night like this," he said, nodding at the furnace.

"Ah, yes," said Neddie.

"Aye, and so is that," said my father, turning to gaze fondly at the jug Johnny Caroline held. "Mulberry Street?"

"Aye," said Neddie. "The bloody voodoo doctor."

Jimmy McNair stirred. "Aye, and what if it is?" he said. "All sweat's the same, black, white, or yellow either. Gie us a drap to shed the bloody cold."

But Johnny Caroline held to the jug, looking, I thought, stupidly if not angrily at Jimmy.

"Come on then, man," said Jimmy. "There's enough for the all of us."

He continued to gaze that way, Johnny Caroline did, and I feared an argument. Neddie looked away and my father frowned. Then Jimmy got up and purposely took the jug from the other man. Yet, he took it carefully, his huge bulk looming over Johnny Caroline and casting him in shadow for a moment before he stepped away.

"Bloody nerve," he said, but he wasn't angry. He tilted the jug to his mouth and drank until his eyes ran tears and his face reddened even more than was natural with him.

"Woosh, damn, woosh," he roared, and I was glad to see that Jimmy McNair was his usual self. "Ye see?" he cried, "still plenty for the all of us."

"Well, James," said my father, and Jimmy turned to him as though he were a stranger. He drank a ltttle more and stood with his mouth closed around the burning liquor.

"Will ye spit it?" asked my father, "or will ye be able to swallow it whole?"

"Just," said Jimmy, choking it down. "And who the hell are you?"

"A man, sonny, what can drink wie the best o' them."

"Oh ho," said Jimmy. "And did ye go into the black dregs of Mulberry Street for yur own poison? Or," he said, looking back and yet not angrily at Johnny Caroline, "will ye pass the bottle once ye've had yur share and no dandle it like a babe on yur bloody knee?"

"It's Jimmy's brought the liquor," said Neddie, smiling at Johnny Caroline. But Johnny Caroline sat with that stupid look still on his face.

"Ah well," said Neddie.

"Noo, are ye the man for this?" asked Jimmy of my father. "It's no made of grapes and oranges, this. This is no bloody eggynoggy Christmas drink, lad. This," he said, "was made by the blackest man on Mulberry Street and my hat's off to him fur sellin' it as cheap as he does, not like those other buggers who ask yur heart

and soul as though they're doin' you a favor. Aye, a poor man
made it fur poor men to forget their bloody aches and pains," he
said, "but it's got his bloody razor mixed wie some o' his sweat and
his own troubles wie the corn that fired it up."

"Hear, hear!" cried my father. "Hud it here and stand by the
guns."

My father took the jug and made the sign of the cross over it
while muttering a facsimile of priestly Latin. He tilted the jug to
his lips, drank too fast and spluttered a fine spray of Michigan
corn hissingly against the furnace.

"Quick, quick," cried Jimmy. "Hud on to yur tongue afore it
melts away and ye'll be speechless."

"Good God!"

Jimmy slapped his knee, laughed and I giggled too, although
watchful of my father. Neddie chuckled too but I saw that Johnny
Caroline did not join in with them. He kept his mournful eyes
steady on the jug.

"Will ye paint the bloody furnace wie guid whiskey?" asked
Jimmy. "Don't tell me ye've tasted better?"

"Och, I'm only warming to the job." Prepared now, my father
tilted the jug and I watched his Adam's apple bob and weave.

"That is guid stuff." His eyes, red with cold before, were red and
wet with whiskey now. He brought a blue bandanna out of his
old, frayed coat and wiped his laughing eyes and blew his nose.

"Gie it to Johnny," said Jimmy. "He's holdin' a wake there all
by himself."

Neddie slipped a dime into the pocket of my brother's old sheepskin as my father made the courtliest of gestures in passing the
jug to Johnny Caroline.

"Thank you," I said, feeling with fingers burning less now with
cold the thin, corrugated wealth of ten cents. I rubbed one finger
luxuriously across Liberty's face. I backed away from where the
men stood, three of them eyeing each other and finding no fault in
what they saw; the other not participating and huddled in on himself. I edged close to the heat of that awful furnace.

My fate was the Emperor's now. Did he challenge me to unlock
my lips, to unfold my hand from about the lucky charm which
opened the secret door leading down into the gold mine below the

palace, I would thrust that arm up to the elbow into the receiving flames. Burned, and in agony but spurning aid, I would keep the secret.

The furnace rumbled and roared and to peer past the peekholes was to look into the sun. I thrust grimy hands toward that power, the chapped wrists showing redly out of the sheepskin.

My father and Jimmy McNair, their bellies hot with whiskey made by a careful-eyed Negro, stood contentedly listening to the sound of hissing steam, of coals roaring afire and of metal expanding hotly in a series of syncopated beats. They thrust hands into pockets and rocked on sweating feet from heel to ball, ignoring Johnny Caroline and quickening to the generosity of Neddie Bates.

"Well," said my father, "all together, lads, eh?"

"Oot o' the bloody cauld," said Jimmy. "Thanks be to our host, the landlord o' the house." He laughed with Neddie and my father over the reference to old times in another land.

"Oh, no thanks to me," said Neddie, shaking his head. "It's glad I am of the company. I never get out much on this bloody seven-day job except to the back alley. Never see anyone but the garbage men twice a week and once of a while they'll make a bloody inspection from above. Them and their inspections," he said.

"And what do they inspect?" said Jimmy.

"It's cleanliness," said Neddie. "But I run a good clean ship down here, as good as any on the P and O line, I'll wager. Oh," he said, looking at Jimmy, "they're no worried about food or coal. They rely on the city food inspector for the refrigerator and it's damn seldom I see him. No, it's a file o' them in their white coaties come walkin' and lookin' and askin' bloody fool questions about the engineering. They're tryin' to cut fuel bills, ye know, damn much good it does them."

"Aye," said my father, "it's the factory all over again."

"Oh," said Neddie, "worse. I sir them yes and I sir them no and it's always a clean bill I get."

I watched Johnny Caroline pick up the jug and run his hands over it. He looked at the others and then uncorked the jug and drank long and deep, as though it were water.

"And how's wee Jeanie?" asked my father. He had his old pipe in his hands.

"Och," said Jimmy, "she's all female worriments, these days. All headaches and cold feet and never giving a man peace to worry himself with.

" 'What will ye do today?' she asks, and what can a man say?

" 'I'll be off to Hudsons,' says I, knowing bloody well I'll never face that line hulking out into the street to have the office close in yur face.

"Or, I'll tell her I'm to see a wee man at Detroit Sheet Metal and the wee man's to interjuce me to the straw boss and maybe the boss has half a heart to take me name and say he'll let me know in a week or so.

"Och," said Jimmy, "I sit on me arse and think of a way to make a dollar without goin' to prison for it."

My father slowly filled his pipe, nodding. Neddie patted Jimmy on the back.

"There's bound to be better times comin'," he said.

"When?" asked my father, looking up from his pipe.

"Oh, I agree," said Jimmy. "It can't last forever. There'll be a bloody revilootion, there will."

Watching Johnny Caroline drink again, I thought of angry men crowding the streets with bricks in their hands and clubs, led by someone big and angry, like Jimmy McNair.

"There'll be no revolution," said Neddie, lighting a cigarette. "The government will change hands first. Throw that bloody Hoover out."

"Hear, hear!" cried my father.

"Ye'll be votin' next time, Alec?"

"That I will, James. I'm a citizen these eight months now of the United States. To hell with the bloody Union Jack."

"Och, don't say that, man," said Jimmy. "I've served me time under that brave flag."

Sleepy and sleek with warmth now, like a cat, I watched Johnny Caroline tilt and drink without speaking, without laughter, without even a look at the others.

"Here," said Jimmy, "Gie us a suck o' that bottle afore it's all gone down yur lug." He gave up the jug quickly this time, but still somewhat ungraciously.

Jimmy looked at him and laughed and drank as though he were sounding charge to that angry mob. He handed the jug to my father.

"Here's to the right to vote and the constytootion and better times in all the forty-eight," said my father and Jimmy said "Hear, hear!" this time.

Neddie drank too, after fastidiously wiping at the neck of the jug, but so as not to offend. Watching him drink, I thought of red liquid trickling into the thermometer to collapse red and glowing where his small, slightly protruding stomach bulged. He handed the jug to Johnny Caroline and when he drank it was, for me, just a man drinking.

Neddie took down the big scoop and went to the coal bunker. Stooping and straining, his little behind out so far I thought he would topple, the stringy muscles of his dead-white arms quivering and his neck-cords tight, he lifted and hauled several shovelfuls to the furnace where, kicking quickly at the metal door to open it, he heaved that coal into the roaring flames without spilling a single nugget.

Then he took the long poker to throw it, like a spear, into the opening and to stir and strike the blaze to frenzy. Satisfied, he banged the door shut, stooped to peer into the heat and then wiped his face with a bandanna while he adjusted gauges and touched at valves.

My father nodded approvingly. I knew that he and Jimmy would have helped but that that was out of the question with Neddie. But they could do the work, I thought, and looking at the other man, I knew that he could not.

Neddie watched Johnny Caroline drink again. Snapping his fingers, he asked:

"Will ye have some cream?"

Johnny Caroline nodded dumbly while Jimmy shrugged his shoulders and my father said he would that.

Half asleep as I was, near all that heat, it seemed to me that Neddie stole away, vanished into shadows and the flickerings of the fire. And, although I watched for him as Jimmy and my father praised Neddie for what he had done for them in the past and for what he would still do, I didn't see him come back through the flickering shadows, bearing four large bowls of chocolate ice cream.

Neddie gave each of us a bowl and a tablespoon. I watched Johnny Caroline dig in first of all. Never before or after have I watched anybody gorge himself as did that silent, morose man:

without joy but with efficiency. My father and Jimmy kept up a running conversation with Neddie who was now peeling an apple for himself, as if he were whittling at something that would prove useful. He used a great butcher's knife on the fruit as though he were perhaps sculpturing a small globe, with intelligence and with infinite patience.

"Yes, yes," he nodded. "I mind ye interjuced me to Claude that time he came down from Flint."

"Aye," said my father. "Took the women to Quebec and ran the car, Bill's Chandler it was, into that bloody Frenchman. 'Parley voo,' says the Frenchman, sitting in the middle o' the lane."

" 'My God, it's a man I've kilt,' says Claudie."

"Cam doon tha lang lane," crooned Jimmy, "and smacked that Chandler into a load of fish."

"Aye, fish," said Neddie, "and no fresh fish either." I looked up from my ice cream. The knife was steady on the apple with the skin coming off in one long peel. Oh, I liked that!

"And didn't the women yell bloody murder," cried my father. "There they were, up to their bums in a load of fish."

"Aye, God's truth," roared Jimmy. "Me old mither, rest her soul, had fish all over her dress. 'What's this,' she said, holding one up by the tail. 'I don't know,' says yur Aunt Nellie, 'but it smells awfully like fish.' "

"Filthy old fish," roared Neddie.

"Wouldn't been so bad," said my father, "but they were old fish going to that Frenchman's farm for fertilizer. It's a guid thing he didn't have a load of the other stuff."

They all roared even though they all knew the story, it had been told so many times before. All but Johnny Caroline, who hadn't heard it before and who didn't laugh now.

I giggled myself but mostly at Jimmy and my father's spontaneity and at the sight of Neddie peeling that apple, breaking off to laugh, and then resuming his paring without breaking the skin. I stopped giggling when I noticed Johnny Caroline had finished his ice cream. He looked at the bowls held by the others and then at mine. I watched him pour liquid fire atop that cold offering.

"By God," said Jimmy, peering down at Johnny's empty bowl, "Yur the boy fur whiskey and ice cream."

His voice, when it came, was a hollow croak. He looked up at Jimmy. "I came away without me sipper," he said.

Jimmy smiled beneficently, as though all riches were his to bestow. He waved a hand as though suggesting a kind of a truce.

Neddie eyed Johnny Caroline from under those bushy eyebrows that were his only hair adornment.

"Oh," he said, "John's had a run of hard luck. Hard luck," he said, shaking his head.

"Och, aye, it can happen." My father looked at Johnny Caroline differently now and so did Jimmy. They didn't ask questions. There was some respect now in the gazes they gave the other man.

I watched Neddie cutting and chewing pieces of that apple with the front teeth that were all he had left. I could feel the threat of sharp metal careful on the tongue, since he was using that large knife, and taste the tart texture of winter apple. It was good to have and to eat and to be warm and with men able to find comfort in such a place. I bent back to my bowl but Neddie, as he chewed the fruit, kept his eyes steadily on Johnny Caroline.

When I looked up again, having finished the ice cream, I saw that Neddie had disappeared somewhere past the clang of the furnace door past which he had thrown the one, long peel. He was back, soon enough, carrying a large package, wrapped in butcher paper. He took it to Johnny Caroline.

"Chops," said Neddie. "A bit o' pork. There'll be supper enough for all of yez."

"There's plenty more," he said, turning to the others. "We'll make up some packages afore ye leave."

"A bit o' coal would be nice, too," said Jimmy. He was embarrassed. "That bloody welfare coal's no bloody good," he said. "It won't burn."

"Aye," said Neddie. "I see ye brought yur scuttle. We'll fill it afore ye leave."

Johnny Caroline sat holding the heavy package. He muttered something that may have been thanks.

"If yur that hungry," said Jimmy, relieved about the coal, "why do ye no get a stick and fry them in the bloody furnace?" He laughed but not uproariously. It was as near to nasty as Jimmy ever became.

My father plucked the jug from near Johnny Caroline's foot.

"That's a good idea," he said. "Meanwhile, I think I'll just have a wee drink afore it's all gone down yur gullet."

Johnny Caroline sat looking dazed and weary. He slowly unwrapped the package and gazed at the limp, dead meat as thick as any book out of the library, I thought, and rich in reds and whites. I could smell them frying in the kitchen at home, hear the sizzling, crackling sound of them being turned in their own juices and see brown and black chops heaped on a plate. My teeth ached for that crisp taste and my mouth watered for the remembered flavor.

"Well, by God," laughed Jimmy, looking from Johnny Caroline to the roaring furnace. "Would they smell them, Ned?" He had a hand raised, a finger extended ceilingward.

"Och, them," said Neddie, but he didn't seem too well pleased at the prospect.

"Is there a way to clean the shovel?"

Neddie didn't like it, but then he considered Johnny Caroline, "I can clean the bloody thing if yur no mind for a bit of coal smoke." Then he laughed, "It wouldn't do for my stomach," he said.

He took the shovel and went around in back of the furnace. I heard the sound of running water off that big shape of metal. When he returned, the shovel was cleansed of dust although still black with usage.

"Are ye serious?" he asked.

"Never more," said Jimmy. "Me own stomach's churning now. Think of a chop, crisp as a biscuit." He took the proffered jug and drank easily in quick, short swallows.

"Och, I don't know," said my father, that blue bandanna to his lips, "In that shovel? Is there no a pan to be had?"

"There's none," said Neddie. "There's so much thievin' upstairs, they lock the kitchen tighter'n a drum."

"Why not in the shovel?" Jimmy passed the jug to Neddie and stood rubbing his big, red hands over his stout frame while he belched, politely excusing himself. "I've et worse in the bloody army, I tell you, and me stomach never the worse for it."

"There's nothing I could find would go in that furnace," said Neddie. Looking again at Johnny Caroline, he said that it couldn't be worse than the maggoty food of a British Navy tug that had ruined his stomach. "We'll do it up in butter," he said. "Half a minute, and I'll get it."

He returned with a great armload of food packages, a pound of butter in one hand.

"Now," said Jimmy. "I'll be the bloody cook I should have been in the British Army."

"Not for me, ye won't," said Neddie. He rubbed his arms where the packages had weighed and said he would stir up the fire.

We gathered around the furnace entrance to watch the cooking of the porkchops on that shovel, larded with a great lump of fine butter. The heat was so intense that Jimmy soon enough passed the shovel to an aroused Johnny Caroline, and fell back wiping at his broad features with his old, cloth cap. He took another drink from the jug.

Johnny Caroline too fell back and my father nearly lost the chops in taking the shovel from the other who staggered backward and half collapsed on Neddie's cot. Soon, my father gave up and passed the shovel to Neddie who held the heavy tool longer than any. He brought the chops out of the furnace to be turned but they saw they were black enough on the other side. Jimmy took the shovel to an orange crate and stood, a moment, looking at them.

"If they ain't the awful lookin' things," he said.

He burned his fingers reaching for one, transferred the chop to the other hand while balancing the shovel and took a bite.

"Damn," he said, his mouth full. "It ain't half bad."

There were ten of the chops and we finished all of them, using the soup bowls as plates. They tasted of coal and they had been overdone in that searing heat, but there was still the taste and feel of meat in the mouth and the satisfaction of swallowing.

The adults ate faster than I did; they washing their food down with gulps of whiskey and I with cold water brought by Neddie in a broken-handled cup. Then they, still hungry, did it all over again while I had had enough.

They tore and chewed and gnawed at the meat and bones as high-spirited as boys munching stolen potatoes cooked in an outdoor fire.

"Phew," said Jimmy, "I'll never be hungry again, again."

My father filled his pipe with the cheap tobacco he would

have smoked had we all been millionaires. He rubbed his stomach and belched contentedly.

But Johnny Caroline sweltered out the cooking of two more chops, hurriedly, as though he believed himself to be running out of time or luck or as if he were storing up, like an animal, for the rest of the long, black winter ahead.

He sat belching after he had finished and, as he raised the jug for another drink, I could see sweat standing on his forehead.

"He's won," said my father. "He's the biggest hog in all Detroit."

"In all Chicagy," said Jimmy.

Neddie laughed, puffing at a cigarette, but said he liked to see a man do well with his food.

They talked more but softer now, as men will who have fed and who have warmth in whiskey. The last quarter of that jug dwindled.

I almost fell asleep, back near the furnace, except that Neddie brought along with more food packages for all a book that had been left behind by some patient. It was short stories by somebody named Jack London. I kept nodding over a story about a cripple who had to work, awakening more at Neddie's story of how it was that he was illegally in the country and didn't dare to go back to Canada any more than he dared apply for legal status here and at Jimmy's tales of evading customs officials.

"Me father," he said, "put the whiskey in his bag-pipes, in the bag, ye ken?"

" 'What's this?' says the American one at the ferry slip. 'Oh,' we says, 'that's jist the pipes. Will ye hear a tune?' The poor man shuddered and waved us on."

I saw that Johnny Caroline was breathing heavily now. He had a long coughing fit while smoking a cigarette he'd taken from Neddie. Later, I awoke to find them shaking him and asking what was the matter. Neddie took my cup and brought him some water. They asked him to lay down but he shrugged them off and sat with his head in his hands.

"I'm locked out, boys," he said. They looked at him and at each other.

"All because the bimbo next door got taken on."

"Where?" asked Jimmy.

"The Chevrolet," said Johnny Caroline. He looked awful to me. "Over Hamtramck way," he said. "I'd been thinkin' to try the wheel company, out yur way, Alec," he said. My father nodded. "But me leg pained me that day and I thought to hell with it."

"It's her tells me the next day the bloody Polack next door; can't even speak English and gets taken on."

"There's no talkin' to them," said Jimmy. "They don't figger on a man's bad luck." My father said it was all the fault of the bloody Southerners coming up and taking jobs at wages no trained man would work for.

"I went out the next day," said Johnny Caroline and then broke off. He seemed to have lost the thread of his thought.

"You mind Tuesday?" he said, at last. "It snowed. It was a bloody cold day and I was at Kurth and Knapp a long, long time in line with dozens ahead of me."

"Aye, Curse and Scrap," said Jimmy. "I've done a turn wie them, Alec, with your Bill. Bloody sweatshop," he said. "Don't tell me they're hirin'."

"Them hirin'," said my father. "It'll be a day afore they hire a man. Yet mind wee Augie, the foreman? Him wie the wee sleekit rat's face? Didn't I work for him? Fired me in two weeks and took on another one ready to work for less."

"Aye," said Jimmy, "the same bloody way with me."

"It's no bloody sweatshop these days," said Johnny Caroline. "Cold, it was and all the men workin' wie mitts and scarves and stampin' their feet. Me own feet were numb and me leg achin' fit to kill.

"Well, they sent us away," he said. "After we'd waited hours. I tramped home to find the bloody door locked and her in the hoose yellin' she won't let me in."

"Bash it in, why didn't ye?" said Jimmy.

"I hadn't the strength," said Johnny Caroline. "She yells oot, 'if ye can no provide, ye can no live here.'"

"A good swift kick," said Jimmy, and Johnny Caroline looked swiftly up at him.

"I'd already done a bit o' that," he said.

"Saturday night," he said, "it was the radio on the blink and the stove doesn't work and there's smoke in the house and the kids fightin' among themselves and she blamin' me for the all of it 'til

I gave her a cuff in the gob. Not," he said, "wantin' to hurt but just to shut her up."

The others looked at each other, with humor and yet with some embarrassment and some shock. They looked back at Johnny Caroline with something of respect.

"Well, she fell," he said. "Broke her false teeth when they fell out." He reached suddenly and took an apple from the sack on a crate. He bit swiftly, swallowed fast and ate the apple without looking at the others.

"She threatened the police," he said. "Ah, but I'd have none of that, I told her. But Tuesday she had me nicely locked out."

"Use yur key, why didn't ye?" asked Jimmy.

"There's no bloody key," said Johnny Caroline. "The lock is long since broke and I've fixed it with snibs and fasteners." He finished the apple and promptly took another.

"I thought of coming here, Neddie," he said. "But, I thought, he has to be careful, Neddie has. Where would we all go for a bit o' fancy meat and butter to balance the bloody dole? I couldn't go crawlin' on me hands and knees to my friends, could I now? I slept downtown in a mission the first night and in a flophouse the second. I was thinkin' she'll soon enough take me back when she finds me satisfied to be gone. Well, I've had enough of it. I thought that if Neddie'd gie us a few packages o' food I'd soon have her openin' the bloody door."

"Aye, true enough," said Jimmy.

"I thought that maybe you'd run me home, Jim. She's always liked you."

"Well," said Jimmy.

My father said that it was getting awfully late and that it was time we were getting along.

"Oot every day, I've been," said Johnny Caroline. "There's no bloody jobs to be had in this bloody city."

It was snowing silently, and silently it was bitter cold when we came along out of the corridor and up the cold concrete into the dark, bitter night. I heard Neddie whisper "so long" and turned to see the metal door close on his bare, bald top. I carried a bag each of apples and potatoes and I had the book down between my belt and stomach for safekeeping.

Jimmy was brightly drunk and so was my father, but neither was like Johnny Caroline who had been sick and for whom only the promise of a ride home given grudgingly by Jimmy and only the promise of my father that we'd see him safely inside his house, had stirred him from the furnace room. He said his sickness would pass.

He staggered up the steps and into the alley, burdened with all those heavy packages. Jimmy and my father were laden too, Jimmy especially, carrying as much as the others plus a scuttle full of good anthracite. They walked ahead of Johnny Caroline and myself, their red faces blowing song in the winter night. The book kept slipping, I was tired and cold now, all the worse for having huddled close to that fire, and the new-laid snow made walking treacherous. I was annoyed too that my father and Jimmy kept singing, after all I'd been told about the need for quietness, what with Neddie's job at stake and all. They walked on ahead.

So it was only I who heard Johnny Caroline's hoarse gasp and turned to see him fall, his parcels scattering and skidding over the alley's slippery surface. He hit the alley floor with a muffled thud and almost immediately, was trying to get up again. Then he lay back and I heard him, as though he were some animal in pain. He clutched at his stomach, folded himself and rolled, his body dark against the white snow.

"Mr. Caroline!" I said. "Is it the stomachache?"

He groaned. Even out in the cold, his smell made me turn away. I looked for my father and Jimmy, but they had already disappeared down the alley, although I thought I could hear them singing still, and laughing.

"Can you get up, Mr. Caroline?" He just lay there and now he was silent and unmoving. I turned and ran for the others.

They had stopped to do what men do in alleys who have drunk much and have night and snow as cover. They were joking, not concerned with either of us.

"A poor man's got to make the bloody best of it," said Jimmy, as I came up. "Never you mind, we've got a bit o' joy in these bags will make the wives smile a bit." Now, I could see him swaying against a rubbish drum as he emptied his bladder.

"Mr. McNair," I said. "Dad!"

"Can a man no have peace attending to nature," laughed Jimmy but my father turned quickly.

"It's Mr. Caroline. He's fallen in the snow."

"Och, the bloody fool," said Jimmy, but my father had already gone past us, grumbling under his breath, and Jimmy followed, not looking at me. I remained, shivering, hunched up against the sudden swirls of snow.

I waited what seemed a long time and then, frightened, I went back down to them. They were standing, silent, shocked, clutching at the packages and looking down at the silent figure.

"Alec," said Jimmy, "there's nothing for it, we've got to get Ned."

"Aye." I was startled at the sound of his voice.

"It'll play hell," said Jimmy.

"Well, then it'll play hell," said my father.

"I think we'd better dump the bloody parcels in the car."

"Aye."

"Then we'll knock up Neddie and tell him."

"A sad story we'll have for him," said my father. Gloomily, he looked down the alleyway.

We took the food parcels to the car, even picking up and taking what had been Johnny Caroline's. Then Jimmy walked back but my father waited a moment while I climbed in the front.

"It couldna be helped," he said. "We'll no be long." He seemed to want to say more but he just closed the door and walked after Jimmy.

After a wait, while I shivered and fought sickness in the car, they came back with Neddie who was dressed now in an old army coat, a cloth cap on his head. I got in the back with the food and coal while Jimmy and my father took the front seats. Jimmy ran down the window on the driver's seat.

"Ye understand?" asked Neddie.

"Oh, aye," said Jimmy.

"I'll call the police after ye've left. Get home as soon as ye can."

"Right," said Jimmy. He had trouble starting the old car. It made a lot of noise, spluttered and caught and then died again. The men hunched anxiously until it started and Jimmy adjusted the choke and let it run awhile.

"That's done it," he said.

"Not a word," said Neddie.

"No bloody fear," said Jimmy and shifted the gear. The car

lurched off, spluttering. Neddie stood there until we turned at the corner.

"It's what we have to do, Alec," said Jimmy. "There's no use getting involved."

"Aye, bloody cruel though it is."

"He'll report it and it'll be another one found in the alley."

"Bloody cruel."

"The poor man hasn't a bloody chance," said Jimmy. "I'll not forget this night."

"Who's to tell her?" asked my father but Jimmy did not answer, and my father did not ask again.

# JAMES ALAN McPHERSON

## Gold Coast

(FROM THE ATLANTIC)

THAT SPRING, when I had a great deal of potential and no money at all, I took a job as a janitor. That was when I was still very young and spent money very freely, and when, almost every night, I drifted off to sleep lulled by sweet anticipation of that time when my potential would suddenly be realized and there would be capsule biographies of my life on dust jackets of many books, all proclaiming: ". . . He knew life on many levels. From shoeshine boy, free-lance waiter, 3rd cook, janitor, he rose to . . ." I had never been a janitor before, and I did not really have to be one, and that is why I did it. But now, much later, I think it might have been because it is possible to be a janitor without becoming one, and at parties or at mixers, when asked what it was I did for a living, it was pretty good to hook my thumbs in my vest pockets and say comfortably: "Why, I am an apprentice janitor." The hippies would think it degenerate and really dig me and people in Philosophy and Law and Business would feel uncomfortable trying to make me feel better about my station while wondering how the hell I had managed to crash the party.

"What's an apprentice janitor?" they would ask.

"I haven't got my card yet," I would reply. "Right now I'm just taking lessons. There's lots of complicated stuff you have to learn before you get your own card and your own building."

"What kind of stuff?"

"Human nature, for one thing. *Race* nature, for another."

"Why race?"

"Because," I would say in a low voice, looking around lest someone else should overhear, "you have to be able to spot Jews and Negroes who are passing."

"That's terrible," would surely be said then with a hint of indignation.

"It's an art," I would add masterfully.

After a good pause I would invariably be asked: "But you're a Negro yourself, how can you keep your own people out?"

At which point I would look terribly disappointed and say: "*I* don't keep them out. But if they get in it's my job to make their stay just as miserable as possible. Things are changing."

Now the speaker would just look at me in disbelief.

"It's Janitorial Objectivity," I would say to finish the thing as the speaker began to edge away. "Don't hate me," I would call after him to his considerable embarrassment. "Somebody has to do it."

It was an old building near Harvard Square. Conrad Aiken had once lived there, and in the days of the Gold Coast, before Harvard built its great houses, it had been a very fine haven for the rich; but that was a world ago, and this building was one of the few monuments of that era which had survived. The lobby had a high ceiling with thick redwood beams, and it was replete with marble floor, fancy ironwork, and an old-fashioned house telephone which no longer worked. Each apartment had a small fireplace, and even the large bathtubs and chain toilets, when I was having my touch of nature, made me wonder what prominent personage of the past had worn away all the newness. And, being there, I felt a certain affinity toward the rich.

It was a funny building, because the people who lived there made it old. Conveniently placed as it was between the Houses and Harvard Yard, I expected to find it occupied by a company of hippies, hopeful working girls, and assorted graduate students. Instead, there was a majority of old maids, dowagers, asexual middle-aged men, homosexual young men, a few married couples, and a teacher. No one was shacking up there, and walking through the quiet halls in the early evening, I sometimes had the urge to knock on a door and expose myself just to hear someone breathe hard for once.

It was a Cambridge spring: down by the Charles happy students were making love while sad-eyed middle-aged men watched them from the bridge. It was a time of activity: Law students were busy sublimating, Business School people were making records of the money they would make, the Harvard Houses were clearing out, and in the Square bearded pot-pushers were setting up their restaurant tables in anticipation of the Summer School faithfuls. There was a change of season in the air, and to comply with its urgings, James Sullivan, the old superintendent, passed his three beaten garbage cans on to me with the charge that I should take up his daily rounds of the six floors, and with unflinching humility, gather whatever scraps the old-maid tenants had refused to husband.

I then became very rich, with my own apartment, a sensitive girl, a stereo, two speakers, one tattered chair, one fork, a job, and the urge to acquire. Having all this and youth besides made me pity Sullivan: he had been in that building thirty years and had its whole history recorded in the little folds of his mind, as his own life was recorded in the wrinkles of his face. All he had to show for his time there was a berserk dog, a wife almost as mad as the dog, three cats, bursitis, acute myopia, and a drinking problem. He was well over seventy and could hardly walk, and his weekly check of twenty-two dollars from the company that managed the building would not support anything. So, out of compromise, he was retired to superintendent of my labor.

My first day as janitor, while I skillfully lugged my three overflowing cans of garbage out of the building, he sat on his bench in the lobby, faded and old and smoking, in patched, loose blue pants. He watched me. He was a chain smoker, and I noticed right away that he very carefully dropped all of the ashes and butts on the floor and crushed them under his feet until there was a yellow and gray smear. Then he laboriously pushed the mess under the bench with his shoe, all the while eyeing me like a cat in silence as I hauled the many cans of muck out to the big disposal unit next to the building. When I had finished, he gave me two old plates to help stock my kitchen and his first piece of advice.

"Sit down, for Chrisake, and take a load off your feet," he told me.

I sat on the red bench next to him and accepted the wilted cigarette he offered me from the crushed package he kept in his sweater pocket.

"Now, I'll tell you something to help you get along in the building," he said.

I listened attentively.

"If any of these sons of bitches ever ask you to do something extra,
be sure to charge them for it."

I assured him that I absolutely would.

"If they can afford to live here, they can afford to pay. The bastards."

"Undoubtedly," I assured him again.

"And another thing," he added. "Don't let any of these girls
shove any cat shit under your nose. That ain't your job. You tell
them to put it in a bag and take it out themselves."

I reminded him that I knew very well my station in life, and that
I was not about to haul cat shit or anything of that nature. He
looked at me through his thick-lensed glasses for a long time. He
looked like a cat himself. "That's right," he said at last. "And if
they still try to sneak it in the trash be sure to make the bastards
pay. They can afford it." He crushed his seventh butt on the floor
and scattered the mess some more while he lit up another. "I never
hauled out no cat shit in the thirty years I been here, and you don't
do it either."

"I'm going up to wash my hands," I said.

"Remember," he called after me, "don't take no shit from any
of them."

I protested once more that, upon my life, I would never, never
do it, not even for the prettiest girl in the building. Going up in
the elevator, I felt comfortably resolved that I would never do it.
There were no pretty girls in the building.

I never found out what he had done before he came there, but
I do know that being a janitor in that building was as high as he
ever got in life. He had watched two generations of the rich pass
the building on their way to the Yard, and he had seen many gov-
ernors ride white horses into that same Yard to send sons and daughters of the rich out into life to produce, to acquire, to procreate,
and to send back sons and daughters so that the cycle would continue. He had watched the cycle from when he had been able to
haul the cans out for himself, and now he could not, and he was
bitter.

He was Irish, of course, and he took pride in Irish accomplish-

ments when he could have none of his own. He had known Frank
O'Connor when that writer had been at Harvard. He told me on
many occasions how O'Connor had stopped to talk every day on
his way to the Yard. He had also known James Michael Curley,
and his most colorful memory of the man was a long-ago day when
he and James Curley sat in a Boston bar and one of Curley's runners
had come in and said: "Hey, Jim, Sol Bernstein the Jew wants to
see you." And Curley, in his deep, memorial voice, had said to
James Sullivan: "Let us go forth and meet this Israelite Prince."
These were his memories, and I would obediently put aside my
garbage cans and laugh with him over the hundred or so colorful,
insignificant little details which made up a whole lifetime of living
in the basement of Harvard. And although they were of little value
to me then, I knew that they were the reflections of a lifetime and
the happiest moments he would ever have, being sold to me cheap,
as youthful time is cheap, for as little time and interest as I wanted
to spend. It was a buyer's market.

In those days I believed myself gifted with a boundless perception and attacked my daily garbage route with a gusto superen-
forced by the happy knowledge that behind each of the fifty or so
doors in our building lived a story which could, if I chose to grace
it with the magic of my pen, become immortal. I watched my tenants fanatically, noting their perversions, their visitors, and their
eating habits. So intense was my search for material that I had to
restrain myself from going through their refuse scrap by scrap; but
at the topmost layers of muck, without too much hand soiling in
the process, I set my perception to work. By late June, however, I
had discovered only enough to put together a skimpy, rather naive
Henry Miller novel, the most colorful discoveries being:

1. The lady in #24 was an alumnus of Paducah College
2. The couple in #55 made love at least 500 times a week, and the
   wife had not yet discovered the pill
3. The old lady in #36 was still having monthly inconvenience
4. The two fatsos in #56 consumed nightly an extraordinary
   amount of chili
5. The fat man in #54 had two dogs that were married to each
   other, but he was not married to anyone at all

6. The middle-aged single man in #63 threw out an awful lot of
   flowers

Disturbed by the snail's progress I was making, I confessed my
futility to James one day as he sat on his bench chain-smoking and
smearing butts on my newly waxed lobby floor. "So you want to
know about the tenants?" he said, his cat's eyes flickering over me.
I nodded.

"Well, the first thing to notice is how many Jews there are."

"I haven't noticed any Jews," I said.

He eyed me in amazement.

"Well, a few," I said quickly to prevent my treasured perception
from being dulled any further.

"A few, hell," he said. "There's more Jews here than anybody."

"How can you tell?"

He gave me that undecided look again. "Where do you think
all that garbage comes from?" He nodded feebly toward my bulg-
ing cans. I looked just in time to prevent a stray noodle from slipping over the brim. "That's right," he continued. "Jews are the
biggest eaters in the world. They eat the best too."

I confessed then that I was of the chicken-soup generation and
believed that Jews ate only enough to muster strength for their
daily trips to the bank.

"Not so!" he replied emphatically. "You never heard the expression: 'Let's get to the restaurant before the Jews get there'?"

I shook my head sadly.

"You don't know that in certain restaurants they take the free
onions and pickles off the tables when they see Jews coming?"

I held my head down in shame over the bounteous heap.

He trudged over to my can and began to turn back the leaves of
noodles and crumpled tissues from #47 with his hand. After a few
seconds of digging, he unmucked an empty pâté can. "Look at that,"
he said triumphantly. "Gourmet stuff, no less."

"That's from #44," I said.

"What else?" he said, all-knowingly. "In 1946 a Swedish girl
moved in up there and took a Jewish girl for her roommate. Then
the Swedish girl moved out and there's been a Jewish Dynasty up
there ever since."

I recalled that #44 was occupied by a couple that threw out a good number of S. S. Pierce cans, Chivas Regal bottles, assorted broken records, and back issues of *Evergreen* and the *Realist*.

"You're right," I said.

"Of course," he replied, as if there were never any doubt. "I can spot them anywhere, even when they think they're passing." He leaned closer and said in a you-and-me voice: "But don't ever say anything bad about them in public. The Anti-Defamation League will get you."

Just then his wife screamed for him from the second floor, and the dog joined her and beat against the door. He got into the elevator painfully and said: "Don't ever talk about them in public. You don't know who they are, and that Defamation League will take everything you got."

Sullivan did not really dislike Jews. He was just bitter toward anyone better off than himself. He lived with his wife on the second floor, and his apartment was very dirty because both of them were sick and old, and neither could move very well. His wife swept dirt out into the hall, and two hours after I had mopped and waxed their section of the floor, there was sure to be a layer of dirt, grease, and crushed-scattered tobacco from their door to the end of the hall. There was a smell of dogs and cats and age and death about their door, and I did not ever want to have to go in there for any reason because I feared something about it I cannot name.

Mrs. Sullivan, I found out, was from South Africa. She loved animals much more than people, and there was a great deal of pain in her face. She kept little cans of meat posted at strategic points about the building, and I often came across her in the early morning or late at night throwing scraps out of the second-floor window to stray cats. Once, when James was about to throttle a stray mouse in their apartment, she had screamed at him to give the mouse a sporting chance. Whenever she attempted to walk she had to balance herself against a wall or a rail, and she hated the building because it confined her. She also hated James and most of the tenants. On the other hand, she loved the "Johnny Carson Show," she loved to sit outside on the front steps (because she could go no further unassisted), and she loved to talk to anyone who would stop to listen. She never spoke coherently except when she was cursing James, and then she had a vocabulary like a drunken sailor. She had great, shrill lungs, and her screams, accompanied by the rabid

barks of the dog, could be heard all over the building. She was
never really clean, her teeth were bad, and the first most pathetic
thing in the world was to see her sitting on the steps in the morning watching the world pass, in a stained smock and a fresh summer
blue hat she kept just to wear downstairs, with no place in the
world to go. James told me, on the many occasions of her screaming, that she was mentally disturbed and could not help herself.
The admirable thing about him was that he never lost his temper
with her, no matter how rough her curses became and no matter
who heard them. And the second most pathetic thing in the world
was to see them slowly making their way in Harvard Square, he
supporting her, through the hurrying crowds of miniskirted summer girls, J-Pressed Ivy Leaguers, beatniks, and bused Japanese
tourists, decked in cameras, who would take pictures of every inch
of Harvard Square except them. Once a hippie had brushed past
them and called back over his shoulder: "Don't break any track
records, Mr. and Mrs. Speedy Molasses."

Also on the second floor lived Miss O'Hara, a spinster who hated
Sullivan as only an old maid can hate an old man. Across from her
lived a very nice, gentle celibate named Murphy, who had once
served with Montgomery in North Africa and who was now spend-
ing the rest of his life cleaning his little apartment and gossiping
with Miss O'Hara. It was an Irish floor.


I never found out just why Miss O'Hara hated the Sullivans with
such a passion. Perhaps it was because they were so unkempt and
she was so superciliously clean. Perhaps it was because Miss O'Hara
had a great deal of Irish pride, and they were stereotyped Irish.
Perhaps it was because she merely had no reason to like them. She
was a fanatic about cleanliness and put out her little bit of garbage
wrapped very neatly in yesterday's *Christian Science Monitor* and
tied in a bow with a fresh piece of string. Collecting all those little
neat packages, I would wonder where she got the string and imagined her at night breaking meat market locks with a hairpin and
hobbling off with yards and yards of white cord concealed under
the gray sweater she always wore. I could even imagine her back in
her little apartment chuckling and rolling the cord into a great
white ball by candlelight. Then she would stash it away in her

bread box. Miss O'Hara kept her door slightly open until late at night, and I suspected that she heard everything that went on in the building. I had the feeling that I should never dare to make love with gusto for fear that she would overhear and write down all my happy-time phrases, to be maliciously recounted to me if she were ever provoked.

She had been in the building longer than Sullivan, and I suppose that her greatest ambition in life was to outlive him and then attend his wake with a knitting ball and needle. She had been trying to get him fired for twenty-five years or so, and did not know when to quit. On summer nights when I painfully mopped the second floor, she would offer me root beer, apples, or cupcakes while trying to pump me for evidence against him.

"He's just a filthy old man, Robert," she would declare in a little-old-lady whisper. "And don't think you have to clean up those dirty old butts of his. Just report him to the Company."

"Oh, I don't mind," I would tell her, gulping the root beer as fast as possible.

"Well, they're both a couple of lushes, if you ask me. They haven't been sober a day in twenty-five years."

"Well, she's sick too, you know."

"Ha!" She would throw up her hands in disgust. "She's only sick when he doesn't give her the booze."

I fought to keep down a burp. "How long have *you* been here?"

She motioned for me to step out of the hall and into her dark apartment. "Don't tell him" — she nodded toward Sullivan's door — "but I've been here thirty-four years." She waited for me to be taken aback. Then she added: "And it was a better building before those two lushes came."

She then offered me an apple, asked five times if the dog's barking bothered me, forced me to take a fudge brownie, said that the cats had wet the floor again last night, got me to dust the top of a large chest too high for her to reach, had me pick up the minute specks of dust which fell from my dustcloth, pressed another root beer on me, and then showed me her family album. As an afterthought, she had me take down a big old picture of her great-grandfather, also too high for her to reach, so that I could dust that too. Then together we picked up the dust from it which might have fallen to the floor. "He's really a filthy old man, Robert," she said in closing, "and don't be afraid to report him to the Property Manager anytime you want."

I assured her that I would do it at the slightest provocation from Sullivan, finally accepted an apple but refused the money she offered, and escaped back to my mopping. Even then she watched me, smiling, from her half-opened door.

"Why does Miss O'Hara hate you?" I asked James once.

He lifted his cigaretted hand and let the long ash fall elegantly to the floor. "That old bitch has been an albatross around my neck ever since I got here," he said. "Don't trust her, Robert. It was her kind that sat around singing hymns and watching them burn saints in this state."

In those days I had forgotten that I was first of all a black and I had a very lovely girl who was not first of all a black. It is quite possible that my ancestors rowed her ancestors across on the *Mayflower,* and she was very rich in that alone. We were both very young and optimistic then, and she believed with me in my potential and liked me partly because of it; and I was happy because she belonged to me and not to the race, which made her special. It made me special too because I did not have to wear a beard or hate or be especially hip or ultra Ivy Leagueish. I did not have to smoke pot or supply her with it, or be for any cause at all except myself. I only had to be myself, which pleased me; and I only had to produce, which pleased both of us. Like many of the artistically inclined rich, she wanted to own in someone else what she could not own in herself. But this I did not mind, and I forgave her for it because she forgave me moods and the constant smell of garbage and a great deal of latent hostility. She only minded James Sullivan, and all the valuable time I was wasting listening to him rattle on and on. His conversations, she thought, were useless, repetitious, and promised nothing of value to me. She was accustomed to the old-rich, whose conversations meandered around a leitmotiv of how well off they were and how much they would leave behind very soon. She was not at all cold, but she had been taught how to tolerate the old-poor and perhaps toss them a greeting in passing. But nothing more.

Sullivan did not like her when I first introduced them because he saw that she was not a beatnik and could not be dismissed. It is in the nature of things that liberal people will tolerate two interracial beatniks more than they will an intelligent, serious-minded mixed couple. The former liaison is easy to dismiss as the dregs of both races, deserving of each other and the contempt of both races; but the latter poses a threat because there is no immediacy of overpowering sensuality or "you-pick-my-fleas-I'll-pick-yours" apparent on the surface of things, and people, even the most publicly liberal, cannot dismiss it so easily.

"That girl is Irish, isn't she?" he had asked one day in my apartment soon after I had introduced them.

"No," I said definitely.

"What's her name?"

"Judy Smith," I said, which was not her name at all.

"Well, I can spot it," he said. "She's got Irish blood all right."

"Everybody's got a little Irish blood," I told him.

He looked at me cattily and craftily from behind his thick lenses. "Well, she's from a good family, I suppose."

"I suppose," I said.

He paused to let some ashes fall to the rug. "They say the Colonel's Lady and Nelly O'Grady are sisters under the skin." Then he added: "Rudyard Kipling."

"That's true," I said with equal innuendo, "that's why you have to maintain a distinction by marrying the Colonel's Lady."

An understanding passed between us then, and we never spoke more on the subject.

Almost every night the cats wet the second floor while Meg Sullivan watched the "Johnny Carson Show" and the dog howled and clawed the door. During commercials Meg would curse James to get out and stop dropping ashes on the floor or to take the dog out or something else, totally unintelligible to those of us on the fourth, fifth, and sixth floors. Even after the Carson show she would still curse him to get out, until finally he would go down to the basement and put away a bottle or two of wine. There was a steady stench of cat functions in the basement, and with all the grease and dirt, discarded trunks, beer bottles, chairs, old tools, and the filthy sofa on which he sometimes slept, seeing him there made me want to cry. He drank the cheapest sherry, the wino kind, straight from the bottle: and on many nights that summer at 2:00 A.M. my phone would ring me out of bed.

"Rob? Jimmy Sullivan here. What are you doing?"

There was nothing suitable to say.

"Come on down to the basement for a drink."

"I have to be at work at 8:30," I would protest.

"Can't you have just one drink?" he would say pathetically.

I would carry down my own glass so that I would not have to drink out of the bottle. Looking at him on the sofa, I could not be mad because now I had many records for my stereo, a story that was going well, a girl who believed in me and who belonged to me and not to the race, a new set of dishes, and a tomorrow morning with younger people.

"I don't want to burden you unduly," he would always preface.

I would force myself not to look at my watch and say: "Of course not."

"My Meg is not in the best health, you know," he would say, handing the bottle to me.

"She's just old."

"The doctors say she should be in an institution."

"That's no place to be."

"I'm a sick man myself, Rob. I can't take much more. She's crazy."

"Anybody who loves animals can't be crazy."

He took another long draw from the bottle. "I won't live another year. I'll be dead in a year."

"You don't know that."

He looked at me closely, without his glasses, so that I could see the desperation in his eyes. "I just hope Meg goes before I do. I don't want them to put her in an institution after I'm gone."

At 2:00 A.M., with the cat stench in my nose and a glass of bad sherry standing still in my hand because I refuse in my mind to touch it, and all my dreams of greatness are above him and the basement and the building itself, I did not know what to say. The only way I could keep from hating myself was to start him talking about the AMA or the Medicare program or beatniks. He was pure hell on all three. To him, the Medical Profession was "morally bankrupt," Medicare was a great farce which deprived oldsters like himself of their "rainy-day dollars," and beatniks were "dropouts from the human race." He could rage on and on in perfect phrases about all three of his major dislikes, and I had the feeling that because the sentences were so well constructed and well turned, he might have memorized them from something he had read. But then he was extremely well read, and it did not matter if he had borrowed a phrase or two from someone else. The ideas were still his own.

It would be 3:00 A.M. before I knew it, and then 3:30, and still he would go on. He hated politicians in general and liked to re-count, at these times, his private catalog of political observations. By the time he got around to Civil Rights it would be 4:00 A.M., and I could not feel responsible for him at that hour. I would be-gin to yawn, and at first he would just ignore it. Then I would start to edge toward the door, and he would see that he could hold me no longer, not even by declaring that he wanted to be an honorary Negro because he loved the race so much.

"I hope I haven't burdened you unduly," he would say again.

"Of course not," I would say, because it was over then, and I could leave him and the smell of the cats there, and sometimes I would go out in the cool night and walk around the Yard and be thankful that I was only an assistant janitor, and a transient one at that. Walking in the early dawn and seeing the Summer School fellows sneak out of the girls' dormitories in the Yard gave me a good feeling, and I thought that tomorrow night it would be good to make love myself so that I could be busy when he called.

"Why don't you tell that old man your job doesn't include baby-sitting with him," Jean told me many times when she came over to visit during the day and found me sleeping.

I would look at her and think to myself about social forces and the pressures massing and poised, waiting to attack us. It was still July then. It was hot, and I was working good.

"He's just an old man," I said. "Who else would listen to him."

"You're too soft. As long as you do your work you don't have to be bothered with him."

"He could be a story if I listened long enough."

"There are too many stories about old people."

"No," I said, thinking about us again, "there are just too many people who have no stories."

Sometimes he would come up and she would be there, but I would let him come in anyway, and he would stand there looking dirty and uncomfortable, offering some invented reason for having intruded. At these times something silent would pass between them, something I cannot name, which would reduce him to exactly what he was: an old man, come out of his basement to intrude where he was not wanted. But all the time this was being communicated, there would be a surface, friendly conversation between them. And after five minutes or so of being unwelcome, he would apologize for having come, drop a few ashes on the rug, and back out the door. Downstairs we could hear his wife screaming.

We endured the aged and August was almost over. Inside the building the cats were still wetting, Meg was still screaming, the dog was getting madder, and Sullivan began to drink during the day. Outside it was hot and lush and green, and the Summer girls were wearing shorter miniskirts and no panties and the middle-aged men down by the Charles were going wild on their bridge. Everyone was restless for change, for August is the month when undone summer things must be finished or regretted all through the winter.

Being imaginative people, Jean and I played a number of original games. One of them we called "Social Forces," the object of which was to see which side could break us first. We played it with the unknown night riders who screamed obscenities from passing cars. And because that was her side I would look at her expectantly, but she would laugh and say: "No." We played it at parties with unaware blacks who attempted to enchant her with skillful dances and hip vocabularies, believing her to be community property. She would be polite and aloof, and much later, it then being my turn, she would look at me expectantly. And I would force a smile and say: "No." The last round was played while taking her home in a subway car, on a hot August night, when one side of the car was black and tense and hating and the other side was white and of the same mind. There was not enough room on either side for the two of us to sit and we would not separate; so we stood, holding on to a steel post through all the stops, feeling all of the eyes, between the two sides of the car and the two sides of the world. We aged. And getting off finally at the stop which was no longer ours, we looked at each other, again expectantly, and there was nothing left to say.

I began to avoid the old man, would not answer the door when I knew it was he who was knocking, and waited until very late at night, when he could not possibly be awake, to haul the trash down. I hated the building then; and I was really a janitor for the first time. I slept a lot and wrote very little. And I did not give a damn about Medicare, the AMA, the building, Meg, or the crazy dog. I began to consider moving out.

In that same week, Miss O'Hara finally succeeded in badgering Murphy, the celibate Irishman, and a few other tenants into signing a complaint about the dog. No doubt Murphy signed because he was a nice fellow and women like Miss O'Hara had always dominated him. He did not really mind the dog: he did not really mind anything. She called him "Frank Dear," and I had the feeling that when he came to that place, fresh from Montgomery's Campaign, he must have had a will of his own; but she had drained it all away, year by year, so that now he would do anything just to be agreeable.

One day soon after the complaint, the little chubby Property Manager came around to tell Sullivan that the dog had to be taken away. Miss O'Hara told me the good news later, when she finally got around to my door.

"Well, that crazy dog is gone now, Robert. Those two are enough."

"Where is the dog?" I asked.

"I don't know, but Albert Rustin made them get him out. You should have seen the old drunk's face," she said. "That dirty old useless man."

"You should be at peace now," I said.

"Almost," was her reply. "The best thing is to get rid of those two old boozers along with the dog."

I congratulated Miss O'Hara and went out. I knew that the old man would be drinking and would want to talk. But very late that evening he called on the telephone and caught me in.

"Rob?" he said. "James Sullivan here. Would you come down to my apartment like a good fellow? I want to ask you something important."

I had never been in his apartment before and did not want to go then. But I went down anyway.

They had three rooms, all grimy from corner to corner. There was a peculiar odor in that place I did not ever want to smell again, and his wife was dragging herself around the room talking in mumbles. When she saw me come in the door, she said: "I can't clean it up. I just can't. Look at that window. I can't reach it. I can't keep it clean." She threw up both her hands and held her head down and to the side. "The whole place is dirty, and I can't clean it up."

"What do you want?" I said to Sullivan.

"Sit down." He motioned me to a kitchen chair. "Have you changed that bulb on the fifth floor?"

"It's done."

He was silent for a while, drinking from a bottle of sherry, and he gave me some and a dirty glass. "You're the first person who's been in here in years," he said. "We couldn't have company because of the dog."

Somewhere in my mind was a note that I should never go into his apartment. But the dog had never been the reason. "Well, he's gone now," I said, fingering the dirty glass of sherry.

He began to cry. "They took my dog away," he said. "It was all I had. How can they take a man's dog away from him?"

There was nothing I could say.

"I couldn't do nothing," he continued. After a while he added: "But I know who it was. It was that old bitch O'Hara. Don't ever trust her, Rob. She smiles in your face, but it was her kind that laughed when they burned Joan of Arc in this state."

Seeing him there, crying and making me feel unmanly because I wanted to touch him or say something warm, also made me eager to be far away and running hard.

"Everybody's got problems," I said. "I don't have a girl now."

He brightened immediately, and for a while he looked almost happy in his old cat's eyes. Then he staggered over to my chair and held out his hand. I did not touch it, and he finally pulled it back. "I know how you feel," he said. "I know just how you feel."

"Sure," I said.

"But you're a young man, you have a future. But not me. I'll be dead inside of a year."

Just then his wife dragged herself in to offer me a cigar. They were being hospitable, and I forced myself to drink a little of the sherry.

"They took my dog away today," she mumbled. "That's all I
had in the world, my dog."

I looked at the old man. He was drinking from the bottle.

During the first week of September one of the middle-aged men
down by the Charles got tired of looking and tried to take a neck-
ing girl away from her boyfriend. The police hauled him off
to jail, and the girl pulled down her dress tearfully. A few days
later another man exposed himself near the same spot. And
that same week a dead body was found on the banks of the Charles.

The miniskirted brigade had moved out of the Yard, and it was
quiet and green and peaceful there. In our building another Jewish couple moved into #44. They did not eat gourmet stuff, and on
occasion, threw out pork-and-beans cans. But I had lost interest in
perception. I now had many records for my stereo, loads of S. S.
Pierce stuff, and a small bottle of Chivas Regal which I never
opened. I was working good again, and I did not miss other things
as much; or at least I told myself that.

The old man was coming up steadily now, at least three times
a day, and I had resigned myself to it. If I refused to let him in, he
would always come back later with a missing bulb on the fifth floor.
We had taken to buying cases of beer together, and when he had
finished his half, which was very frequently, he would come up to
polish off mine. I began to enjoy talking politics, the AMA,
Medicare, beatniks, and listening to him recite from books he had
read. I discovered that he was very well read in history, philosophy,
literature, and law. He was extraordinarily fond of saying: "I am
really a cut above being a building superintendent. Circumstances
made me what I am." And even though he was drunk and dirty
and it was very late at night, I believed him and liked him anyway because having him there was much better than being alone.
After he had gone I could sleep, and I was not lonely in sleep; and
it did not really matter how late I was at work the next morning
because when I thought about it all, I discovered that nothing
really matters except not being old and being alive and having potential to dream about, and not being alone.

# JOHN R. MILTON

## *The Inheritance of Emmy One Horse*

(FROM THE SOUTH DAKOTA REVIEW)

### I

AND THE WATER of life flowed past his door.

He pushed the short stick into the sand between his bare feet. He drew a circle around it with his forefinger, and added several wiggly lines, apparently aimless in direction, each one ending at the circle. From the pouch at his waist he withdrew a tuft of hair — lynx or bobcat, he thought, although the memory was dim — and carefully placed the hair on top of the stick, not pushing this time but letting it rest easily and precariously. He was ready again. He would get five more before sundown.

He heard the car bearing down upon the approach to the bridge, then speeding across, and as the car was directly above him he muttered the words and hit sharply at his stick with the tuft of hair on it and sent it all flying into the river. The car sped off into the distance. No matter — it would crash at the next bridge and fall into the water. All of its occupants would drown. He chuckled. In the past years — he did not know how many — he must have killed over a thousand white people. The spell was infallible.

What more could he ask.

Crazy, they called him, and cast him out from the tribe. He could not remember how long he had lived under the bridge. Or how long ago it was that Samuel Big Medicine had become Samuel Talks-in-Circles. Or just Sam TIC. The young braves in their beat-up

Fords and Chevvies laughed at him, and the women turned their
eyes away as though he had been forever expelled from the Yank-
tonnais. So he had. No longer shaman, no longer powerful, no
longer useful — so they said. A judge — white — came to the reservation and ordered him taken to a big house. Sam refused to go.
His people honored his request and took matters into their own
hands, into tradition, into the old way which said that a tribe member no longer useful must be sent away to die by himself.

He survived.

Stumbling across the prairie, walking blindly into fences that cut
him and angered him, avoiding towns except once when he did not
expect to find a town out in the middle of nowhere, he fell,
exhausted, down an embankment at the end of a bridge and rolled
into the water. Had it been deep at that point he would have
drowned, gladly. But his head remained on the sand, and he raised
it as proudly as he could and took command of the territory, a small
place, under a highway bridge.

He slept all night with his body partly in the water, rising the
next morning with wrinkled skin, shivering in the early chill of
dawn, noticing driftwood along the river bank. Without moving
his lips he smiled at the thought of making a fire without the white
man's matches. He knew of no Indian who could still do it.

At this point in his life, Sam TIC decided to wage war upon the
whites again, as his people had done successfully generations ago,
being defeated ultimately only through the numbers and weapons
brought to bear against them. He was still shaman. He had established his territory; like holding a pass against the invaders in the
old days, he would now hold the bridge. They would not see him.
He would work his magic, alone, unseen, and all would die.

Deep under the bridge he lived.

A foray into the nearest town — it became necessary — yielded
matches and several cans of beans. He got away unseen. From the
driftwood along the river he selected those pieces which could
be propped against each other and the bridge support to make a
shelter. Other pieces he burned, for heat and for cooking the
beans.

They had said he was crazy: formerly revered, formerly respected
in the inner circles of the tribe, a member of the council, now
outcast, now isolated from two civilizations. He had taken his

old hunting knife with him. Its new use was inglorious — cutting into the tin cans of beans. He dreamed at night of sprinting across the prairie and through the brush along the river, knife in hand, upraised, needing only a swift strike to bring down a deer. But, in the daytime, awake, prowling up and down the river, Sam saw no deer, no rabbits, no game of any kind.

Crazy. A hermit. He liked it, more than he would admit to himself. He became a scavenger, invading the town with all the stealth of a Sioux warrior, returning with a board, a few bent nails, a piece of tar paper, and soon he had a respectable and portable shack built and set upon two runners. When he needed sunshine in the winter, he pulled the shack out into the open. When he wanted shade in the summer, he pulled it back under the bridge.

He was tolerated, after they found him there, because he did no harm.

Little did they know, the palefaces, that he was the power which was destroying them, one by one, as their cars went off the highway in fatal accidents, either at the next curve or at the next bridge. Twice he had literal proof of the strength of his medicine. A car full of noisy young whites failed to make the turn at the other approach to the bridge — the one Sam could see across the river from him — and careened into the river. There was much excitement then, and much wailing and mourning for the lost young people, but no one suspected that it was Sam's particular talent which had dealt the blow. Again, after yellow signs with crosses on them were erected at the curve, a car came speeding at the bridge and went through the rail and into water deep enough to cover all traces of the accident. Only Sam saw that one.

It was no accident.

Let it be said that Sam was no murderer. He was engaged in legitimate warfare; other than that, he was — at least in his own sight — a good and responsible man. He even acquired an odd kind of love for the bridge itself, after seven or eight years of living under it. He loved the bridge in the way that a man loves a woman, seeing her always as she was when first she became a part of his life. The bridge grew old, and Sam did not notice. It was wrinkled and stiff and had more than one aching joint — all unnoticed, because Sam took the bridge for granted, as a man does his wife.

Others had noticed — civil engineers of the highway department.

In town, those people (all of them) who did not know that Sam TIC had caused the highway deaths through his making of medicine, who, indeed, had never heard of Sam, complained to the state highway department, to the governor, that six yellow cross signs at the old bridge were quite enough. A new bridge, with new approaches, was needed. And, the old bridge was getting dangerous for other reasons also — it might fall into the river.

And so one day some strange men came and prowled around the bridge, poking at it, looking at it, and talking constantly in numbers and formulas. Sam did not understand what was taking place, and he simply told the men to quit, to move away, to get out of there. Damn it.

They did not go, until toward evening. Sam found his knife, opened a can of beans, and contemplated what kind of spell he would cast upon the men if they ever returned.

He had almost forgotten them when they came back. This time they were followed by a swarm of trucks and machines and gadgets which Sam had never seen before, and there were many more men. Every one of them marched to the edge of the bridge, stood hesitantly above the river, and looked down at Sam. He decided that the best thing was to ignore them. At that very moment he was jarred by the loudest voice he had ever heard, from a giant in a leather jacket: "Hey, old man," the voice roared, "you'll have to pull out of there!"

Sam slowly turned his head in the direction of the voice and peered wonderingly but a little belligerently at the giant. "I ain't go-un anyplace."

The giant did not move, but his roar increased: "Oh yes you are! Get out! Scram! Vamoose! We got work to do, redskin, and you're in the way."

"Work?" Sam could hardly utter the word. "There ain't no work to do here. I am here eight years and no work." He thought for a moment. "Go away. You must be crazy."

A small man, with glasses pushed up on his forehead, stepped in front of the big man and told Sam that he must at least move his shack out from under the bridge. It was dangerous to remain under the bridge, he said.

Sam tried to think about the little man, but he could not comprehend the necessity of moving his shack. It was early summer, he guessed, very warm, and he wanted to be in the shade. He would move the shack later on, perhaps in October.

The men did not talk any longer. Four of them half slid down the embankment from the bridge, walked in a group to the shack — as though afraid to act individually — took hold of the ropes which Sam used to move the shack, and pulled it to the edge of the river. The very edge. Sam looked at the men and said nothing. Two men got behind the shack and pushed, tipping it on its side into the water. In less than a minute the current got hold of the boards and they drifted down the river, a rough, weather-beaten, flimsy box with the open door gaping blackly like a mouth open in protest.

Sam did not protest. If he could have known that the old bridge would not be demolished until the new one was completed, he might have stayed awhile longer — but he did not know and he did not stay. He still had his knife and his personal totem bag. He still had a firm belief in his powers as shaman.

Samuel Big Medicine walked slowly, head up, toward the little town upriver.


## II

"You ain't got all of your head!"

The little brown devils were buzzing around her, coming at her and yet not coming. They made her head spin and her heart beat too fast. She thought she was crying out "stop it!" but she could not hear her words. Something was wrong again.

"Emmy is crazy, Emmy is crazy, Emmy is crazy!"

The little brown devils (or were they red? or copper?) changed color and swirled about as leaves do in a stiff autumn wind. Colored leaves — brown, yellow, blue — but leaves were not blue. Always something was wrong. Blue leaves fluttering in her face, but leaves could not be blue, and they could not strike out at her as these blue things did.

"Go home, Emmy One Horse, and find the rest of your head!"

"Let me alone."

"Yah, yah, Emmy's crazy!"

She stumbled, and the blue leaves (only now they were definitely dark red) retreated from her. The wind must have changed, because now she could hear her voice, her own voice, far away yet, but she heard it. "Let me alone," the voice cried. "Go away and let me alone."

She swung her arms up to defend herself and beat wildly at her tormentors. "I hate you!" she screamed. "I'll kill you!" And the brown devils which weren't really brown at all fell back and hesitated and fell back again. The red and black and blue became blurred and mixed up as the colors on little boys' jackets do when the little boys are crowded together and pushing each other in their haste to get away from something they suddenly fear. And Emmy began to remember now, and she turned and ran away from the boys.

As she ran, the fresh new air streamed into her lungs and her eyes and worked itself down into her legs so that she ran faster; and as she ran her head cleared and she realized that she was running toward the big white house at the end of the street. And in the house, the white frame house, she knew that she was running up the stairs toward the big white room at the back, the room with the sunshine flooding through the windows and the sturdy door was there and she could shut it against the devils no matter what color they were.

Here she was safe.

"You're crazy, Emmy."

She leaned from the bed and flung open the door. The hall was empty. "I hate you!" she screamed. "I'll kill you!" She ran to the closet, pushing aside the dresses, dumping the hatboxes to the floor. No one was there. She fell to the floor, landing too hard on one knee, and searched under the bed. Only dust and a bit of lint. One canvas shoe with the lace missing. She wondered what had happened to the shoelace, and then her knee hurt and she looked at it to find blood seeping through the scraped skin.

Emmy watched as the blood oozed, red across her brown skin, dark red because of the brown underneath, oozing, then moving slowly down the leg and over the little bumps she had gotten during the morning from the brown devils. The bumps had not killed her but the blood might — if enough came out. If her blood ran all over the floor until it dripped, pluht, pluht, pluht, down the stairs and out the front door — then the brown devils would see that she could no longer be bothered. No more devils if the red water flowed fast enough and far enough.

It stopped.

She went outdoors again. The blood had not even reached her ankle. There was perhaps enough for the boys to smell it. They would go away.

She was safe.

It was good to be lazy in the April sun, late April. Fluffy white clouds chased each other across a pale blue sky that was picking up a little more color, a deeper blue, each day. There were no black or brown or copper-red clouds. No devils in the sky. That was where Emmy wanted to live, in the sky, in white clouds, in whiteness like when a woman went to live with a man, or a lake froze peacefully in the winter, or the popcorn was heaped for the children in the park. But Emmy did not dare go to the park anymore, and ice made her cold, and she was an Indian.

Partly at least.

She heard her father call, voice muffled from the kitchen, and she stretched out on the steps and stayed where she was. Her eyes closed to the afternoon sun as she waited for energy, for purpose. It did not come. The boys were gone and Emmy suddenly felt lazy, not exactly lazy either, just more peaceful than anything else. Her head had stopped spinning.

Finally.

Why had Bill and Les and the Riley boys wanted her to go fishing with them? She had gone with them before, but only as a child, when she was some kind of toy or curiosity to them. That was long ago. She didn't always remember because sometimes her head felt fluffy like the clouds only not white but brown and black and sometimes red and green and yellow and brown. She remembered that the boys had asked her to go fishing this morning.

"I'm too old to play with boys."

"Aw c'mon Emmy," pleaded Les.

"No."

"What's the matter?" asked one of the Riley boys, and she could not remember which one it was, but they were Rileys.

"Nothing's the matter," she answered. "I don't want to go fishing." Then she had arrived at the inspiration of the young lady who is superior to her tormentors: "Nice ladies don't do that."

Bill threw his head back so hard that his cap fell off; he guffawed and hollered and pranced around, then doubled over and held his stomach as though he had cramps — laughing all the time. The Riley boys stared first at Emmy and then at Bill, as though they could believe neither one. But it was Les who stood sullenly off to the side and said so quietly that no one heard it for a moment, "Nice lady, hell. Your old man's an Injun, or had you forgotten?"

"My mother was white," she screamed back at him, and her head began to pound again. "White! White! Do you understand?"

"Yeah." Les continued to speak softly, as though to keep anyone else from hearing. "But she's gone. And you're old enough to come down to the river with us now. Get what I mean?" The boys all stood quietly now, facing Emmy expectantly, not certain that they had said the right thing but wanting to find out.

She fled. It was not clear to her now, but she must have run, because the only visual image remaining was the line of boys advancing upon her, and the only sound was the chant that followed her from an earlier year,

> *Half-a-head Emmy*
> *Can't think worth a penny,*

and the rest was mixed up with the colored but mostly brown things that buzzed around her and frightened her.

She was on the porch.

Had she gone to the river? She could not remember.


### III

Samuel (Big Medicine) Talks-in-Circles and Emmy One Horse sat together on a grassy knoll seven feet above the swirling brown water. The river current was strong at this point and had deposited a tangle of driftwood below the bank. The bare rooted end of a tree lying in the water, looked like a horse's head.

*We are the last two, Sam said.*

*My mother was white, Emmy insisted.*
*I have killed many whites.*
*You should not do that. I think you have not done it.*
*See my totems.*
*There is only some hair in there (fur?), and a few sticks.*
*You know nothing of the old ways. You listened too much to your*
mother.
*She was white.*
*I know. That was her trouble.*
*How could you know about her?*
*I know.*
*Don't you have any troubles, old man?*
*No, no, only with the bridge.*
*Yes, you told me that. You were foolish.*
*Don't say that.*
*I just said that you were . . .*
*No. I ain't crazy.*
*I didn't say that.*
*You think. You no say. You think.*
*Talk straight. Maybe you are crazy after all.*
*We are all crazy.*
*Not me.*
*No. You ain't crazy.*
*I mean it.*
*We are the last two, Sam said.*
*What shall we do? Emmy asked.*
*They will put us in the big house now.*
*I won't go. My father can stop them.*
*He is Inyan.*
*Yes, but my mother was . . .*
*. . . white. I know.*
*It makes a difference.*
*Make-un you crazy is what it did.*
*No, I only have headaches. They go away.*
*Inyans go away too. All go away. None left.*
*They're on the reservation.*
*They go away. None left. Only whites.*
*But my mother . . .*

*. . . was white. I know. Too bad.*
*What shall we do? Emmy asked.*
*Make medicine, Sam said.*
*The sticks?*
*And the hair of the cat.*
*Will it work on me, too, because I'm white?*
*You Inyan.*
*Are you that sure?*
*Sure.*
*Will it kill many?*
*Watch. All the hair left, on all the sticks. Big totem. We kill all the whites in the land, keep land for Inyans, everything will die except our people, and our land.*
*I'm afraid.*

Sam emptied his medicine bag on the grass. He pushed the sticks into the ground and capped each one with a piece of fur. He took more time than usual to utter his words, his incantation, his final work of magic. He was the big shaman of the Sioux and would return to his tribe in honor as soon as he kicked the sticks into the river. He became excited at the thought, and he jumped to his feet as quickly as his stiff legs would allow, drawing back his right foot — the kicking foot — and lashing out with all his remaining vigor at the hair-topped sticks. He kicked too hard and lost his balance. He fell over the edge of the bank and dropped heavily into the river. Emmy started for the edge and drew back when she saw that Sam had hit his head on the wood which looked like a horse and was floating unconscious, drifting rapidly downstream as the current caught him and took him away from her.

There was nothing she could do except return to the big white house.

For a while her headaches increased as she wondered if Sam TIC had killed her mother on the old bridge. She went back to the grassy knoll one day and kicked tentatively at one of Sam's sticks, still there. Nothing happened. She kicked one stick so hard that it flew into the river, but there were no accidents that day either.

By October, when the leaves were blowing across the town — almost all of them were yellow this time — the new bridge had been built and dedicated and the old one demolished. Some of the pieces floated down the river. Emmy's headaches were less frequent, and she was able to talk to the Riley boys without upsetting either them or herself. The boys found the rest of the sticks, with their hairlike caps, and Emmy persuaded them to set the sticks gently in the river and let them float downstream. The act was performed with reverence, and the procession moved on the water with dignity.

And the water of life flowed past, as it always had.

# JOYCE CAROL OATES

## By the River

(FROM DECEMBER)

HELEN THOUGHT: "Am I in love again, some new kind of love? Is that why I'm here?"

She was sitting in the waiting room of the Yellow Bus Lines station; she knew the big old room with its dirty tile floor and its solitary telephone booth in the corner and its candy machine and cigarette machine and popcorn machine by heart. Everything was familiar, though she had been gone for four months, even the old woman with the dyed red hair who sold tickets and had been selling them there, behind that counter, for as long as Helen could remember. Years ago, before Helen's marriage, she and her girl friends would be driven in to town by someone's father and after they tired of walking around town they would stroll over to the bus station to watch the buses unload. They were anxious to see who was getting off, but few of the passengers who got off stayed in Oriskany — they were just passing through, stopping for a rest and a drink, and their faces seemed to say that they didn't think much of the town. Nor did they seem to think much of the girls from the country who stood around in their colorful dresses and smiled shyly at strangers, not knowing any better: they were taught to be kind to people, to smile first, you never knew who it might be. So now Helen was back in Oriskany, but this time she had come in on a bus herself. Had ridden alone, all the way from the city of Derby, all alone, and was waiting for her father to pick her up so she could go back to her old life without any more fuss.

It was hot. Flies crawled languidly around; a woman with a small sickly-faced baby had to keep waving them away. The old woman selling tickets looked at Helen as if her eyes were drawn irresistibly that way, as if she knew every nasty rumor and wanted to let Helen know that she knew. Helen's forehead broke out in perspiration and she stood, abruptly, wanting to dislodge that old woman's stare. She went over to the candy machine but did not look at the candy bars; she looked at herself in the mirror. Her own reflection always made her feel better. Whatever went on inside her head — and right now she felt nervous about something — had nothing to do with the way she looked, her smooth gentle skin and the faint freckles on her forehead and nose and the cool, innocent green of her eyes; she was just a girl from the country and anyone in town would know that, even if they didn't know her personally, one of those easy, friendly girls who hummed to themselves and seemed always to be glancing up as if expecting something pleasant. Her light brown hair curled back lazily toward her ears, cut short now because it was the style; in high school she had worn it long. She watched her eyes in the mirror. No alarm there really. She would be back home in an hour or so. Not her husband's home, of course, but her parents' home. And her face in the mirror was the face she had always seen — twenty-two she was now, and to her that seemed very old, but she looked no different from the way she had looked on her wedding day five years ago.

But it was stupid to try to link together those two Helens, she thought. She went back to the row of seats and sat heavily. If the old woman was still watching, she did not care. A sailor in a soiled white uniform sat nearby, smoking, watching her but not with too much interest; he had other girls to recall. Helen opened her purse and looked inside at nothing and closed it again. The man she had been living with in the city for four months had told her it was stupid — no, he had not used that word; he said something fancy like "immature" — to confuse herself with the child she had been, married woman as she was now, and a mother, adulterous married woman . . . and the word *adulterous* made her lips turn up in a slow bemused smile, the first flash of incredulous pride one might feel when told at last the disease that is going to be fatal. For there were so many diseases and only one way out of the world, only one death and so many ways to get to it. They were like doors, Helen thought dreamily. You walked down a hallway like those in movies, in huge wealthy homes, crystal chandeliers and marble floors and . . . great sweeping lawns . . . and doors all along those hallways; if you picked the wrong door you had to go through it. She was dreamy, drowsy. When thought became too much for her — when he had pestered her so much about marrying him, divorcing her husband and marrying him, always him! — she had felt so sleepy she could not listen. If she was not interested in a word her mind wouldn't hear it but made it blurred and strange, like words half-heard in dreams or through some thick substance like water. You didn't have to hear a word if you didn't want to.

So she had telephoned her father the night before and told him the three-fifteen bus and now it was three-thirty; where was he? Over the telephone he had sounded slow and solemn, it could have been a stranger's voice. Helen had never liked telephones because you could not see smiles or gestures and talking like that made her tired. Listening to her father, she had felt for the first time since she had run away and left them all behind — husband, baby girl, family, in-laws, the minister, the dreary sun-bleached look of the land — that she had perhaps died and only imagined she was running away. Nobody here trusted the city; it was too big. Helen had wanted to go there all her life, not being afraid of anything, and so she had gone, and was coming back; but it was an odd feeling, this dreamy ghostliness, as if she were really dead and coming back in a form that only looked like herself . . . She was bored, thinking of this, and crossed her bare legs. The sailor crushed out a cigarette in the dirty tin ashtray and their eyes met. Helen felt a little smile tug at her lips. That was the trouble, she knew men too well. She knew their eyes and their gestures — like the sailor rubbing thoughtfully at his chin, now, as if he hadn't shaved well enough but really liked to feel his own skin. She knew them too well and had never figured out why: her sister, four years older, wasn't like that. But to Helen the same man one hundred times or one hundred men, different men, seemed the same. It was wrong, of course, because she had been taught it and believed what she had been taught; but she could not understand the difference. The sailor watched her but she looked away, half-closing her eyes. She had no time for him. Her father should

be here now, he would be here in a few minutes, so there was no
time; she would be home in an hour. When she thought of her father the ugly bus station with its odor of tobacco and spilled soft
drinks seemed to fade away — she remembered his voice the night
before, how gentle and soft she had felt listening to that voice, giving in to the protection he represented. She had endured his rough
hands, as a child, because she knew they protected her, and all
her life they had protected her. There had always been trouble,
sometimes the kind you laughed about later and sometimes not,
that was one of the reasons she had married Paul, and before Paul
there had been others — just boys who didn't count, who had no
jobs and thought mainly about their cars. She had called her father from a roadhouse sixty miles away once, when she was fifteen;
she and her best friend Annie had gotten mixed up with some men
they had met at a picnic. That had been frightening, Helen
thought, but now she could have handled them. She gave everyone
too much, that was her trouble. Her father had said that. Even
her mother. Lent money to girls at the telephone company where
she'd worked; lent her girl friends clothes; would run outside when
some man drove up and blew his horn, not bothering to get out
and knock at the door the way he should. She liked to make
other people happy, what was wrong with that? Was she too lazy to
care? Her head had begun to ache.

Always her thoughts ran one way, fast and innocent, but her
body did other things. It got warm, nervous, it could not relax.
Was she afraid of what her father's face would tell her? She pushed
that idea away, it was nonsense. If she had to think of something,
let it be of that muddy spring day when her family had first moved
to this part of the country, into an old farmhouse her father had
bought at a "bargain." At that time the road out in front of the
house had been no more than a single dirt lane . . . now it was
wider, covered with black top that smelled ugly and made your
eyesight shimmer and sweat with confusion in the summer. Yes,
that big old house. Nothing about it would have changed. She did
not think of her own house, her husband's house, because it
mixed her up too much right now. Maybe she would go back and
maybe not. She did not think of him — if she wanted to go back
she would, he would take her in. When she tried to think of
what had brought her back, it was never her husband — so much

younger, quicker, happier than the man she had just left — and
not the little girl, either, but something to do with her family's
house and that misty, warm day seventeen years ago when they had
first moved in. So one morning when that man left for work her
thoughts had turned back to home and she had sat at the breakfast
table for an hour or so, not clearing off the dishes, looking at the
coffee left in his cup as if it were a forlorn reminder of him — a
man she was even beginning to forget. She knew then that she
did not belong there in the city. It wasn't that she had stopped
loving this man — she never stopped loving anyone who needed
her, and he had needed her more than anyone — it was something
else, something she did not understand. Not her husband, not
her baby, not even the look of the river way off down the hill,
through the trees that got so solemn and intricate with their bare
branches in winter. Those things she loved, she hadn't stopped loving them because she had had to love this new man more . . . but
something else made her get up and run into the next room and
look through the bureau drawers and the closet, as if looking for
something. That evening, when he returned, she explained to
him that she was going back. He was over forty, she wasn't sure
how much, and it had always been his hesitant, apologetic manner
that made her love him, the odor of failure about him that mixed
with the odor of the drinking he could not stop, even though he
had "cut down" now with her help. Why were so many men afraid,
why did they think so much? He did something that had to do with
keeping books, was that nervous work? He was an attractive man
but that wasn't what Helen had seen in him. It was his staring at
her when they had first met, and the way he had run his hand
through his thinning hair, telling her in that gesture that he
wanted her and wanted to be young enough to tell her so. That
had been four months ago. The months all rushed to Helen's
mind in the memory she had of his keen intelligent baffled eyes,
and the tears she had had to see in them when she went out to call
her father . . .

Now, back in Oriskany, she would think of him no more.

A few minutes later her father came. Was that really him? she
thought. Her heart beat furiously. If blood drained out of her
face she would look mottled and sick, as if she had a rash . . .
how she hated that! Though he had seen her at once, though the

bus station was nearly empty, her father hesitated until she stood
and ran to him. "Pa," she said, "I'm so glad to see you." It might
have been years ago and he was just going to drive back home
now, finished with his business in town, and Helen fourteen or fifteen, waiting to go back with him.

"I'll get your suitcase," he said. The sailor was reading a magazine, no longer interested. Helen watched her father nervously.
What was wrong? He stooped, taking hold of the suitcase handle,
but he did not straighten fast enough. Just a heartbeat too slow.
Why was that? Helen took a tissue already stained with lipstick and
dabbed it on her forehead.

On the way home he drove oddly, as if the steering wheel,
heated by the sun, were too painful for him to hold. "No more
trouble with the car, huh?" Helen said.

"It's all right," he said. They were nearly out of town already.
Helen saw few people she knew. "Why are you looking around?"
her father said. His voice was pleasant and his eyes fastened seriously upon the road, as if he did not dare look elsewhere.

"Oh, just looking," Helen said. "How is Davey?"

Waiting for her father to answer — he always took his time
— Helen arranged her skirt nervously beneath her. Davey was her
sister's baby, could he be sick? She had forgotten to ask about
him the night before. "Nothing's wrong with Davey, is there, Pa?"
she said.

"No, nothing."

"I thought Ma might come, maybe," Helen said.

"No."

"Didn't she want to? Mad at me, huh?"

In the past her mother's dissatisfaction with her had always
ranged Helen and her father together; Helen could tell by a glance
of her father's when this was so. But he did not look away from the
road. They were passing the new high school, the consolidated
high school Helen had attended for a year. No one had known
what "consolidated" meant or was interested in knowing. Helen
frowned at the dark brick and there came to her mind, out of nowhere, the word "adulterous," for it too had been a word she had
not understood for years. A word out of the Bible. It was like a
mosquito bothering her at night, or a stain on her dress — the kind
she would have to hide without seeming to, letting her hand fall

accidentally over it. For some reason the peculiar smell of the old car, the rattling sun shades above the windshield, the same old khaki blanket they used for a seat cover did not comfort her and let her mind get drowsy, to push that word away.

She was not sleepy, but she said she was.

"Yes, honey. Why don't you lay back and try to sleep, then," her father said.

He glanced toward her. She felt relieved at once, made simple and safe. She slid over and leaned her head against her father's shoulder. "Bus ride was long, I hate bus rides," she said. "I used to like them."

"You can sleep till we get home."

"Is Ma mad?"

"No."

His shoulder wasn't as comfortable as it should have been. But she closed her eyes, trying to force sleep. She remembered that April day they had come here — their moving to the house that was new to them, a house of their own they would have to share with no one else, but a house it turned out had things wrong with it, secret things, that had made Helen's father furious. She could not remember the city and the house they had lived in there, but she had been old enough to sense the simplicity of the country and the eagerness of her parents, and then the angry perplexity that had followed. The family was big — six children then, before Arthur died at ten — and half an hour after they had moved in the house was crowded and shabby. And she remembered being frightened at something and her father picking her up right in the middle of moving, and not asking her why she cried — her mother had always asked her that, as if there were a reason — but rocked her and comforted her with his rough hands. And she could remember how the house had looked so well: the ballooning curtains in the windows, the first things her mother had put up. The gusty spring air, already too warm, smelling of good earth and the Eden River not too far behind them, and leaves, sunlight, wind; and the sagging porch piled with cartons and bundles and pieces of furniture from the old house. In that old dark house in the city, the grandparents had died — her mother's parents — and Helen did not remember them at all except as her father summoned them back, recalling with hatred his wife's father — some little confused argument they had had years ago, that he should have won. That old man had died and the house had gone to the bank some- where mysterious, and her father had brought them all out here to the country. A new world, a new life. A farm. And four boys to help, and the promise of such good soil . . .

Her father turned the wheel sharply. "Rabbit run acrost," he said. He had this strange air of apology for whatever he did, even if it was something gentle; he hated to kill animals, even weasels and hawks. Helen wanted to cover his right hand with hers, that thickened, dirt-creased hand that could never be made clean. But she said, stirring a little as if he had woken her, "Then why didn't Ma want to come?"

They were taking a long, slow curve. Helen knew without look- ing up which curve this was, between two wheat fields that belonged to one of the old, old families, those prosperous men who drove broken-down pickup trucks and dressed no better than their own hired hands, but who had money, much money, not just in one bank but in many. "Yes, they're money people," Helen remem- bered her father saying, years ago. Passing someone's pasture. Those ugly red cows meant nothing to Helen, but they meant something to her father. And so after her father had said that — they had been out for a drive after church — her mother got sharp and impatient and the ride was ruined. That was years ago, Helen's father had been a young man then, with a raw, waiting, untested look, with muscular arms and shoulders that needed only to be directed to their work. "They're money people," he had said, and that had ruined the ride, as if by magic. It had been as if the air itself had changed, the direction of the wind changing and easing to them from the river that was often stagnant in Au- gust and September, and not from the green land. With an effort, Helen remembered that she had been thinking about her mother. Why did her mind push her into the past so often these days, she only twenty-two (that was not old, not really) and going to begin a new life? Once she got home and took a bath and washed out the things in the suitcase, and got some rest, and took a walk down by the river as she had as a child, skipping stones across it, and sat around the round kitchen table with the old oil cloth cover to listen to their advice ("You got to grow up, now. You ain't fif- teen anymore" — that had been her mother, last time), then she

would decide what to do. Make her decision about her husband
and the baby and there would be nothing left to think about.

"Why didn't Ma come?"

"I didn't want her to," he said.

Helen swallowed, without meaning to. His shoulder was thin
and hard against the side of her face. Were those same muscles
still there, or had they become worn away like the soil that was
sucked down into the river every year, stolen from them, so that
the farm Helen's father had bought turned out to be a kind of
joke on him? Or were they a different kind of muscle, hard and
compressed like steel, drawn into themselves from years of resist-
ing violence?

"How come?" Helen said.

He did not answer. She shut her eyes tight and distracting, eerie
images came to her, stars exploding and shadowy figures like those
in movies — she had gone to the movies all the time in the city,
often taking in the first show at eleven in the morning; not because she was lonely or had nothing to do but because she liked
movies. Five-twenty and he would come up the stairs, grimacing
a little with the strange inexplicable pain in his chest: and there
Helen would be, back from downtown, dressed up and her hair
shining and her face ripe and fresh as a child's, not because she
was proud of the look in his eyes but because she knew she could
make that pain of his abate for a while. And so why had she left
him, when he had needed her more than anyone? "Pa, is something wrong?" she said, as if the recollection of that other man's
invisible pain were in some way connected with her father.

He reached down vaguely and touched her hand. She was surprised at this. The movie images vanished — those beautiful people she had wanted to believe in, as she had wanted to believe in
God and the saints in their movie-world heaven — and she opened
her eyes. The sun was bright. It had been too bright all summer.
Helen's mind felt sharp and nervous as if pricked by tiny needles, but when she tried to think of what they could be no explanation came to her. She would be home soon, she would be able
to rest. Tomorrow she could get in touch with Paul. Things could
begin where they had left off — Paul had always loved her so
much, and he had always understood her, had known what she
was like. "Ma isn't sick, is she?" Helen said suddenly. "No," said

her father. He released her fingers to take hold of the steering wheel again. Another curve. Off to the side, if she bothered to look, the river had swung toward them — low at this time of year, covered in places with a fine brown-green layer of scum. She did not bother to look.

"We moved out here seventeen years ago," her father said. He cleared his throat: the gesture of a man unaccustomed to speech. "You don't remember that."

"Yes, I do," Helen said. "I remember that."

"You don't, you were just a baby."

"Pa, I remember it. I remember you carrying the big rug in the house, you and Eddie. And I started to cry and you picked me up. I was such a big baby, always crying . . . And Ma came out and chased me inside so I wouldn't bother you."

"You don't remember that," her father said. He was driving jerkily, pressing down on the gas pedal and then letting it up, as if new thoughts continually struck him. What was wrong with him? Helen had an idea she didn't like: he was older now, he was going to become an old man.

If she had been afraid of the dark, upstairs in that big old farmhouse in the room she shared with her sister, all she had had to do was to think of him. He had a way of sitting at the supper table that was so still, so silent, that you knew nothing could budge him. Nothing could frighten him. So, as a child, and even now that she was grown up, it helped her to think of her father's face — those pale surprised green eyes that could be simple or cunning, depending upon the light, and the lines working themselves in deeper every year around his mouth, and the hard angle of his jaw going back to the ear, burned by the sun and then tanned by it, turned into leather, then going pale again in the winter. The sun could not burn its color deep enough into that skin, which was almost as fair as Helen's. At Sunday school she and the other children had been told to think of Christ when they were afraid, but the Christ she saw on the little Bible bookmark cards and calendars was no one to protect you. That was a man who would be your cousin, maybe, some cousin you liked but saw rarely, but he looked so given over to thinking and trusting that he could not be of much help; not like her father. When he and the boys

came in from the fields with the sweat drenching their clothes
and their faces looking as if they were dissolving with heat, you
could still see the solid flesh beneath, the skeleton that hung onto
its muscles and would never get old, never die. The boys — her
brothers, all older — had liked her well enough, Helen being the
baby, and her sister had watched her most of the time, and her
mother had liked her too — or did her mother like anyone, having been brought up by German-speaking parents who had had no
time to teach her love? But it had always been her father she had
run to. She had started knowing men by knowing him. She could
read things in his face that taught her about the faces of other
men, the slowness or quickness of their thoughts, if they were beginning to be impatient, or were pleased and didn't want to show
it yet. Was it for this she had come home? — And the thought surprised her so that she sat up, because she did not understand. Was
it for this she had come home? "Pa," she said, "like I told you on
the telephone, I don't know why I did it. I don't know why I
went. That's all right, isn't it? I mean, I'm sorry for it, isn't that
enough? Did you talk to Paul?"

"Paul? Why Paul?"

"What?"

"You haven't asked about him until now, so why now?"

"What do you mean? He's my husband, isn't he? Did you talk
to him?"

"He came over to the house almost every night for two weeks.
Three weeks," he said. Helen could not understand the queer
chatty tone of his voice. "Then off and on, all the time. No, I
didn't tell him you were coming."

"But why not?" Helen laughed nervously. "Don't you like him?"

"You know I like him. You know that. But if I told him he'd of
gone down to get you, not me."

"Not if I said it was you I wanted . . ."

"I didn't want him to know. Your mother doesn't know either."

"What? You mean you didn't tell her?" Helen looked at the
side of his face. It was rigid and bloodless behind the tan, as if
something inside were shrinking away and leaving just his voice.
"You mean you didn't even tell Ma? She doesn't know I'm coming?"

"No."

The nervous prickling in her brain returned suddenly. Helen rubbed her forehead.

"Pa," she said gently, "why didn't you tell anybody? You're ashamed of me, huh?"

He drove on slowly. They were following the bends of the river, that wide shallow meandering river the boys said wasn't worth fishing in any longer. One of its tributaries branched out suddenly — Mud Creek, it was called, all mud and bullfrogs and dragonflies and weeds — and they drove over it on a rickety wooden bridge that thumped beneath them. "Pa," Helen said carefully, "you said you weren't mad, on the phone. And I wrote you that letter explaining. I wanted to write some more, but you know . . . I don't write much, never even wrote to Annie when she moved away. I never forgot about you or anything, or Ma . . . I thought about the baby, too, and Paul, but Paul could always take care of himself. He's smart. He really is. I was in the store with him one time and he was arguing with some salesmen and got the best of them; he never learned all that from his father. The whole family is smart, though, aren't they?"

"The Hendriks? Sure. You don't get money without brains."

"Yes, and they got money too, Paul never had to worry. In a house like his parents' house nothing gets lost or broken. You know? It isn't like it was at ours, when we were all kids. That's part of it — when Paul's father built us our house I was real pleased and real happy, but then something of them came in with it too. Everything is spost to be clean and put in its place, and after you have a baby you get so tired . . . but his mother was always real nice to me. I don't complain about them. I like them all real well."

"Money people always act nice," her father said. "Why shouldn't they?"

"Oh, Pa!" Helen said, tapping at his arm. "What do you mean by that? You always been nicer than anybody I know, that's the truth. Real nice. A lot of them with those big farms, like Paul's father, and that tractor store they got — they complain a lot. They do. You just don't hear about it. And when that baby got polio, over in the Rapids — that real big farm, you know what I mean?

— the McGuires. How do you think they felt? They got troubles just like everybody else."

Then her father did a strange thing: here they were seven or eight miles from home, no house near, and he stopped the car. "Want to rest for a minute," he said. Yet he kept staring out the windshield as if he were still driving.

"What's wrong?"

"Sun on the hood of the car . . ."

Helen tugged at the collar of her dress, pulling it away from her damp neck. When had the heat ever bothered her father before? She remembered going out to the farthest field with water for him, before he had given up that part of the farm. And he would take the jug from her and lift it to his lips and it would seem to Helen, the sweet child Helen standing in the dusty corn, that the water flowed into her magnificent father and enlivened him as if it were secret blood of her own she had given him. And his chest would swell, his reddened arms eager with muscle emerging out from his rolled-up sleeves, and his eyes now wiped of sweat and exhaustion. . . . The vision pleased and confused her, for what had it to do with the man now beside her? She stared at him and saw that his nose was queerly white and that there were many tiny red veins about it, hardly more than pen lines; and his hair was thinning and jagged, growing back stiffly from his forehead as if he had brushed it back impatiently with his hand once too often. When Eddie, the oldest boy, moved away now and lost to them, had pushed their father hard in the chest and knocked him back against the supper table, that same amazed white look had come to his face, starting at his nose.

"I was thinking if, if we got home now, I could help Ma with supper," Helen said. She touched her father's arm as if to waken him. "It's real hot, she'd like some help."

"She doesn't know you're coming."

"But I . . . I could help anyway." She tried to smile, watching his face for a hint of something: many times in the past he had looked stern but could be made to break into a smile, finally, if she teased him long enough. "But didn't Ma hear you talk on the phone? Wasn't she there?"

"She was there."

"Well, but then . . ."

"I told her you just talked. Never said nothing about coming home."

The heat had begun to make Helen dizzy. Her father opened the door on his side. "Let's get out for a minute, go down by the river," he said. Helen slid across and got out. The ground felt uncertain beneath her feet. Her father was walking and saying something and she had to run to catch up with him. He said: "We moved out here seventeen years ago. There were six of us then, but you don't remember. Then the boy died. And you don't remember your mother's parents and their house, that goddam stinking house, and how I did all the work for him in his store. You remember the store down front? The dirty sawdust floor and the old women coming in for sausage, enough to make you want to puke, and pig's feet and brains out of cows or guts or what the hell they were that people ate in that neighborhood. I could puke for all my life and not get clean of it. You just got born then. And we were dirt to your mother's people, just dirt. I was dirt. And when they died somebody else got the house, it was all owned by somebody else, and so we said how it was for the best and we'd come out here and start all over. You don't remember it or know nothing about us."

"What's wrong, Pa?" Helen said. She took his arm as they descended the weedy bank. "You talk so funny, did you get something to drink before you came to the bus station? You never said these things before. I thought it wasn't just meat, but a grocery store, like the one in . . ."

"And we came out here," he said loudly, interrupting her, "and bought that son of a bitch of a house with the roof half rotted through and the well all shot to hell . . . and those bastards never looked at us, never believed we were real people. The Hendrikses too. They were like all of them. They looked through me in town, do you know that? Like you look through a window. They didn't see me. It was because hillbilly families were in that house, came and went, pulled out in the middle of the night owing everybody money; they all thought we were like that. I said, we were poor but we weren't hillbillies. I said, do I talk like a hillbilly? We come from the city. But nobody gave a damn. You could go up to them and shout in their faces and they wouldn't hear you, not even when they started losing money themselves. I prayed to God during them bad times that they'd all lose what they had, every bastard one of them, that Swede with the fancy cattle most of all! I prayed to God to bring them down to me so they could see me, my children as good as theirs, and me a harder worker than any of them — if you work till you feel like dying you done the best you can do, whatever money you get. I'd of told them that. I wanted to come into their world even if I had to be on the bottom of it, just so long as they gave me a name . . ."

"Pa, you been drinking," Helen said softly.

"I had it all fixed, what I'd tell them," he said. They were down by the river bank now. Fishermen had cleared a little area and stuck Y-shaped branches into the dried mud, to rest their poles on. Helen's father prodded one of the little sticks with his foot and then did something Helen had never seen anyone do in her life, not even boys — he brought his foot down on it and smashed it.

"You oughtn't of done that," Helen said. "Why'd you do that?"

"And I kept on and on; it was seventeen years. I never talked about it to anyone. Your mother and me never had much to say, you know that. She was like her father. — You remember that first day? It was spring, nice and warm, and the wind came along when we were moving the stuff in and was so different from that smell in the city — my God! It was a whole new world here."

"I remember it," Helen said. She was staring out at the shallow muddy river. Across the way birds were sunning themselves stupidly on flat, white rocks covered with dried moss like veils.

"You don't remember nothing!" her father said angrily. "Nothing! You were the only one of them I loved, because you didn't remember. It was all for you. First I did it for me, myself, to show that bastard father of hers that was dead — then those other bastards, those big farms around us — but then for you, for you. You were the baby. I said to God that when you grew up it'd be you in one of them big houses with everything fixed and painted all the time, and new machinery, and driving around in a nice car not this thing we got. I said I would do that for you or die."

"That's real nice, Pa," Helen said nervously, "but I never . . . I never knew nothing about it, or . . . I was happy enough any way I was. I liked it at home, I got along with Ma better than anybody did. And I liked Paul too, I didn't marry him just because you

told me to. I mean, you never pushed me around. I wanted to
marry him all by myself, because he loved me. I was always happy,
Pa. If Paul didn't have the store coming to him, and that land
and all, I'd have married him anyway — You oughtn't to worked
all that hard for me."

In spite of the heat she felt suddenly chilled. On either side of
them tall grass shrank back from the cleared, patted area, stiff
and dried with August heat. These weeds gathered upon themselves in a brittle tumult back where the vines and foliage of trees
began, the weeds dead and whitened and the vines a glossy, rich
green, as if sucking life out of the water into which they drooped.
All along the river bank trees and bushes leaned out and showed
a yard or two of dead, whitish brown where the waterline had once
been. This river bent so often you could never see far along it.
Only a mile or so. Then foliage began, confused and unmoving.
What were they doing here, she and her father? A thought came to
Helen and frightened her — she was not used to thinking — that
they ought not to be here, that this was some other kind of slow,
patient world where time didn't care at all for her or her girl's
face or her generosity of love, but would push right past her and go
on to touch the faces of other people.

"Pa, let's go home. Let's go home," she said.

Her father bent and put his hands into the river. He brought
them dripping to his face. "That's dirty there, Pa," she said. A
mad dry buzzing started up somewhere — hornets or wasps. Helen
looked around but saw nothing.

"God listened and didn't say yes or no," her father said. He was
squatting at the river and now looked back at her, his chin creas-
ing. The back of his shirt was wet. "If I could read him right it
was something like this — that I was caught in myself and them
money people caught in themselves and God Himself caught in
what he was and so couldn't be anything else. Then I never thought
about God again."

"I think about God," Helen said. "I do. People should think
about God then they wouldn't have wars and things . . ."

"No, I never bothered about God again," he said slowly. "If he
was up there or not it never had nothing to do with me. A hail-
storm that knocked down the wheat, or a drought — what the
hell? Whose fault? It wasn't God's no more than mine so I let

him out of it. I knew I was in it all on my own. Then after a while
it got better, year by year. We paid off the farm and the new machines. You were in school then, in town. And when we went into
the church they said hello to us sometimes, because we outlasted
them hillbillies by ten years. And now Mike ain't doing bad on his
own place, got a nice car, and me and Bill get enough out of the
farm so it ain't too bad, I mean it ain't too bad. But it wasn't money
I wanted!"

He was staring at her. She saw something in his face that mixed
with the buzzing of the hornets and fascinated her so that she
could not move, could not even try to tease him into smiling too.
"It wasn't never money I wanted," he said.

"Pa, why don't we go home?"

"I don't know what it was, exactly," he said, still squatting. His
hands touched the ground idly. "I tried to think of it, last night
when you called and all night long and driving in to town, today.
I tried to think of it."

"I guess I'm awful tired from that bus. I . . . I don't feel good,"
Helen said.

"Why did you leave with that man?"

"What? Oh," she said, touching the tip of one of the weeds, "I
met him at Paul's cousin's place, where they got that real nice tavern and a dance hall . . ."

"Why did you run away with him?"

"I don't know, I told you in the letter. I wrote it to you, Pa. He
acted so nice and liked me so, he still does, he loves me so much
. . . And he was always so sad and tired, he made me think of
. . . you, Pa . . . but not really, because he's not strong like you
and couldn't ever do work like you. And if he loved me that much
I had to go with him."

"Then why did you come back?"

"Come back?" Helen tried to smile out across the water. Slug-
gish, ugly water, this river that disappointed everyone, so familiar
to her that she could not really get used to a house without a river
or a creek somewhere behind it, flowing along night and day: perhaps that was what she had missed in the city?

"I came back because . . . because . . ."

And she shredded the weed in her cold fingers, but no words
came to her. She watched them fall. No words came to her, her

mind had turned hollow and cold, she had come too far down to this river bank but it was not a mistake any more than the way the river kept moving was a mistake; it just happened.

Her father got slowly to his feet and she saw in his hand a knife she had been seeing all her life. Her eyes seized upon it and her mind tried to remember: where had she seen it last, whose was it, her father's or her brother's? He came to her and touched her shoulder as if waking her, and they looked at each other, Helen so terrified by now that she was no longer afraid but only curious with the mute marble-like curiosity of a child, and her father stern and silent until a rush of hatred transformed his face into a mass of wrinkles, the skin mottled red and white. He did not raise the knife but slammed it into her chest, up to the hilt, so that his whitened fist struck her body and her blood exploded out upon it.

Afterward, he washed the knife in the dirty water and put it away. He squatted and looked out over the river, then his thighs began to ache and he sat on the ground, a few feet from her body. He sat there for hours as if waiting for some idea to come to him. Then the water began to darken, very slowly, and the sky darkened a little while later, as if belonging to another, separate time, the same thing as always, and he had to turn his mind with an effort to the next thing he must do.

# NANCY PELLETIER PANSING

## The Visitation

(FROM INTRO #1)

FOR FOUR DAYS the letter lay unnoticed on the hall floor. It lay there mixed with magazines and circulars and bills, all of which had been slipped through the mail slot to come sliding on to the worn, oriental runner where they fell in disarray. Mrs. McClure never even noticed them, and of course it was not Colonel McClure's chore to gather in the mail. It was unfortunate that the letter had been delivered on Saturday, because weekends were usually the worst. Since the yardman came on Tuesday, Mrs. McClure tried to pull herself together to be able to deal with him. Sometimes the Colonel was able; sometimes he wasn't.

Now the back doorbell was ringing, and Hazel McClure knew that the yardman was here and that it was Tuesday morning. Pulling herself up from the couch, she fumbled at the front of her cotton robe and pulled it together. She looked at the desk clock to see what time it was, but her vision was blurry and she couldn't focus. Her head throbbed and she felt nauseated. The television was still on, slipping dizzily. As she stooped to switch it off, she lurched into the set and then caught herself against it.

The doorbell sounded again.

"I'm coming, I'm coming," she muttered, and her voice sounded strange to her own ears. She had heard no voices but those on television for some time. She glimpsed herself quickly in the hall mirror, and saw only her disheveled, short gray hair and her blurred, red face. After sliding the door chain and holding the Yale lock, she managed to open the door.

"Mrs. McClure, ma'am, it's me, Henry. Just wanted you all to know ah was here. Guess ah'll start by mowin' the yard. If there's anything extra you wants done, you all can tell me later."

"Yes, yes, Henry. All right, glad you're here. Just woke up."

She tried to distinguish Henry's black features, but he only looked dark and shadowy in the dimness of the back porch. Narrowing her eyes, she squinted after him as he walked down the steps. Yes, it was a bright day, sunshiny. She wished she felt better. Coffee. That's what she needed. Coffee. And while she was about it she would make some tea for the Colonel.

Turning into the kitchen, she hit her hip painfully against the breakfast table. She reached for the coffeepot which sat on the small gas range, looked inside it only to find the greasy remains of the last pot of coffee. She couldn't remember when she had made it. Friday morning? Oh, well. The problem now was to wash out the grounds and rinse the pot and measure new. Leaning on the sink, she rested her head on the cool enamel cabinet above. It was such an effort. Maybe if she just had a little drink, she could cope. Just a half a juice glass full would steady her hands, and get at the pain in her head. Then she could make the coffee and the tea and maybe even fix some bacon and eggs. This afternoon she would go out in the yard and work with Henry. Letting the coffeepot fall with a rattling clatter into the sink, she opened the left-hand lower cupboard hurriedly. Vodka. There was no vodka, only a bottle of vermouth and an old vinegary bottle of Chianti. Mrs. McClure's hands shook with fear and apprehension. There had been some there. Now where could it be? The living room?

Lurching anxiously, she returned to the living room. With the shades drawn and the draperies pulled, it could have been night. In the faint light that came from the kitchen, she could distinguish the rumpled couch where she had slept and the coffee table with a welter of magazines and glasses. Sitting on the couch heavily, she checked through the glasses for any remnants, just a taste. The first two glasses were completely dry, but the third and fourth each had a swallow. At least she had never diluted her liquor with ice. Whatever she found would be pure vodka. She swallowed the liquid quickly, careful to hold the glass with both shaking hands so as not to spill. Such a little bit, but it was better than nothing. The hot, stinging flavor cut through the fuzzy, dried-out feel of her mouth, and she savored it. She could feel the little trickle of warmth slide down her throat, feel it open up her stomach. She sighed. Getting up from her couch, she opened the front drape and raised the blind a careful twelve inches. The bright sun penetrated the room slowly and reluctantly. As she accustomed her eyes to the light, she looked for a bottle. Beside the couch? Behind it? On the TV? There wasn't one. Maybe there would be a bottle in the bedroom. Besides, she should check on the Colonel.

This time she walked with more assurance through the front hall, stepped over the mail, went past the bathroom to the bedroom. Her chest still felt warm and reassured. As she opened the bedroom door, she wrinkled her nose in disgust. The strong, stale odor of cigarette smoke hung in the gray-blue air. Hazel wished that the Colonel wasn't such a heavy smoker. From the bed she heard the deep snoring, the heavy breathing. He would be hard to wake this morning. Again she raised a shade. The air conditioner hummed steadily, and she shivered from its chill, unreal air. With a start of pleasure she saw a not quite empty bottle of vodka on the bedside table. Hurrying toward it, she half stumbled over the corner of the bed, reached for the bottle, unscrewed the top, tilted her head back and drank the clear liquid in a long, smooth gulp. Her eyes watered; her throat burned, and she coughed. In the bed Colonel McClure whinnied softly at the disturbance.

She lay down on the bed beside him and curled her body contentedly around him. There wasn't anything that she had to do, and he was sleeping so soundly that it was a shame to wake him. Just a short nap, that's all she'd take, and then she'd make breakfast.

Hazel didn't know how long she'd been there or what time it was. Outside she could hear the whirr of the gasoline mower so she knew that Henry was still working. Focusing as hard as she could, she saw that the little electric clock by the bed said 11:30. On the floor was the empty bottle. Beside her the Colonel still snored.

"Colonel. Randolph." She shook him gently. "It's Tuesday. Henry's here. Colonel."

He stirred and reached past her for a cigarette. His eyes were still tightly closed.

"Randolph, I was just thinking about making you some tea. Would you like that?"

With a sudden snort, he raised up, opened heavy, bloodshot eyes and looked at her.

"What, what? Tuesday? Tea? What the devil are you talking about?"

His gray hair was rumpled, and his yellow-gray mustache needed washing and trimming. Hazel thought that he looked bad, and for a fleeting moment she was concerned. Struggling up from the bed, she started out to the kitchen once more.

"One of us is going to have to go to the liquor store today," she called back. And it was just then that she saw and recognized the mail.

Hazel squatted down on her haunches and sorted through it. She muttered to herself about the junk mail, tossed aside a copy of *Gourmet,* picked out the bill from Dr. Hillman (that would be for the iron shots), the one from Halsey's grocery (they were expensive but they did deliver), the one from the wine shop (sometimes it was easier to have a bit of wine or beer delivered than to go out and get it). There was a circular from St. James Episcopal Church. One of these days they would go. And there was the letter, a personal letter. She squinted closely at the return address, but she'd have to have her glasses to read it. After groping around in the murkiness of the hall closet, she found her purse where she was always careful to hide it, and then, inside her purse, her glasses. She took the glasses and the letter into the kitchen.

With great exactitude, like a child with a new task, she measured the water, fitted in the stem, the basket, measured the coffee, one, two, three, four, and one for the pot, put on the basket lid, the top. She turned on the front right burner and set the pot on the blue flame. Reaching to the back of the stove, she picked up the tarnished tea kettle, shook it, found that it had water already in it. She lit the back left burner for the kettle. With satisfaction she watched the two busy fires and listened to the spitting crackle of the flame hitting the water drops on the coffeepot. Inspired by her industry, she took a small package of bacon from the refrigerator, two eggs, a dab of margarine. Then she saw the letter again lying on the breakfast table.

"Who in the world would be writing to me?" she mused. Her

head had begun to ache again, and the heat of the stove with the heat of the outdoors that came from the open back door oppressed her. Fitting the dark-rimmed glasses on, she looked closely at the envelope.

"Summit, New Jersey. Mrs. Donald L. Wyman. I can't imagine."

Slowly she tore the letter open. An edge of the envelope cut her forefinger, and she swore under her breath. She read dully. The coffee began to perk. She reread. The tea kettle whistled, and she got up to turn it off.

"Oh, dear God, what will we do? What will we do?" She began to cry haltingly, ponderously. She sat down at the breakfast table and put her head down until the tears stopped. Unwittingly she had crumpled the letter in her hand. Now she smoothed it out and read it again.

*July 19, 1967*

MY DEAR COLONEL AND MRS. MC CLURE,

*It has been such a long time since I have seen you both. Of course we keep up with our Christmas cards, although I didn't hear from you this past Christmas at all. I do hope that you are both well.*

*Don and I have been transferred from Chicago to the New York office and have bought a home here in Summit. Now that we are fairly well settled, we have planned a vacation to Virginia Beach. We realized that our trip would bring us near Richmond, and we would love to stop to see you. It would only be for an afternoon, just a short visit. We will be passing through Richmond on the 27th of July. I do hope this isn't too short notice. Please don't hesitate to write me if it is not convenient.*

*The children—Don, Jr., is seven now and Ben is five—will be along and I can't wait to have you meet them. I think of you both so often and remember how wonderful and good you were to me.*

*I am keeping my fingers crossed that everything will work out and that we will be able to see each other. My dearest love to you both.*

EMILY

Emily. The name echoed and reechoed in her throbbing head. With the name came a flood of memories, pictures, happinesses that seemed now to belong to someone else. Army bases, an officers' club, parties and flowers and silver and laughter, Emily golden and smiling. And Randy. Her heart lurched, stopped, started to beat painfully. Randy, her son, the Colonel's son, their son. Randy who was lean and suntanned and loving. Randy, who loved them and who loved Emily. Everything had been so good, so right, so complete. Already Hazel was envisioning grandchildren, and knitting sweaters and smocking dresses. Randy and Emily would have beautiful children, bright children. They would have many because they wanted them. That was the fashion now — big families. She and Randolph had had only Randy. That was the fashion then, in the lean thirties. She was sorry now that there had been no more, but so be it. Randy was all that they could have expected. It hadn't been easy moving from base to base, never settled, always new schools and a new climate. And there had been the war years when the Colonel had been in Europe and she and Randy had been in the States. But they had managed, and the years had been good, and Randy had grown and thrived, and they were happy.

Emily. She had loved Emily because she was exactly right for Randy. There was an old-fashioned tenderness about the girl, an involvement with people that was refreshing in a person so young. She was almost ashamed to think the thoughts that she did of Emily swollen with child — her grandchild. Maybe there would be girls now in the McClure family.

But that was all a long time ago, and this letter was from that same Emily, that sweet girl who was now a woman and who was — she turned the envelope over — Mrs. Donald L. Wyman. And there was no Randy, no Mrs. Randolph McClure, Jr., anywhere, and there never would be. For a minute she hated Emily for reminding her. And there were no grandchildren and no hand-knit sweaters or smocked dresses. There was only Mrs. Wyman and a husband and their two little boys. And, God help them all, there was only Hazel and Randolph McClure here in this stifling little house in Richmond, Virginia, in this hot kitchen with the nauseating odor of strong, over-perked coffee. Mrs. McClure gagged, held her hand over her mouth, and ran for the sink. Retching and vomiting painfully, she clutched the sink with white-knuckled hands. When she was finished, she drank a glass of water, blew her nose. Her eyes watered, and her stomach ached.

She would have to get a letter off right away to Emily to say that she and the Colonel were both ill and unable to see her and her family. No, she'd say that they were going to be out of the city at that time. Then a sharp fear pierced her clouded mind. How long had the letter been in the hall? What day was it? She picked up the letter from the table and checked the postmark — July 20th — and today was — she stumbled to the wall calendar — Tuesday, July 25th. Frantically she looked again at the letter. "We will be passing through Richmond on the 27th of July." That was Thursday. Oh, God. That was day after tomorrow. She couldn't do it; she just couldn't. The house was a mess. Every other Friday there was Lottie who came in to clean, and she was due this Friday but that would be too late. Lottie was booked solidly doing day work. She could never get her on Wednesday or even on Thursday. She and the Colonel would just leave home for the day. No. That wasn't right. Where could they go? She could call her, but how explain calling so late? She just couldn't cope with a conversation yet. A wire? How would she know for sure Emily had gotten it?

"Help me, please, God, help me."

But there was no help, no answer to her dilemma. She'd have to manage, have to pull herself and the Colonel together, have to straighten the house. Maybe she could do it. There could be no vodka for either of them for two days. Well, maybe just a little. She'd have to manage that, too. From somewhere inside came the stirrings of purpose. Fumblingly she got out a tea bag, two cups. She poured herself a cup of the bitter coffee and brewed a cup of tea for the Colonel. She could get him up, get him into the kitchen instead of taking it to him in bed. Somehow she would get through to him. He had always loved Emily, too. Her head was beginning to ache again.

The Colonel snorted at being aroused, but he was obedient when he realized that his wife meant business.

"I said, Randolph, Emily is coming for a visit. Please, do you understand? I need your help. Randolph!" she shouted at him.

"All right, all right," he groused pulling himself up on his elbows. Even Hazel could smell the sourness of his breath as he swore. "My God, my head. How about a Bloody Mary? Would that help?"

"Absolutely nothing, Randolph. Do you understand what I

said? The day after tomorrow Emily, Randy's fiancée, is coming for a visit. We have to get ready."

This time he understood. The puffy eyes opened slowly, and his hand went automatically to the unkempt mustache.

"Emily? Oh, no, you can't mean it. When?"

"Day after tomorrow. Thursday."

"This is Tuesday?"

"It is."

"Lord help us. I feel wretched, absolutely wretched."

"Well, so do I. But, Randolph, we positively cannot have another drink while we get ready."

With a great effort Hazel helped him extricate himself from the limp, soiled sheets. Once they both fell backward onto the bed, but Hazel tugged and pulled until they were both standing. Walking to the door, the Colonel leaned against the door jamb.

"You'll have to help me, my dear," he muttered, and Hazel was startled by her protectiveness. He was so old, so feeble, and he didn't eat properly. She took hold of him by his armpit and his elbow and guided him down the hall and into the kitchen. They fell against the table, but Hazel caught them both and then seated him. Both were breathing heavily. She sugared his tea for him and set it in front of him. Opening a cupboard door, she took out a bottle of aspirin and measured out three for him, three for herself. Taking out another bottle, this time tranquilizers, she measured out two, one for her, one for him.

"Here, take these. And drink your tea. It's a start. There's Emily's letter. Do you want me to read it to you?"

He nodded, and she began to read in a cracked, husky voice. When she had finished, she looked up. The Colonel sat stooped and still while two lines of tears slid from his rheumy eyes into his mustache.

"We'll never be able to carry it off," he hiccupped.

For a moment Hazel put her head down on the table. It was too much. They were too far gone to rally now. But Emily was coming. There was no getting around it. She remembered young Randy laughing and hugging her and saying, "What a mother! Hazel can do anything when she sets her mind to it!" When had he said it and why? Was it when he brought the two roommates home from college without telling her? Or the time that the flowers weren't de-

livered for the engagement party, and she made the table arrangements from unbudded forsythia and pussy willows? Or was it when
she had the going-away party for him after he was drafted? It
didn't matter now. Emily was coming to visit her and the Colonel,
and they had to receive her — for Randy.

"Colonel," she whispered as she got up and walked around to
him. "Colonel, we'll do it. We have to."

There were moments when she doubted, when she gave up completely. The vacuum cleaner was stubbornly complicated, and the
nozzle would not stay on. She couldn't find clean sheets for the
bed. There was so much trash that needed carrying out. Frantically she pressed Henry into service.

"Henry, you hurry up with that yard and come help me in the
house. I can't work the vacuum, and there's this trash. And I want
you to neaten up this back porch. It's a sight."

"Yes, ma'am!"

As her brain cleared, she realized that she was not clean. If she
was not, then the Colonel wasn't either. She would have to help
him bathe. Tomorrow she would clean herself up. The bathroom
was a sight. Towels, sour and mildewed, were tossed on the floor.
There were glasses and two empty bottles on the sink counter. The
toilet needed flushing. First she would clean the bathroom; then
she would bathe the Colonel. Gathering up the soiled rug, the
smelly towels, she carried them to the utility room. She would have
to order some laundry soap. There was none. She could hear the
Colonel retching and gagging. Food. They both must eat. The
bacon was still lying on the counter from her earlier effort. She
dampened a tea towel and took it to the Colonel along with a fresh
cup of tea. With dismay she discovered that he had thrown up
on the bed. Putting him on a chair, she stripped the soiled bed.
Her whole body was trembling. The smell of the vomit made her
gag again. She couldn't be sick — too much to do. No matter
where she went, no matter which room she approached, there was
something pressing at her from another direction. The bacon, the
bathroom, the bottles, the Colonel. Too much. Outside she heard
tires squeal on the curving road in front of their little house. Or-
dinarily she shut out all sounds, but now she thought that on
Thursday tires would squeal and she would see a car drive up the

little gravel driveway and it would be Emily. She had to remember; she could not manage if she forgot.

There was laundry to do. The sheets she would send out, but she had to wash out a blouse for herself and underwear for Randolph. Using hand soap, she made a lather and did her little laundry. She was careful to wash out the sink at the same time. She searched out a handful of clothespins and walked into the glaring afternoon sunlight. With extreme fastidiousness she hung the three dripping pieces on the line. Only once did she sag to her knees. Back in the house, she realized that she was sweating heavily and that her hands trembled. A drink would help. For now it would help, but what about later? She had to be careful. Food. That was the next thing. She lit a fire under the dirty skillet and put in the wet, warm bacon. Again she gagged. They had to eat.

By evening, Hazel was exhausted. Somehow she had managed to feed them and to bathe the Colonel. The bathroom was clean. Most of the bottles had been gathered up and put in the empty trash container in the mop closet. She had been careful to do this after Henry had left. Tomorrow she would do the living room and the kitchen, and she would order supplies. She still wasn't hungry, but she forced herself to open a can of tomato soup and scramble some eggs. Since there was no vodka in the house, she had thought it safest to keep it that way. But she had ordered an eight-pack of beer from the wine shop. The Colonel was watching TV and sipping a beer right now. If his hands could stop shaking, he would look almost like his former self. She would have one careful beer while she was fixing their supper. She sighed heavily. There was one more day; she might pull it off.

Wednesday was hot and humid. If anything, Hazel felt worse. There was still so much to do, and it closed in on her as soon as she wakened. Beside her Randolph snored. Where to begin? Coffee and tea, groceries, the living room, the kitchen. She didn't dare think about it. She pulled herself out of bed. Now it was her whole body that ached. Maybe she had flu. But she had to be honest. The muscles were sore from yesterday's vomiting. She knew the feeling. She set a goal for herself. If she got everything done, she would go to the liquor store. By afternoon she should be well enough to take the car out. Neither of them had drunk anything but that beer for the past twenty-four hours. They would be entitled to a vodka and tonic.

By evening Hazel had accomplished a great deal. The living room was straight and the furniture dusted, the magazines and newspapers sorted through. On the desk Randy's picture smiled securely. In the kitchen Hazel had swept, wiped the counters, and washed the accumulation of dishes and glasses. An order from Halsey's had filled a few of the empty shelves of the refrigerator. There were lettuce and tomatoes and a package of cold cuts and a carton of potato salad. A quart of milk stood by the two remaining beers. The bathroom was clean. Hazel had always liked to clean bathrooms because they showed such a good return for her effort. As yet she hadn't touched the bedroom, but there would be plenty of time in the morning. She made a mental note to put out her best guest towels.

Everything had taken more time than she had anticipated, but considering her headache and the still-present stirrings of nausea, Hazel was proud of her day. The Colonel had been no help, but then she didn't expect him to do much. He never had been a man to help out around the house. That was her job. She was glad that he hadn't nagged for a drink and had been content with a beer for lunch and one during the afternoon. But now they had earned a drink. At the thought, Hazel's heart beat faster. The goal was in sight.

"Colonel," she stated when she had finally found him puttering with the lawn trimmer in the garage, "I think we should have a little something in the house in case Emily or her husband should want a drink. I'll just run down to the liquor store now."

"Fine, my dear. Of course we should. Be sure to get enough. How about groceries? Have you ordered any?"

"A few. Enough, I think."

The trip to the store was harrowing. There was the need to travel over the four-lane expressway, and after that there was the maze of the shopping center. Hazel had taken twenty-five dollars with her. That would be enough for four bottles of vodka and some mix. Pulling up to a parking place near the liquor store, she took a deep breath and then got out of the car into the sweltering July sun. A wave of heat from the pavement assaulted her. Pulling herself up straight, she entered the store. Something about the clerks always put her on the defensive.

"Four bottles of vodka, please, Haller's," she ordered.

When the bottles were sacked, she carried them carefully to the car. After placing them on the back seat, she locked the car and went two doors down to the supermarket. She shivered in the vast, bright, air-conditioned store. There were the mingled smells of coffee, onions, soap. From hidden speakers came the soothing sound of music. What were they playing? It was familiar. She couldn't place the song, but it made her remember — good times, easy and secure, times when marketing was natural and effortless and even exciting. Before Korea, before Heartbreak Ridge. Funny how this was the only name that she could remember out of all those strange, faraway sounds that she and the Colonel had followed with colored pins on the map after Randy had gone to Korea. Once she had known them all, understood the 38th parallel, known the strategy. Then when it was all over, after the telegram had come, then she could think of none of it — only Heartbreak Ridge and that wasn't even the place where her Randy was killed. But she could never forget Randy's dislike of service, of being an army brat, his resolve to be a civilian, his plans for a future of college and maybe teaching. She could never forget that Randy had never got far enough to make a firm decision. After all his resolve against war, she could never forget that the army got him — got him once and for all on a strange battlefield in a strange war that was not a war, in a country that she did not even understand.

Someone bumped her basket, and Hazel realized that she had been standing obliviously in front of the frozen foods. Still heavy with recollection, she moved slowly till she came to the soft drinks and mixes. A carton of tonic water, one eight-pack of beer, a carton of mixed pop for Emily's boys. That should do it. She pushed the cart lethargically to the checkout counter and stood unseeing, moving up with the line. Tomorrow Emily would be here. She mustn't forget.

Home again, Hazel fixed herself and the Colonel a drink. "Just one," she thought, "and then I'll fix supper." The vodka warmed her, encouraged her, steadied her. While the Colonel watched the news on the television, she fixed cold cuts and tomatoes and salad.

She was surprised that her glass emptied so fast. She sweetened it with a dollop from the bottle.

"Careful," she cautioned herself. "Emily is coming."

Together she and the Colonel ate their summer supper in front of the TV.

"My dear, I'm very tired. I believe that in view of tomorrow, I'll make my good-nights and retire." The Colonel bowed slightly toward Hazel. "Tomorrow will be quite a day. I wonder if our Emily has changed. Probably not. She was a beauty."

"Good night, Randolph. I'll just straighten the kitchen and follow you to bed." She watched him shuffle through the hall toward the bedroom.

When the dishes were cleaned, she wanted a drink, a nightcap. Did she dare? Yes, she would make a long drink with ice and tonic, and she would sip it slowly till she slept. And she would take a sleeping pill to be sure. Lying in bed she thought with satisfaction about her accomplishments. Once she had kept a fine house, a house of hospitality and warmth and welcome. Maybe she still could. But it was an effort. Was it old age? Or was it drinking? When had drinking become so important? There had always been plenty of it in the old days — cocktail parties, before dinner drinks, table wine. But it was fun. Was it the Colonel's retirement? Was it the loss of Randy? Perplexing thoughts floated at random through her relaxing mind. When had the evenings become fuzzy? When had the days begun to run together? What could she do now? A hopeful feeling of respectability filled her body. The house was clean. There was food. The grass was cut. Tomorrow there would be company.

Hazel awakened early on Thursday. There was something special she knew, but for a while she drifted heavily. There was still the headache and just an edge of nausea. She was almost hungry this morning — breakfast hungry, bacon-and-egg hungry. Then she remembered that this was Emily's day. Gently, so as not to disturb the Colonel, she swung her feet to the floor. Pulling her robe on, she looked around the bedroom. In the dim light, she saw the confusion of clothes and papers and full wastebaskets. She began to neaten, to hang up clothes, to straighten the dresser tops. There were towels to be got for the bathroom, her blouse to be pressed, coffee and tea to be made.

"I wonder what time she will arrive," Hazel murmured aloud, and, with her arms full of dirty clothes, she hurried to the bathroom. Stopping briefly, she brushed her teeth, splashed water over her face, gathered up some more soiled towels. Once in the kitchen she realized that it was raining, and she was dismayed. Somehow she had expected the day to be brilliant. But there was a coziness about the house. She started a simple breakfast and wakened the Colonel.

Hazel was shaky, and even the tranquilizers couldn't seem to stop the trembling. In the basement she set up the ironing board and heated the iron. The iron felt awkward in her hand. With great care she pressed the collar, then the sleeves, then the body of the blouse. If only the trembling would stop. Once her hand slipped, and the iron burned the inside of her arm viciously. Tears filled her eyes. Just ironing a blouse was a chore — why, once she had ironed all the Colonel's uniform shirts. He had insisted — and now look at her. She hated her ineptness.

When she was finished, she dressed. The Colonel was already dressed and was sitting on the front terrace, and she was proud of him. She chose her skirt, a blue linen, got out a girdle, hose, blue-and-white spectators. Throwing down the dirty cotton robe and the sour nylon nightgown, she stood naked and cool in the bedroom. She looked in the mirror at her body, at the bloated thickness of her abdomen, the sagging breasts. There were bruises, some purple, some red, some fading and yellow, on her arms and her hips and her buttocks. Her face and neck looked flushed and red compared to the gray skin of the rest of her body. Unable to look at herself any longer, she dressed and then ran a brush through her hair. Would the nausea never leave her completely? A drink would settle it. With a sudden movement she gathered up the little pile of soiled clothes and hurried to the kitchen. She took out a juice glass, half filled it with vodka, drained it in one gulp. That was all she would have. She felt the warm relief of the alcohol, the steadiness. Her burn didn't hurt as much now. Her heart beat more slowly. She looked at the clock. 12:30. Any time now. Emily could arrive any time.

By three o'clock Hazel was pacing the floor. Suppose she didn't come. Oh, but she would. Emily was dependable. What if she'd been in a wreck with her husband and her boys? Oh, God, that was unthinkable. What if they came for dinner? She ran to the refrigerator and checked it again. There wasn't enough. But Halsey's would cut her a good thick steak. That was it — a good, big sirloin. And there was the potato salad, and she could make a tossed salad. Maybe she should order bread or rolls, too. The Colonel always said he never wanted his house to be without food and drink for guests. Probably Emily wouldn't stay, but Hazel should be prepared nevertheless. She hurried to the phone and called the grocer. It was almost three-thirty. The Colonel was fussing with a trowel in a pot of straggly geraniums. He had always liked flowers. Now the rain had stopped and a gray and sticky dampness hung in the air accentuating smells of mustiness in the house. Hazel got a room deodorant from under the kitchen sink and sprayed a false pine smell through the kitchen and living room. Furtively she put the spray back, took out the vodka, poured about two inches into the glass, sipped it carefully, then suddenly tossed it off. If only they would arrive. But now she could wait more calmly.

At four o'clock they arrived. Just as Hazel had imagined, car tires squealed in front of the house, and the gravel of their driveway crunched, and car brakes grabbed, and voices spilled out of the car. Hazel ran to the front door calling to the Colonel as she went.

"They're here, Randolph! They're here! Oh, Emily!"

As she watched Emily, still blond but with short hair now, still lithe but with a slightly thicker figure, she was filled with tenderness. Emily would have been her daughter-in-law now, and they would have loved Randy together. How pretty she still was! She held out her arms toward her.

"Oh, Mrs. Mac! How wonderful to be here, to see you!"

For a minute Hazel wondered about her breath. She kissed her cautiously on the cheek.

"And just as wonderful to see you, Emily," Hazel said. "Randolph, doesn't she look young and lovely? Certainly doesn't look like the mother of these two big boys."

Emily turned and put her arms around the Colonel who stood smiling in anticipation. Hazel watched the husband — what was his name? Don — and the two boys walk toward the porch. Randy would have been a much handsomer man. Don was short, a little heavy. And the boys, Emily's sons. They favored their father. Shy, too.

"And you're Don," she called to him. "I met you once a long time ago — soon after you were married. How wonderful of you to take time to see us. And you are Don, Jr., and you must be Ben." Don smiled. "I hope this isn't an imposition. Emily assured us it wasn't. Can't you boys tell Mrs. McClure hello?"

The boys stood sturdy and unyielding. Hazel's head began to ache. Such strange little boys. She stooped down.

"I have some pop in the kitchen. How about it? Wouldn't that taste good now after all the driving?" She stood up dizzily. "Come in, come in, all of you. We'll have a good visit and catch up."

Everyone moved into the tiny hall. Hazel took the Colonel by the arm, and she could feel him trembling. This was all wrong. She wished she had called Emily, made an excuse of some kind.

"The bathroom is there to the right. Come out to the kitchen, boys, when you're through, and pick out what you want to drink."

Hurrying to the kitchen, Hazel reached for her glass, filled it, quaffed it. She leaned against the refrigerator and waited for the strength and the warmth. She took two aspirin. Then she took out ice trays, emptied them into an ice bucket. The boys ran into the kitchen.

"I want cherry, I want cherry," the younger one chanted.

"Orange for me."

"How do you ask?" Hazel reprimanded, annoyed by their demanding whines. "That's right, boys." Don had just come into the room. "Mrs. McClure wants you to be polite."

"Please," they chorused obediently.

"Here, let me help you," Don offered.

She stooped down again to give the glasses to the children. "You smell funny. Yuch."

"Ben!"

Hazel laughed nervously. "That's all right. Maybe it's the vodka. I had a little drink while I was waiting this afternoon. Which reminds me — would you and Emily like a little something refreshing — vodka and tonic?"

While Don checked with his wife and the Colonel, Hazel got

out more glasses. She turned just in time to see the boys opening the mop closet.

"Hey, look," yelled Don. "Look at all the empty — "

"Close that closet door right now," Hazel said venomously. What possessed them to snoop around like that?

The boys hastily closed the closet door and looked back at her with enmity. Everything was wrong. If her head would just stop throbbing; if she just weren't so tired. It must be the humidity.

"A vodka and tonic all the way around, Mrs. Mac," Emily called out. "I'll help you and let the men visit for a bit." She lowered her voice. "The Colonel looks so fragile, is he well? I remember him dapper and gallant. Oh, I hope you are both well." Emily put her arm around Hazel. All Hazel could remember was Ben's comment about how she smelled. She turned away. "We're both just getting older, dear. You know how it is, and of course retirement is hard on all men. The Colonel just doesn't have enough to do, but he's happy. Here's Don's drink. I'll take the Colonel's in." Hazel hoped no one would notice the anticipatory tremble of the Colonel's hand. He hadn't had a drink except his beers for two and a half days. She steadied his hands around the glass and smiled casually at the younger couple. Emily and Don were sitting on the couch, the Colonel in his TV chair. She sat in the little velvet side chair. She heard the kitchen door slam and knew that the boys had gone outside. What could she say?

"You've been transferred, Don?"

"Yes. We like the East a great deal."

"I'm very proud of Don, Mrs. Mac. This move made him the youngest man in the New York office. He's doing very well."

"That's wonderful, Don."

"Yes, yes, fine," mumbled the Colonel who had nearly finished his drink. He wiped his moist mustache with a somewhat steadier hand.

With a sudden stab of horror, Hazel saw an empty bottle neck protruding from the flounce of the couch. How had she missed it? She prayed that no one would notice it. Maybe she could get close enough to kick it all the way under. What was Emily saying?

"I said, are you still active with the garden club? You always had a way with flowers — not only growing them but arranging them."

"Why, no. Not very much. I just haven't gotten too involved here in Richmond. It's sort of a relief after all the social life of the army just to stay unencumbered." She wished she had at least one bowl of flowers here in the living room. She'd meant to fix some, but she'd forgotten. In the garage she could hear a banging sound. What were the boys doing? Didn't anyone else notice it?

"Is anyone ready for another drink?" The Colonel held his glass up and clinked the ice cubes. "My dear, could you freshen mine up?"

Hazel looked at Emily and Don with a questioning smile.

"I don't think so, thank you. I've still quite a bit of driving to do today," replied Don.

"I still have plenty, thank you," Emily answered.

The banging noise had gotten plainer and louder.

"Better check on the boys. Can't ever tell what they'll think up next." Don left the room.

Hazel took the two empty glasses to the kitchen. She poured a half of her highball glass full of vodka, put a jigger and a half in the Colonel's. As she opened up the tonic, she sipped at the straight vodka in her glass, replenished it and topped it off with tonic. After adding the tonic water to the other glass, she squirted in some lemon. She was feeling better. After all, no one would expect a retired couple who never spent any time around children to take young ones in stride immediately.

Returning to the living room with the drinks, she heard Emily exclaim, "You mean you all don't belong to a club or have any friends or go out anywhere? Why, Colonel, that's terrible. I can't imagine you both cut off like that."

What business was it of hers? Hazel was annoyed. If they chose to live a life of seclusion, whose business was it but theirs? Emily had forgotten Randy, but she and the Colonel would never get over it. Let her live her suburban housewife's life with her successful husband and her two children that were someone else's grandchildren. She took a long drink from her glass.

"Here, Randolph. And don't drink this one so fast. Do you want Emily to think you have a drinking problem?"

Her words jarred her ears, and she wished she hadn't said them. Was she imagining or did Emily look at her strangely? She looked down at the foot of the couch to where the bottle had stuck out, but it was gone. She hadn't removed it. Where was it? Maybe Emily or Don had kicked it by mistake. Yes, that was it. The living room seemed warm and close. Hazel wanted to sleep. She wished the company would go. But that wasn't right.

"Oh, by the way, Emily, I have a nice, big steak and all the trimmings, and we'd be delighted if you four would stay for dinner."

"No, no, Mrs. McClure, we wouldn't think of it. I told you that it would be just a short visit, and I meant it."

"Maybe another time, then," Hazel replied with relief.

The room was quiet. Outside she could hear Don laughing at something with his boys. She didn't think that she liked them very much. She took another long drink. Why was it so hard to talk to Emily? She'd changed. It was sad, and she could feel tears springing hot and sudden. Life was never what was expected. Maybe Randy would have married someone else, after all.

"Let's see, Emily, you must be about thirty-four or thirty-five now. Doesn't seem possible."

"No point in trying to fool you, Mrs. Mac. You've known me too long. I'm thirty-six. This summer."

The room was quiet again. Outside it began to rain softly. The back door slammed, and Don and the children came in.

"With this rain and the driving ahead of us, well, I hate to rush you, Emily, but I do think we'd better get going."

Standing slowly to her feet Emily nodded her head yes. She walked over to the Colonel, leaned down and kissed him on his cheek.

"I've enjoyed seeing you, sir. You were always one of my favorite men. Now don't stand up. Well, if you insist, I'll help you." Emily pulled him to his feet, and Don hurried to assist.

"Nice to have seen you again, sir. If you're ever up our way, we'll expect a visit."

The boys walked over, held out pudgy, brown hands, shook the Colonel's trembling, freckled one.

Suddenly Hazel couldn't bear to have them leave. Why, they had hardly discussed anything. What were Emily's interests? What was her house like? What grades were the children in? She stumbled to her feet. Emily walked over quickly and put her arms around Hazel. Hazel's face felt hot and wet.

"Oh, Mrs. Mac, everything changes, doesn't it? I love you and the Colonel. I do. Good-bye."

In a flurry of gathering up and toileting, Emily and her family were in their car. Don pushed all the door locks down proprietorily. Hazel felt excluded, confused. Holding on to the Colonel's arm with one hand, she waved farewell with the other. Everyone waved back to them. Slowly the car crunched down the driveway, tooted twice, and pulled smoothly and finally out to the black-topped street.

Hazel and the Colonel stood a moment in the soft summer rain. In the distance Hazel could hear sounds of traffic, of children's voices. She could smell onions cooking in some neighbor's house. In the twilight the yard looked smooth and vividly green.

"Come on, Randolph. We'd better go in. It was a nice little visit, wasn't it? I have that big steak. I'll fix part of it. And I'll make a salad. But I need a drink first. Let's each have one and we'll talk."

Together they walked to the dark house, and Hazel noticed that the Colonel was crying too.

# SYLVIA PLATH

## Johnny Panic and the Bible of Dreams

(FROM THE ATLANTIC)

EVERY DAY from nine to five I sit at my desk facing the door of the office and type up other people's dreams. Not just dreams. That wouldn't be practical enough for my bosses. I type up also people's daytime complaints: trouble with mother, trouble with father, trouble with the bottle, the bed, the headache that bangs home and blacks out the sweet world for no known reason. Nobody comes to our office unless they have troubles. Troubles that can't be pinpointed by Wassermanns or Wechsler-Bellevues alone.

Maybe a mouse gets to thinking pretty early on how the whole world is run by these enormous feet. Well, from where I sit I figure the world is run by one thing and this one thing only. Panic with a dog-face, devil-face, hag-face, whore-face, panic in capital letters with no face at all — it's the same Johnny Panic, awake or asleep.

When people ask me where I work, I tell them I'm assistant to the secretary in one of the outpatient departments of the Clinics Building of the City Hospital. This sounds so be-all, end-all they seldom get around to asking me more than what I do, and what I do is mainly type up records. On my own hook though, and completely under cover, I am pursuing a vocation that would set these doctors on their ears. In the privacy of my one-room apartment I call myself secretary to none other than Johnny Panic himself.

Dream by dream I am educating myself to become that rare character, rarer, in truth, than any member of the Psychoanalytic Institute: a dream connoisseur. Not a dream-stopper, a dream-explainer, an exploiter of dreams for the crass practical ends of health and happiness, but an unsordid collector of dreams for themselves alone. A lover of dreams for Johnny Panic's sake, the Maker of them all.

There isn't a dream I've typed up in our record books that I don't know by heart. There isn't a dream I haven't copied out at home into Johnny Panic's Bible of Dreams.

This is my real calling.

Some nights I take the elevator up to the roof of my apartment building. Some nights, about 3 A.M. Over the trees at the far side of the Common the United Fund torch flare flattens and recovers under some witchy invisible push, and here and there in the hunks of stone and brick I see a light. Most of all, though, I feel the city sleeping. Sleeping from the river on the west to the ocean on the east, like some rootless island rockabying itself on nothing at all.

I can be tight and nervy as the top string on a violin, and yet by the time the sky begins to blue I'm ready for sleep. It's the thought of all those dreamers and what they're dreaming wears me down till I sleep the sleep of fever. Monday to Friday what do I do but type up those same dreams. Sure, I don't touch a fraction of them the city over, but page by page, dream by dream, my Intake books fatten and weigh down the bookshelves of the cabinet in the narrow passage running parallel to the main hall, off which passage the doors to all the doctors' little interviewing cubicles open.

I've got a funny habit of identifying the people who come in by their dreams. As far as I'm concerned, the dreams single them out more than any Christian name. This one guy, for example, who works for a ball bearing company in town, dreams every night how he's lying on his back with a grain of sand on his chest. Bit by bit this grain of sand grows bigger and bigger till it's big as a fair-sized house and he can't draw breath. Another fellow I know of has had a certain dream ever since they gave him ether and cut out his tonsils and adenoids when he was a kid. In this dream he's caught in the rollers of a cotton mill, fighting for his life. Oh, he's not alone, although he thinks he is. A lot of people these days dream they're being run over or eaten by machines. They're the cagey ones who won't go on the subway or the elevators. Coming back from my lunch hour in the hospital cafeteria I often pass them, puffing up the unswept stone stairs to our office on the fourth floor. I wonder, now and then, what dreams people had before ball bearings and cotton mills were invented.

I've got a dream of my own. My one dream. A dream of dreams.

In this dream there's a great half-transparent lake stretching away in every direction, too big for me to see the shores of it, if there are any shores, and I'm hanging over it looking down from the glass belly of some helicopter. At the bottom of the lake — so deep I can only guess at the dark masses moving and heaving — are the real dragons. The ones that were around before men started living in caves and cooking meat over fires and figuring out the wheel and the alphabet. Enormous isn't the word for them; they've got more wrinkles than Johnny Panic himself. Dream about these long enough, and your feet and hands shrivel away when you look at them too closely; the sun shrinks to the size of an orange, only chillier, and you've been living in Roxbury since the last Ice Age. No place for you but a room padded soft as the first room you knew of, where you can dream and float, float and dream, till at last you actually are back among those great originals and there's no point in any dreams at all.

It's into this lake people's minds run at night, brooks and gutter-trickles to one borderless common reservoir. It bears no resemblance to those pure sparkling blue sources of drinking water the suburbs guard more jealously than the Hope diamond in the middle of pinewoods and barbed fences.

It's the sewage farm of the ages, transparence aside.

Now the water in this lake naturally stinks and smokes from what dreams have been left sogging around in it over the centuries. When you think how much room one night of dream props would take up for one person in one city, and that city a mere pinprick on a map of the world, and when you start multiplying this space by the population of the world, and that space by the number of nights there have been since the apes took to chipping axes out of stone and losing their hair, you have some idea what I mean. I'm not the mathematical type: my head starts splitting when I get only as far as the number of dreams going on during one night in the state of Massachusetts.

By this time, I already see the surface of the lake swarming with snakes, dead bodies puffed as blowfish, human embryos bobbing around in laboratory bottles like so many unfinished messages from the great I Am. I see whole storehouses of hardware: knives, paper cutters, pistons and cobs and nutcrackers; the shiny fronts of cars looming up, glass-eyed and evil-toothed. Then there's the spider-man and the web-footed man from Mars, and the simple, lugubrious vision of a human face turning aside forever, in spite of rings and vows, to the last lover of all.

One of the most frequent shapes in this large stew is so common-place it seems silly to mention it. It's a grain of dirt. The water is thick with these grains. They seep in among everything else and revolve under some queer power of their own, opaque, ubiquitous. Call the water what you will, Lake Nightmare, Bog of Madness, it's here the sleeping people lie and toss together among the props of their worst dreams, one great brotherhood, though each of them, waking, thinks himself singular, utterly apart.

This is my dream. You won't find it written up in any casebook.

Now the routine in our office is very different from the routine in Skin Clinic, for example, or in Tumor. The other clinics have strong similarities to each other; none are like ours. In our clinic, treatment doesn't get prescribed. It is invisible. It goes right on in those little cubicles, each with its desk, its two chairs, its window, and its door with the opaque glass rectangle set in the wood. There is a certain spiritual purity about this kind of doctoring. I can't help feeling the special privilege of my position as assistant secretary in the Adult Psychiatric Clinic. My sense of pride is borne out by the rude invasions of other clinics into our cubicles on certain days of the week for lack of space elsewhere: our building is a very old one, and the facilities have not expanded with the expanding needs of the time. On these days of overlap the contrast between us and the other clinics is marked.

On Tuesdays and Thursdays, for instance, we have lumbar punc-tures in one of our offices in the morning. If the practical nurse chances to leave the door of the cubicle open, as she usually does, I can glimpse the end of the white cot and the dirty yellow-soled bare feet of the patient sticking out from under the sheet. In spite of my distaste at this sight, I can't keep my eyes away from the bare feet, and I find myself glancing back from my typing every few min-utes to see if they are still there, if they have changed their position at all. You can understand what a distraction this is in the middle of my work. I often have to reread what I have typed several times, under the pretense of careful proofreading, in order to memorize the dreams I have copied down from the doctor's voice over the audograph.

Nerve Clinic next door, which tends to the grosser, more unimaginative end of our business, also disturbs us in the mornings. We use their offices for therapy in the afternoon, as they are only a morning clinic, but to have their people crying, or singing, or chattering loudly in Italian or Chinese, as they often do, without break for four hours at a stretch every morning is distracting to say the least. The patients down there are often referred to us if their troubles have no ostensible basis in the body.

In spite of such interruptions by other clinics, my own work is advancing at a great rate. By now I am far beyond copying only what comes after the patient's saying: "I have this dream, Doctor." I am at the point of re-creating dreams that are not even written down at all. Dreams that shadow themselves forth in the vaguest way, but are themselves hid, like a statue under red velvet before the grand unveiling.

To illustrate. This woman came in with her tongue swollen and stuck out so far she had to leave a party she was giving for twenty friends of her French-Canadian mother-in-law and be rushed to our emergency ward. She thought she didn't want her tongue to stick out, and to tell the truth, it was an exceedingly embarrassing affair for her, but she hated that French-Canadian mother-in-law worse than pigs, and her tongue was true to her opinion, even if the rest of her wasn't. Now she didn't lay claim to any dreams. I have only the bare facts above to begin with, yet behind them I detect the bulge and promise of a dream.

So I set myself to uprooting this dream from its comfortable purchase under her tongue.

Whatever the dream I unearth, by work, taxing work, and even by a kind of prayer, I am sure to find a thumbprint in the corner, a bodiless midair Cheshire cat grin, which shows the whole work to be gotten up by the genius of Johnny Panic, and him alone. He's sly, he's subtle, he's sudden as thunder, but he gives himself away only too often. He simply can't resist melodrama. Melodrama of the oldest, most obvious variety.

I remember one guy, a stocky fellow in a nail-studded black

leather jacket, running straight into us from a boxing match at Mechanics Hall, Johnny Panic hot at his heels. This guy, good Catholic though he was, young and upright and all, had one mean fear of death. He was actually scared blue he'd go to hell. He was a pieceworker at a fluorescent light plant. I remember this detail because I thought it funny he should work there, him being so afraid of the dark as it turned out. Johnny Panic injects a poetic element in this business you don't often find elsewhere. And for that he has my eternal gratitude.

I also remember quite clearly the scenario of the dream I had worked out for this guy: a Gothic interior in some monastery cellar, going on and on as far as you could see, one of those endless perspectives between two mirrors, and the pillars and walls were made of nothing but human skulls and bones, and in every niche there was a body laid out, and it was the Hall of Time, with the bodies in the foreground still warm, discoloring and starting to rot in the middle distance, and the bones emerging, clean as a whistle, in a kind of white futuristic glow at the end of the line. As I recall, I had the whole scene lighted, for the sake of accuracy, not with candles, but with the ice-bright fluorescence that makes the skin look green and all the pink and red flushes dead black-purple.

You ask, how do I know this was the dream of the guy in the black leather jacket. I don't know. I only believe this was his dream, and I work at belief with more energy and tears and entreaties than I work at re-creating the dream itself.

My office, of course, has its limitations. The lady with her tongue stuck out, the guy from Mechanics Hall — these are our wildest ones. The people who have really gone floating down toward the bottom of that boggy lake come in only once, and are then referred to a place more permanent than our office, which receives the public from nine to five, five days a week only. Even those people who are barely able to walk about the streets and keep working, who aren't yet halfway down in the lake, get sent to the outpatient department at another hospital specializing in severer cases. Or they may stay a month or so in our own observation ward in the central hospital, which I've never seen.

I've seen the secretary of that ward, though. Something about her merely smoking and drinking her coffee in the cafeteria at the ten o'clock break put me off so I never went to sit next to her again. She has a funny name I don't ever quite remember correctly, something really odd, like Miss Milleravage. One of those names that seem more like a pun mixing up Milltown and Ravage than anything in the city phone directory. But not so odd a name, after all, if you've ever read through the phone directory, with its Hyman Diddlebockers and Sasparilla Greenleafs. I read through the phone book, once, never mind when, and it satisfied a deep need in me to realize how many people aren't called Smith.

Anyhow, this Miss Milleravage is a large woman, not fat, but all sturdy muscle and tall on top of it. She wears a gray suit over her hard bulk that reminds me vaguely of some kind of uniform, without the details of cut having anything strikingly military about them. Her face, hefty as a bullock's, is covered with a remarkable number of tiny maculae, as if she'd been lying underwater for some time and little algae had latched onto her skin, smutching it over with tobacco-browns and greens. These moles are noticeable mainly because the skin around them is so pallid. I sometimes wonder if Miss Milleravage has ever seen the wholesome light of day. I wouldn't be a bit surprised if she'd been brought up from the cradle with the sole benefit of artificial lighting.

Byrna, the secretary in Alcoholic Clinic just across the hall from us, introduced me to Miss Milleravage with the gambit that I'd "been in England too."

Miss Milleravage, it turned out, had spent the best years of her life in London hospitals.

"Had a friend," she boomed in her queer, doggish basso, not favoring me with a direct look, "a nurse at St. Bart's. Tried to get in touch with her after the war, but the head of the nurses had changed, everybody'd changed, nobody'd heard of her. She must've gone down with the old head nurse, rubbish and all, in the bombings." She followed this with a large grin.

Now I've seen medical students cutting up cadavers, four stiffs to a classroom about as recognizably human as Moby Dick, and the students playing catch with the dead men's livers. I've heard guys joke about sewing a woman up wrong after a delivery at the charity ward of the Lying-In. But I wouldn't want to see what Miss Milleravage would write off as the biggest laugh of all time. No thanks and then some. You could scratch her eyes with a pin and swear you'd struck solid quartz.

My boss has a sense of humor too, only it's gentle. Generous as Santa on Christmas Eve.

I work for a middle-aged lady named Miss Taylor who is the head secretary of the clinic and has been since the clinic started thirty-three years ago — the year of my birth, oddly enough. Miss Taylor knows every doctor, every patient, every outmoded appointment slip, referral slip, and billing procedure the hospital has ever used or thought of using. She plans to stick with the clinic until she's farmed out in the green pastures of social security checks. A woman more dedicated to her work I never saw. She's the same way about statistics as I am about dreams: if the building caught fire she would throw every last one of those books of statistics to the firemen below at the serious risk of her own skin.

I get along extremely well with Miss Taylor. The one thing I never let her catch me doing is reading the old record books. I have actually very little time for this. Our office is busier than the stock exchange with the staff of twenty-five doctors in and out, medical students in training, patients, patients' relatives, and visiting officials from other clinics referring patients to us, so even when I'm covering the office alone, during Miss Taylor's coffee break and lunch hour, I seldom get to dash down more than a note or two.

This kind of catch-as-catch-can is nerve-racking, to say the least. A lot of the best dreamers are in the old books, the dreamers that come in to us only once or twice for evaluation before they're sent elsewhere. For copying out these dreams I need time, a lot of time. My circumstances are hardly ideal for the unhurried pursuit of my art. There is, of course, a certain derring-do in working under such hazards, but I long for the rich leisure of the true connoisseur who indulges his nostrils above the brandy snifter for an hour before his tongue reaches out for the first taste.

I find myself all too often lately imagining what a relief it would be to bring a briefcase into work, big enough to hold one of those thick, blue, cloth-bound record books full of dreams. At Miss Taylor's lunchtime, in the lull before the doctors and students crowd in to take their afternoon patients, I could simply slip one of the books, dated ten or fifteen years back, into my briefcase, and leave the briefcase under my desk till five o'clock struck. Of course, odd-looking bundles are inspected by the doorman of the Clinics Building, and the hospital has its own staff of flatfeet to check up on the multiple varieties of thievery that go on, but for heaven's sake, I'm not thinking of making off with typewriters or heroin. I'd only borrow the book overnight and slip it back on the shelf first thing the next day before anybody else came in. Still, being caught taking a book out of the hospital would probably mean losing my job and all my source material with it.

This idea of mulling over a record book in the privacy and comfort of my own apartment, even if I have to stay up night after night for this purpose, attracts me so much I become more and more impatient with my usual method of snatching minutes to look up dreams in Miss Taylor's half hours out of the office.

The trouble is, I can never tell exactly when Miss Taylor will come back to the office. She is so conscientious about her job she'd be likely to cut her half hour at lunch short and her twenty minutes at coffee shorter if it weren't for her lame left leg. The distinct sound of this lame leg in the corridor warns me of her approach in time for me to whip the record book I'm reading into my drawer out of sight and pretend to be putting down the final flourishes on a phone message, or some such alibi. The only catch, as far as my nerves are concerned, is that Amputee Clinic is around the corner from us in the opposite direction from Nerve Clinic, and I've gotten really jumpy due to a lot of false alarms where I've mistaken some pegleg's hitching step for the step of Miss Taylor herself returning early to the office.

On the blackest days when I've scarcely time to squeeze one dream out of the old books and my copy work is nothing but weepy college sophomores who can't get a lead in *Camino Real,* I feel Johnny Panic turn his back, stony as Everest, higher than Orion, and the motto of the great Bible of Dreams, "Perfect fear casteth out all else," is ash and lemon water on my lips. I'm a wormy hermit in a country of prize pigs so corn-happy they can't see the slaughterhouse at the end of the track. I'm Jeremiah vision-bitten in the Land of Cockaigne.

What's worse: day by day I see these psyche-doctors studying to win Johnny Panic's converts from him by hook, crook, and talk, talk, talk. These deep-eyed, bush-bearded dream-collectors who preceded me in history, and their contemporary inheritors with their white jackets and knotty-pine-paneled offices and leather couches, practiced and still practice their dream-gathering for worldly ends: health and money, money and health. To be a true member of Johnny Panic's congregation one must forget the dreamer and remember the dream: the dreamer is merely a flimsy vehicle for the great Dream-Maker himself. This they will not do. Johnny Panic is gold in the bowels, and they try to root him out by spiritual stomach pumps.

Take what happened to Harry Bilbo. Mr. Bilbo came into our office with the hand of Johnny Panic heavy as a lead coffin on his shoulder. He had an interesting notion about the filth in this world. I figured him for a prominent part in Johnny Panic's Bible of Dreams, Third Book of Fear, Chapter Nine on Dirt, Disease, and General Decay. A friend of Harry's blew a trumpet in the Boy Scout band when they were kids. Harry Bilbo'd also blown on this friend's trumpet. Years later the friend got cancer and died. Then, one day not so long ago, a cancer doctor came into Harry's house, sat down in a chair, passed the top of the morning with Harry's mother, and on leaving, shook her hand and opened the door for himself. Suddenly Harry Bilbo wouldn't blow trumpets or sit down on chairs or shake hands if all the cardinals of Rome took to blessing him twenty-four hours around the clock for fear of catching cancer. His mother had to go turning the TV knobs and water faucets on and off and opening doors for him. Pretty soon Harry stopped going to work because of the spit and dog droppings in the street. First that stuff gets on your shoes, and then when you take your shoes off it gets on your hands, and then at dinner it's a quick trip into your mouth and not a hundred Hail Marys can keep you from the chain reaction. The last straw was, Harry quit weight lifting at the public gym when he saw this cripple exercising with the dumbbells. You can never tell what germs cripples carry behind their ears and under their fingernails. Day and night Harry Bilbo lived in holy worship of Johnny Panic, devout as any priest among censers and sacraments. He had a beauty all his own.

Well, these white-coated tinkerers managed, the lot of them, to talk Harry into turning on the TV himself, and the water faucets, and to opening closet doors, front doors, bar doors. Before they were through with him, he was sitting down on movie-house chairs, and benches all over the Public Garden, and weight lifting

every day of the week at the gym in spite of the fact another cripple took to using the rowing machine. At the end of his treatment he came in to shake hands with the clinic director. In Harry
Bilbo's own words, he was "a changed man." The pure Panic-
light had left his face; he went out of the office doomed to the
crass fate these doctors call health and happiness.

About the time of Harry Bilbo's cure a new idea starts nudging
at the bottom of my brain. I find it as hard to ignore as those bare
feet sticking out of the lumbar puncture room. If I don't want to
risk carrying a record book out of the hospital in case I get discovered and fired and have to end my research forever, I can really
speed up work by staying in the Clinics Building overnight. I am
nowhere near exhausting the clinic's resources, and the piddling
amount of cases I am able to read in Miss Taylor's brief absences
during the day are nothing to what I could get through in a few
nights of steady copying. I need to accelerate my work if only to
counteract those doctors.

Before I know it I am putting on my coat at five and saying good
night to Miss Taylor, who usually stays a few minutes overtime to
clear up the day's statistics, and sneaking around the corner into
the ladies' room. It is empty. I slip into the patients' john, lock
the door from the inside, and wait. For all I know, one of the
clinic cleaning ladies may try to knock the door down, thinking
some patient's passed out on the seat. My fingers are crossed.
About twenty minutes later the door of the lavatory opens and
someone limps over the threshold like a chicken favoring a bad
leg. It is Miss Taylor, I can tell by the resigned sigh as she meets
the jaundiced eye of the lavatory mirror. I hear the click-cluck
of various touch-up equipment on the bowl, water sloshing, the
scritch of a comb in frizzed hair, and then the door is closing with
a slow-hinged wheeze behind her.

I am lucky. When I come out of the ladies' room at six o'clock
the corridor lights are off and the fourth floor hall is empty as
church on Monday. I have my own key to our office; I come in first
every morning, so that's no trouble. The typewriters are folded
back into the desks, the locks are on the dial phones, all's right
with the world.

Outside the window the last of the winter light is fading. Yet

I do not forget myself and turn on the overhead bulb. I don't want to be spotted by any hawk-eyed doctor or janitor in the hospital buildings across the little courtyard. The cabinet with the record books is in the windowless passage opening onto the doctor's cubicles, which have windows overlooking the courtyard. I make sure the doors to all the cubicles are shut. Then I swtich on the passage light, a sallow twenty-five-watt affair blackening at the top. Better than an altarful of candles to me at this point, though. I didn't think to bring a sandwich. There is an apple in my desk drawer left over from lunch, so I reserve that for whatever pangs I may feel about one o'clock in the morning, and get out my pocket notebook. At home every evening it is my habit to tear out the notebook pages I've written on at the office during the day and pile them up to be copied in my manuscript. In this way I cover my tracks so no one idly picking up my notebook at the office could ever guess the type or scope of my work.

I begin systematically by opening the oldest book on the bottom shelf. The once-blue cover is no-color now, the pages are thumbed and blurry carbons, but I'm humming from foot to topknot: this dream book was spanking new the day I was born. When I really get organized I'll have hot soup in a thermos for the dead-of-winter nights, turkey pies, and chocolate eclairs. I'll bring hair curlers and four changes of blouse to work in my biggest handbag Monday mornings so one one will notice me going downhill in looks and start suspecting unhappy love affairs or pink affiliations or my working on dream books in the clinic four nights a week.

Eleven hours later. I am down to apple core and seeds and in the month of May, nineteen thirty-four, with a private nurse who has just opened a laundry bag in her patient's closet and found five severed heads in it, including her mother's.

A chill air touches the nape of my neck. From where I am sitting cross-legged on the floor in front of the cabinet, the record book heavy on my lap, I notice out of the corner of my eye that the door of the cubicle beside me is letting in a little crack of blue light. Not only along the floor, but up the side of the door too. This is odd since I made sure from the first that all the doors were shut tight. The crack of blue light is widening and my eyes are fastened to two motionless shoes in the doorway, toes pointing toward me.

They are brown leather shoes of a foreign make, with thick elevator soles. Above the shoes are black silk socks through which shows a pallor of flesh. I get as far as the gray pinstripe trouser cuffs.

*"Tch, tch,"* chides an infinitely gentle voice from the cloudy regions above my head. "Such an uncomfortable position! Your legs must be asleep by now. Let me help you up. The sun will be rising shortly."

Two hands slip under my arms from behind, and I am raised, wobbly as an unset custard, to my feet, which I cannot feel because my legs are, in fact, asleep. The record book slumps to the floor, pages splayed.

"Stand still a minute." The clinic director's voice fans the lobe of my right ear. "Then the circulation will revive."

The blood in my not-there legs starts pinging under a million sewing machine needles, and a vision of the clinic director acid-etches itself on my brain. I don't even need to look around: the fat potbelly buttoned into his gray pinstripe waistcoat, woodchuck teeth yellow and buck, every-color eyes behind the thick-lensed glasses quick as minnows.

I clutch my notebook. The last floating timber of the *Titanic*. What does he know, what does he know?

Everything.

"I know where there is a nice hot bowl of chicken noodle soup." His voice rustles, dust under the bed, mice in the straw. His hand welds onto my left upper arm in fatherly love. The record book of all the dreams going on in the city of my birth at my first yawp in this world's air he nudges under the bookcase with a polished toe.

We met nobody in the dawn-dark hall. Nobody on the chill stone stair down to the basement corridors where Jerry the Record Room boy cracked his head skipping steps one night on a rush errand.

I begin to double-quickstep so he won't think it's me he's hustling. "You can't fire me," I say calmly. "I quit."

The clinic director's laugh wheezes up from his accordion-pleated bottom gut. "We mustn't lose you so soon." His whisper snakes off down the whitewashed basement passages, echoing among the elbow pipes, the wheelchairs and stretchers beached for the night along the steam-stained walls. "Why, we need you more than you know."

We wind and double, and my legs keep time with his until we come, somewhere in those barren rat tunnels, to an all-night elevator run by a one-armed Negro. We get on and the door grinds shut like the door on a cattle car and we go up and up. It is a freight elevator, crude and clanky, a far cry from the plush one in the Clinics Building.

We get off at an indeterminate floor. The clinic director leads me down a bare corridor lit at intervals by socketed bulbs in little wire cages on the ceiling. Locked doors set with screened windows line the hall on either hand. I plan to part company with the clinic director at the first red exit sign, but on our journey there are none. I am in alien territory, coat on the hanger in the office, handbag and money in my top desk drawer, notebook in my hand, and only Johnny Panic to warm me against the Ice Age outside.

Ahead a light gathers, brightens. The clinic director, puffing slightly at the walk, brisk and long, to which he is obviously unaccustomed, propels me around a bend and into a square, brilliantly lit room.

"Here she is."

"The little witch!"

Miss Milleravage hoists her tonnage up from behind the steel desk facing the door.

The walls and the ceiling of the room are riveted metal battleship plates. There are no windows.

From small, barred cells lining the sides and back of the room I see Johnny Panic's top priests staring out at me, arms swaddled behind their backs in the white ward nightshirts, eyes redder than coals and hungry-hot.

They welcome me with queer croaks and grunts as if their tongues were locked in their jaws. They have no doubt heard of my work by way of Johnny Panic's grapevine and want to know how his apostles thrive in the world.

I lift my hands to reassure them, holding up my notebook, my voice loud as Johnny Panic's organ with all stops out.

"Peace! I bring to you . . ."

The Book.

"None of that old stuff, sweetie," Miss Milleravage is dancing out at me from behind her desk like a trick elephant.

The clinic director closes the door to the room.

The minute Miss Milleravage moves I notice what her hulk has been hiding from view behind the desk — a white cot high as a man's waist with a single sheet stretched over the mattress, spot-less and drumskin tight. At the head of the cot is a table on which sits a metal box covered with dials and gauges. The box seems to be eyeing me, copperhead-ugly, from its coil of electric wires, the latest model in Johnny-Panic-Killers.

I get ready to dodge to one side. When Miss Milleravage grabs, her fat hand comes away a fist full of nothing. She starts for me again, her smile heavy as dogdays in August.

"None of that. None of that. I'll have that little black book."

Fast as I run around the high white cot, Miss Milleravage is so fast you'd think she wore roller skates. She grabs and gets. Against her great bulk I beat my fists, and against her whopping milkless breasts, until her hands on my wrists are iron hoops and her breath hushabys me with a love-stink fouler than Undertaker's Basement.

"My Baby, my own baby's come back to me . . ."

"She," the clinic director says, sad and stern, "has been making time with Johnny Panic again."

"Naughty naughty."

The white cot is ready. With a terrible gentleness Miss Miller-avage takes the watch from my wrist, the rings from my fingers, the hairpins from my hair. She begins to undress me. When I am bare, I am anointed on the temples and robed in sheets vir-ginal as the first snow. Then, from the four corners of the room and from the door behind me come five false priests in white sur-gical gowns and masks whose one lifework is to unseat Johnny Panic from his own throne. They extend me full-length on my back on the cot. The crown of wire is placed on my head, the wafer of forgetfulness on my tongue. The masked priests move to their posts and take hold: one of my left leg, one of my right, one of my right arm, one of my left. One behind my head at the metal box where I can't see.

From their cramped niches along the wall, the votaries raise their voices in protest. They begin the devotional chant:

*The only thing to love is Fear itself.*
*Love of Fear is the beginning of wisdom.*
*The only thing to love is Fear itself.*
*May Fear and Fear and Fear be everywhere.*

There is no time for Miss Milleravage or the clinic director or the priests to muzzle them.

The signal is given.

The machine betrays them.

At the moment when I think I am most lost the face of Johnny Panic appears in a nimbus of arc lights on the ceiling overhead. I am shaken like a leaf in the teeth of glory. His beard is lightning. Lightning is in his eye. His Word charges and illumes the universe.

The air crackles with the blue-tongued, lightning-haloed angels.

His love is the twenty-story leap, the rope at the throat, the knife at the heart.

He forgets not his own.

# MIRIAM RUGEL

## Paper Poppy

(FROM THE KENYON REVIEW)

IT IS ONLY by the most curious indirection that one comes to realize what is happening to other people. Their crises. Their passions. Common to all, these are the keys to all, if one's gaze is focused at the proper time and position. Yet how often the crises pass unseen and unsuspected, by intimates, closest family, friends. It is difficult at times even to recognize one's own. One does not always hear the sound of the key, turning.

If I had not met Katherine, perhaps I would not have seen what I saw at the health club. And, if I had not looked into my husband's face then, I might not have followed Mister Robert with such absorption. Into this danger. Terrible danger.

Was I a little in love in the beginning with Mister Robert? It is easy for an older woman, married young to the wrong husband — through no fault, no fault of his — to be touched by a beautiful boy. By eyes with the color and movement of a star sapphire, by golden hair. It was not always golden, Mister Robert's hair. That was the pity.

It has been nearly forty years since I met Katherine. The daughter of my aunt's seashore neighbor, she was an unsuccessful girl in the terms of that period, an isolate, without dates or friends, therefore without identity. I was told to help Katherine. Newly engaged, at eighteen preoccupied with trousseau-hunting and bridal showers, I had no desire to help anyone. But an evening was arranged; in the living room of her summer home I met

Katherine. I was introduced, quite obviously, as blueprint of the girl Katherine should, and if she tried, could become. We spent only that evening together. But she has companioned me, as a sonata learned in childhood remains in the repertoire, over all the years since.

She was a sturdy, pallid girl with a heavy presence. Her dark hair was short, worn straight, an anomaly in the thirties; her face was plump, smooth, the skin waxy, mauve-white as moonflowers that open only to darkness. That evening she was dressed in white, stout canvas skirt, white blouse, white jacket cut severely as a hospital intern's.

We walked on the boardwalk for an hour, saw a movie, stopped for a soda, went home. I have no memory of the movie; our conversation was inconsequential.

What has stayed with me for thirty-six years is the supporting pressure of Katherine's square hand under my elbow at every street crossing, the naturalness with which she took the curb side of every pavement, a flat, grained wallet, plain, that appeared whenever money was needed.

These have stayed and the way, in a dark, salty-smelling street as we walked homeward, her hand lifted once, almost helplessly, to touch my pearls and, again helpless, to linger for a moment on my throat. I remember how I recoiled, not so much before a girl's caress, as at a stranger's. And I have remembered how, saying good night before the circular porch that ran around my aunt's house which was darkened except for a dim entrance light, Katherine bent and kissed me. If I close my eyes I can still feel the sweetness of that tentative kiss, soft and strange on my lips, its contact blind as an infant's moist mouth trailing across one's cheek. I remember how, as my surprised eyes met hers, open, I saw in the latter a complete unawareness, an innocence total as any I have ever known. In the instant before she fled I caught the edge of her wonder and the first faint hint of baffled desire.

And though I did not see her again during my visit, evading my aunt's suggestions and keeping the secret I felt Katherine did not know, I asked regularly about her in later years. She was no more successful as she grew older, my aunt reported; she was a trial to her parents; she was a college dropout; she moved away from home; she left her city; only in her work at some marine station — she had majored in biology — I heard she was brilliant. I have thought often about her, the moonglow skin, the clarity in her eyes, and I have trembled for the time of her lost innocence. The turning of the key. I have hoped she would find a gentle lover, someone who would be faithful and who would love her very long.

The health club. I do not know why the one show I saw there last August returns to me, compulsively, like an illness that is over except for recurrent sieges of weakness and malaise. There could have been nothing more pleasant than that evening in the open, the pool set high, placid, clean, blue, the sky an echoing color, windswept by clouds, the audience still dressed in shorts, fresh slacks, cottons.

Each summer the season is ended by this event, the selection of a member who has achieved, through the club's direction and facilities, the most striking physical improvement.

I sat beside my husband and our two sons, folding chairs close to the posing platform, facing the half-dozen assorted judges, around us many families from this edge of suburbia. The evening's prospect amused me — patronizingly so — although, myself a club member, I had for several years welcomed the hours prescribed for women, the individual instruction, the bicycles and rowing machines, a small indoor pool usually empty and always very cold. My work is sedentary; I was grateful for the opportunity of stirred blood.

I was grateful that evening, too, for my husband's obvious enjoyment. A long line of contestants had filed onto the platform, each assuming classic stances, "full-front, profile and optional," according to the master of ceremonies, "three poses of muscular display."

"Like Greek sculpture," my younger boy said.

"With granite heads," replied his brother, and we all laughed.

Then, as the interviewing began — student or non-student, married or bachelor, occupation — I lost the scene. I frequently do, when I go with my husband to these events. I enjoy his enjoyment. This is a great part of his charm for me, this talent for find-

ing pleasure, the directness with which he meets living, an
uncomplicated emotional climate overlaying a capacity for sound
judgment. It is his directness — almost a simplicity — that has
helped to keep him erect, given him a show of virility, a face unlined in spite of the white in his brisk mustache, his springing
black hair. I have learned to appreciate this absence of complica-
tion and indeed many other of his qualities.

"Ah, nice," I hear him say, as a young giant sprouts enormous
pectorals. "Very nice." He speaks quietly as at a cricket match.

Yes. I appreciate my husband, even though unexpectedly my
own life has more and more suspended itself between book covers
and he has not opened a magazine in thirty years. There are
values other than literature in a marriage. And other than sex.
Tenderness can be a touchstone. Tenderness has been his gift to
me, which I have held precious for its immenseness.

I hear his shout of laughter at some pun on biceps, triceps, and
I smile.

Tenderness has been the ground upon which we have met,
in the evenings, after our separate days, tenderness, the respect
due one from another human being, and the anchor, the warm-
ness, of a hand in one's own through living. Tenderness and the
slow learning of mutuality have overbalanced all. If this is not as
much as others have known, it is a great deal more than nothing.
Which, grimly committed by my own commitment, I expected
after my first month of marriage.

And so I watched him that evening, glad of his relaxation, as
I sometimes do when he sits before television, enough engrossed
in *Tarzan* that his head moves without his knowing. As indeed
he watches me, when we go to an experimental play, or when we
visit my Bohemian friends, or while he waits endlessly in some
library as I track a reference in a paper by one of my physician
employers — work grown into accidentally, unneeded in any finan-
cial way, necessary only to me.

And as I thought this the show continued, a ballet on the platform now, done by a professional member, all fluidity and grace.
It had turned nearly dark. A spotlight had been thrown on the
contestants, fewer than in the beginning. While I watched I became aware of a changed atmosphere, a suspensefulness, as semi-

finalists were chosen, proportions and symmetry discussed, the pronouncement of a winner approached. At a signal, those remaining in line went taut, tiny bikinis slipping on contracted waists, the play of their huge muscles astonishing. And, really seeing for the first time, I inspected the bodies before me, noting with surprise and some distaste that they were shaved, glistening. Oiled. Like great birds, ostriches, peacocks, they preened themselves, slowly revolving for the judges, highlights reflected under the yellow spotlight. The feeling of a game lessened. The women in the audience faded. There was only the tension of competitiveness. And the maleness.

It had gone quite dark. Quite silent. I saw the game was over. Before me the figures — flexed, arms bent, forefingers oddly folded — seemed to expand, grow larger, until the corded legs, the great chests, loomed. Until instead of men they seemed animals. About to lunge. To spring.

And suddenly my amusement vanished. I felt threatened, afraid; a giddiness gripped me. Instinctively protecting, I turned to my sons. They were absorbed. I faced away from the contestants, fighting nausea, trying to lose the dizziness in the audience. And their faces were familiar. I had seen these faces before. At a wrestling match, when a hooded figure had seized his opponent's head and pounded it, repeatedly, on the concrete floor. And though I knew then that the thuds, the grunts of the victim, were part of play acting, those spectator faces had been real, what I saw in them was real, the shouts for a killing were no mockery. I had been sick then, but not as now.

In these faces was the same fascination and something more, beyond brutality or covetousness, something salacious, obscene, that could almost be smelled, and which I did not care further to name. In the massed masculinity, I tried to swallow, breathe, stand and leave . . . And I could do none of these. The smell, the sourness, rose in my throat, filled my mouth beyond containing. I groped for my husband, for his reassurance, comfort, help. And I saw his head was moving. He was engrossed. His gaze, focused, shining, traveled each fantastic body. And as a hand was raised over the first young giant, as a trophy was wheeled onto the platform, I saw my husband bend forward, straining. He belonged to the scene; he was part of it. I stretched out my hand to recall him, to reach the tenderness of which I had been so lately thinking. And I could not. I did not want to touch him. He was ugly.

When I think of Mister Robert — in the salon his name carried a Gallic accent — I see his medieval head suspended against taupe velvet. There are places where heads belong: the carrot-haired girl with twin-peaked desperate eyebrows immobilized before the movie cashier's window, purple eyes imploring comfort as she buys a ticket, her secrets forever impenetrable . . . a leonine face, male, with painted lips and brilliant eyes burdened by mascara, ruffling the paper poppy heading his cane, his wand, fixed against an old city door.

I am trying to evade Mister Robert.

Mister Robert's texture was smooth nap and subtle color, as his essential quality was one of grave sweetness. A fine face, features large but chiseled, cheeks touched with pink, tan hair.

He was my hairdresser for many years. Talented, expensive, less than voluble. As quietly dressed as mannered. Only gradually, as we became friends, he talked a little: he loved his dog, he visited his mother. There was no mention of friends, hobbies, activities. He discussed neither clients nor confreres. The reticence gave him dignity.

Then a bout of virus turned into pneumonia, and he was hospitalized for lack of home nursing. His poodle, mad with loneliness, was shot by a kennel owner. It was on his return to the salon, as he talked of his dog, that I discovered how alone Mister Robert really was, a solitude to be deepened when, shortly thereafter, his mother died.

Mister Robert did not display his grief. With his inheritance, he bought a small country house which he painted and papered himself, although he spoke not at all of his choices. He did begin to ask domestic questions. How did one empty a vacuum? Roast a turkey? I could hear him, with other clients, talk of salad dressings and orange sauce. I hoped, with his mother's passing, he had found himself a girl. It is only now, as I think of him intensely, that I realize my interior picture of Robert at home was one of a slender figure tied about the middle with a Hans Christian Andersen apron.

Inevitably, as is the way with talented hairdressers, Mister Robert became indispensable to me. My hair had never been so audibly admired. I had only to appear regularly, sit for an hour, and pay the exorbitant fee to have my usually careless self transformed into a woman almost pretty, *soignée*.

It was natural, in this shop where a grateful client might furnish a few rugs for her operator's new apartment, that I began to show my appreciation. At Christmas I gave Robert a good tie, at Thanksgiving a bottle of wine or a liqueur.

This Christmas, long before the holiday, he mentioned a men's boutique newly opened in the locality. Beyond his means, he admitted cheerfully, but with a superior collection. I went there immediately, freshly coiffed, feeling attractive.

The boutique was certainly superior. Mink tails covered a circle of sofa; within this a raised dais displayed an impractical pale suit, creamy boots, and a man's fur sports jacket. Mister Robert? I was discomfited.

I looked about and saw the shop was crowded with customers and a full audience — expensively dressed men, hippies with their long-haired existentialist girl friends, many carrying infants in what seemed pink-and-blue coal scuttles. A strange milieu for an aging square with teased hair and heels. At once I felt fifty. Which I was.

The exquisite young man who bore down upon me with an offer of help identified himself as assistant manager. He was approximately twenty. The manager was older, perhaps by a year. Both were beautiful: they each wore the displayed suit and stood with boot toes as correctly pointed as any model. And both were promptly appropriated by another customer in pipe-stem trousers and jacket neatly vented to accommodate bulbous buttocks.

"Your suits!" he shrilled. "They're stunning!"

"I love them," his blue-jeaned girl friend breathed. "Can we afford —— "

"$160.00, on special order."

And they were plunged into discussion of the costume's details.

Ignored, I took my unsuitable coiffure to a rack of shirts, saw their fabric, a transparent voile, and dropped one as I noticed its lace-trimmed cuff. And again I thought, incredulous, Mister Robert?

"Pardon," a voice said beside me. "Do you mind if I talk to you?"

I looked at a counterpart of myself, older I hoped, wearing, of all things, a hat. Hers was not a head I would care to place in my gallery.

"I have to talk to someone," she said. "I can't, to my son." She indicated a healthy appearing youngster, only a trifle soiled, whom a maid should have gone over with a chamois. "What do you make of all this?"

I hesitated. "The clothes are divine. They must be . . . fun . . . to wear. And I think I'm going to be sick soon."

"Thank Heaven!" She examined her son. "I wouldn't dare say this to him. I'd alienate him. But if his father were here he'd kill him!"

With this grammatically obscure judgment I perfectly agreed, and bought Mister Robert for $12.00 a shocking pink pullover that came sealed in a Swedish aluminum tube to be attacked, the instructions read, with a can opener.

Mister Robert said he liked his gift greatly. I thought the color must have complemented his hair, which seemed, week by week, to be changing. Turning brighter. The shade was really quite becoming, although I was slow to determine the reason for the heightened attractiveness. I had merely noticed he was looking younger and — dared I think it? — prettier. It was as if his head were in perpetual sunlight. And his lashes, were they always so abundant?

I must say at once these things did not repel me. I was interested. I liked Mister Robert. There were few people outside the shop, within my own life, I liked as well. I liked the books I saw in his booth, *Ulysses* and James Baldwin, his Chagall print, my private favorite; I liked him for his quietness, his sweetness; for his immaculate grooming; undeniably for his beauty. Most of all I liked his reticence and the dignity that persisted in spite of dyed hair. It was my fondness that increased my dismay. For now, week by week, I began to see the careful training of a forehead forelock. I saw it become bolder, separate itself from the rest of the hair until it fell, carefully casual, to the eyebrows. Until it was brightened almost to flamboyance. And I heard more talk of food. A filet baked in pastry, a pheasant. One does not prepare pheasant for a solitary dinner. And then, one week when I was early, I waited for Mister Robert and could see him from a distance as he walked toward the booth. And I felt shock. The forelock was a blatant gold. It was a signal and a banner. A call to arms. An invitation to an old waltz.

With its change, Robert's manner altered. He talked more loudly. He was vivacious. He was also much interested now in diets: for the first time I heard him sharp, malicious, in his disdain of a fellow worker careless enough to show a waistline bulge. At the same time he pressed me for more recipes, fast depleting my small epicurean store. Somewhere he had become expert on apéritifs, confiding matter-of-factly the aphrodisiac properties of several. With his new expertise he discussed rich soups, requiring long preparation. Hardly fare for a dieter.

About this time, too, American women began to buy wigs in substantial numbers. Robert was interested in wigs, although he had no part or profit in their sale. During one of my appointments the shop was showing a new model, auburn, a cap of tumbled curls. This one tempted me. I was drawn by the thought of saving time and weekly fees. I asked to have it brought to my booth, but by the time it arrived I was set and combed, ready to leave.

"Next time," I told Robert. "I'll try it before you do my hair."

Still he stood, silent, almost stubborn, one bony hand reaching out to fondle red tendrils. And he smiled, sweetly.

"I'll try it for you, Mrs. H," he said. And he had snatched the wig, pulled the booth curtains, before I could speak the first word of my refusal.

"I'm not really serious," I said, brusquely. And I left, shaken, walking fast. I tried to dismiss the matter. But I could not truly dismiss it. Because, oddly, in the single space of standing there while he spoke, in the second before my leaving, I had seen as vividly as though it were actual Mister Robert's face framed in curls. I had seen his face. Grotesque and beautiful.

All through the afternoon I felt uneasy, out of equilibrium. I went early to an appointment with my husband. We had a long dinner. Afterward, turning out of the mid-city restaurant, we strolled a bit, since it was not yet theater time. And as we rounded a corner our attention was simultaneously caught by a figure at the street's end. A ludicrous figure, dressed in white corduroys that outlined every contour, the hair in extravagant pompadour, one hand coquettishly flipping its forehead forelock, the other outstretched with fingers daintily pointed and the whole gait girlish — one foot carefully placed at the other toe, achieving a studied sway of hips.

"It's a girl!" I said, involuntarily.

"No," my husband corrected me, "it's a boy."

And since we had halted, naively, my husband's appraisal was heard by its subject, who had, by now, overtaken us.

"It *was* a boy," the creature said sweetly.

Only then, because of a quiet remonstrance, I saw there was a second figure. A man, older, ordinary, dressed in conservative suit and tie, hardly noticeable.

And before I took my husband's arm, grateful for its solidity, I stood stockstill on the pavement, watching until the pair had passed into twilight. For a moment I thought I had recognized Mister Robert. Perhaps the afternoon's episode had disturbed me unduly. Of course it wasn't Mister Robert. This boy was much too short for Mister Robert. It was just the flip of the forelock, so like Robert's gestures, I now realized. It was just the way the hips swayed, accentuated in this creature. Of course it wasn't Robert.

But now something began to change. I began to worry about Mister Robert. Too much. I slept badly. Odd pictures came to me; I did not enjoy my thoughts. During the day I could not work with concentration. What could one do to help?

He was growing so much thinner. Week by week he turned more incorporeal. And his position at the chair was strange. He had always been a boy of small fondnesses, a pat on the shoulder of the blue robe, shop-supplied, a hand under one's chin to tilt the head . . . Now he stood artificially away from his client, angled awkwardly forward at the middle, touching one nowhere except as was necessary.

Nor was he working well. My coiffure was unchanged in style, but it had become one of such stiffness and precision that its purpose seemed to turn me plain. I looked like an English judge. The spontaneity had left his fingers, the skill which in a single movement could give the whole head a flattered sweep. I didn't care about the hair: it was his thinness that concerned me. His diet had been too successful. His chest was without human thickness, the jacket as though on a coat hanger, the waist ring-size. He had the thinness of a spider. Or of a praying mantis, set on end.

I decided to talk to my Mister Robert. Tell him that even a golden forelock could not hide wasted features. Nor lipstick conceal fatigue. Could it be lipstick I was now seeing? Most certainly it was lipstick. I would talk to Mister Robert. He could not misunderstand the intentions of a woman well past fifty. After all, I had known this boy for twenty — I smiled at the appellation. Even though he had never seemed to age, I could hardly claim boyhood for him. But when I was in the shop my courage failed me. His reticence, since the wig incident, had grown formidable. Perhaps because of the wig he wished me gone. Perhaps he was doing my hair badly with deliberation. To discourage my coming. I knew from the ease with which I could choose my time for appointments that he had lost many customers. Perhaps he wished to lose me.

And then, one day, I thought he was about to voice this desire. Finishing a botch of a job, I heard his voice, treble, waspish, above me.

"I simply cannot do you any longer, Mrs. H!" I heard him say. "Unless you move to the new side of the shop. This booth is unbearable!"

Faced into the mirror, I stared.

"Don't you feel it?" (in complete exasperation). "The heat here?"

The enclosure was glassed, reflecting sun rays, the day hot. But in air conditioning I was comfortable.

"Why, of course, Mister Robert, I'll —— " I stood, turning toward him. I saw his face covered, running, with drops of perspiration big as pearls. Above his lips, around his nostrils, under his hairline. "Why, you poor boy!" I said. "You *are* hot."

"I am indeed!" he returned bitterly.

And impelled to save him embarrassment, in distress myself, I turned back to the mirror and held out his tip behind me, blindly. But he had flung out of the cubicle.

I sprayed my hair myself, although it scarcely merited the effort, and left. Still feeling the bony fingers fumble at the nape of my neck. Feeling something more disturbing, which I had tried for some time to discount, to consider temporary — an uncontrollable quivering through his arms, conveyed to his clients through every fingertip.

He was ill.

I saw him only twice more. The first time in a park near the shop, a favorite of sandaled beatniks, folk singers, the city's love children. And of mine. I circled the famous stone goat one noon, searching an empty bench. On the third try I glimpsed Mister Robert, sitting on the fringe of the fountain, spreading a picnic lunch. He looked appalling.

But he smiled with what seemed genuine pleasure and leaped to his feet when he saw me. He indicated cheese, crackers, carrot strips, celery.

"Why, Mrs. H! Would you care for some refreshment? Do you like sangria? Just burgundy and Perrier —— "

I was about to accept, gladly, when I heard another greeting. Male. Distracted momentarily by the blush that mantled Robert's cheeks, I glanced at length beside me and saw a man, older, ordinary, dressed in conventional suit and tie, hardly noticeable. The man I had seen in that early twilight. Surely it was that man. Hastily I made excuses and left. Telling myself this proved nothing. Except by the bride's blush on Mister Robert's face. And the discreetly veiled satisfaction of the stranger at my departure.

I missed my next two appointments, a coward. Then, with routine broken, I telephoned in the middle of the third week. The girl on the line hesitated.

"I don't know, Mrs. H. Mister Robert hasn't been feeling at all well lately. He's been leaving early. Do you think you could be here by 8:30 tomorrow morning?"

I was prompt. And promptly ushered into the shop's new wing.

"How is Mister Robert?" I asked the girl who shampoos my hair.

"Not good," she answered.

The manicurist was more communicative.

"What a pity! This is his last working day — he's taking an

early vacation. Everyone will miss him. Nerves, I'd say. Though he calls it high blood pressure."

I thought of the perspiration. "Nerves?" I questioned vaguely.

And Robert stood beside us. "Try to keep up with the schedule." He addressed the girls without acknowledging me. "The desk promised no late shampoos and no run-ins."

The last, I knew, was a term for customers accommodated without appointments.

Today Mister Robert had a helper to hand him rollers and lotion. Or to protect him from clients. And today there was no forelock: his hair was combed severely, a dull even brown. Only his brows were touched with pencil, making them thicker, turning his eyes more deeply blue. Before my head was half finished, he was blotting his cheeks with a handkerchief.

It was stupid to sit there in silence. Especially when the girl left us.

"I hear I'm to lose you for a while, Robert. I'm sorry you're not well . . ." I was quiet. There was such vulnerability in the tremoring fingers; the whole figure was strung so high it seemed at any hint of aggression its parts would shiver and disconnect. I felt anxious only that he stay together, be able to finish this last day. And yet I was the older of us, with the privilege of a twenty-year friendship.

"Robert, I want you to listen. I'm concerned about you."

"It's just blood pressure!" he said with desperation. "It's — I can't stand this place anymore."

"I've felt that way, Robert. Sometimes it helps to talk to a friend. Or, perhaps, to a doctor."

"It hasn't helped me," he answered flatly. And with his trembling fingers he undid all my rollers and started from the beginning again.

I sat under the dryer, miserable, bidding myself to stop the chivvying. But when Mister Robert returned I held a note in my hand. And, when he had fumbled with my hair sufficiently, I spoke to him once more.

"Where are you going on your vacation?"

"I haven't made any plans."

I folded my note into his palm.

"This is the address of our shore apartment," I said. "It's in a little place, Robert. No mail. No telephone. Only ocean. I can write to have it ready. Go there. Please. It's helped me. Just a few days may give you perspective."

Only politeness kept him from handing back the paper. "I . . . don't know. I don't want to promise —— "

"Consider it. Please."

He looked at me and saw my concern. It was a measure of his gentleness that he could answer what he saw. He almost reached for my hand, although he couldn't quite bear to touch it. Instead, he managed a kind of jocoseness.

"Well, thank you, Mrs. H! Now you take care until we meet again, whenever that may be. Whenever the fortunes of life bring us together . . ." And the torturing perspiration moved, rolled down his face like a blanket, and, horribly, his eyes filled with tears. "It's just that — I've lost something very dear to me — that I can't get back again . . ." He turned toward the wall. "I — hope I can get over it. It's either that — or not going on."

I think that is what he said. The words were hardly audible. I told myself to go no further. I felt his balance would disappear utterly.

"Try," I said, nonetheless. "It depends on you. How intelligently you handle yourself."

I am ashamed that I turned then and left him. Without help or comfort.

I did not see him in the shop again. He did not take my apartment. I heard nothing about a catastrophe.

I keep telling myself there was nothing I could do to help him. As I could do nothing for Katherine. As I had no right to resent my husband at the health club. There is no excuse for interference. Or for presumption. There is no legitimate reason. One's passions are one's own.

It is only that every day, every night, I see Mister Robert before me. I see his face framed in curls. Grotesque and growing daily more beautiful. I know I am in love. For the first time in my life — old, past fifty — my thighs, my womb know love's fever. I am not in love with Mister Robert. Not that boy. Naturally. I love

the face in the auburn wig. I long for the touch of a hand I
know and that I feel I soon will find. When I go out, I search for
auburn curls. At home, I dream of a kind of seraglio with drawn
curtains and a narrow bed. I am perfumed. Sitting crosslegged
and smiling, in flowing sleeves, I gaze at my laced fingers, upturned
palms. I await the one who I know will come.

I wait the touch of her hand on my pearls.

# MARGARET SHIPLEY

## The Tea Bowl of Ninsei Nomura

(FROM THE DENVER QUARTERLY)

*And the dragon was wroth with the woman and went to make war with the remnant of her seed . . .*
— Revelation

THE SUBDIVISION which had grown up around the country home of the Furman Powells in the Santa Clara Valley neither aggravated nor pleased them: they were indifferent to it. It seemed to their new neighbors, who had never been invited into the Powell living room or, as a matter of fact, into the Powell yard, that the cloistered life the Powells led behind their high redwood fence and shaggy eucalyptus trees bore little relationship to the neat tract homes and circular drives that had crept down the valley from San Francisco for the past five years and had now passed around them, leaving them unmolested on their weedy, overgrown island.

The Powells' activities in the world outside of their island were well known to anyone who was curious enough to inform himself: Furman had retired from the fine arts department of the University, where he had been a teacher for thirty years, and had spent a total of nine years on sabbatical leaves in and out of the Orient, his most recent one as artist in residence at the University of Kyoto. Teresa, six years his junior and also an artist, taught in the local high school when not accompanying her husband into voluntary exile. They had lived for brief academic periods in Taiwan, Bangkok, Calcutta, Hong Kong, and, before the advent of Red China, in Peking, and were known, each in his own right, as authorities on oriental art. Furman, in particular, was in demand throughout the country as a lecturer to students and cultural groups, but accepted few such invitations since his retirement. Their paintings had toured the country in one-man shows and were individually hung in art galleries in Paris, London, and New York. During the thirty years of their life together they had raised two children, a boy and a girl, who had married and gone to live in the Bay area, where they contrived problems of their own which they did not share with their parents.

Such was the state of balance between the Powell ethnic and that of the peach-and-plum valley that the high redwood fence surrounding the Powell island had to be more than a fence. It had to be a cultural barrier between oriented and non-oriented minds. Until the day with which this account is concerned, it had served well in its dual role. It had protected the Powells from the banality of newly paved streets and tonsured lawns, and had dissuaded adventurous children (and adults) from exploring the grounds. In one or two instances, of which the Powells were contentedly unaware, it had talked a neighbor out of making that most quotidian of gestures, the afternoon call.

In the final test of its weather-resistant impregnability, however, the redwood fence proved unable to divide two purely inapposite minds one from the other. To appreciate the purity of those minds and the interstellar space which separated them physically and intellectually from each other — a space in which a sturdy redwood fence becomes a straw in the wind — requires a look at two respective ways of life, inside and outside of the fence.

To begin with Furman Powell, with the internal life of the man which a neighbor might never hope to discover: visualize a wild, untended approach to the house (once inside the gate) along a gravel path and a sudden debouchement into a clipped, grassy clearing adjacent to a flagged area partly roofed by a grape-laden arbor joined to the house. Beyond the patch of grass, where a deck chair, boat cushions, and weathered table are in comfortable, worn disarray, the ground goes deliberately into fine chipped rock the depth of the west yard until it ends, as it begins, in a patch of grass backed by a dense stand of brush and untended fruit trees. Designed into the clean, shadowless length of rock-chip are large boulders placed in five groups of three, several stone jars and bowls, a small stone bridge over a cement-lined pond, and a stone lantern piped to the Powells' gas line to burn an eternal flame — a light invisible by day but which creates living shadow patterns at night.

The rock-chipped area is Furman's Japanese garden. Its piano curved margins are bordered in iris which stand tall and colorful in early summer. It is a place of light, shadow, and subtlety, and is a graphic representation of the artist's mind; he created it, a miniature copy of the stone garden at Ryuan-ji, with some additions of his own, so that he could see truth as well as know it. His twentieth-century mind longed for the thirteenth-century clarity of the eye of Muso Kokushi. No trees, no colors, no grasses. Yet, sprawled in his deck chair facing it, he could gaze at it the whole of a summer afternoon and still turn away, at dusk, puzzled. The image of those shapes stayed before his eyes afterward whether he waked or slept, and still he could not fathom the mystery of form, composition, and light, which to him were more vital than blood and flesh.

There were other ways in which his mind was mirrored in his surroundings: atop the two gateposts of the redwood fence were the round, cool, onion-shaped Giboshu so commonly seen on the bridge posts of Kyoto. How silent they were, even lonely, yet watchful, so watchful of the people outside who hurry and chatter and wave like reeds! He had carved them out of a solid redwood trunk he had bought in Oregon and had fastened them with decorated brass bolts he had brought from Nara.

Inside the house, his and Teresa's art works shared the walls with paintings of the images of Buddha — the god of thunder and the god of winds, and the genre pictures of Utamaro Kitagawa. Shelves were crowded with Kiyomidzu wares — teacups, rice bowls, vases and those ordinary little "antiques" Teresa could never keep from buying in the Sanneizaka above their Kyoto apartment near Kiyomidzu.

One truly ancient tea bowl supposed to have been glazed in the seventeenth century by Ninsei Nomura himself occupied an ebony pedestal of its own. This artifact was Furman's indoor Ryuan-ji, the object of his long, fixed gaze through a winter afternoon or evening when he was not painting: the *cha-wan* made him feel calm, deeply happy, peaceful, contented. The secret was to leave it alone, untouched; to let it live its own life; not to disturb that ever-fresh something that emanated from it.

Furman had built a roof light into the north exposure of his house, and here, in a clutter of canvases, sculptures, screens and scrolls, he and Teresa worked in the evenings and on weekends. He liked to paint while she was there. When she was teaching he liked to lie in his deck chair contemplating the stones of Ryuan-ji or sit in the house, weather forbidding, considering the pure *cha-wan.*

Most of his days after his retirement were spent outdoors trimming the edges of the little patch of grass, cutting the curled heads off the iris, or simply meeting the peaceful stone shapes of his garden on their own terms.

His outdoor occupations he usually performed unencumbered by clothes, which he considered unnecessary in the fruit-growing sun of a country where a day in January could feel like one in June. Furthermore, the air playing over the skin of his entire body served as a natural conductor between himself and the forms around him. Through its medium, uninterrupted by cloth or the restricting notions of propriety, he was able to receive in peace the secret emanations from his garden forms and from nature. They were real, they were pure, and they brought him a clarity of mind that approached — but never quite attained — understanding.

Teresa, knowing his mind, tolerated his natural state with wary amusement. For herself, she was in agreement that the trivia of material things must be brushed away in order to communicate unencumbered with the truth. She was not convinced, however, that the milkman or the postman would understand, and indeed, on their first encounter with Furman in the nude, they had proved themselves unworthy. The milk was no longer left at the house door but beside the gate, on the inside; as for the mail, if it was too cumbersome to go in the box outside, it was tied with string around the fat neck of one of the Giboshu.

An unfortunate visit by a young woman representing Wonderglo cosmetics had resulted in embarrassment for the lady and ennui for the artist. With a tiny, piercing scream she had beat a retreat to the outside. One other female had been exposed to Furman

*au naturel:* she was a middle-aged lady of their acquaintance, a
member of the board of deacons of the Methodist church, who
was that day soliciting gifts for the foreign missions drive. As she
emerged from the overgrown path and stepped onto the grass
she was confronted with the artist seated in an attitude of
Buddha trimming the grass edge with a pair of hand clippers.
With a rotation of her heel she promptly directed herself toward
the back door as if the Buddha, who was experiencing undiluted
scorn for her hypocrisy, were not there. On the return trip he
made no effort to remove himself from her view, nor did he place
himself in her way; he was bored by the whole kit and baggage of
subterfuge. She exited without acknowledging his presence.

"After all," Teresa chided him, "you're not very pretty in your
birthday suit, dear. You can't expect Minetta Flickmann to think
you are."

He was fifty-nine, fleshy of middle and spindly of leg, blessed
with an extremely white skin that never tanned, although his chest
was covered with curly black hair.

On the day that all barriers of false pride were to dissolve in the
pure light of truth, Furman, relaxing in his deck chair and watching the afternoon shadows move over the fifteen stones of Ryuan-ji,
was the image of a slightly sour and over-fed Adam camping in an
oriental Eden. He was at peace. A procession of Minetta Flick-
manns bent on ignoring him could not have budged him from his
nudity nor from his conviction that nature was truth and truth
nature, or have caused him to alter one jot his unsophisticated pos-
ture in the chair. It was thus that truth, in the shape of Bertha
Otterburgh, sought him out that day and found him.

Bertha had moved into a new house one street over and two
doors down from the Giboshu gate in January when her foster parents, along with several hundred other local and alien folk, had
signed on for jobs at the Splendimart Shopping Center on Fifty-
ninth Avenue — a super bazaar that had sprung full-blown from
the earth while the Powells were in Kyoto. Bertha had not quite
finished high school: one night in her junior year she had attended
an evangelistic movie in which a young drag racer had given up his
worldly goods to join a youth group called In His Footsteps. After
the show an agile young man had jumped to the stage and invited

those who wanted to be saved to exit on the left (the unbelievers to exit on the right). Bertha had chosen the left, because she felt herself called.

The call proved to be valid. Bertha became the most ardent evangelist of her local group. She gave up school to devote her mornings to reading to the blind, and spent her afternoons and evenings writing and distributing the IHF bulletin, *The Gleam.* Occasionally she worked as a checker in the Splendimart Supermarket in order to pay for room and board with her foster parents, or to pay the printer. She had a flair for reciting a biblical phrase and was thought by her peers to be an able witness to the Word.

Bertha was tall and looked out of place everywhere she went. Her 36-24-36 person was encased in a skin of ivory that took on olive tones in the sun. Above her oval face her black hair was wound high in a shining crown she kept scrupulously clean and smooth because it was a gift of God and should therefore be tended as a priestess would tend an altar. Her second-generation Italian mother had married an immigrant Moravian laborer who had imparted to Bertha his rather heavy features and a tendency to take on weight, but Bertha was an ascetic, and had inherited her mother's fine bones.

She appeared beside Furman's recumbent body as soundlessly as a fawn might appear from the brush. His awareness of her presence (he lay with his eyes closed now against the low sun) came only when she said, "It's a real nice day for sunburning, ain't it?"

He had embarked on an exploration of alternative compositions for a mural he planned for the city library. Indeed, his consciousness of time and place had so receded behind his eyelids that he felt himself to exist only as a projection of his critical mind wandering over the imaginary fresco from one shape to another much as a beetle would crawl over the stone mosaic design set into his patio.

He opened his eyes and turned his head toward that sudden, polite voice. She stood where she had apparently emerged from the path, in the full light of the glowing late afternoon, a purely oriental image in her straight-cut shift with high collar, her face as bland and unlined as the face of Buddha, her glossy head a genuine Utamaro. She regarded him thoughtfully, and he could only stare back.

"When He comes," she said pleasantly, looking beyond him now, "He'll feel real at home in that garden. It's so uncluttered."

He knew how the stones of Ryuan-ji appeared in this light: solid, true, simple, each an individual yet each related to the others. He had never seen a human being take on this simplicity until now — sculpture, pottery, yes, but never a living creature. Life was impure; it did not readily isolate itself from its heartbeat to become an art form. This young woman, however — whoever she was — was carved in white jade. The light shining from her was cleaner than the light that lay like an interference on her bare arms.

Her attention returned to him but she spoke of the garden. "Christ is the chief cornerstone, like the big one there," she pointed, "elect, precious. He that believeth on Him shall not be confounded."

Ah, one of those Bible girls. He hunched himself upright, the better to see her. No, she was not "one of" anything. Something unique lay about her like incense. He said cautiously (he was rusty on these things), "Yes. Wasn't it Peter who said on this rock I will build my church."

She smiled. "And we can be but priests, or 'lively stones,' Peter says, in this spiritual building."

He thought, there's no flaw in the timbre of the voice, either, or in the person behind the voice. This is fantastic. I mustn't scare her away.

She offered him a pamphlet from the raffia bag on her arm. "Here's your copy of *The Gleam*. It don't cost you nothing, but we ask for a contribution, if your spirit is eager to become a part of Christ's church on earth."

His spirit was not eager, but he took the literature and reached for his pants pocket. He had no pants. He was nude. A glance at her told him only that she was waiting courteously for the quarter, or dime, whatever he might be moved to give. It irritated him that he was now going to have to make a production of getting her the money, but there was nothing for it.

He heaved himself out of his chair with a grunted excuse and went to the house feeling singularly undressed. In the kitchen cupboard he fumbled in the teapot reserved for milk and newspaper change, took out a quarter, changed his mind and exchanged it for the newly minted Kennedy half dollar he had promised the paper boy. The boy would have to go without. Something in this experience was going to stay with him for life. He wasn't sure what it was, but it merited at least a token of recognition from the teapot.

Teresa called as he shut the cupboard, "Is it getting cool out there? I'll make tea." She appeared in the door. Across her face glinted the suppressed amusement it always cost him when she found him puttering about the place nude. "What are you after?"

"Some change for the IHF. They're sending their saints around the neighborhood." Why did he feel sarcastic? A moment before he had been deeply moved.

"Not one of those young girls, surely." She opened the louvers and looked out. "Really, Furman. There's a limit. Here." She snatched a smock from its hook and thrust it at him.

"Don't be a fool, Terry. She would be insulted." He went out of the back door leaving his wife, for the first time in years, nonplussed. It would have been disastrous for him to go out there in the smock — like looking down when you're on a ledge forty stories above Broadway and Forty-second Street. An act of faith was in the process; it wouldn't do to frighten it off. Let Terry witness the little drama, perhaps it would help her understand what he could not explain.

If the young woman had wanted to be spared embarrassment she could have slipped away as quietly as she had come. But she had not: she was standing at the edge of the iris border staring at the stones of Ryuan-ji. She smiled as he approached and said, as one might say at a reception in an art gallery, "It's like the tablet of Moses. Each one is a Commandment."

He answered as he would have in an art gallery, "It all depends on the individual's point of view. Yours is biblical." He handed her the half dollar, which she acknowledged with a matter-of-fact little gesture and dropped in her bag. She was not thinking about the money.

"Not just biblical, sir. A pure woman depicts a pure church, a vile woman a false church. I try real hard to keep the testimony of Jesus Christ."

His irritation was forgotten as he made an interesting conclusion: when she quoted Scripture her speech was perfect; in her own speech she was not exactly refined. This, he further noted, was not a mark of impurity; it only meant that her light shone through a raw-cut stone. He felt a gentle warmth for her sincerity, although he could never offer himself to be "saved."

"You do very well," he said. "It shows."

"Do you really think so?" She regarded him anxiously. "Am I free from spots, wrinkles, or any other disfigurement, holy and perfect like the church?"

How quaint, how naive. And how laughable, if it had not been so revealing. She stood as unclothed as himself in her utter truthfulness, while he, to her, must be hopelessly costumed in the trappings of duplicity, since he had no intention of ever giving his life to the Word of God.

"Yes, I really think so," he reassured her, adding, "You are very lovely." Then he wished she would go.

She made a move to leave, but a new mood was on her and she hesitated. She was concerned. "You can be cleansed, you know," she told him. "You can be baptized."

A very perceptive child indeed. He said, "I know. But I have my gods."

She considered this with a frown. Before she could form words to give him hope he indicated the path and led her to the gate, where she gave him a stiff little goodbye under the blank faces of the Giboshu.

Teresa acknowledged the miracle with a few caustic-gentle remarks over tea. She thought she understood, she said. He was not so sure, for himself. He only knew that he felt compelled to resurrect his crimson dragon-encrusted robe, which he had bought in Nanking in 1941 and had not worn in years, and that he could not drink his tea until he had it on.

# ISAAC BASHEVIS SINGER

*The Colony*

(FROM COMMENTARY)

IT WAS ALL like one long dream: the eighteen-day boat trip to Argentina, the encounter with my Polish *landsleit* in Montevideo and Buenos Aires, my speech in the Theater Soleil, and then the trip by car to the old Yiddish colony in Entrerios where I was scheduled to lecture. I went there in the company of a Yiddish poetess who was to read her poems, Sonya Lopata. The spring Sabbath day was a warm one. We passed by sleepy little towns bathed in sunlight, everywhere the shutters closed. The dusty road stretched itself between huge wheat fields and ranches where thousands of oxen fed without being tended. Sonya kept on talking to the chauffeur in Spanish, a language which I do not know. At the same time she patted, pinched, and pulled my hand; she even dug the nail of her index finger into it. The calf of her leg she pressed against mine. It was all both strange and familiar: the bright sky without a single cloud, the wide horizon, the midday heat, the smell of orange trees which drifted God knows from where. Sometimes it seemed to me that I had experienced all this in a former life.

About two o'clock the car stopped before a house which was supposed to be a hotel or an inn. The chauffeur knocked at the door, but nobody came to open it. After he had banged and cursed a long time the owner appeared, a sleepy little man. We had awakened him from his siesta. He tried to get rid of us with all kinds of excuses but the chauffeur refused to be cheated of his dinner. He argued with him profusely. After much haggling and many reproaches we were let in. We passed through a patio paved with colored stones and decorated with cactuses planted in large tubs. We entered a darkish hall which held tables without a single guest. It reminded me of the story by Reb Nachman Bratslaver about a palace in the desert where a feast for demons was prepared.

Finally the owner came to and went to wake the cook. Again we heard talk and complaints. Then the cook woke his assistant. It took three hours till we finished the meal. Sonya said to me, "This is Argentina."

There was a long trip in a ferry over a river as wide as a lake. The car approached the Jewish colony. The wheat fields swayed in the heat like a green sea. The road became even dustier. A Spanish cowboy on horseback drove a herd of cattle to slaughter. He chased the animals with wild cries and whipped them to make them run. They were all lean, covered with scales of dirt, and one could see the fear of death in their distended pupils. We passed the carcass of an ox of which nothing was left but hide and bones. Crows still tried to get the last bit of nourishment from it. In a pasture a bull copulated with a cow. He mounted her high, his eyes bloodshot and his long horns protruding.

All day long I did not notice the Sabbath, but when the sun began to set I suddenly felt the closing of the Sabbath day and remembered my father chanting "The Sons of the Mansion" and my mother reciting "God of Abraham." I was overcome by sadness and longing. I grew tired of Sonya's caresses and moved away. We passed a synagogue by the name of Beth Israel. There was no candle to be seen and no voice to be heard. Sonya said to me, "They are all assimilated."

We came to the hostel where we were to stay. In the patio stood a billiard table and barrels filled with torn books. A Spanish-looking woman was ironing a shirt. Along the patio, on both sides, doors led into rooms without windows. I was given a room, Sonya one near me. I had expected someone to receive us, but nobody came. Sonya went to change her clothes. I came out to the patio and stopped at one of the barrels. Great God! It was full of Yiddish books with library markings on them. In the dusk I read the titles of books which had enchanted my youth: Sholom Aleichem, Peretz, L. Shapiro, and translations from Hamsun, Strindberg, de Maupassant, Dostoevsky. I remembered the bindings, the paper, the print. Although it is unhealthy to read in twilight, I strained

my eyes and read. I recognized each description, every phrase, even
the misprints and transposed lines. Sonya came out and explained
it all to me. The old generation of colonists had spoken Yiddish.
There had been a library here; they had organized lectures, had
invited Yiddish actors. The new generation was raised on Spanish.
However, from time to time they still brought in a Yiddish writer,
a reciter, an actor. A special fund was set aside for this. It was done
mostly to avoid the criticism of the Yiddish press in Buenos Aires.
There still remained two or three old people who might enjoy
these activities.

After a while a member of the committee showed up. He was
short, broad, with black hair which was almost blue, and with the
black shining eyes of a Spaniard or an Italian. He spoke to us in a
broken Yiddish. He winked at the hotel owners and joked with
them. His cheeks had a mango redness. The night fell black and
thick, with a darkness that no lamp could penetrate. The crickets
seemed to make a different sound than in Europe or in the United
States where I now lived. The frogs croaked differently. The stars
had different formations. The southern sky pressed low with its
unfamiliar constellations. I imagined I heard the whining of jack-
als.

Two hours later I gave my speech. I spoke about Jewish history,
Yiddish literature, but the boorish men and fat women in the
audience seemed not to understand what I said. They didn't even
listen. They ate peanuts, talked, screamed at their children. Bee-
tles, butterflies, all kinds of insects flew through the broken win-
dowpanes and cast flying shadows on the walls. The electricity went
off and then on again. A dog had entered the hall and began to
bark. After my lecture Sonya read her poems. Then they gave us
a supper of extremely fatty and spicy foods. Later somebody took
us back to the hostel. The colony was badly lit, the ground full of
ditches and mounds of earth. The man who led the way told us
that the colonists had become rich in recent years. They didn't
farm anymore but hired Spaniards or Indians to do their work.
They themselves went often to Buenos Aires. Many of them had
Gentile wives. Their main amusement was playing cards. The
colonies which Baron de Hirsch had built to take the Jews away
from their insubstantial businesses and turn them into useful farm-
ers were falling apart. As the man spoke, passages from the Bible

came into my mind. I thought of Egypt, the Golden Calf, and the two calves which Jeroboam the son of Nebat established in the cities of Beth-el and Dan saying, "Behold thy God, O Israel." There was something biblical in that abandoning of one's origins, forgetting the efforts of the fathers. To this spiteful generation there should have come a prophet, not a writer of my kind. When the man left us, Sonya went to her room to wash up for the night, and I returned to the barrels of books. I could not read them now, but I touched their covers and pages. I breathed in their moldy smell. I dug a book out of the pile and tried to read its title by the light of the stars. Sonya came out in night-robe and slippers, her hair loose.

"What are you doing?" she asked. And I answered, "I am visiting my own grave."

The night was dark and long. Tepid breezes wafted through the open door. From time to time I heard what seemed to me the steps of a beast lurking in the darkness, ready to devour us for our sins. All the endearments, the whole game and procedure of love had passed, but I could not fall asleep. Sonya was smoking and she was overcome by a garrulousness which I sometimes suspect is the passion number one with women. She spoke in a nagging tone.

"What does a girl of eighteen know? He kissed me and I fell in love with him. He immediately began to talk about practical details: getting married, children, an apartment. My father was no longer alive. My mother had gone to live with her sister, a widow, in Rosario. She was actually her maid. Men ran after me, but they were all married. I worked in a textile factory. We made sweaters, jackets, all kinds of knitted goods. We were paid pennies. The workers were all Spanish women, and what went on there I cannot describe to you. They were always pregnant and they seldom knew by whom. Some of them supported their lovers. The climate in this country makes you crazy. Here sex is not a caprice or a luxury. It attacks you like hunger or thirst. In those days the pimps still played a big part in our community. They were the bosses in the Yiddish theater. When they didn't like a play it was immediately taken off the boards. The struggle with them had already begun. The others isolated them completely. Here the elders of the burial society are the real leaders. They refused to sell them plots in the cemetery. They were not let into the synagogue on the New Year and Yom Kippur. They had to establish their own cemetery and their own synagogue. Many of them were already old, has-been pimps, their wives former whores.

"What was I saying? Yes, then they still played a big role and tried to get hold of every woman who was alone. They had special men who did the seducing. As a matter of fact, my own boss was after me. I began to write — but who needs poetry here? Who needs literature? Newspapers, yes. Even the pimps read the Yiddish papers every day. When one of them died whole pages of obituaries appeared. You came here in the best time of the year, spring. But all year round the climate is terrible. In summer the heat is unbearable. The rich go to Mar del Plata or to the mountains, but the poor remain in Buenos Aires. In winter it's often bitter cold, and modern heating didn't exist in those days, not even the kind of ovens they used to have in Poland. One simply froze. Now there is already steam heat in the new buildings, but the old houses still have stoves which give out smoke, but no heat. It seldom snows, but it sometimes rains for days and the cold gets into your bones. There is no lack of sickness here and the women suffer even more than the men, bad livers, kidneys, what not. This is the reason the burial society is so strong.

"A writer does not write just for his files. I tried to find recognition in the newspapers and magazines, but when they see a young girl, and in addition not an ugly one, they're drawn to her like flies to honey. The big shot who himself led the war against the pimps became interested in me. He had a wife, but she had a lover. Why he consented to such conduct I will never know. He must have loved her immensely. Here there is not much religion. They go to synagogue only on the Days of Awe. The Gentiles have many churches, but only the women worship there. Almost every Spaniard here has a wife and a mistress.

"To make it short, I came to the editor, and he said to me almost openly, 'If you sleep with me, I will publish your work.' The critics disguised their meaning, however they wanted the same thing. I wasn't so holy, but a man has to please me. To go to bed with someone cold-bloodedly, this I cannot do.

"And there was Leibele, my present husband. He also wrote poems and had published some of them. He had even brought out a little book. In those times when somebody's name was printed black on white he appeared to me like a genius. He showed me a review by some critic in New York. He had a job with the burial society. Till today I don't know what he did there. Most probably he was somebody's assistant. We went to the rabbi and got married. We moved into the Jewish section on Corrientes. It soon appeared that his job wasn't worth a penny. He earned little and what he earned he spent. He had a whole bunch of friends, little writers, beginners, amateurs who attach themselves to Yiddish culture. I never knew that such creatures exist. He was never alone, always with them. They ate together, drank together, and if I had allowed it, he would have slept with them as well. Not that he was a homo-sexual. Far from it — he was not sexual altogether. He was one of those who cannot stay alone for a minute. Every night I had virtually to drive out his cronies, and every night my husband begged me to let them stay a little longer. They never left before two o'clock. In the morning I had to go to work. Wherever he took me, to the theater, to a restaurant, to a lecture, even just for a walk, his bunch of *shlemiels* followed. They could babble and dis-cuss each bit of nonsense forever. Some men are jealous, but he didn't even know that jealousy existed. When one of his colleagues kissed me, he was overjoyed. He wouldn't have minded if they had gone further. This is how he was and how he still is. When he heard that I was going with you on this lecture he was in seventh heaven. You are to him a god, and no one can be jealous of a god.

"We had no children and things might have come to an end, but a divorce only makes sense if you are in love with somebody else. However, the years passed and I didn't fall in love with anyone. The few affairs I had were with married men. In the beginning I had a high opinion of my husband's writing, but then he disap-pointed me in this too. I grew as a poetess — at least the critics praised me — but my husband stagnated. He began to be more and more enthusiastic about my poems. Everyone wants to be admired, but his admiration irritated me. He infected the others too. My house became a kind of temple, and I, its idol. One thing he for-got, we had to eat and pay rent. I still went to work and came home in the evening dead tired. I was a second Georges Sand, just the same, I had to cook supper for him and his parasites. I stood over the pots and they analyzed my verses and marveled at each word. Funny, isn't it?

"Lately things are a little easier. I stopped going to work. Once in a while I get a subsidy from the community — we now have a few patrons of the arts. From time to time I publish something in a newspaper, but basically everything remains the same. Occasionally he earns a little money, not enough!"

"Why don't you have children?"

"What for? I don't even know if he can father children. I suspect that we are both barren."

Sonya laughed. "If you remained here I would have a child with you."

"What for?"

"Yes, what for? Women have such a need. A tree wants to give fruit. But I need a man to look up to, not someone I have always to apologize for. Recently we even stopped sleeping together. It's all platonic."

"Does he consent?"

"He doesn't need it. All he wants is to discuss poetry. Isn't that strange?"

"Everything is strange."

"I have castrated him spiritually, that is the truth."

At dawn Sonya returned to her room. I covered myself and fell asleep. I was awakened by sounds I had never heard before. I imagined that I heard the voices of parrots, monkeys, and birds whose beaks are shaped like bananas. Through the open door there drifted in the fragrance of oranges mingled with the scent of fruits and plants which I could not identify. The breeze which blew in was warmed by the sun and seasoned with exotic herbs. I breathed deeply. Then I washed at the faucet and stepped outside. The barrels with books still stood there, waiting for a Yiddishist redemption. I left the patio and saw women and children dressed in Sunday finery — the mothers with mantillas on their heads and lace on their sleeves, prayer books in hand — riding to church on horseback. In the distance I could hear the ringing of church bells. All around me stretched the wheat fields and pastures. The grass was full of flowers: yellow, white, all colors and shapes, and the grazing oxen blithely chewed up all these wonders.

A sound played in the air, a mixture of birds' song and breezes in the trees. It reminded me of the story from the Talmud about the North Wind playing on King David's lyre and awakening him to

midnight studies. Sonya came out in a white dress embroidered
with red and blue. She looked fresh and was in a playful mood. It
seemed to me that only now I saw her for the first time as she really
was: small and broad, with high cheekbones and the slanted eyes
of a Tartar. She had a high bosom, rounded hips, and muscled
calves like the magician's helpers who used to come to our court-
yards to roll barrels on their soles and swallow fire.

Who knows from where she came, I thought. Perhaps from the
Khazars. What doesn't a people go through in two thousand years
of exile? But nature has a memory.

Sonya gave me a sideways glance. She smiled questioningly,
knowingly, with a wink. I remembered the passage in Proverbs,
"Such is the way of an adulterous woman: she eats, and wipes her
mouth, and says, 'I have done no wrong.'" Yes, the Enlighten-
ment which our poets praised in such lofty phrases and called "The
Daughter of Heaven" has made us all into lechers and harlots.
Nobody cared about serving us breakfast and we went to look for a
coffee shop. We strolled like honeymooners. The chauffeur who
had brought us here was to come for us at one o'clock. We were told
that he had a mistress among the laborers in the colony. Most
probably he would be hours late. After walking a few minutes, we
came upon a house. On the porch sat an old man in a gray jacket
and gray cap, the kind they used to wear in Warsaw. The color of
his face reminded me of the Warsaw porters: reddish, bluish, with
the stubble of a gray beard. His hairy throat with its pointed
Adam's apple was heavily veined. Although he was without prayer
shawl or phylacteries, he rocked back and forth as he recited from a
prayer book. As we came nearer he lifted up his eyes which might
have once been blue, but were now yellowish, spotted, and bloodshot.

I said to him, "You are praying, aren't you?"

The old man hesitated, and answered hoarsely (I imagined that
I recognized a Warsaw voice): "Do I have something better to do?
You are the speaker, isn't that right? I was at your lecture last night.
Did they let you talk, the scoundrels? They need a speaker like I
need a boil. All they need is to stuff themselves and play cards.
May their guts rot in hell! And you, young lady — what is your
name? — I heard your poems, yes, I heard them. I couldn't under-
stand them all. I am a simple fellow, but . . ."

He closed the prayer book and rose, "You will eat with me."

We tried to decline; the old man lived alone. But he said, "When will I have a chance like this? I am already eighty-one years old. When you visit again I will be lying there," and he pointed toward a grove of trees which must have hidden the cemetery.

The old man's house was full of broken-down furniture. His dishes seemed not to have been used for a long time. On an uncovered table in the living room there lay fresh eggs, still encrusted with the dirt of chickens. He prepared an omelet for us. He cut thick slices of whole wheat bread, full of bran and kernels. On his half-paralyzed legs he hobbled back and forth bringing us more things to eat: gooseberry jam, stale cookies, dried cheese. As he served us, he spoke.

"Yes, I had a wife. Fifty-four years we lived together like doves. I never heard a bad word from her. Suddenly she lay down and it was all over. The children wandered off. What was there for them here? One son is a doctor in Mendoza. A daughter is married in Brazil and lives in São Paulo. One son died and left three orphans. I always thought that I would be the first to go. But what can you do? If one is destined to live, one must live. A woman is not so helpless when she is alone. As you see, I am one of the first colonists. When I came here it was all wasteland. You couldn't even buy a piece of bread. While on the ship we all sang Zunser's hymn, 'The Lord's Blessing is in the Plough.' We were told that peasants are healthy because they live in the lap of nature, and that kind of poppycock. But the moment we arrived an epidemic broke out. Children fell ill and died. Older people also became sick. There was talk that the water was poisoned or who knows what. The Baron sent us delegates who were supposed to be agriculturalists, but they couldn't tell wheat from rye. They gave us endless advice; nothing helped. We all wanted to leave but didn't have the fare. We had signed contracts and were debtors. They bound us hand and foot; still they were — what do you call it — philanthropists. A great man came to us from Paris and spoke only French. We didn't understand a word he said. Of Yiddish they were ashamed, these charity lords.

"The Spanish people in the neighborhood hated us. They always shouted, 'Go back to Palestine!' One day a rain started and

continued for eight days without stopping. The rivers overflowed
their banks. There was a flood. In the middle of the day it became
as dark as night. There was such thundering and lightning that
we thought the world was coming to an end. It hailed too. The
hailstones were as large as goose eggs. One chunk of ice made a
hole in a roof and destroyed the house. How does ice come from
the sky? There were among us a few elderly people and they began
to recite their confessions. They believed the Messiah was about
to come and that this was the war between Gog and Magog. Those
who could write wrote long letters to the Baron, but he never answered. The women did one thing, they cried. There came to us
a young man, Hershelle Moskver. They called him — how do you
say? — an idealist. He had long hair and wore a black blouse with a
sash. He had already been to the Holy Land and had left it.
'There,' he said to us, 'is a desert. Here the earth is fat.' He brought
with him a young woman. Her name was Bella. She was beautiful, black like a gypsy, with a mouth full of white teeth. All the
men fell in love with her. When she entered a room it became
brighter. She comforted and helped everyone. When a woman
gave birth, she was the midwife. But the women began to complain that she had come here to seduce their husbands. There was
a lot of gossip and fighting. In the middle of all this Bella contracted typhoid fever and could not be saved. Her enemies had put
a curse on her. Hershelle Moskver stood at her grave and refused
to recite the Kaddish. Three days later he was found hanged. Do
you want another cup of coffee? Drink, my good friends, drink.
When will I have such an honor again? If you want, come with
me to the cemetery. It's right here. I will show you everything.
The whole colony is buried there."

Our breakfast finished, the old man took his cane and we walked
to the cemetery. The fence was broken. Some headstones were
bent, others had toppled over. They were all grown over with
weeds and wildflowers, the engraved letters green with moss and
half-erased. Here and there protruded a rotting wooden tablet.
The old man pointed toward a hill. "There lies Bella, and next
to her, Hershelle Moskver. They lived together, and . . . how is
it in the Bible?"

I helped him out. "Lovely and pleasant in their lives, and in
their death they were not divided."

"Yes, you remember. My memory has weakened. What took place seventy years ago is clear to me like yesterday. What happened yesterday seems far away. It's all the years, the years. I could sit with you seven days and seven nights and I wouldn't be able to tell you a tenth of what we suffered. And does the younger generation know it? They don't want to hear a thing. Everything was prepared for them. All work is now done with machines. They get in a car and drive to Buenos Aires. Are you two husband and wife?"

"No, we are friends."

"Why don't you get married?"

"He already has a wife." Sonya pointed to me.

"Well, I will sit down here."

The old man sat on a bench. Sonya and I walked among the graves and read the inscriptions on the headstones. The air smelled sweet, like honey. Bees hummed as they flew from flower to flower. Huge butterflies such as I had never seen before fluttered over the graves. The wings of one butterfly had the black and white stripes of a prayer shawl. Sonya and I came over a hill and saw a stone with two names, those of Bella and Hershelle Moskver.

Sonya took my hand and began to pinch, and pull. She dug her nails into the flesh. We stood by the stone and could not move away. Every few moments another kind of bird sounded his call. A strong perfume filled the air. In Sonya's hair all sorts of insects gathered. A ladybug landed on my lapel. A caterpillar fell into the cuff of my pants. The old cemetery teemed with life, death, love, vegetation. Sonya said, "If only we could remain here like this."

After a while we returned to the bench where the old colonist waited. He had fallen asleep. His toothless mouth was open and he looked as stiff as a corpse. But his eyes under his shaggy brows seemed to smile. A butterfly had settled on the vizor of his cap. It remained still, congealed in thoughts as ancient as its species. Then it shook its wings and flew off in the direction of the hill where Bella and Hershelle lay buried — the Romeo and Juliet of Baron de Hirsch's grandiose dream to turn Russian Jews into Argentine peasants.

# JOYCE MADELON WINSLOW

## *Benjamen Burning*

(FROM INTRO #1)

BENJAMEN A. (for Amos) Israelovitch, six years old, was standing on Delancey Street in Brooklyn with his arms raised straight up over his head. The three middle fingers on each hand Benjamen criss-crossed and like this with his arms and six fingers he was standing on Delancey Street. It was Saturday, sundown. There was a Kosher dill pickle smell from the delicatessen and the Spanish music from the tenements above the stores. There were the people out walking and the men talking outside the fish cellar about what tomorrow's business would be like if it was like last year this time, God forbid! The men wore yamalkas and mezuzahs and pais. The women you could not see — they stayed inside. The Spanish, Puerto Ricans, beat rugs against the walls of the buildings from inside their windows, cleaning for tomorrow. The house must be clean for after church. Their women you heard yelling for a child mostly. The Jewish women you wondered where they were.

In front of the iron grating of Katz's dry goods stall, locked against thieves on the Sabbath, Arnie Frankel played with seven other boys. Arnie was seven, the oldest, he could be the Rabbi. Jared was only a week younger but he couldn't be the Rabbi, the Cantor he could be. So he was the Cantor and sang the responses and Arnie got to lead the congregation or scold the boys for not knowing their Hebrew lesson. Michael, David, Micah, Jon, David S. and E-li, as he was called, were the congregation sometimes

and sometimes the bad pupils. Right now they were the congregation.

"Benjamen, come on and play," Eli called.

"E-li, you're not supposed to yell in Schul," Arnie scolded.

"Don't call me E-li. Call me right."

The Rabbi made a face at Eli. "Hey, Benjamen," the Rabbi
called. "Come here. You can help make a minyon."

Benjamen didn't answer. He was thinking of Aunt Reisa and
Uncle Art's when he was there a whole weekend alone.

The Rabbi asked again. "Benjamen, come here."

"Can't," Benjamen answered, looking at his fingers. "I'm not
through yet."

"What are you doing?"

"I'm burning."

"Why?"

" 'Cause I'm a Havdalah candle."

Arnie nodded, and turned back to his congregation. He started
davening, and they all followed, rocking back and forth on their
heels chanting. They said the Sh'ma, the Hatzi-Kaddish, and the
Adoration. They did the reading from the Torah, the Kiddish,
and heard a brief sermon from Jared on singing louder and coming to Schul on time, and finished the service with three verses
of Ayn Kelohenu and a benediction from Arnie. Then the women
started coming to collect their sons for bed — tomorrow would be
a big day. They'd have to get up early to go visit Aunt Reisa and
Uncle Art in the country, or Cousins Harry and Hope on the Island, or go with Marion and the boys to the shore.

"Say good night, Cantor," Jared's mother said. She was proud of
his game. Someday, for real, who knows? "Benjamen," she said,
"your mother wants you home now, too. What's with the hands,
Benjamen?"

"I'm a Havdalah candle."

"Ah, yes, three wicks, very good, Benjamen, just like a real Havdalah candle. Did you help your mother light hers at sundown?"

"Paul did it. I watched him."

"Good boy. It will burn all night while you sleep and tomorrow when you wake up it will be a puddle of wax. Come. Your
mother sent me to get you. Stop playing Havdalah candle now and
come home."

Benjamen politely followed Jared's mother home, his arms raised up over his head, his six middle fingers crossed. She looked back at him. "Benjamen, are you still playing Havdalah candle?"

"I *am* a Havdalah candle. I'm not through burning."

"Mmm. Well, burn on the way home. Hurry up." She walked briskly, looking back over her shoulder every so often at Benjamen burning, at Jared, glad he was a Cantor and not a candle. God bless Benjamen he was such a serious little boy. Oh well, don't butt in where you're not asked.

At home, Benjamen's mother was helping him into pajamas. Benjamen had not lowered his arms once.

"Benjamen, you would help me get this shirt off if you would please untwist your wick," his mother asked.

"I can't. The flame would go out."

"Benjamen, I've almost had it with this Havdalah candle game. Stop burning and take off that shirt *now*. And then get into the bathroom so you can wash up before you go to bed."

"Would you brush my teeth?"

"Benjamen! Harold! Harold, would you come in here and tell your son to behave and mind his mother. Benjamen, I want you to put your arms down at once and get into pajamas and brush your teeth, or no trip to the country tomorrow. Do you hear me?"

"I'm not through burning," Benjamen snuffled.

"All right. Burn. Burn. You can go into bed with your play-clothes on and burn all night, but don't expect to visit Aunt Reisa tomorrow." She went out of the room muttering, "Just like his brother at his age, thought he was a Kiddush cup and drank everything in the house. What are we raising here, a pulpit or a family?" Benjamen kicked off the covers, maneuvered between them and fell asleep.

Mrs. Israelovitch came in later to tuck him in and saw Benjamen fast asleep with his arms raised high above his head, the three middle fingers on each hand criss-crossed. At eleven P.M., just before she went to bed, she checked on him. He was asleep, still burning. At six A.M. just before she started breakfast she looked in. Same.

Benjamen got up at six-thirty, ran to the front door, got the funny sheets out of the Sunday paper, ran into his parents' bedroom and plopped onto his father's stomach.

"Umph!" said Mr. Israelovitch.

"Morning," kissed Benjamen. "Read me Dagwood first."

Mr. Israelovitch rubbed his face, kissed his son. "Well, so you stopped burning? Your mother will be happy."

"The flame went out early this morning. For a while I thought it would never go out."

"Neither did we. What happened, your arms got tired?"

"No, the candle burned to the bottom. You know about Havdalah candles. What does this say?"

"It says, Alexander, tell Cookie breakfast is ready and we better eat or we'll never get to Aunt Reisa's and Uncle Art's."

"It does not," Benjamen laughed. Then pouted, "Can I go?"

"We'll have to ask your mother."

Mr. Israelovitch and Benjamen went into the kitchen where Mrs. Israelovitch was laying out lox, bagels, whitefish, cream cheese, meunster cheese, and onion rolls on the table. Benjamen's older brother, Paul, ten, got up early to beat the line at the delicatessen. He'd also gotten some halavah, chocolate, for Aunt Reisa like his mother said.

"Can I go to Aunt Reisa's?" Benjamen asked his mother.

"You'll have to ask your father."

"Can I?"

"Will you stop burning the next time your mother asks you?"

"I wanted to but I couldn't. I couldn't. The flame wouldn't go out till it burned away and I wasn't finished burning yet."

"Benjamen," his mother said, "you must learn the difference between a game and being Benjamen. Candles do not eat breakfast. You could have stopped burning."

"I wasn't playing a game. I *was* a Havdalah candle. Honest."

"Benjamen," his mother said . . .

"Oh, Mom, let him go," Paul said. "Benjamen, you won't be a Havdalah candle anymore, will you?"

"I don't think so."

"OK. Just tell Mom you're sorry and let's eat, huh?"

"I'm sorry."

"OK," said his mother. "This time OK. But not again."

That night in the car on the way back from Aunt Reisa's, about sundown, Benjamen quietly lifted both arms above his head, his palms together.

"Put your arms down before they see you," Paul whispered fiercely.

"I can't."

"Benjamen, you promised Mom you wouldn't be a Havdalah candle anymore."

"I'm not."

"Well, then what are you doing with your arms, anyway," whispered Paul who hated to see his brother hit because he was usually hit for something, too, afterwards.

"I'm burning," Benjamen explained out loud.

"You're *what?*" Mrs. Israelovitch exclaimed, turning around.

"Benjamen," his father tried, "there are no Havdalah candles on Sunday. Saturday only."

"I'm not a Havdalah candle. I'm a Yarzeit candle."

"If you think you're going to burn for twenty-four hours like this, you're wrong," his mother yelled. "Harold, stop the car at once. I am going to finish this burning once and for all."

"Don't hit him," pleaded Paul.

"I can't help it," Benjamen cried. "I just can't help it. God said I have to burn."

"*God* said," Mr. Israelovitch said slowly. "When did God say this?"

"Just now. He tells me to burn at sundown and I don't know what I am till then."

"All right, Benjamen," said his father. "You may burn. We won't try to stop you. If God said, that's all there is to it. Esta, this is something for the Rabbi, not us. Go to the Rabbi tomorrow."

Mrs. Israelovitch explained to the Rabbi Monday.

"Thank God he thinks he is a candle and not a bush," the Rabbi consoled.

"He doesn't have enough fingers to be a bush. I'm telling you, Rabbi, I don't know what to do. All night long he burned. For all I know, he's at home still burning. Breakfast he didn't eat."

"He'll live."

"Wash up he didn't do."

"A little dirt never hurt."

"To school he didn't go."

"What! He didn't go to school?! That's not good. That's no-ot good! Why didn't he go to school?"

Mrs. Israelovitch threw up her hands. "Because he's burning!"

Mr. Israelovitch closed the cosmetics store early to come home and hear what the Rabbi said.

"He said don't worry."

"What don't worry with my son in there burning. He doesn't eat or go to school today and I'm not supposed to worry?"

"He says it will pass."

"What did he say about God telling him?"

"He said be glad that's all He asked."

Benjamen burned till just before sundown, then came out of his room and ate three cheese blintzes, a plate of macaroni salad, a plate of potato salad, a pickle, a glass of chocolate milk and some strudel. Then some more chocolate milk. His mother fed, looked worried, was quiet. The Rabbi said to humor it, it would go away.

"More?" his father asked gently. Benjamen shook his head.

"Where's Paul?"

"At Jared's watching the color television. Benjamen, how, ah, how do you feel?"

"Fine."

"Nothing hurts?"

"No. Can I go to Jared's?"

"*May* I go to Jared's," his mother corrected.

"May I go to Jared's?"

His father looked lovingly at him. "Ah, Benjamen, Benjamen. The youngest is supposed to be the easiest. Benjamen, a question. Will you burn anymore?"

"Harold!"

"Forgive me, Esta, I cannot ignore. Benjamen, do you like this burning? It hurts me so to see you not eat or go to school, and be so unhappy."

"I *have* to," he yelled and ran out the front door, slamming it hard. A little later Paul called to say Benjamen said to say he was at Jared's, too, and he was sorry for slamming the door. They'd be home after Cisco Kid.

Wednesday and Thursday went by. Benjamen walked to school
with Paul, and walked back with him. They played after school,
Benjamen winning two steelies and four cat's-eyes, Paul winning at
stickball from Peter Bashkin who claimed gutter balls don't count.
Mr. Israelovitch smoked his pipe after dinner, Mrs. Israelovitch
massaged his shoulders. They discussed the day's business, the boys,
and wondered why they could find the time to work and write
their eldest, Alan, at the college and he could let two weeks go by
and not a word.

"When he wants money, *then* we hear," Mr. Israelovitch puffed.

"He's a good boy, he's busy," Mrs. Israelovitch said. She defended
him, but still, she thought a letter would be nice. She would write
and tell him to write his father at once.

"Wait till I tell Reisa about the Yarzeit candle," Mrs. Israelovitch
said. "She may have some ideas about this."

"First you better explain to her what is a Yarzeit candle."

"Harold! My own sister raised in my mother's house knows a
Yarzeit candle."

"Hmm? Then she's forgotten maybe, like she forgets to keep
Kosher and to pray in the Schul and to keep the head covered.
What is Arthur, a pagan he prays without his head covered?
We get a little money, a little acceptance, a home in the high-fa-
lootin' neighborhood, and so soon we forget!"

"So soon we forget? So soon we forget? *You* forget you're talking about my only sister? And while we're on the subject of forgetting, did you forget a little common courtesy at supper? Since
when do you go to someone's house and eat off their table and then
throw it up to their faces that the food you are eating isn't good
enough for you because it isn't Kosher? You knew they weren't
Kosher before you sat down! You had to yell at them in front of
Benjamen?"

"I didn't want to eat there in the first place! Who made me eat
there? If I had my way, we wouldn't have gone at all."

"She's my sister and I wanted to see her. You'd begrudge me
my own sister? And it does Benjamen no harm to run in a little
grass for a change, to play with their dog. Where in the city can
he play with a dog?"

"He likes dogs? I'll take him to the pound."

"Harold, don't pick up just one word. You're stubborn as a

mule. They have not been blessed with children and they are very good to Benjamen."

"You call it good to Benjamen when Arthur takes him to their Temple, it should burn, and they wear no Yalmakas? This you call good? We send him to Hebrew School and teach him here so he can go there and pray without a Yalmaka? Next you'll let him eat pork at their table!"

"They wouldn't serve him pork!"

"Aach! Just because there's a mezuzah on their door you don't call that a Jewish home. A cat can have kittens, it doesn't make it a mother."

"They're Jewish the way they think Jewish is. She's my sister, Harold, and I love her."

"Esta, I love your sister dearly, and her husband, he's a good man, but Jewish the way Jewish is they are not. Jewish you light the candles and break chalah and pray with the head covered. You don't drink a glass wine, then take the empty glass and call it a glass wine. You leave out the wine, it's an empty glass only. Esta, no more do I want Benjamen visiting that pagan. He doesn't need this."

"Harold, you're getting entirely too carried away. What is this 'no more'? You don't make bad relations between my sister and me because you don't like their Temple. No one asked you to go to their Temple. So we won't let Benjamen visit their Temple anymore, it upsets you so. Everytime they talk about their Temple or their young Rabbi you give such a look you scare him half to death."

"Esta, I said no more and I mean it. And I want no consulting with her on this burning. We can handle this ourselves without their help, and not another word said!"

They kissed and made up before they went to sleep because they promised they would never go to sleep angry. But a honeymoon it was not.

Friday, when Mr. and Mrs. Israelovitch came home from Schul, Paul met them at the door crying.

"What's the matter?"

"I can't make him stop," Paul cried. "He was crying all night and he won't stop."

Mr. and Mrs. Israelovitch ran into the bedroom. Benjamen was on his bed with his train and silky blanket, all cried out. Up in the air he held five fingers, and four fingers.

"Nine fingers? What has nine candles, Benjamen?"

"One is the Shamos."

"A menorah," his father slumped. "Are you going to burn eight days and nights, Benjamen?"

"He can't burn for eight days, he'll starve to death," his mother said. "Benjamen, enough! Enough!"

His father sat on the bed next to Benjamen and looked like he would cry.

"I *have* to," whispered Benjamen.

"When did you start burning, Benjamen?"

No answer.

"A little after you left," Paul cried.

"Benjamen, you're making your brother cry. *Please* stop burning," his father pleaded.

"I can't."

"Why can't you?" his mother asked.

"God said I have to." Benjamen tried to cry but he was too tired out. He hiccuped crying.

His father sighed. "Go to sleep, Benjamen." He lifted him up, tucked him in, kissing him good night with a hug. He shepherded his family out of the room. "He's never burned for more than a day. Tomorrow he'll forget he was a menorah and will eat supper again." He put his hand on Paul's head. "Don't worry, Paul. It'll be all right." Paul went to bed troubled, but not worried. Mother and Father were home. Everything would be all right.

But everything was not all right. Benjamen ate nothing Saturday. Nothing on Sunday. Despite pleading. Despite threats. Despite crying.

The supper table Monday night was lonesome again. Only three people where four should be. Mrs. Israelovitch put silverware at Benjamen's place, but he was not there. She would keep putting silver though. The day I don't put silver is the day I give up and die, she thought. Mr. and Mrs. Israelovitch and Paul stayed within their places. They did not spread out more comfortable over Ben-

jamen's part of the table. Benjamen's part of the table was for
Benjamen, no two ways about it.

"You'll pass the salt, please?" Mr. Israelovitch asked.

It was passed.

There was a lot of sighing and dipping the bread into the natural gravy, and eating and as for talking not much. Paul never
heard before the cup into the saucer make such a loud noise. He
was very frightened.

After supper, Paul snuck some gefilte fish with a carrot slice in
to Benjamen. If his mother caught him he'd get hit: "It hurts me
as much as it hurts you," she said. "He'll get so hungry, he'll eat,
you'll see and everything will be all better. Trust me." Paul
waited till his parents left Benjamen's room and were talking in
the living room.

"Benjamen, I'll feed you some fish," Paul said. "Open your
mouth."

"I don't want any."

"You *love* gefilte fish. Come on, please eat some fish."

"I don't want any. I don't want anything. Just leave me alone."
Benjamen was sitting on his bed with his silky blanket, nine fingers up in the air.

"Aren't you hungry? I'll get you some candy. Don't you even
want some candy?"

"No." Benjamen was very white, very quiet, very unhappy.

"Oh Benjamen, what's the matter?" Paul sat down next to him
and put his arm around him. Benjamen did not flinch away like
he usually did when someone got mushy. Benjamen looked very
little, very different.

"I've got to keep burning," he whispered. "If the flame goes
out we die."

"We won't die," Paul promised.

"Because I'm keeping it burning," Benjamen said.

Paul picked up the carrot with the fork and held it close to Benjamen. "Carrot?" He talked like Mrs. Israelovitch. "A nice
piece carrot, Benjamen?"

Benjamen shook no.

"*Please* eat the carrot. Just the carrot."

Benjamen shook no.

Paul cried almost. He didn't know what to do, what to do. All

of a sudden he screamed, "NO!" He stabbed the fish with the
fork and flung it, plate, carrot, fork, everything crash to the floor
screaming, "Awful fish! I hate you fish!"

Mr. Israelovitch came running in. He scooped Paul up, held
him tight.

"I hate you fish," Paul sobbed. "I hate you fish!"

"I know," Mr. Israelovitch soothed. He looked at Mrs. Israelovitch standing worried in the doorway. "It's all right shanevelt,
it's all right." Later in the week Benjamen let Paul feed him some
rye bread and butter, but Paul only. From his mother and father
he would eat nothing.

On the fifth day the doctor came and worried over Benjamen.
He knew the Israelovitches well. He'd seen the children through
measles, German measles, chicken pox, scarlet fever, a nail in the
foot, a broken nose, and the polio scare. He knew how they were
doing in school, he celebrated with the family bar mitzvah, and his
own daughter Nancy was in college with their oldest, Alan. This
with Benjamen worried him. He was thinking how to say what he
thought to Harold and Esta.

"Nu?" Mrs. Israelovitch said.

"Esta, there are some things we need a different kind medicine."

"I don't care how much it costs," Mr. Israelovitch said. "Get it."

The doctor tried again. "There are some things there are no
shots, no pills." He stopped. How to go on? He knew this family,
he loved and understood them. Understood? Felt, more like. His
own grandparents raised his parents this way and it was a good
way, they were good people. But change, even for their own good,
they did not do. "There are some things," he said to the anxious, unblinking eyes, "we help by talking, listening."

"I try to talk to him, doctor," Mrs. Israelovitch said. "Me he
won't answer."

"Of course," the doctor said. She had given him an opportunity. "You know some times you get angry, you don't know why
and you talk to a friend, a complete stranger in the market, maybe?
You talk, you feel better. Maybe Benjamen would talk to a
stranger, someone new who knows special how to understand
him?" He waited. They did not understand yet. He'd have to do

this the best he could so Benjamen could be helped. "I have a friend," he continued, "who is very good with children, with this kind of problem like Benjamen is having."

"You know other children who burn?" Mrs. Israelovitch asked.

"Not always burn, but don't talk, don't eat. Deep down inside is something bothering them."

"This is a personal friend?"

"A man I trust," the doctor said. "A very good doctor downtown."

"Oh *ho!*" Mr. Israelovitch exclaimed. The doctor cringed slightly. "Comes the dawn! I know what it is you're saying. A doctor with the couches, yes? A what do you call him — a *headshrinker!*" He pounced on the word. "A headshrinker! No! No son mine goes to a headshrinker."

The doctor nodded sadly. He knew it. No changing. There was only one thing he could say here, the question that always commanded attention, respect and consideration. "Harold, what can it hurt to try?"

Mr. Israelovitch was shaking his head back and forth, back and forth.

"We'll discuss it," Mrs. Israelovitch said firmly. They started discussing the second the doctor walked out the door.

"I don't know, I just don't know," Mrs. Israelovitch began. "My mother, may she rest in peace, never had this problem with us. Did we do something wrong? Alan, God bless him, is a healthy, smart boy. Paul is a good boy. What did we do wrong with Benjamen?"

"What is this with the headshrinker?" Mr. Israelovitch said. "Did we ever go to headshrinkers? We got a good hit, no more problem. Or we went to the Rabbi and we did what he said. No couches, no books on raising the children. My father couldn't read the English if he had such a book. Now, so different. Who's changed, I ask you? The children or the parents?"

"Maybe it's the only thing to do," Mrs. Israelovitch sighed. "For the first time I can't help mine own child." She began to cry. "I can't help mine own child. What kind mother am I?!"

"Maybe I expected too much?" Mr. Israelovitch said sadly. "Alan, God bless him, was always saying I expect so much from him he was afraid to bring home a bad mark."

"We never expected all A's. Just the best they can do. They knew we never got angry if it is the best they can do. Is it too much to expect the best from your children?"

"We should thank God we got two healthy sons. With two such sons it's only fair there are problems with the third. Who else has two such boys? Oh, Benjamen. Oh, my little one."

"Now what was good is bad. It used to be you heard drink more milk. Drink more milk. No more. Is bad for the skin. It used to be eggs was good for you — good for the shine on the hair. Now no more. Is bad for the heart. And butter. If mine mother, may she rest in peace, cooked with butter it was a luxury it was so expensive, so delicious. Now, no! Margarine they say to use. I'm telling you, first the milk, then the eggs, then the butter is all bad. The next thing you know, they'll say your own parents is no good for you!"

"They said it! What do you think the doctor was saying? Who goes to a headshrinker? Someone who hates his parents!"

"No! Someone who hates his parents?"

"What do you think — someone is going to pay fifty dollars to tell a headshrinker he is happy at home? What do you think the doctor was saying before?"

"He thinks Benjamen hates us? Oi Gottenu! It should come to this!" She started to sob into her handkerchief, rocking back and forth, back and forth in the rocker. Mr. Israelovitch wept inside.

Benjamen burned till the menorah burned out. He grew feverish. He didn't seem to hear when you spoke to him, he didn't cry, he never smiled. He stayed in his room and sat still with his silky blanket. He seemed to be waiting for something.

Alan flew home Saturday. He'd never heard his mother so upset. He knew the story from letters, now from the phone. His mother had half-cried, half-laughed it, trying to minimize it for him Benjamen saying over and over in a fever he was going to keep the flame alive, going to burn forever going to be the Eternal Light over and over he says this, Alan, he has 104° fever, he is in Mt. Sinai Hospital your father is beside himself God help us he is so sick over and over he says he is the Eternal Light God says he must burn forever I don't know what all this is maybe you better come home — .

Alan, Paul, Mr. and Mrs. Israelovitch, Jared's mother and the doctor sat at a table in the doctors' dining room of the hospital, no one touching his coffee. Paul was quiet, still. Alan was stunned. Yesterday he was listening to a lecture in sociology. Today he had just seen his little brother in a hospital bed packed with ice, the doctor shaking his head back and forth, back and forth, and the nurse looking with compassion at his mother. The Rabbi had already left to see other patients. He told Alan to pray, to be a strength for his poor parents, for Paul. Alan looked at Paul. I wonder how much he understands of this, he thought. I wonder how it will affect him. My God! he thought. Benjamen! He hardly knew him. He was away at the University for two of Benjamen's growing-up years. He got pictures Benjamen drew for him while he was at school, he sent Benjamen little presents, he didn't even know his own brother. How selfish to take and take. While he was dating girls Benjamen was burning inside, burning up with something while he was sure his mother's letters exaggerated, while he laughed over her spelling errors.

"What kind of a God lets this happen?" he burst out. "What kind of a God lets a little boy — "

"Sha!" Mr. Israelovitch commanded. "You do not speak of God in such a tone."

"It's natural to want to blame," Mrs. Israelovitch soothed. "Sha, Alan, my baby, my precious baby." She hugged Paul to her, covering him with tears, he was the closest to her. Jared's mother got up and put her arms around Mrs. Israelovitch. She sobbed against Jared's mother. Paul edged away.

"Why did he have to burn? Why did he have to burn?" Mrs. Israelovitch sobbed.

"He said God told him," Mr. Israelovitch said hoarsely. "I don't understand. I never heard such a thing."

Paul was restless. He wanted to run. He wanted to cry. He wanted to be home eating supper all of them together. He wanted to sit on his father's lap. He didn't like this. He felt like he had to run.

"He said we would all die if he stopped burning," Paul said.

"What's this?" said his father. "When did he say this?" They all listened carefully.

Paul was frightened. Maybe he shouldn't have told. "He said it when I took him the fish."

"What else did he say?"

"Nothing."

"Where does he get an idea like this?" Mrs. Israelovitch said.

"Who knows where children get ideas?" Jared's mother said. "They get an idea in their heads, it takes forever to find out from where."

"We would all die if he stopped burning," the doctor said. He thought. He tapped the table.

"Paul," the doctor said, "do you know what he meant?"

Paul shook his head. He started to cry.

"Mom, let's get him home," Alan said. "Let's all go home. There's nothing we can do here." He wanted to get out of the hospital smell, the doctors getting their supper in the hospital. Maybe he could bring a toy or a stuffed animal to Benjamen tomorrow. Maybe he could understand all this if he were at home, he never did enough for Benjamen.

"I'm staying," his mother said. "What if the fever breaks, if he wants to see me? I stay here all night if I have to." Her voice got louder. "You come home from the college, you right away give orders."

"No, no, I just — "

"Don't just me. Who sent you to college? Who scrimped so you could go to school take girls to shows? And you don't even write a letter to your father once a week who waits to hear from you. You know how he loves you."

"Mom, I'm sorry. I — "

"I'm sorry. I'm sorry. You think that settles everything?" She wiped the corner of her eye. "You get some new ideas you think you know everything, you use God's name in vain in front of us you forget you are Alan Israelovitch, you forget where you come from like my sister, God bless her. Next you'll forget the Sabbath, you'll forget to keep Kosher, you'll forget everything like you forget your own parents. Maybe sending you to the college wasn't such a smart idea. Maybe we made a mistake with you, Alan, letting you have so much. I swore I'd never say this in front of your father but I'm saying it. All this new, you forget your own home.

I didn't go to college, Alan, but I still know more about life than you."

"I never forgot you, Mom, believe me, I never forgot you."

"Not even a letter once a week that's asking too much."

"I'm sorry about the letters. I didn't realize — "

"Big shot! New ideas."

"There's nothing wrong with new ideas."

"Oh, no?"

"No! There's nothing wrong with change if it makes you better!"

"So now we're no good, eh? Your family made you, Alan. Your family you run to when you are in trouble or lonely. The old family you don't think is so bad then."

"The old family is fine. But new ideas, new ideas let you see more. Mom, I never knew what was going on in the world till I went to college. I thought the world began and ended with Delancey Street. Other people aren't so different, you know? They just have different ways of saying the same things."

"You mean to tell me," Mr. Israelovitch said with remarkable control, "you are no different from Reisa, Art, from forgetting the Sabbath, the Covenant? This is what I get after all these years of trying to teach you — "

"I knew you'd get back to them. It always gets back to them, doesn't it? Well, there's nothing wrong with them. They're different. OK. But it's what they want, the way they want to live. So let them. We live the way we live. The whole world doesn't have to do what you do just because you think it's right. Who are you anyway?"

There was a silence. Alan swallowed. Drank some cold coffee. He wasn't going to take it back. He was tired of being different, of fighting prejudice, other ideas. They had to know sooner or later.

"Alan," the doctor said, "we're all very emotional and excited here. Maybe you owe your father an apology?"

"I'm sorry," Alan said.

"Ach!" Mr. Israelovitch turned away, disgusted, defeated, sick at his heart. "I can see it all happening before mine own eyes. Our way of life is dying with our own children. With mine own generation, all the Jews will be dead. My own son doesn't keep up the faith, God help us!"

The doctor leaned forward as Mr. Israelovitch was speaking. "Harold," he said quickly, "did you ever say that in front of Benjamen?"

"Say what?"

"All the Jews will be dead."

"I don't know."

"Oh, Dad, you always say that whenever you talk about Reisa and Art."

"Maybe I did. You remember that, eh? Too bad you don't remember as well the other things I've been trying to teach you."

"Mr. Freund says something like that all the time," Paul said.

"What does he say?" the doctor asked.

"He says the flame will go out if we don't keep the faith strong. He says it when we give the wrong answer."

"Oh, my God," Mrs. Israelovitch breathed. "I understand." She shuddered. "A pox be on my house."

Mr. Israelovitch was stricken. He mumbled something, at first incredulous, horrible, then louder, "I've killed my own son? Esta, forgive me. I've killed my own son?"

"Bite your tongue. He isn't dead." She put her hand over her heart, rocking back and forth, back and forth in the cold hospital chair.

Upstairs, Benjamen dreamed of candles, tall candles of red, yellow, orange, bright gold candles and all the candles were people, Mr. Freund, Aunt Reisa and Uncle Art, Paul, his mother and father all gloriously burning, big, tall, strong flames, thousands of red flames, swirls and arcs of hot, fiery light in front of Katz's delicatessen, candle smells and black smoke, hotter, all the people melting into hot puddles of wax, his father dripping hot melted faces of flame to his feet the hiss of sliding wax bodies mirrors and mirrors of blinding heat a wall of fire he was surrounded by blue-hot flame yellow spots running exploding run Benjamen run! Benjamen plunging through the wall of fire, sickening heat, fire in his hands and feet. Upstairs Benjamen kept burning till the flame went out.

# BIOGRAPHICAL NOTES

# Biographical Notes

MAEVE BRENNAN was born in Dublin, Ireland, on January 6, 1917. *In and Out of Never Never Land,* a collection of her short stories, was published by Scribner's in 1969. *The Long Winded Lady,* a collection of notes and comment from *The New Yorker* magazine, was published by Morrow in 1969.

JACK CADY was born in 1932 and raised in the South and Midwest. He has worked as an over-the-road trucker, an auctioneer, a tree climber and a sailor. He is currently teaching English and short story writing at the University of Washington, Seattle, as an assistant professor.

His publication credits include "The Burning," winner of the *Atlantic Monthly* "First" award, 1965. The story also appeared in *The Best American Short Stories 1966.* He has published in *The Yale Review* and elsewhere and is currently working on a novel.

MARK COSTELLO was born in 1936. His work has appeared in *Epoch, North American Review* and the *Transatlantic Review.* He now teaches in the Department of English at the University of Illinois and is working on a novel.

JOHN BART GERALD was born in 1940 in Manhattan. He received his B.A. from Harvard and has served as a medic with the Air Force Reserves. His first novel, *A Thousand Thousand Mornings,* appeared in 1964.

MARY GRAY HUGHES was born in Brownsville, Texas, in 1930. She was educated at the University of Texas and Barnard College, and did graduate work in anthropology at Oxford University. She has published short stories and poetry. Her father is the writer Hart Stilwell.

NORMA KLEIN was born in New York City in 1938. She graduated from Barnard College in 1960 and received an M.A. in Slavic Languages from Columbia in 1963. She has published fifty short stories in such magazines as *Mademoiselle, Cosmopolitan, Grecourt Review, Southwest Review, Northwest Review, Canadian Forum, Nimrod, MSS, Malahat Review, Prairie Schooner.* One of these stories was included in *Prize Stories 1963: The O. Henry Awards,* another in 1968. She is married to a biochemist and has a two-year-old daughter.

MARY LAVIN, the author of nine volumes of short stories and two novels, was born in East Walpole, Massachusetts. She went to Ireland at the age of ten and has lived there ever since although she has returned for many visits to the United States. Miss Lavin was educated in Dublin, receiving her M.A. from the National University of Ireland, where she also received the degree D. Litt (*honoris causa*) in 1968. She is a member of the Irish Academy of Letters. In 1960 and 1962 she was the holder of a Guggenheim Fellowship. She was awarded the James Tait Black Memorial Prize for *Tales from Bective Bridge* and the Katherine Mansfield Prize for *The Great Wave.* Her most recent collection, *In the Middle of the Fields,* was published in March 1969. Widowed in 1954, Miss Lavin, who is the mother of three daughters, recently married Michael MacDonald Scott. They live on a farm in County Meath and have a small mews-house in Dublin.

ALISTAIR MACLEOD currently lives in Fort Wayne, Indiana. He was born in North Battleford, Saskatchewan, but did most of his growing up in Dunvegan, a small community in Nova Scotia's Inverness County. He has worked at various times as a milkman, logger, miner and teacher in a one-room school. He graduated, also at various times, from St. Francis Xavier University, the University of New Brunswick and Notre Dame. He has published fiction and poetry in several small magazines, and is at present an assistant professor of English with Indiana University at Fort Wayne.

DAVID MADDEN was born in 1933 in Knoxville, Tennessee, where he was raised and has wandered over much of the United States —

as a student and as a teacher he has lived in Connecticut, California, North Carolina, Kentucky, Ohio, Boston and New York. Crown will publish his second novel, *Cassandra Singing*, this fall, and Illinois University Press is bringing out a collection of his essays on imaginative writing, *The Poetic Image in Six Genres*. Louisiana State University Press will publish *The Singer*, a collection of his stories. His short stories, essays and poems have appeared in major literary quarterlies. Many of his plays have been produced outside New York. He is the author of a study of Wright Morris, and of *Tough Guy Writers of the Thirties* and *Proletarian Writers of the Thirties*.

Writer-in-residence at Louisiana State University, Mr. Madden has a Rockefeller Grant this year to enable him to finish *Bijou*, a novel in progress.

BERNARD MALAMUD was born in 1914 in Brooklyn, and studied at The City College (A.B., 1936), and Columbia University (M.A., 1942). A member of the Bennington College faculty since 1961, Mr. Malamud has also taught for two years at Harvard.

Mr. Malamud was a Partisan Review Fellow in fiction during 1956–57. In 1958, he received the Rosenthal Award of the National Institute of Arts and Letters; in 1958, the Daroff Memorial Award; in 1959, the National Book Award for fiction for *The Magic Barrel*; and both the Pulitzer Prize and the National Book Award in 1967 for *The Fixer*. He was one of the eleven recipients of the first Ford Foundation grants to creative writers. He is a member of the National Institute of Arts and Letters.

His novels are *The Natural* (1952), *The Assistant* (1957), *A New Life* (1961), and *The Fixer* (1967). *The Magic Barrel* (1958) and *Idiots First* (1963) are collections of his short stories.

He is married and the father of two children.

MATTHEW W. MCGREGOR was born in 1920 in Montreal, Canada, and grew up in Detroit, Michigan. He is a veteran of the Civilian Conservation Corps, James Hoffa's Teamsters Union 299 and of the U.S. Navy. He attended Wayne University, Detroit, and was graduated from the University of Michigan where he won an Avery Hopwood Award. He has worked for newspapers in Detroit, in Westchester County, New York, and in Arizona, Minnesota, Connecticut and Pennsylvania, and was in 1956 nominated for a Pulitzer Prize in news reporting. He spent one year writing in

Bideford, Devonshire, England. Currently living in Harrisburg, Pa., with wife and infant daughter, he is working on a book of short stories.

JAMES ALAN MCPHERSON was born in Savannah, Georgia, in 1943. He grew up there and attended Morris Brown College in Atlanta, and Morgan State College in Baltimore. He entered Harvard Law School in 1965 and received an LL.B in 1968. Currently he is working on an M.F.A. at the Writer's Workshop at the University of Iowa.

He is now teaching a course at Iowa in Afro-American Literature, and in September he will begin a new job as a contributing editor to the *Atlantic*. His first book, *Hue and Cry*, a collection of short stories, will be published in May 1969, and he is presently at work on a novel.

JOHN R. MILTON was born in Minnesota in 1924. He received his B.A. and M.A. from the University of Minnesota and his Ph.D. from the University of Denver. He has taught in Minnesota, North Dakota, Colorado, and is currently in South Dakota. In 1965 he was Resident Writer in fiction at the Helene Wurlitzer Foundation, Taos, New Mexico. His critical writing has been largely in the areas of the American novel, Western American literature, modern drama, and esthetics, and he has published four books of poems, *The Loving Hawk*, *Western Plains*, *The Tree of Bones* and *This Lonely House*.

JOYCE CAROL OATES's sixth book, a novel entitled *Them*, will be published in the fall of 1969. Her previous novel, *Expensive People*, was nominated for a National Book Award, and other fiction of hers has appeared in *Esquire, Atlantic Monthly, Southern Review* and elsewhere.

NANCY PELLETIER PANSING was born in 1923, and, since her father was a construction engineer, she traveled all over the eastern United States with her family; in 1944 she graduated from Duke University, married Joseph Pansing, and started traveling some more. Now, four children later, the Pansings are settled permanently in Marietta, Ohio. Mrs. Pansing started back to school several years ago when she enrolled in a creative writing class at Marietta College. Since then she has gone on to get a teaching certificate at Marietta College and will soon have completed a

Master's degree in English at Ohio University. "The Visitation," which appeared in *Intro,* is her first published story.

SYLVIA PLATH was born in 1932 in Boston, Massachusetts, and was educated at Wellesley High School and Smith College. While on a Fulbright scholarship to Newnham College, Cambridge, she met the English poet Ted Hughes, whom she married in 1956. After a period in the United States she settled in England where her two children were born. "Johnny Panic and the Bible of Dreams," perhaps the finest of her few short stories, was unpublished during her lifetime. Her poetry books are *The Colossus* (Random House) and the posthumously published *Ariel* (Harper & Row). A novel *The Bell Jar* is published by Faber and Faber, London. A book of critical studies by various hands, together with some hitherto unpublished prose and poetry and a checklist of criticism and bibliography, entitled *The Art of Sylvia Plath,* will be published by Indiana University Press this year.

MIRIAM RUGEL was born in Philadelphia and studied short story writing at Columbia. She has published more than a hundred stories and articles, her fiction having appeared in *Harper's, Epoch, Mademoiselle, Kenyon Review, Saturday Evening Post* and *Good Housekeeping.* Her works have also been sold in England, Canada, Africa, Italy, Norway and Sweden, and have been used on television and radio. Her stories have been reprinted in the *O. Henry Prize Award Stories* and in such collections as Bread Loaf's *American Accent* and Harold Ribalow's *The Chosen,* and in several supplementary school reading texts. For eight years she led an adult writing class and currently lives in Philadelphia with her husband, son and daughter. She has just finished (vicariously) law and medical school with the last two. At present she is working through a novel.

MARGARET SHIPLEY was born in California and has lived in New York City, France and Greece. She now makes her home in Boulder, Colorado, with her husband and two teen-age sons. She is an editorial writer for the University of Colorado and is the author of a novel, *The Sound of the Sun.* Her poems and short stories have appeared in a number of literary journals.

ISAAC BASHEVIS SINGER, the son and grandson of rabbis, was born in Radzymin, Poland, in 1904. Although he was a student at the

Rabbinical Seminary in Warsaw, he chose not to become a rabbi and went to work as a journalist for the Yiddish press in Poland after the completion of his studies. In 1935, Mr. Singer came to the United States and since that time he has worked as a journalist and book reviewer for the *Jewish Daily Forward* in New York City.

Although he originally wrote in Hebrew, Mr. Singer long ago adopted Yiddish as his medium of expression. His published works in English include *Satan in Goray, Gimpel the Fool, The Family Moskat, The Magician of Lublin, The Spinoza of Market Street, Short Friday, The Slave, In My Father's Court,* and *The Manor. The Seance,* his most recent book, was published in 1968 by Farrar, Straus & Giroux.

Isaac Singer has been the recipient of literary awards which include the Louis Lamed Prize and a grant from the American Academy and National Institute of Arts and Letters. He is a member of the National Institute of Arts and Letters. Mr. Singer's works have appeared in *Commentary, Midstream, Mademoiselle, Esquire, Partisan Review,* and other national magazines.

JOYCE MADELON WINSLOW was born in July 5, 1946, and has lived primarily in Fairfield, Connecticut. She received her B.A. in English from the University of Michigan, Ann Arbor, in 1968, and will receive her M.A. in English from the University of Wisconsin in Madison in 1969. She plans to go into advertising copywriting. "Benjamen Burning" won the Avery Hopwood Creative Writing Award at the University of Michigan in 1968. She is currently at work on a series of short stories.

# THE
# YEARBOOK
## OF THE
# AMERICAN SHORT STORY

*January 1 to December 31, 1968*

# Roll of Honor, 1968

## I. *American Authors*

ALGREN, NELSON
   Home to Shawneetown. Atlantic, Aug.

BARBA, HARRY
   A Letter to the Corinthians. North American Review, Nov.-Dec.
BELLOW, SAUL
   Mosby's Memoirs. New Yorker, Sept. 20.
BLAKE, GEORGE
   A Modern Development. Kansas Magazine, Winter.
BRENNAN, MAEVE
   The Children Are There Trying Not to Laugh. New Yorker, Jan. 13.
   *The Eldest Child. New Yorker, June 23.
BRODKEY, HAROLD
   Bookkeeping. New Yorker, April 27.
BROWN, GEORGE MACKAY
   Five Green Waves. Atlantic, April.

*CADY, JACK
   Play Like I'm Sheriff. Twigs, IV.
   The Shark. Yale Review, Spring.
CASSILL, R. V.
   The Rationing of Love. New American Review, No. 3, April.
CHAY, MARIE
   I Like It Better That Way. Southwest Review, Winter.

CHEEVER, JOHN
   Playing Fields. Playboy, July.
CHENEY, BRAINARD
   Get On Board Little Children. Sewanee Review, July-Sept.
CONNORS, THOMAS E.
   Death and the Man. North American Review, Sept.-Oct.
CORRINGTON, JOHN WILLIAM
   A Time to Embrace. Denver Quarterly, Winter.
*COSTELLO, MARK
   Murphy's Xmas. Transatlantic Review, Winter.

DOXEY, WILLIAM S.
   In the Days of Joseph. Cimarron Review, June.
DUNFORD, NELSON JAMES
   Teams of Many Men. Chelsea, June.

EPSTEIN, LESLIE
   The Disciple of Bacon. New American Review, No. 4, Aug.
   Playground. Yale Review, Winter.

FRANCIS, H. E.
   The Rate of Decomposition in a Cold Climate. Southwest Review, Summer.
FRIEDMAN, PAUL
   An Evening of Fun. Perspective, Autumn.

* Stories marked with an asterisk are reprinted.

*GERALD, JOHN BART
Walking Wounded. Harper's, Aug.
GOULET, JOHN
Captain Robin. Intro #1, Sept.

HALL, JAMES B.
While Going North. Virginia Quarterly Review, Winter.
HARRINGTON, DONALD
Artificial Respiration. Esquire, Nov.
HAUSER, MARIANNE
The Seersucker. Carleton Miscellany, Fall.
HENDERSON, ROBERT
Cockcrow. New Yorker, July 6.
HERMANN, JOHN
Penates. Virginia Quarterly Review, Spring.
*HUGHES, MARY GRAY
The Foreigner in the Blood. Esquire, Feb.

KELLY, BERNARD
Game Called on Account of Darkness. Denver Review, Spring.
*KLEIN, NORMA
The Boy in the Green Hat. Prairie Schooner, Summer.

*LAVIN, MARY
Happiness. New Yorker, Dec. 14.

*MACLEOD, ALISTAIR
The Boat. Massachusetts Review, Spring.
MACMILLAN, IAN T.
Light and Power. Georgia Review, Spring.
*MADDEN, DAVID
Nothing Dies But Something Mourns. Carleton Miscellany, Fall.
The Day the Flowers Came. Playboy, Sept.
*MALAMUD, BERNARD
Pictures of Fidelman. Atlantic, Dec.
MATTHEWS, JACK
The Yard Man. Prism International, Summer.
*MCGREGOR, MATTHEW W.
Porkchops with Whiskey and Ice Cream. Virginia Quarterly Review, Spring.

MCMARTIN, SEAN
The God in the Middle. South Dakota Review, Autumn.
*MCPHERSON, JAMES ALAN
Gold Coast. Atlantic, Nov.
*MILTON, JOHN R.
The Inheritance of Emmy One Horse (under the pseudonym Christopher Garrard). South Dakota Review, Spring.
A Small Betrayal. Western Review, Winter.
MOAT, JOHN
Sam. Panache, No. 2.

*OATES, JOYCE CAROL
A Story of an Ordinary Girl. Texas Quarterly, Summer.
Out of Place. Virginia Quarterly Review, Summer.
By the River. December.

PAINTER, CHARLOTTE
Sandbox. Massachusetts Review, Autumn.
PALEY, GRACE
Two Stories from Five Boroughs
I. Samuel Who Died
II. The Burdened Man Who Came Alive . . . Esquire, March.
*PANSING, NANCY PELLETIER
The Visitation. Intro #1, Sept.
PERRY, RONALD
Three Laotian Tales. Hudson Review, Summer.
PHELPS, EVERETT DEAN
You Know What They Say. Virginia Quarterly Review, Summer.
*PLATH, SYLVIA
Johnny Panic and the Bible of Dreams. Atlantic, Sept.
PRICE, REYNOLDS
The Knowledge of My Mother's Coming Death. Southern Review, Summer.

ROGIN, GILBERT
What We See Before Us. New Yorker, July 6.
ROOKE, LEON
Load Every Rift With Ore. Carolina Quarterly, Fall.

ROTHBERG, ABRAHAM
The Sand Dunes. Southwest Review, Spring.
*RUGEL, MIRIAM
Paper Poppy. Kenyon Review, No. 4.

SANDBERG-DIMENT, ERICK
The Golden Mirrors of Yesterday. South Dakota Review, Summer.
SCHILLER, MARVIN
In the Bosom of the Family. Carleton Miscellany, Summer.
*SHIPLEY, MARGARET
The Tea Bowl of Ninsei Nomura. Denver Quarterly, Summer.
*SINGER, ISAAC BASHEVIS
The Letter Writer. New Yorker, Jan. 13.
The Colony. Commentary, Nov.
SKILLINGS, R. D.
Native Son. South Dakota Review, Summer.
STACTON, DAVID
Notes Written in the Self of a Man with a Singular Distaste for Writing Anything Down. Transatlantic Review, Spring.
STERLING, THOMAS
Bedlam's Rent. Paris Review, Winter-Spring.

STONE, PHILIP ALSTON
The Dead. Southern Review, Autumn.
STUART, JESSE
Our Sammie. Esquire, Oct.

VEDER, BOB
Black Betty. Literary Review, Spring.

WEILER, P. GARRETT
Cut-Hand. South Dakota Review, Summer.
*WINSLOW, JOYCE MADELON
Benjamen Burning. Intro #1, Sept.
WOIWODE, L.
The Boy. New Yorker, Aug. 31.

YU-HWA, LEE
The Bomb-Proof Inn. The Literary Review, Spring.

ZIMPEL, LLOYD
Ovenmen. Massachusetts Review, Autumn.
They Lay There Bleeding. December.

## II. *Foreign Authors*

BETTI, UGO
Three Stories. The Malahat Review, July.
BREWSTER, HARRY
Sappho's Leap. The Sewanee Review

DONLEAVY, J. P.
Rite of Love. Playboy, Oct.
A Fair Festivity. Playboy, Nov.
A Small Human Being. Saturday Evening Post, Nov. 16.

GILLIATT, PENELOPE
What's It Like Out? New Yorker, Oct. 26.
Albert. New Yorker, Oct. 5.
GORDIMER, NADINE
A Satisfactory Settlement. Atlantic, Jan.
Abroad. Southern Review, Summer.

HOUSEHOLD, GEOFFREY
Exiles. Saturday Evening Post, Dec. 14.
HURREH, ISMAEL
I, You, the Whorehouse. Intro #1, Sept.

IK, KIM YOUNG
From Here You Can See the Moon. Texas Quarterly, Summer.

JOYCE, JAMES
Giacomo, Joyce. Harper's, Jan.
JUMP, BARBARA
The Fool Discovered. Malahat Review, July.

LALIC, MIHAILO
The Snow Is Melting. Literary Review, Winter.

LESSING, DORIS
Side Benefits of an Honorable Profession. Partisan Review, Fall.
LITVINOV, IVY
Babushka. New Yorker, July 20.

MCMAHON, BYRON
Green Reflections. Occident, Spring-Summer.
MULISCH, HARRY
Spit and Image. Transatlantic Review, Spring.

RUORO, PETER
End of Month. Literary Review, Summer.

TAYLOR, ELIZABETH
In and Out the House. Saturday Evening Post, Dec. 14.
TEMPLETON, EDITH
The Darts of Cupid. New Yorker, Nov. 2.

WARNER, SYLVIA TOWNSEND
The Perfect Setting. New Yorker, Sept. 21.
Truth in the Cup. New Yorker, Dec. 7.
WATKINS, ROY
The Criminal. Intro #1, Sept.
WIESEL, ELIE
The Madman of Sighet. Commentary, May.

# Distinctive Short Stories, 1968

## I. *American Authors*

ABDOU, ELIAS
Beauty Is Truth, Truth Beauty. Quartet, Winter.

ALLEN, JOHN HOUGHTON
The Long Ride. Southwest Review, Autumn.

ASTRACHAN, SAMUEL
Katherine Weaver. Carleton Miscellany, Summer.

AUKEMA, CHARLES
Climbing Jacob's Ladder. Intro #1, Sept.

BANKS, RUSSELL
The Drive Home. New American Review, No. 4, Aug.

BARBER, PATRICIA
Flagstop. Intro #1, Sept.

BAUM, THOMAS
A Friend in Need. Transatlantic Review, Autumn.

BEAL, M. F.
Survival. New American Review, No. 3, April.

BENNETT, JOHN Z.
The Coil. North American Review, Sept.-Oct.

BISHOP, CHRISTOPHER
A Point of Navigation. Sewanee Review, Oct.-Dec.

BONAZZI, ROBERT
Light Casualties. Transatlantic Review, Spring.

BRASHERS, H. C.
Growing Pains. Michigan Quarterly Review, Summer.

BRENNAN, MAEVE
The Sofa. New Yorker, Mar. 2.

BUCHAN, PERDITA
It's Cold Out There. New Yorker, Sept. 14.

BURROUGHS, WILLIAM
Wind Die, You Die, We Die. Esquire, Aug.

CHAFFIN, LILLIE D.
Beyond the Curve. North American Review, Sept.-Oct.

CHARYN, JEROME
The Changeling. Transatlantic Review, Winter

CHEEVER, JOHN
The Yellow Room. Playboy, Jan.
Percy. New Yorker, Sept. 21.

COOK, BRUCE
The Goyische Garfield. December.

CONNORS, THOMAS E.
Death and the Man. North American Review, Sept.-Oct.

CORRINGTON, JOHN W.
The Night School. Massachusetts Review, Summer.

DE LANUX, EYRE
Cot No. 11. New Yorker, Oct. 26.

DESMOND, JOHN F.
  Tender Years. Michigan Quarterly Review, Summer.
DICKSON, J. W.
  The Wall. Denver Quarterly, Summer.
DILLARD, LEONA M.
  The Brothers. Kansas Quarterly, Winter.
DISTLER, ALAN
  White and Fast Water. New American Review, No. 4, Aug.
DORAN, JEFFREY
  Under Another's Sky. Atlantic, Jan.
DOXEY, WILLIAM S.
  Sailing Westward. DeKalb Literary Arts Journal, Spring.
DUNFORD, NELSON JAMES
  Teams of Many Men. Chelsea, June.

ELLIOTT, GEORGE P.
  Tourist and Pilgrim. Harper's, April.
ELMAN, RICHARD M.
  Turn on Guatemala Story. Evergreen, Oct.
EMERY, THOMAS
  The Kill. Georgia Review, Fall.
EPSTEIN, SEYMOUR
  Think of Green. Harper's, July.
EUSTIS, HELEN
  Miss Bird and I. Redbook, Nov.

FINEMAN, MORTON
  Sunday Is a Narrow Place. Saturday Evening Post, Mar. 23.
  Journey to the Fishing Waters. Saturday Evening Post, July 13.
FITZGERALD, BILL
  The Midnight Movie Director. Saturday Evening Post, May 4.
FLOOD, CYNTHIA
  On California Street. Wascana Review, Vol. 3, No. 2.
FOWLER, WILL
  The Red Carpet Treatment. Prairie Schooner, Summer.
FOX, ROBERT
  Some of Them Were Boys. December.
FREITAG, GEORGE H.
  Something No One Ever Sees. New Yorker, Mar. 23.

FRIEDMAN, ALAN
  International Love. Partisan Review, Summer.

GALLANT, MAVIS
  Malcolm and Bea. New Yorker, Mar. 23.
  Saturday. New Yorker, June 8.
GOLD, HERBERT
  Girl Getting Educated. Playboy, June.
GRAU, SHIRLEY ANN
  The Burglar. Saturday Evening Post, Oct. 19.
GRINSTEAD, DAVID
  A Day in Operations. Literary Review, Autumn.
GRISEWELLE, G. W.
  Robert Melendez. Texas Quarterly, Summer.
GROPPE, JOHN
  A Shred of Decency. Western Humanities Review, Spring.

HALPERIN, IRVING
  The Jew and the Easter Eggs. Phylon, Spring.
HARRIS, MACDONALD
  Ammazzafiori. Western Humanities Review, Spring.
HARTER, EVELYN
  Greet You with Garlands. Southwest Review, Autumn.
HEBERT, H. V.
  Screw. Transatlantic Review, Spring.
HOFFMAN, A. C.
  The Landmarks. Literary Review, Autumn.
HOWLAND, MARY
  Spring in a Strange Land. California Review, Spring.
HUMPHREY, WILLIAM
  The Human Fly. Esquire, Sept.
  A Home Away from Home. Saturday Evening Post, Sept. 7.
HUNT, HUGH ALLYN
  Ciji's Gone. Transatlantic Review, Autumn
HURLBUT, KAATJE
  The Secret. Redbook, July.

JACOBS, MARJORIE
Sins of Fathers. Phylon, Summer.
JOHNSON, SIKES
The Loser. Denver Quarterly, Autumn
JONES, THOMAS G.
A Family Privation. Georgia Review, Spring.

KAPLAN, JOHANNA
Sickness. Commentary, Dec.
KATZ, STEVE
The Sweet Salento, with Edmond Kulik, and Peter Stern Among the Woptimists. Paris Review, Winter-Spring.
KEISTER, LORRIE
Breakfast Out. Red Cedar Review, Winter.

LARGE, THOMAS
Mrs. Bluefoot's Radio. Intro #1, Sept.
LARNER, JEREMY
They Are Taking My Letters. Harper's, Oct.
LEE, LAWRENCE
An Alliance of Strangers. Sewanee Review, Oct.-Dec.
LURIE, MORRIS
Home Is. Transatlantic Review, Autumn.
LOMAX, ALMENA
In the Faraway Country of Montgomery, Alabama. Harper's, Sept.

MADDEN, DAVID
Love Makes Nothing Happen. Southwest Review, Summer.
MAIN, J. M.
Lillian. Perspective, Autumn.
MALAMUD, BERNARD
My Son the Murderer. Esquire, Nov.
An Exorcism. Harper's, Dec.
MALTZ, ALBERT
The Spoils of War. Saturday Evening Post, Oct. 5.
MASON, MICHAEL
A Good Education-Spontaneous Demonstration. Evergreen, Oct.
MATTHEWS, JACK
Love Song for Doris Ballinger. Carleton Miscellany, Fall.

MCMAHON, JEREMIAH
Mr. Swift and His Remarkable Thing. Playboy, Oct.
MEETER, GLENN
Don't You Remember Me? South Dakota Review, Spring.
METCALF, JOHN
The Children Green and Golden. Wascana Review, Vol. 3, No. 1.
MOLYNEUX, THOMAS
Jimmy Outlaw. Shenandoah, Summer.
MORGAN, BERRY
The Flower Gully. New Yorker, Aug. 24.
MOUNTZOURES, H. L.
An Examination. New Yorker, Jan. 20.
Twigs. New Yorker, May 4.

NISSENSON, HUGH
The Crazy Old Man. Esquire, Aug.

OATES, JOYCE CAROL
Shame. Atlantic, June.
The Heavy Sorrow of the Body. Northwest Review, Summer.
OSIER, JOHN
The Ritual. Georgia Review, Winter.
OSTROW, JOANNA
Used in the Highlands Since Time Immemorial. New Yorker, Nov. 30.

PARRA-FIGUEREDO, A.
The Lake at Hamilton's Bluff. Kansas Quarterly, Winter.
PETRAKIS, HARRY MARK
Dark Eye. Playboy, Dec.
PIERCY, MARGE
Love Me Tonight, God. Paris Review, Summer.
PORTER, JOHN ASHBY
Destruction of Gods. Occident, Spring-Summer.
PRICE, NANCY
The Invisible Ones. Virginia Quarterly Review, Winter.
PRICE, REYNOLDS
Scars. Esquire, Dec.

REYNOLDS, LAWRENCE JUDSON
That Grand Canyon. Intro #1, Sept.

RINDFLEISCH, NORVAL
A Cliff of Fall. Epoch, Autumn.
ROBINSON, FRED MILLER
Chimera. Minnesota Review, No. 4.
ROGIN, GILBERT
The Something of the World. New Yorker, Mar. 2.
ROTH, HENRY H.
Family Jacobs. Transatlantic Review, Winter.
Confrontations. South Dakota Review, Autumn.

SANDBERG, PETER
The Rhyme of Lancelot. South Dakota Review, Autumn.
SCOTT, VIRGIL
Home Is Where the Heart Is. Red Cedar Review, Winter.
SERNAKER, RICHARD
The Incendiaries. Occident, Spring-Summer.
SHEFNER, MARY
Mary Johnson, I Know You. Denver Quarterly, Summer.
SINGER, ISAAC BASHEVIS
The Dead Fiddler. New Yorker, May 25.
Zeitl and Rickel. Hudson Review, Spring.
Yanda. Harper's, May.
SKILLINGS, R. D.
Silly Buffalo and His Friends. Carleton Miscellany, Summer.
SORRELLO, ROBERT T.
Drowning. Western Humanities Review, Winter.
SPICEHANDLER, DANIEL
The Race of Scorpions. Transatlantic Review, Spring.
SPIELBERG, PETER
Palimpsest. Wascana Review, Vol. 3, No. 1.
SPINGARN, LAWRENCE P.
An Autumn Journey. Denver Quarterly, Autumn.
STAFFORD, JEAN
The Philosophy Lesson. New Yorker, Nov. 16.
STARR, B. J.
Coming of Age in Korea. The Smith, No. 10, Nov.

STUART, JESSE
The Best Years of Our Lives. Forum, Summer.

TABAK, MAY NATALIE
Small Change. Kenyon Review, Issue 5, Mar.
TARGAN, BARRY
And Their Fathers Who Begat Them. Esquire, Jan.
TAYLOR, HARRY H.
The Cage. South Dakota Review, Spring.
TURCO, LEWIS
The Catalogue Idea. The Quest, Summer-Fall.
TYLER, ANNE
The Common Courtesies. McCall's, June.

UPDIKE, JOHN
Man and Daughter in the Cold. New Yorker, March 9.
Eros Rampant. Harper's, June.

VACHON, JOHN
You Can Make a Million. Panache, No. 2.
VEDER, BOB
One for Almost None. Prairie Schooner, Summer.

WEST, JESSAMYN
The Birthday Suit. Saturday Evening Post, Oct. 5.
WILLIAMS, JOAN
Spring Is Now. Virginia Quarterly Review, Autumn.
WOIWODE, L.
The Long Trip. New Yorker, July 13.
The Horses. New Yorker, Dec. 28.

ZANDER, WILLIAM
A Lack of Grace. December.
ZIMPEL, LLOYD
Burying Blackie. Carleton Miscellany, Summer.

## II. *Foreign Authors*

AIDOO, AMA ATA
Other Versions. Literary Review, Summer.

ARMAH, AYI KWEI
Yaw Manu's Charm. Atlantic, May.

BANVILLE, JOHN
Summer Voices. Transatlantic Review, Spring.

BETTI, UGO
The People of the Via Lungagna. Prism International, Summer.

BORGES, JORGE LUIS
The Other Death. New Yorker, Nov. 2.
The Intruder. Atlantic, Oct.

BROPHY, BRIGID
The Woodcutter's Upright Son. Atlantic, Nov.

BRYAN, ELIZABETH
Rag and Bone Man. California Review, Spring.

ĆOPIĆ, BRANKO
Love and Jealousy. Literary Review, Winter.

GILLIATT, PENELOPE
Fred and Arthur. New Yorker, June 15.

HOOD, HUGH
It's a Small World. Tamarack Review, Winter.

KIELY, BENEDICT
A Great God's Angel Standing. New Yorker, Aug. 24.

LITVINOV, IVY
She Knew She Was Right. New Yorker, Sept. 28.

MÁRQUEZ, GABRIEL GARCÍA
Balthazar's Marvelous Afternoon. Atlantic, May.

NARAYAN, R. K.
Seventh House. New Yorker, Aug. 3.

OHIDO, NATHANIEL
They Stole Our Cattle. Literary Review, Summer.

SHRUBB, PETER
Life Abroad. Transatlantic Review, Spring.

SMART, PETER
All Good Things, the Best of Friends. Intro #1, Sept.

THEROUX, PAUL
Two in the Bush. Atlantic, July.

VIMAL, G. P.
The Eucalyptus. Western Humanities Review, Summer.

VIVANTE, ARTURO
The Lighthouse. New Yorker, Jan. 20.

WALKER, TED
Something of a Miracle. New Yorker, May 18.
The Peaches. New Yorker, Oct. 12.

WARNER, SYLVIA TOWNSEND
A Pair of Duelling Pistols. New Yorker, Feb. 17.

# Addresses of American and
# Canadian Magazines Publishing
# Short Stories

Alphabet, 276 Huron Street, London, Ontario, Canada
Ann Arbor Review, 115 Allen Drive, Ann Arbor, Michigan
Ante, Box 22915, Los Angeles, California 90029
Antioch Review, 212 Xenia Avenue, Yellow Springs, Ohio 45387
Argosy, 205 East 42nd Street, New York, New York 10017
Arizona Quarterly, University of Arizona, Tuscon, Arizona 85721
Atlantic, 8 Arlington Street, Boston, Massachusetts 02116
Ave Maria, Notre Dame, Indiana 46556
California Review, 280 East Mountain Drive, Santa Barbara, California 91303
Canadian Forum, 30 Front Street West, Toronto 1, Ontario, Canada
Canadian Home Journal, 71 Richmond Street, Toronto, Ontario, Canada
Carleton Miscellany, Carleton College, Northfield, Minnesota 55057
Carolina Quarterly, Box 1117, Chapel Hill, North Carolina
Catholic World, 304 West 58th Street, New York, New York 10019
Cavalier, 67 West 44th Street, New York, New York 10036
Chicago Review, Reynolds Club, University of Chicago, Chicago, Illinois 60637
Cimarron Review, 203B Morrill Hall, Oklahoma State University, Stillwater, Oklahoma 74074
Colorado Quarterly, University of Colorado, Boulder, Colorado
Colorado State Review, 360 Liberal Arts, Colorado State University, Fort Collins, Colorado 80521
Commentary, 165 East 56th Street, New York, New York 10022
Critic, 180 North Wabash Avenue, Chicago, Illinois 60601
December, Box 274, Western Springs, Illinois
Denver Quarterly, University of Denver, Denver, Colorado 80210
Descant, Texas Christian University, Forth Worth, Texas 76129
Edge, Box 4067, Edmonton, Alberta, Canada
Ellery Queen's Mystery Magazine, 505 Park Avenue, New York, New York 10022

Epoch, 252 Goldwin Smith Hall, Cornell University, Ithaca, New York 14850
Esquire, 488 Madison Avenue, New York, New York 10022
Evergreen Review, 80 University Place, New York, New York 10003
Evidence, Box 245, Station F., Toronto, Ontario, Canada
Fantasy and Science Fiction, 347 East 53rd Street, New York, New York 10022
Forum, Ball State University, Muncie, Indiana
Four Quarters, LaSalle College, Philadelphia, Pennsylvania 19143
Gentleman's Quarterly, 488 Madison Avenue, New York, New York 10022
Georgia Review, University of Georgia, Athens, Georgia 30601
Glamour, 420 Lexington Avenue, New York, New York 10017
Good Housekeeping, 959 Eighth Avenue, New York, New York 10019
Greensboro Review, University of Greensboro, Greensboro, North Carolina
Harper's Bazaar, 572 Madison Avenue, New York, New York 10022
Harper's Magazine, 2 Park Avenue, New York, New York 10016
Holiday, 641 Lexington Avenue, New York, New York 10022
Hudson Review, 65 East 55th Street, New York, New York 10022
Husk, Cornell College, Mount Vernon, Iowa 52314
Inland, Box 685, Salt Lake City, Utah
Intro, Bantam Books, 271 Madison Avenue, New York, New York
Kansas Quarterly, Denison Hall, Kansas State University, Manhattan, Kansas 66502
Kenyon Review, Kenyon College, Gambier, Ohio 43022
Ladies' Home Journal, 641 Lexington Avenue, New York, New York 10022
Laurel Review, West Virginia Wesleyan College, Buckhannon, West Virginia 26201
Literary Review, Fairleigh Dickinson University, Teaneck, New Jersey 07666
McCall's, 230 Park Avenue, New York, New York 10017
MacLean's, 481 University Avenue, Toronto, Ontario, Canada
Mademoiselle, 420 Lexington Avenue, New York, New York 10017
Mainstream, 832 Broadway, New York, New York 10018
The Malahat Review, University of Victoria, Victoria, British Columbia, Canada
Manhattan Review, 229 East 12th Street, New York, New York 10003
Massachusetts Review, University of Massachusetts, Amherst, Massachusetts 01003
Michigan Quarterly Review, University of Michigan, Ann Arbor, Michigan 48104
Midstream, 515 Park Avenue, New York, New York 10022
Minnesota Review, Box 4068, University Station, Minneapolis, Minnesota 55414
Motive, Box 871, Nashville, Tennessee 37202
MSS, 670 Fifth Avenue, Chico, California 95926
New American Review, 1301 Avenue of the Americas, New York, New York

New Campus Review, Metropolitan State College, Room 608, 250 West 14th Avenue, Denver, Colorado
New Renaissance, 9 Heath Road, Arlington, Massachusetts 02174
New Yorker, 25 West 43rd Street, New York, New York 10036
North American Review, University of Northern Iowa, Cedar Falls, Iowa
Northwest Review, Erb Memorial Union, University of Oregon, Eugene, Oregon 97403
Occident, Eshelman Hall, University of California, Berkeley, California 94720
Ohio University Review, Athens, Ohio
Panache, 153 East 84th Street, New York, New York 10028
Paris Review, 45-39 171 Place, Flushing, New York 11358
Partisan Review, 22 East 17th Street, New York, New York
Per Se, Box 2377, Stanford, California 94305
Perspective, Washington University Post Office, St. Louis, Missouri 63130
Phoenix, Ida Noyes Hall, 1212 East 59th Street, Chicago, Illinois
Phylon, Atlanta University, Atlanta, Georgia 30314
Playboy, 232 East Ohio Street, Chicago, Illinois 60611
Prairie Schooner, Andrews Hall, University of Nebraska, Lincoln, Nebraska 68508
Prism International, University of British Columbia, Vancouver, British Columbia, Canada
Quarterly Review of Literature, Box 287, Bard College, Annandale-on-Hudson, New York 12504
Quartet, 346 Sylvia Street, West Lafayette, Indiana 47906
Queens Quarterly, Room 524, Humanities Building, Queens University, Kingston, Ontario, Canada
Quest, Post Office Box 207, Cathedral Station, New York, New York 10025
Red Cedar Review, 325 Morrill Hall, Michigan State University, East Lansing, Michigan 48823
Redbook, 230 Park Avenue, New York, New York 10017
Red Clay Reader, 2221 Westminster Place, Charlotte, North Carolina 28207
Reflections, Box 109, Chapel Hill, North Carolina 27514
Reporter, 660 Madison Avenue, New York, New York 10021
Roanoke Review, Box 268, Roanoke College, Salem, Virginia 24153
Rogue, 1236 Sherman Avenue, Evanston, Illinois
San Francisco Review, Box 671, San Francisco, California
Satire, State University College, Oneonta, New York 13820
Seventeen, 320 Park Avenue, New York, New York 10022
Sewanee Review, University of the South, Sewanee, Tennessee 37375
Shenandoah, Box 722, Lexington, Virginia 24450
Sound, 15918 60th West, Edmonds, Washington 98020
South Dakota Review, Box 111, University Exchange, University of South Dakota, Vermillion, South Dakota 57069
Southern Humanities Review, Auburn University, Auburn, Alabama
Southern Review, Louisiana State University, Baton Rouge, Louisiana 70803

Southwest Review, Southern Methodist University, Dallas, Texas 75222
Tamarack Review, Box 159, Postal Station K, Toronto, Ontario, Canada
Texas Quarterly, Box 7527, University Station, Austin, Texas 78712
Transatlantic Review, Box 3348, Grand Central P.O., New York, New
  York 10017
Tri-Quarterly, Northwestern University, Evanston, Illinois 60201
Twigs, Hilltop Editions, Pikeville College Press, Pikeville, Kentucky
University Review, University of Kansas City, Kansas City, Missouri
University Review, University of Missouri, 5100 Rockhill Road, Kansas
  City, Missouri 64110
Vagabond, Collierstrasse 5, 8 Munich 12, Germany
Virginia Quarterly Review, I West Range, Charlottesville, Virginia 22903
Voyages, 2034 Allen Place, N.W., Washington, D.C. 20009
Wagner Literary Magazine, Grymes Hills, Staten Island, New York
Wascana Review, Wascana Parkway, Regina, Saskatchewan, Canada
Weird Tales, 9 Rockefeller Plaza, New York, New York 10020
West Coast Review, Simon Frazer University, Burnaby 2, British Columbia,
  Canada
Western Humanities Review, University of Utah, Salt Lake City, Utah
  84112
Wisconsin Review, Wisconsin State University, Oshkosh, Wisconsin
Yale Review, Box 1729, New Haven, Connecticut 06520
Yankee, Dublin, New Hampshire 03444